Wareham, MA

Cover and Book Design: Nauset Press

Illustrations Copyright © 2023 Karyn Kloumann

ISBN: 979-8-9859692-3-8

Library of Congress Control Number: 2022912984

Excerpts from this novel appeared in *The Hye-Phen Magazine*, *Newtown Literary*, *Sunday Salon*, *KGBBarLit*, and *The Armenian Review*.

NANCY AGABIAN

The Fear of Large and Small Nations

— a novel —

NAUSET PRESS
WAREHAM, MASSACHUSETTS

And though the words 'I must get away' do not
actually pass across your lips, you make a leap
from being that nice blob just sitting like a boob
in your amniotic sac of the modern experience to
being a person visiting heaps of death and ruin
and feeling alive and inspired at the sight of it ...
—Jamaica Kincaid, *A Small Place*

✿

I am so close and yet so far from the strange life that
throbs around me. A thousand threads connect
me to my homeland, yet its life seems to be shrouded
in mystery. Will I ever penetrate that mystery and
acquire a clear insight into its existence?
—Zabel Yessayan, *Prometheus Unchained*

CONTENTS

Glossary   vii

Prologue: Motherland   ix

I

1. To Collage   2
2. A Portrait of the Artist as an Infant   20
3. Outside In   34
4. Triangles   53
5. Acting Out a Rescue   70
6. Reflections of a Dead Twin   88
7. Free to Be Armenian   103
8. Ask Your Body   123
9. You Say Tradition, We Say Codependence   140

II

10. Dealing   161
11. Ethnic Cleansing   178
12. Sorry about the Violence   193
13. Women's Month   212
14. One for the Eavesdropper   230
15. Us and Them   245
16. Power Plays   262
17. I'll Take Your Pain Away   281

III

18. Time Warps   293
19. Recognition   303
20. Changing the Story   323

Acknowledgments   332

GLOSSARY

Most meanings of Armenian words that aren't readily deduced by context can be found by Googling the word with the term "in Armenian" after it. Listed below are some terms and Western Armenian spellings that aren't as easy to find online.

abush / ապուշ – idiot (Eastern Armenian: apush)

che / չէ – no (casual)

Digeen / Տիկին – Mrs. (Eastern Armenian: Tikin)

ha /հա – yes (casual)

mi vargyan / մի վարգյան – just a moment

poghots / փողոց – street

Spiurkahye / Սփյուռքահայ – an Armenian from the diaspora

tavloo/ թավլու – backgammon (Eastern Armenian/Russian: nardi/ նարդի)

vochinch / ոչինչ – literally: nothing. Colloquially: no problem.

yorghan / յորղան – (Turkish) quilt stuffed with wool

If no distinction is made between Eastern and Western transliterations, the spelling is the same for both dialects.

PROLOGUE: MOTHERLAND

Look, my child, wherever you are,
Wherever you go under this moon,
Even if you forget your mother,
Do not forget your mother tongue.

—Silva Gaboudikian

I don't remember the first time I saw Mother Armenia wielding her heavy sword across her narrow hips. It was likely from a distance, while walking the streets in the center of Yerevan, that I initially glimpsed her blocky military figure, an upright soldier guarding me from her perch above the city. Eventually, I ascended the hill where she stood and learned that she had replaced a statue of Stalin in the sixties and that her likeness was inspired by actual Armenian mother-warriors. But most of the time her stark figure hovered in the back of my consciousness, never really engaging my imagination. Instead, my preferred symbol of the motherland was an apparition named Fimi whom I encountered during the final hours of my very first trip to Armenia.

She appeared in the middle of the night, an otherworldly vision among the stray dogs that regularly wandered the outskirts of the cafés by the Opera. I wouldn't have noticed her if Gharib hadn't announced, "Oh, look who is here!" as Fimi glided toward our patio table under an umbrella of light. She was wearing a little rhinestone crown pinned into the nest of reddish hair piled atop her head, and her face was framed by spit curls that twirled at her temples. Bright-red lipstick lit up her lips and blue eyeshadow arched over her lids. She wore a white fur capelet over a glittering baby-blue brocade dress, with chunky costume jewelry clustered on her fingers, up her arms, and around her neck. With a boozy smile, Fimi stepped further into the light, and I could see that her capelet was dingy and her jewelry was tarnished with gemstones missing. Had I encountered her alone on the streets, I might have guessed she was a prostitute. Taking cues from my friends as we sat near the Opera, I regarded her as an artist.

It seems odd to call the people at the table my friends when I'd been in Yerevan merely a week, but I did feel close to them. In Armenia, even as people struggled and subsisted, it was impossible not to feel embraced and nurtured. I had been invited to participate in a feminist conference along with a handful of visiting artists and intellectuals from Europe. The Armenians had taken us in as their own: feeding us, taking us on tours, welcoming us into their homes, and imparting their unique sense of togetherness, going so far as to stay up all night to shepherd us to the airport in the early morning. For the few hours left before my flight brought me back to New York, I was a member of a family of Armenian artists in exile from their sleeping counterparts.

The café was the kind of commercial venture once loathed during the advent of capitalism after the Soviet collapse, but now begrudgingly accepted at the time in 2005. More than a few people had lamented that this area was once a beautiful park during the Soviet era before its current iteration as a string of overpriced tourist traps; the complaints didn't preclude anyone from spending hours at a time smoking and drinking once they plopped into a patio chair, though. The artists had collectively decided this was the least objectionable establishment, based on its lower prices and less boorish waiters. They now passed Mother Armenia a glass and poured her some cognac.

Fimi was unlike any woman in Armenia I had seen. All week I had been confronted by conformity on the streets of Yerevan: armies of thin young virgins in uniforms of long dark hair, sleek skirts, and high heels. Scattered among them were the matrons who had already raised their children, wearing boxy leopard-print blouses and shapeless black skirts, their unkempt hairdos a rainbow of hues and gray roots. The women of transitional age—like me—lacked a visible presence, probably because they were caring for children in their homes or working long hours in menial jobs—or both (which I had learned about at the feminist conference). Fimi seemed to belong to another class entirely: the international tribe of artists. It turned out she was a singer, though not an operatic one; she professed to love music from all cultures, entertaining us with songs in Russian, Arabic, Ladino, Georgian, and Armenian. With her sweet, deep, and soulful voice, she performed passionately, twirling her arms and pushing her bosom toward the moon.

Luckily, Fimi knew a little English. In between songs, she told me her story.

"I am hated," she said, "because I am so different from everyone." She told me she had two young daughters who lived with her mother and sister—a highly unusual arrangement here, since breaking the bonds of family was synonymous with tearing apart the nation. I wondered if her family had taken her daughters away, but all Fimi said was that she needed to live her life as an artist. Without a job, she was destitute, surviving on small loans from friends. One of the Western artists was recording Fimi's singing on a MacBook, hatching a plan for her to tour Europe, insisting she would be loved and adored.

"I'll go to Europe, darling," she confided in me. "Why not? I live in a cold water flat, even in the winter. Do you know how hard that is? To take a cold bath in December?"

"No, you can't go to Europe!" Mardi interrupted her. "They will exploit you! It will ruin you!" His warning seemed ironic after he and Gharib had confessed that it was next to impossible to be an artist in Armenia. They were the generation left behind during the "brain drain," when their ostensible mentors had fled through a crack in the Soviet Union's Iron Curtain, initiating a stream of expatriation, the so-called "bloodless genocide" of economic survival that razed the nation of people. Mardi and Gharib told me that economic and social pressures made it difficult to be creative, to be seen or heard. Because of the closed borders with Turkey and Azerbaijan, cultural access was constricted, with little selection in films and music; books were even more limited because of the dearth of translation. And forget about owning a computer; they were prohibitively expensive. Gharib told me that it felt as though even ideas were blockaded.

And yet, the conference, organized by a diasporan Armenian living in Holland, had exposed me to thinkers I had yet to read: Walter Benjamin, Hannah Arendt, Gayatri Spivak. I held an MFA in writing from an Ivy League university and had never heard of these people. Students were more interested in learning how they could get published than having impassioned conversations about art, how it related to love, if it should be influenced by politics, and how it might bring change. Armenia was in flux, actively shaping itself as best it could, caught in a rush of free-market capitalism yet cautious about abandoning its communal culture. The charged conversations throughout the week prompted me to reconsider my role as a writer: how I might help to bring change to this place, but also how I might be changed in the process. In New York, I operated on the outskirts of the Armenian community. Being embraced here, a place where "real" Armenians debated their future, made me feel validated and challenged at once.

As everyone argued her fate, Fimi turned to me with a raised glass. "Art forever!" she shouted. "I only live for love!"

I was practically mute, entranced by this larger-than-life figure, though I was a performer too. A few days before, I had recounted to an audience how I had once taken a woman on a date to an Armenian church in New York, while the cult of all-male priests—in their own bejeweled brocade ensembles—chanted their arcane liturgy. Fimi might have been a troubled soul with a complex history, but I could see her only through the window of my wonder. In her freedom from the typical roles for Armenian women, she was an aberration, a pariah-princess, a painted Anti-Mother who materialized only under the cover of darkness. Here I was, flown in to represent feminist liberation, yet single and miserable, a third-generation Armenian American in my late thirties, unaware of how trapped I was by my own mind. I could only admire Fimi's defiant spark of expression.

The artists felt stuck between destitution if they stayed and irrelevance or exploitation if they left, but I was awakened by what I saw, by the puzzling combination of the culturally familiar and the socially foreign. The government was corrupt, fashioning tradition into a nationalist weapon to wield power. And yet the creativity of the people could not be stopped.

In poetry and the collective imagination, Mother Armenia fiercely protects her brood so that they will defend the homeland, a martyr passing on songs that her children should always remember, even if they forget her. After two generations of estrangement, I returned to reacquaint myself, only to discover that Mother Armenia had been debased, her songs so beautiful because she really was a prostitute whose children had been taken away from her by the world.

Fimi wouldn't be Fimi if she were anywhere else, a fear that spoke to me. I never saw her, my Mother Armenia, again, but it was then that I decided to come back to Yerevan to live, to find art and love—no matter what.

I

1. TO COLLAGE

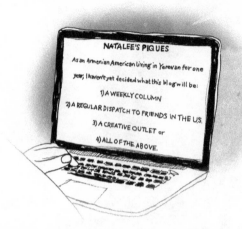

BLOG POST: SEPTEMBER 1, 2006
GREENPOINT, BROOKLYN

What I Can Bring on the Plane >>> On my flight overseas I cannot take any liquids or gel-like substances in my carry-on luggage. This new security measure must be making the product development people over at Dr. Scholl's miserable. Their state-of-the-art gel shoe inserts are now a forbidden item listed on the website of the Transportation Security Administration. Other items on the list also seem questionable as security threats: liquid mascara, for one. I highly doubt there's enough room in such a tiny bottle for a harmful amount of explosive material. The TSA may as well ban Magic Markers. But they don't. They also don't prohibit toy Transformer robots.

I find it difficult to believe that enough Americans had a question about toy Transformers to require an entry on the companion list of allowable items. Instead, I think the TSA is throwing us a bone, hoping that a plaything will distract us from not having our own bottle of water on a transatlantic flight. The Transformers can also help us imagine that we are cyborgs, impervious to terrorism.

The TSA must think that American travelers are confused about whipped cream, too. It's certainly necessary for air travel, the Reddi-Wip, so it's understandable why that would be a big question mark. Sorry, you can't pack dessert toppings in your carry-on luggage. No jelly or Jell-O, either. But you can wear a gel-filled bra. And you can take up to 4 oz of K-Y Jelly. I understand there are many health and personal reasons to enhance and lubricate, but I can also imagine a bunch of TSA dudes deciding that women must have big boobs and wet pussies at all costs.

I also discovered that you cannot squeeze a saber into your carry-on. Bows and arrows are also off-limits, as are meat cleavers and cattle prods. You can't take incendiaries, explosives, and firearms or *realistic replicas* of incendiaries, explosives, and firearms.

Who are all these Americans, trying to get onto planes with simulacra of dangerous weaponry? Perhaps they are Civil War reenactors, back from a vacation, packing their props. Nearly 150 years later, the Civil War is still with us, restaged as theater, as if we can never get it out of our systems.

Perhaps I'm reading too much into the TSA list of permitted and prohibited items, but I can't help but look at it as a poem about what government officials think we're afraid of and what we desire. Someone from another planet reading it might think Americans are addicted to dessert, fixated on women as sex objects, and driven to violence. The guidelines are meant to protect us, but they also indicate the dangers we pose to each other.

When I lamented to my mother that I can't take toothpaste with me on my red-eye to Europe, she advised, "Bring a travel toothbrush, you know, the kind with a case? And squeeze a little toothpaste onto the brush part. What, are they going to take your toothbrush away?"

Yes, they might. I've had my fantasies: "Hey, Middle Eastern woman, hand over the dentifrice!" For after all our lessons about race, we still believe that appearance is most central in designating who we are, the reason the TSA has institutionalized racial profiling.

I told my mother, "I read in the news that this guy at JFK was wearing a T-shirt that said in Arabic and English, 'We will not be silent,' and the TSA actually made him take it off."

"Well," my mother explained, "that's because they don't want people on the plane to get upset."

I'm about to journey to Armenia, to live for a year among people who I resemble. As a child I learned our history in Armenian school, represented by slides of colorful shrinking maps: we were an ancient people who reigned over our share of kingdoms but mostly suffered under the conquest of others. Under an increasingly brutal Ottoman Empire, we finally managed to defend ourselves, only to arrive at a terrible point in history: our grandparents were children when the catastrophe befell them in 1915, when the Young Turk regime shot their fathers and brothers, then marched their mothers, sisters, aunts, and grandmothers through the desert where they were raped, abducted, or left to desiccate and die.

During the slideshow, there was no time to grieve the wounds of our grandparents, depicted as lost little children in white clothing standing in rows outside the front steps of their orphanage. Soon we were viewing the next frame: Russia, recognizing an opportunity, stepped in and swept what was left of Armenia into the Soviet Union. But our grandparents had fled across continents and created our far-flung diaspora, where we were left to remember our silent cousins living in captivity behind the Iron Curtain, who mouthed an Eastern variation of our language, who ate different food, but who basically looked like us.

When the Soviet Union finally broke open, my friends and family trekked back to the closest thing we had to a homeland, then returned to report on the emotional power of being in a place where your Armenian countenance was, for once, not unusual. I am curious to feel what this is like, but I am also wary of attaching so much importance to appearance, like simplified images in a slideshow. Our history marched on, after all, once the Soviet Union collapsed, to a war with neighboring Azerbaijan. Before the conflict started in 1988, some villages in Armenia contained a majority of Azerbaijanis, who now are all gone. No Armenians are left in Azerbaijan, either. The border is closed, and there is virtually no interaction or exchange. The people of these two nations don't look very different from each other, but thirteen years later, war is not out of their system.

So as Armenia approaches a parliamentary election this coming spring, and I get ready to board a plane in the coming days, I wonder what the government of Armenia will think of its people. I wonder what words will be banned and what odd poems I will encounter.

STORY: EARLY SEPTEMBER, 2006
YEREVAN, ARMENIA

Na couldn't figure out how to call home on the cordless phone. After she had arrived in Yerevan in the wee hours of the morning and slept into the early afternoon, she decided that the first thing she needed to do was call her parents to inform them of her safe arrival. But she couldn't find the code to call the U.S. anywhere in the informational packet from the embassy. Unnerved, she searched for clues by the phone, then around the apartment, which she had rented from a diasporan family she knew in New York. The place was huge and modern, fitted with all the amenities and stocked with plastic bins filled with medicine for diarrhea. The code to call home, however, was nowhere to be found. And the cupboards and fridge were bare.

As Na ventured outside to find something to eat, she discovered the apartment building was part of a complex of four massive structures situated around a central courtyard. Constructed of a pinkish tufa stone native to the region, the buildings appeared to be dry, dull, and dusty. Every window was different, ranging from double-pane glass to black plastic garbage bags. Laundry hung from the balconies, and electrical cables threaded through hacked holes in the walls. Na imagined that if there were an earthquake, all nine stories precariously stacked atop her ground-floor apartment would crush her like a cockroach.

She wandered away from the buildings down a dusty unpaved alley. The day was sunny, the air dry, the high altitude felt in her shallow breaths. She sensed a tension in the air, in the eyes of the people she encountered lumbering among the low-boughed, little trees. Following the alley to a busy road, she soon found a small store. She peered around the few shelves of cans, cabbages, and tomatoes, the sound of street traffic filling up the small space of the aisle. Stacked on shelves on the wall were fresh loaves of bread, flat and round and light brown. Na was relieved to remember the word for bread, and the word for butter, too, from the once weekly Armenian language classes that her parents had forced her to take throughout her childhood. She had long forgotten the nouns, then relearned them as a graduate student when she formally studied Western Armenian, only for them to lie dormant again since she never used them in conversation. Now she didn't know how to make a sentence to ask for what she wanted—or if it would even be understood in Eastern Armenian, which sounded to her like a rollercoaster instead of the melody of her grandmother's voice. The translation of the Armenian expression in the imperative mood was, "Give me the bread," which seemed rude. Saying, "I want the bread" sounded primitive, and she thought it attracted too much attention to her foreignness. In English, she probably would have said, "Could I get a loaf of bread?" but the modal form in Armenian was beyond her. Finally, she pointed to a loaf behind the clerk's head and said, "Hahts?" very softly, her voice sounding like that of a very young child. The clerk stared at Na, a fully grown woman. Na was so embarrassed by her fear and inability to speak Armenian that she lowered her eyes and wordlessly slipped out the open door.

Luckily, she discovered a larger store nearby, where the food was readily displayed and within reach. She picked an oval loaf of bread, the size of a notebook, from the shelf and brought it up to the counter. The butter was in a glass case, so she pointed to it and said, "Garac." The clerk was a broad woman in an apron, revealing a gold tooth when she asked which brand Na wanted. A pause and Na's furrowed brow caused the clerk to point and say, "This one?" in Armenian, to which Na nodded. Then she went home, let out a deep breath, and ate her bread and butter. The bread was equally light in texture and heavy in taste, settling at the back of her tongue, the butter slightly sour and soft. As she chewed, the pliability relieved her nerves.

Feeling frozen by her lack of language reminded Na of being a child in Armenian school, unable to answer simple questions in class. A top student in her public grammar school in the leafy Rhode Island town where she grew up, she found the Armenian language impossible to learn. She hated those classes with immigrant children who could speak Armenian perfectly and who rolled their eyes when she couldn't keep up. The teachers, also immigrants, seemed impatient with Na, too, staring at her expectantly whenever they asked a question she couldn't answer, loath to offer encouragement. Language was a key to her people's survival. So it was very stressful for Na to fail at Armenian school, to be bad at what she was. She would spend many years avoiding the Armenian community, throughout high school, college, and young adulthood, until she was thirty, when she decided she needed to know her history. Her grandmother had survived the Armenian Genocide, but she had told Na about it only in brief fragments, so Na's understanding of what her grandmother had endured, and the event itself, was limited. And yet, she had a theory that centuries of oppression had filtered through her blood—one of the reasons her coming-of-age had been so difficult. She went to graduate school for writing and found her way to her Armenian identity through extensive research and the writing of a book about her family history—but apparently, it wasn't enough. Now she was in the country where she was bad at what she was, and there was no way to avoid it, the language surrounding her, voices and signs bombarding her on the streets.

The Fulbright orientation hadn't prepared her for this. Most of the scholars were visiting a country they were studying, not one they had an ancestral link to. She was expecting more worldly advice, but the scholars received instruction along the lines of a Fodor's guide: *learn the basic vocabulary of the language, like numbers, please, hello, and thank you; don't walk alone anywhere at any time of day because you will be a target as an American; embassy-sponsored bus trips into the countryside can be a great way to experience the nation.* Emphasis was placed on what the Americans could teach the natives, rather than what they could learn from each other. She was critical of the orientation and George W. Bush's imperialist State Department, regarding herself as much more adventurous.

After all, she could have come to Armenia many years before with one of the "Young Professional" tour groups of the diaspora, which her parents had offered to pay for, but she always refused. Such tours tooled around Armenia, informing the young professionals that the fledgling nation was the size of Maryland and had a population of three million; the group visited orphanages, schools, the military, an astronomy observatory, and ancient churches, ostensibly so that young Armenian Americans would be able to see firsthand how the struggling homeland was faring. But it seemed to Na that the unstated purpose of the tour was to offer diasporans the chance to meet each other as possible mates in heterosexual matrimony. Her brother had participated in the late nineties and had a great time—though he was gay and remained closeted—but Na was insistent about coming to Armenia on her own terms.

The opportunity arrived when a young Armenian lesbian Amal, who was studying in the States, discovered Na's first book of poems and translated a couple of the proto-riot grrrl ones for a new literary journal, which brought Na an unexpected audience in Yerevan. She was soon invited to perform her work at a feminist conference in 2005, exactly one year before. The week before the trip, she came down with the flu and spent her days in bed, watching the coverage of New Orleans's decimation by Katrina. In her bleary state, she felt a duty to witness the hell that was taking place: no food, no water, no sanitary conditions, no medicine for those who were too poor or sick to evacuate. Throughout Bush's first term, she had become dismayed by war upon war, fear upon fear, and she joked like other liberals that she would move to Canada if he was reelected on his platform of gay-marriage bashing and pro-choice demonizing. She was so disgusted by her government's negligence of its own people that she was glad to leave it all behind and flee to Armenia. She thought the desperation of the people in New Orleans, Black and poor and disenfranchised, paralleled something of what Armenians had experienced in the Ottoman Empire, and she found the timing of the disaster ironic upon her first trip to the homeland. She was that privileged, that removed from racism in the U.S. to watch the actual suffering of others unfolding on TV and compare it to a history she had mostly read about, even if that history was in her blood. In her compartmentalized mind, Armenia was a site of escape because it was the only other place in the world she felt she had any claim to.

Na had still been somewhat sick as she boarded the plane, but she managed to tour around Armenia, sit in on panels with feminists from Europe, perform her piece, and socialize with her host and guide, a man her age named Mardi who wore large dark-framed glasses, his features vaguely Asian—smooth black hair, narrow eyes, high forehead, short and flat nose. He was rather foxy, Na thought, and she soon learned he was a filmmaker, divorced, and living with his mother. Water was available for only a few hours a day at their flat, so Na took baths in the tub, pouring cups of water over her head from a bucket of water saved from the day before, which sparked a sense memory of how her grandmother had bathed her as a child. Mardi's mother, Digeen Sargsyan, was also familiar: with her critical heavy-lidded visage, she questioned Na about her life in America and why she wasn't married. Such interrogations were typical in Armenian American families, too. Na's mother often asked why Na wasn't dating men and expressed shamed distress that she didn't have grandchildren.

Na was protective of the fact that she had been single for five years because she feared something was inherently wrong with her. She was very pained by these feelings, more so than any loneliness she experienced. So she wondered if Armenia would be the place where she would fall in love. Maybe she wasn't unlovable or incompetent at finding love; maybe she'd been looking in the wrong place and was meant to find someone here, just as the diasporan Young Professionals trips had suggested. In fact, she had a little crush on Mardi, though he could be surly as he accompanied her around the city to the conference sites. She had to be informed by one of the European feminists that he was gay and that he was in a relationship with Gharib, a jovial pear-shaped political scientist who was moderating panels at the conference. Na was the president of the Queer Armenians of New York group, but her gaydar had failed her. She sensed that Mardi might be queer when she saw him primping in the mirror one morning, but she had assumptions about LGBT Armenians—that they weren't aware of their own sexuality, that they repressed their identities to survive. It didn't occur to Na that she might think this way because she was in the habit of burying her own desires.

As she tore off pieces of bread from the loaf, slicing them through the middle to add little chunks of butter, Na glanced across the sterile, renovated apartment, taking in its many tones of beige, wishing she were still at the flat with Mardi and his mother with their seventies-era furniture and faded wallpaper. They lived nearby, on Tigran Mets Poghots, around the corner from her complex in a building that surrounded a busy inner courtyard of cars, makeshift garages, and grape arbors. Neighbors hung out the windows and called to each other and watched the comings and goings below. She remembered breakfasts in their small kitchen and how Mardi's mother had once served a special treat brought back from her ancestral village in the countryside. The fig preserves in honey were so tender and sweet on her tongue that Na actually blushed with embarrassment.

Mardi didn't seem to appreciate such simple pleasures; instead, he often seemed annoyed by his mother and how much she questioned his life, how she stared out the window waiting to see when he came home. But he clearly cared for her; she suffered from a bad back, and he periodically lifted her up off the ground in an awkward chiropractic maneuver. There wasn't enough money for proper medical treatment for Digeen Sargsyan; Mardi did not have a job, and his mother worked a couple of days a week as a teaching assistant at a local school. Na was eager to learn more, but she didn't want to pry into their seemingly difficult lives, and she was ashamed to call attention to her privilege.

Na worried she had upset the balance of the household when Mardi's mother read an interview of Na in a local feminist magazine, in which she divulged that she was bisexual. When Na came home that evening, Mardi's mother seemed disappointed as she glared at her, which reminded Na of her own parents' disapproval of her sexuality. The next morning, however, Digeen Sargsyan asked Na, through Mardi, about her orientation.

First off, she wasn't sure what *bisexual* meant. There was no word for it in Armenian. "I tell her you have boyfriend and girlfriend," Mardi said.

If Na hadn't been more mortified, she would have been flattered that someone thought she could have relationships with two people at the same time. "No, no!" she said, explaining that she'd been attracted to both sexes for about as long as she could remember. She was single now, she told him, but in the past, her relationships had been with either a man or a woman. (Though having partners of both genders simultaneously wasn't unappealing to her.)

"It's a difficult life," Digeen Sargsyan responded.

"Not really," Na lied. She certainly didn't feel it was easy to be out or to find partners who readily accepted her. It didn't help that the Armenian American community was largely hostile to LGBT Armenians. But she didn't want her orientation to be demonized. "In America, it's quite normal," she claimed.

"It's special in Armenia," Digeen Sargsyan said. Then she went on to tell Na that Cher was a prostitute. Of Armenian descent, the superstar might have been a respectable woman, Digeen Sargysan purported, had she grown up in Armenia. Mardi laughed and shook his head. Na thought perhaps his mother was making the Cher non sequitur because the topic of gayness was hitting too close to home. Na attributed Digeen Sargsyan's open curiosity to the fact that Na was an outsider; being gay was a terrible deviancy in Armenian society, one that she might have trouble tolerating in her own son.

From her activist work with the Queer Armenians of New York, Na knew of terrible crimes against gay and lesbian Armenians. The organization had helped secure amnesty for a straight woman, a psychologist, who helped gay teens who had been kicked out of their homes and were subsequently assaulted, raped, and blackmailed by the Yerevan police. Na had also advocated for an acquaintance in Armenia when he was implicated in the murder of a gay American man who had been teaching English at one of the universities; the police investigated the crime as one of passion, using it as an excuse to identify, round up, and harass any gay man in Yerevan. At the time, a new human rights bill protecting LGBT people had been enacted into law, reversing the old Soviet penal code against homosexuality, but it was an empty diplomatic technicality to appeal to the Council of Europe. The reality was that it was physically dangerous to be a gay man, and queer women were invisible.

When Na did her performance piece at the conference, in which she referenced going on a date with a woman, a progressive journalist approached her and claimed that she was the first person in Armenia to publicly come out. In his article, he interviewed Beatris, a prominent outlier poet, who said that she had expected Na to be a much more forceful person based on the style of her poems. "I did not imagine her to be so passive. It was a surprise for me to see her so seemingly defenseless," Beatris stated. "A desire to protect her rose up inside me. But after her performance, I suddenly realized that this vulnerable creature herself was defending us." As much as Armenia had felt foreign on her first trip, Na was offered space to voice her reality in a world where she had never imagined she would be embraced—or needed.

Na had forgotten this sense of purpose on her first day back in the country, now that she was here to teach creative writing and to research social change. It was as if time had collapsed the years between now and when she was thirteen years old, begging her mother to let her quit Armenian school, everything triggering her fears from childhood of not being Armenian enough. She wasn't sure why this was happening. Perhaps it was because she wasn't staying with a family, like during her last visit, but rather occupying a family-sized apartment on her own.

Right as she was finishing up her bread and butter, the phone rang. It was Mardi and Gharib, checking in after receiving an email from her a few days before. She asked them for the code to call the U.S., which they didn't know, but they told her to meet them at Miasin, the hip and trendy restaurant with track lighting, concrete walls, and wooden tables where she had performed the year before and which was currently hosting the feminist conference. The guys told her she would be able to use the internet at the restaurant to email her parents. Na unfolded her map and traced a route to walk there. As she maneuvered down familiar streets through the main square, with its grand Soviet architecture and side streets with old homes and tin roofs, she felt somewhat more competent.

META-WRITING:

I didn't set out to write like this, in disjointed sections. Weblogging had been the latest internet sensation at the time, before social media. On my blog, I fancied myself a sly reporter, crafting dispatches filled with arch observations. Eventually, when I lost my way, these texts became more significant than a lark.

I also hadn't intended to portray myself in the third person. But at some point in writing about what happened to me when I lived in Armenia, I needed distance from all the inexplicable ways I had acted, including why I had an identity crisis.

My public and private selves, which I thought I had integrated over the years as a bisexual feminist Armenian American woman, became refractured in Armenia. Simultaneously, I witnessed how the locals shuffled multiple selves. When Mardi showed me his bedroom where I would be staying during my first visit, I was confronted by a large, life-sized black-and-white photograph on his wall of a topless woman with dirty-blond, teased hair and thick, fake eyelashes. Her arms were open wide as if she were dancing, stretching open a crocheted spiderweb of a top. I tried not to be startled by her breasts, which were perfect and pert, and noticed that her face seemed strained. The next morning, Mardi told me, "She was a child psychologist in Germany who was also a stripper during the sixties. She killed herself. She was tormented by her double life. I am interested in this, in subjugating identity."

When Mardi and Gharib took me to the Sergei Parajanov Museum a few days later, I viewed many artifacts from the life of the famed director, not to mention his curious collages of doll parts, buttons, found objects, and scraps of paper, which he created during the years the Soviets banned him from filmmaking and imprisoned him for being gay, which he never actually admitted to, which the wall labels did not explain. Years after Parajanov completed his sentence, the museum was built as a residence by the Soviets for him to live in, which I had trouble understanding: would he be on exhibit, like an animal in his own zoo? There were two bedrooms and a kitchen, but they had never been used because Parajanov died in 1990 before it was completed. Perhaps he sensed the strange fate awaiting him.

As we rested in Parajanov's courtyard, Gharib started singing suddenly, slowly and sweetly, what sounded like a hymn. I was captivated by what he told me was an ancient pagan song that was usually played on the duduk. When I expressed that I hadn't known he was a singer, he explained, "Yes, I am classically trained. You know, I also sing in persona," and he belted out a few lines of Gloria Gaynor's "I Will Survive" in a completely different tone, then scatted, bebop style. "I'm recording an album of jazz standards with her voice," he said.

I came to discover such collaging of selves, styles, and voices among artists who were borrowing references and other source materials. It seemed that after the Soviet Union collapsed deconstruction took a spot in Armenian literary consciousness. I often wondered if it enabled people to express themselves—their feelings, ideas, and sexualities—indirectly, and thus, safely.

Three days after I landed in Yerevan for my second visit, looking for bread and butter, I met a young Armenian man who created poems by collaging porn, Armenian classical texts, and British song lyrics. I somehow fell in love, and at the end of my year in Armenia, I returned to New York with him. Whenever we had troubles, I wrote in my journal; three years into the relationship, I was turning to it every day.

JOURNAL: AUGUST 2, 2009
ASTORIA, QUEENS, NY

Breaking Up with Seyran

Pros	Cons
more time to write	loneliness
less stress	shame of failing
more dignity	guilt for not helping him

I feel stupid, resorting to this kind of a list. I never thought it would take this long to figure out whether to break up with him. I guess this is what happens when you get involved very quickly—it was like we committed to each other after one date. I was charmed by Seyran when he showed me around Yerevan, taking me to restaurants only locals frequented and out-of-the-way outdoor markets with endless stalls of stuff underneath loosely hung blue tarp canopies—clothes and shoes and nuts and housewares. There was that market he called "the petting place" because the aisles were so narrow people nearly rubbed up against each other. When we shopped, we saw life in the markets. Families and children, old folks in slippers. Farmers from the countryside with their ruddy hands and seller's gazes. Some woman skirting around with a tray of little cups of black foamy coffee to serve to vendors. I miss all of that.

Now we go to the Marshalls on Northern Boulevard in Long Island City. The fluorescent lights and piped-in advertisements can't compare. Seyran is obsessed with shopping, with collecting and consuming America. We've spent countless hours in malls, shops, and thrift stores, looking for shoes or pants or rucksacks. I find it soul sucking, though it can be bonding when he buys stuff for the kitchen, like pots, pans, and long-handled spoons; I think they appeal to him because they help to make our house a home.

I also think that he likes the measure of control he has over shopping: you don't like an item, you put it back on the rack. You don't like a store, you leave. It has given him solace in a place that is foreign and unfriendly. I can understand because when he took me shopping and helped me find the things I needed in Yerevan, I was finally able to breathe. Now when he needs to buy something, he does extensive research into the product, reading everything he can, trying to find the lowest price. Then he orders it online and it arrives at our door. There is a process and a secure outcome. And if it's not exactly what he wants, he can send it back. Mostly he has kept the guitars, amps, cords, pedals, hard drives, keyboards, mic stands—equipment he couldn't get in Armenia. But he also keeps some crap: incense created by Tibetan monks, a book on how to disappear completely, and size-ten men's sandals. The one thing that distinguishes our little apartment, here on the second floor of a brick house, attached to a chain of houses exactly like it, is the constant stream of deliveries from UPS, FedEx, and the USPS.

The second or third time we went to a Yerevan supermarket, which was a relatively new and expensive concept to him—since people were still going to the butcher, the baker, the cheese shop, the fruit market—he told me, "You turn me into consumer." At the time, his English vocabulary wasn't that expansive, so the word *consumer* really stood out. It struck me as a post-Soviet construct as I'd never even thought of it as an identity before. I did not consider myself a consumer. When a lawyer briefly sublet my grad school apartment, he told me that he couldn't live the way that I did—without a TV, stereo, microwave, or fancy kitchen. I'm used to living on a low income as a writer. But in Armenia, I had money from the United States government, and the dollar was strong. Food for the week cost ten dollars. Jeans cost five dollars. We were able to eat out whenever we wanted.

We also entertained our friends. I'm trying to keep up the practice here as much as I can. This is when Seyran is at his best, eager to make people happy. I love how much he loves to help friends with their computers, to play music on his guitar, to burn CDs, to serve food on neatly arranged plates, to light up the hookah; his pointed face gleaming in its sculpted, angled features. (I still find myself astonished at how handsome he is, even dashing at times.) His benevolent nature goes beyond the typical Armenian cultural imperative of hosting with as much generosity as possible. It truly seems to bring him joy.

But when he is apart from people, he becomes dark and mean. I'm tired of being told how much he doesn't like my friends, and I don't appreciate how he makes fun of them behind their backs. Also, he doesn't understand that in New York, where friendships take place mostly over email and phone, that his kind of temperament is deadly. Within this bubble, he takes out his frustrations on me, calling me names. When he first called me stupid, I lectured him on how destructive it was. But now we call each other stupid all the time, and I hardly ever notice. There's no point in telling him that he doesn't understand the concept of emotional support. That Americans have conceptualized such a thing is laughable to many Armenians. And I kind of get the joke. But when I think about being in a relationship and how, like any commitment, you do it for someone who loves and cares about you, I wonder what I am doing it for.

The thing is, I am not sure when and how to call it quits. I have never broken up with someone whom I've lived with, married, and brought to America. Every time I suggest it after a particularly impossible fight, he tells me, "I'm not ready." He still seems to need me. Besides the emotional component, there are all the legal issues; he'll lose his green card since it's based on his marriage to me. If he goes back, he'll face dangers that I can't even think about right now. As the granddaughter of a genocide survivor, who knows all the stories of rescue and survival, who has been taught how precious every single Armenian life is, how am I going to build up my American boundaries to turn a young Armenian out?

Even though it's clear to me that it's over, I wonder whether it really is. The problem is that I haven't fully figured out our complex knot of troubles, and so I can't let go. And part of the reason is that he is all wrapped up in Armenia for me, in trying to understand that rough and troubled place. We were in love and wanted to be together in the same place, so we got married. We've made a commitment, and he feels like family to me. I feel responsible for him, and I want him to have a good life. Which, come to think of it, is sort of how diasporans feel toward Armenia.

The other day I was depressed, so he asked me to take a walk with him to Sports Authority: "Let me buy you a new pair of sneakers." I've been wearing the same ones I brought with me to Armenia when they were new, and now they are worn out from all the walks we have taken since. As I tried on sneakers in the aisles of the store, lacing and unlacing, he told me that he knows he does not make a lot of money as an IT guy, but when he finds himself complaining about his life, he stops and realizes, "I have money to buy things, I get to live in a nice place." After I finally decided on New Balance, I followed him around the store for an hour or more as he examined water bottles, shirts made with SPF material, sleeping bags for subzero freezing temperatures, and other stuff he didn't need. I was thinking about how bored I was, how disconnected I felt from him, but later, after dinner, he said, "I had fun with you today." He hugged me and said, "I love you," which he very rarely does anymore.

When I think of what a good, healthy relationship looks like and realize mine is far from it, I tell myself that I wouldn't like a good relationship; I would be bored or fuck it up or feel like I wasn't measuring up. There are enough sustaining elements: we do the laundry, we eat sushi, we like the same kinds of movies, we have people over for dinner, we take long walks around Queens. Raised in expressive, critical Armenian families, we feel that when we are mean to each other, at least we are being honest. And then of course there are all the things that I take for granted, that I can't even see or identify since I am in the thick of it: all the ways we have learned and accepted each other's eccentricities.

He is always asking me to wash his back when he is taking a shower. I don't like how my hand gets wet and sudsy, and he usually asks when I am in the midst of doing something else. Tonight, when I was grading papers, he took a shower and summoned me; as I pressed the washcloth slowly across his wide back, I realized that I had this task, and it involved another person, and it filled up my life.

"I love you, too," I told him.

STORY: EARLY SEPTEMBER, 2006
YEREVAN

Once outside the center of Yerevan, Na watched from the van window as the lively streets gave way to a desolate landscape: a few scrawny trees interspersed among concrete block hovels. Now with Gharib, Mardi, and Hankist, the leader of the feminist conference, Na felt somewhat at ease, but she still hadn't been able to email her parents. When she arrived at Miasin, Na had asked if she could use Hankist's laptop to check her email. "Ha," Hankist said, squinting at the screen through the smoke of her cigarette. "Mi vargyan." After a moment, Hankist invited Na to come along on a trip through the countryside to show her latest coterie of visiting artists a glimpse of Armenia.

As Na marveled at the nearly postapocalyptic landscape, the minivan encountered a strange oasis: a grotesque mansion under construction, the garden studded with dozens of fountains and populated by hundreds of statues of Armenian heroes. Gharib said the owner had made his money by monopolizing sugar imports with the help of his connections to the government. "This man is lawless," Gharib said. "A police officer stopped him for driving too fast, and he locked the cop in the truck of his car and dumped him off at the station. And the police did nothing. They let him go. Can you imagine?"

Now ten minutes outside of the city center, the tour stopped to examine Shant, an ostentatious restaurant with fountains and mirrors. After they passed through the restaurant and crossed a manicured courtyard, they encountered a small zoo. The animals faced each other in two lines of small concrete cages meant to look like caves. Monkeys and peacocks and bears and raccoons and birds Na had never heard of before were isolated and exhibited behind hand-painted signs in Armenian, Russian, and English. The creatures seemed despondent; the monkey, uncharacteristically lethargic, slumped in a corner of his cave. Mardi told Na that the owner of the complex was a member of parliament, another oligarch. He described those greedy men who swooped in during the transition to capitalism and took what they could get, leaving the rest of the country in squalor. "Asshole," Mardi said, echoing her thoughts. Na asked who dined at the restaurant. He looked at her with contempt and explained, "The rich and the fucking rich." Na wondered aloud if the corrupt clientele ate the exotic animals. "Maybe," Gharib told her. "It's more about the oligarch's pathetic attempt to exhibit his dominance."

The next item on the tour was the nuclear power plant, Metsamor. An Uzi-wielding guard in a halo-sized policeman's cap, greeted them and allowed them to pass by the four reactors letting off steam. Na was intrigued with their outer surface, covered in a crosshatched pattern like a spider's web. "The plant was shut down after the earthquake in 1988 but was turned back on a few years later, during the dark times," Gharib said. He meant the years from 1991 to 1994, when Armenia had first become independent and was at war with Azerbaijan, when heat and electricity were so scarce that the trees in the parks were cut down for firewood. "Now that Armenia has stabilized, there is pressure from the EU to close the plant down," Gharib said, "since it is deemed unsafe by an earthquake fault." But Armenia had no gas or oil of its own, and there was reluctance to be so dependent on Russia's fossil fuel energy imports. Because its borders with Azerbaijan and Turkey had been closed since the war, oil pipelines from Azerbaijan to Turkey went out of their way to bypass Armenia. "The nuclear power plant provides 40 percent of the country's electricity," Gharib said as Na gazed out the window at the silhouette of the chimneys, reminding her of the nuclear meltdown at Three Mile Island. It seemed to her that the only way for Armenia to survive was to gamble with the possibility of a wide-scale disaster.

Eventually, the group began to wonder how much radiation they were soaking in. Noticing a large crack in the concrete surface of one of the chimneys, they hightailed it back to the city. By the time they returned, Na was exhausted. She sat with Hankist on a park bench and tried to gain her bearings. When a vendor came around, they bought some ice cream. Na realized that she hadn't eaten since the bread and butter, and she was starving. She had had no way of knowing that by taking Hankist up on her invitation, she would be spending her entire day touring obscene monuments of the corrupt. So much for her goal to call or email home. She realized it had been comforting to play the tourist again, being driven around and cared for, her only obligation to look. But she was disturbed by the juxtaposition of images she had seen, the misspent wealth pasted alongside abject poverty, forming a landscape of geopolitical vulnerability. As she ate her ice cream, she looked down and noticed the wrapper in her hand. It read *Shant*, the name of the zoo-restaurant. In Armenian it was a male name, meaning "lightning," while in English it was a contraction of "shall not," an old-fashioned way to say *won't*. It wouldn't be the last time she found herself in dissonance—or between raw power and polite prohibition.

2. A PORTRAIT OF THE ARTIST AS AN INFANT

Artists Are Depressed Here, Too >>> "I was reading in the newspaper about a man in Russia who worked very hard and saved his money to such an extent that he wore his clothes until they were threadbare, and he had not eaten meat since before World War II ... " Moussi announced, out of the blue. We were standing in an apricot orchard by the ruins of Zvartnots Cathedral.

"And now he is eighty-four and wondering what to do with the million dollars that he has saved. And you know what he did? He burned it! I could not understand this. It made me sick!"

It seemed to me that if someone lived with austerity his whole life, it would be difficult to change. "Maybe he didn't want the responsibility that comes with that amount of money," I offered.

"My wife and I always say that if we got a lot of money, we would still stay in our apartment; we would not spend on material things," Moussi said. He was wearing a silk tie featuring a stylized crane hand-painted by his wife. "Instead, we would invest it in art and cultural projects. This man could have done so much good with the money. I think he was sick," Moussi said, "to choose a life of deprivation."

It was only a few days after I had arrived in Armenia, and we were standing by a banquet table under the apricot trees eating ripe, tasty grapes and peaches on an outing sponsored by the Ministry of Culture. Moussi, a friend of one of my friends from New York, had invited me. For my Fulbright project to write about art and social change in Armenia, I thought it would be helpful to attend an expedition to a cultural site. It was unclear to me who the other people were, but they were Armenian, dressed in their best, and looked mighty bored as they waited for the bus to take them back to Yerevan. They'd likely been here before, but to a newcomer like me, Zvartnots (which means Cathedral of the Angels) was an incredible sight: built in the seventh century, it was the only Armenian church of a circular design, constructed in three levels, like a layered wedding cake. It was destroyed by an earthquake in the tenth century, and the ruins now consisted of several columns and fragments of bas-reliefs. I was captivated by the designs on the fragments: leaves, grapes, pomegranates, and eagles. Kings, queens, and priests. I touched them with my hands, thinking about the artist stoneworkers who had carved them 1,400 years ago. As an Armenian American who often feels her culture exists in negative space, I appreciated the hardness of the stone: here was something made by Armenians so far back that I couldn't even imagine what their lives were like, if they had lived with sacrifice or plenty. But they existed—the proof was in the carvings.

The next evening, I had another opportunity to think about responsibility and deprivation at a lecture by a white American man living in Berlin, an independent scholar and "interventionist" at the Aragats Gallery. Speaking of protests in which he'd participated against globalization and the G8 conferences in Europe in the nineties, he explained that the territory of the street could be a site of action. He said that activism that "puts your body on the line" can be very effective. I wondered why the need for his lecture; after all, massive street protests in Yerevan and Stepanakert were what had prompted the dissolution of the Soviet Union. My friend Mardi, a filmmaker, claimed during the Q and A that it was very difficult to enlist Armenians in any kind of activism.

The discussion became very heated. From what I heard translated into English, it seemed that one camp thought that if your art wasn't political, then you weren't a true artist. But others claimed the opposite—that politics violated art, turning it into propaganda; they insisted that artists must practice activism separately from their work. But, the first camp argued, won't your political views inevitably inform your art?

The debate became even more incendiary, with raised voices in rushed Armenian. It seemed that people were provoked by a political definition of art because it was a throwback to the years when art was controlled by the state and used as a tool of the authoritarian government. But those artists who were desperate to fight government corruption were angry and frustrated by those who seemed reluctant for their art to have a political orientation. What was strange to me was that no one seemed to be saying, "Well, we can have different motivations for creating art; you can have your opinion and I can have mine ... " Instead, a differing artistic intention was treated as a personal assault. There was urgency to this debate, but I wondered if it was because solidarity had been forced on the culture for so long that subjectivity was still seen as a threat.

Another theory: because artists are now caught up in their own day-to-day survival, as they try to make change, challenge perceptions, get their work seen, and eke out a living, they feel intense stress. I've been told that there are personal grievances among these artists who are vying for limited opportunities for funding.

At one point, one large man, Medzig, spontaneously stomped on an upside-down plastic wine cup in response to a comment on the Soviet years. It was clear he was making a point that if you expressed yourself, you would be stamped out, violently and quickly. But the act was overshadowed by an even more absurd farce. When Medzig sat back down in his seat, the cheap folding chair buckled beneath him. Both acts, intentional and accidental, seemed like a commentary on the trauma people were expressing. The Soviet Union could crush you, but corrupt, capitalistic Armenia was so unstable now that you could crumple simply by the weight of your own existence.

Gushag, a young, chocolate-bearded philosophy student, said that he thought the issue was memory: "We struggle with memory, so we've put urgency on the practices. We believe that we are the ones who are speaking, but it's really our memories." I took him to mean that there are historical traumas trapped inside of Armenians from their years of surviving the particular violence of the Soviet Union and from suffering during the "dark years," when they endured a war with Azerbaijan. If art that changes the world compels you to put your body on the line, what do you do when your body has been attacked? What do you do when you haven't been used to having a body, when you've long been told your strength is collective and not individual? When denying your own body has been the method by which you, your family, and your culture have been able to survive the empires and the dark times?

Later, alone at my apartment, when I put the ideologies aside, I realized how much the event troubled me. Being here in Armenia is like being an infant again. I don't know the language, everything is new, and I'm with a bunch of Armenians who are yelling like my family. I recalled the first person to hug me after I arrived: Mardi. I was so happy to see him, a familiar face, that I gave him a huge embrace. But in reality, I don't know him very well, and after the first moment I could sense in his body an emotional slackness. It felt pretty embarrassing.

At one point the discussion turned to the salvation of the Armenian people. At a café catching up with some of the artists later, a poet acquaintance, Beatris, told me that after the Genocide, some Armenians hoped that communism would provide salvation. At first, rescued Armenians were able to build a society on their ancestral land with Soviet Russian overseers who let them survive according to their rules. But now, eighty years later, communism has been extinguished. During the café conversation, Medzig told me that when the Soviet system collapsed, a couple of ideas emerged that had been previously repressed: salvation through religion or salvation through the power of the individual. This doesn't sound so different from the diasporic mindset—either you tie yourself to church, community, and family, or you break away to express your own identity. How many stories had I heard from Armenia and the diaspora about queer Armenians coming out, only to be shunned by their families? Soviet pressure to adhere to the state parallels the conditional pressure of Armenian families to conform to heteronormativity. *You're either one of us, or you're against us. We can abandon you at any moment.* Here was the source of my discomfort, amplified through families, bodies, art, and politics: the pressure to deprive oneself of an individual self.

After the lecture, I met a young man named Seyran who told me he liked my poems. He had read a few that had been translated into Armenian last year which were published on a local online literary website. He seemed shy and excited, and I felt like a rock star. More than a handful of Armenian artists, upon meeting me, recognized my name from reading those few poems. I never imagined such an audience existed when I wrote them ten years ago. This, in my mind, is the kind of connection that can bring salvation.

The sculptors at Zvartnots now seemed to come into focus: they put their bodies into their work to create a message for others to see, chiseling hard stone with their instruments over days, months, years. Perhaps they were slaves to a system, perhaps they were independent artists; we don't know their level of sacrifice. In any case, it seems that no matter where, when, or how artists live, the way their art touches other lives is ultimately outside of their control. The fact that those ancient artists could reach an alienated Armenian, centuries into a future they could hardly imagine, gave me hope.

META-WRITING:

I didn't mention that I was brought to tears when I was back at the sterile diasporan apartment, alone, thinking about the conflict among the artists. Raised as an assimilated American, I was apt to conflate Armenian strangers with my family; their eyes, voices, and gestures were indistinguishable in a place where I felt so alone. I thought of my mother and her stories of marrying so young after losing her mother, then being left alone to care for little children when her husband went away on business trips. Growing up, I often felt my mother was there but not really there: going through the motions. Similar to many women of her generation, she avoided discussing issues of the body, and when she did they were broached in hushed tones. As I grew older and interacted with the Armenian community, I sensed this shame to be a cultural inheritance—so many other Armenians my age had experienced their parents abruptly changing the channel when a couple made out on TV. As I learned about the centuries of oppression leading up to the Genocide, it became clearer just how much having an Armenian body put you at risk for being killed.

In Yerevan I felt like a failure since I hadn't been able to publish my memoir about this legacy of my Armenian family history. Thus, the work of ancient, unknowable artists was enticing for me to project upon, and Seyran's attention was ego-boosting.

A few years later, when I was writing this account of trying to break up with Seyran that you now hold in your hands, he downloaded a strange TV show: The Earth Without People: 10,000 Years Later. *Through computer animation, ominous music, dramatic voice-over narration, and the testimony of various scientists, the program depicted how domesticated animals like cats and dogs, with no humans to take care of them, would inhabit the abandoned skyscrapers of New York City. Great world monuments like the Taj Mahal and the Great Wall of China would gradually crumble over time.*

I had to wonder about this premise. How could it be that all the human beings would die, but not the dogs and cats? It seemed the production was inspired by the evangelical Christian concept of the rapture: when all the good souls go to heaven and the rest of us will be sent to hell (but our pets will populate purgatory). Seyran agreed it was totally stupid. Americans in their shiny, safe paradise are obsessed with destruction, while Armenians, though they have existed for much longer, are aware of their near annihilation, past, present, and future; there's no need to fantasize about it.

There was one idea that oddly appealed to me, though: all the books in libraries turning to dust. Even the stuff we put on hard drives and plastic discs will disintegrate in ten thousand years.

Shakespeare, the Mona Lisa, Bach: all of it gone. Human intellectual production is fleeting and irrelevant, the show purported.

The idea was comforting: none of these words about our troubled and misguided relationship, typed into the memory of a hard drive, would ever matter. My written thoughts will dissipate, with no better chance to survive than Shakespeare's canon. If you don't have a culture, or words to write down, or a body, or even a self—then they cannot be abandoned.

STORY: EARLY SEPTEMBER, 2006
YEREVAN

Na was standing in the crowd outside Aragats Gallery after a lecture on art and activism, feeling overwhelmed. It was only three days after she had arrived in Armenia, and she was jet-lagged, stimulated by the discussion, and taking in her surroundings. The people on the sidewalk were greeting each other on this side street of newly built high-rises. Na noticed a range of young and old along with less conventional types. In the rest of the city, many Armenians costumed themselves according to strict gender-specific rules: men sported Members Only jackets with pointy shoes and cut their hair very short, no longer than half an inch; the women adorned themselves in layers of make-up, skirts, and heels, their dark hair ironed-straight down to the center of their spines. In contrast, the artist crowd streaming onto the sidewalk from Aragats Gallery consisted of balding men with longish sideburns and women with short hair of multiple colors. People wore jeans with tears in them, outdated glasses worn unironically, glints of gold teeth from Soviet-era dentists. In their individuality, they seemed at one with each other. It was ironic since they had just been engaged in fierce debate.

As she glanced around the crowd, Na spotted an acquaintance from her last visit the year before, Beatris the outlier poet, who had published some of Na's poems, translated into Armenian, in her online literary journal. Beatris, with her short red hair, nose ring, couture overalls and combat boots, was now standing in a group of five or six people, including Moussi, who had taken Na to Zvartnots the day before. Na approached shyly and Beatris enthused, "Natalee jan! What are you doing in Yerevan?" as she kissed Na on both cheeks.

Na told her about the creative writing classes that she would teach at the university, and Beatris asked if anyone could participate, pointing out the young man standing to Na's right. His name was Seyran, and he had published poems in Beatris's journal, too.

"I read your poems," he said. "I really like them." To Na he seemed like a nice young man, smiling broadly, a little geeky. Chiseled angles to his nose and jaw, short dark hair combed over his forehead like Napoleon—a typical Armenian male hairstyle. Na looked away for a moment to ponder if he'd be able to attend her class. She started to tell him that she didn't know if unregistered students could audit. When she looked back at him, to tell him he probably couldn't, Seyran was still smiling.

Moussi interrupted to talk about their trip to Zvartnots the day before, and soon the conversation moved to another topic and into Armenian. Na felt herself shy away. As she peered through the windows of the gallery, she could see the back of the American lecturer, in his khakis, talking to people, and she realized that she wanted to tell him how Armenians had started the first protests that led to the fall of the Soviet Union; they *had* put their bodies on the line. She went back inside to look for him but suddenly felt too bashful to approach. *He is here to talk to Armenians*, she thought, *not me*.

Na then caught Seyran out of the corner of her eye, making his way around the perimeter of the crowd inside the gallery. She had a feeling he was following her. He intercepted Na in the doorway as she was on her way out, underscoring how much her poems meant to him. "They are like Nirvana lyrics. They have voice of the teenager, which is very important because we all have teenagers inside of us." She smiled. Then he asked, "Are you popular in the U.S.?" She was flattered that anyone would think so and felt sorry to disappoint him. He didn't seem to mind, however, and asked, "How do you keep inspired?" Na was impressed; amidst all the arguing, no one had addressed personal motivation to create.

As they ambled back outside, Beatris invited them to dinner with a big group of folks. Happy to be included, Na walked down the street with Seyran and continued their conversation. He spoke heavily accented English, awkwardly syncopating his syllables, so she had to twist her ear to understand him, but she was happy to feel a connection to someone—anyone—since she had been feeling so lonely lately.

At the subterranean restaurant, with white floor tiles, brown tables, and a nondescript ambiance, Seyran sat next to Na, right in the middle of the long table, but he soon became very quiet. It was subtle, but Na felt a twinge of responsibility for him, as if he had silently attached himself to her. The group ordered khachapuri, a Georgian dish, which took on various meal-sized configurations of dough, cheese, and eggs. When Na's order came, it was a giant triangle of phyllo dough, larger than her head, filled with salty cheese. She cut it with her knife and fork, listening to the conversation as she took bites. Periodically, people translated into English for her. The group was criticizing the younger generation for their apathy, for not agitating for change. *Why haven't they changed with their new freedom?* they asked.

"Why don't you ask him?" Na said, jutting her thumb sideways at Seyran, the only young person at the table. When everyone's eyes focused on Seyran, however, he turned red. In Armenian he said that young people did care about Armenia, and they wanted it to be different, like Europe, a more open society, but such a change could mean losing Armenian tradition and culture. Then he looked at Na and said in English, "Your poems are going toward Europe." She guessed that he meant her poems expressed her feelings freely.

As people decided to make their way home, she realized that she didn't exactly know what to take, a taxi or a marshrutka, one of the numbered white vans with set routes. She told people where she was going, and they directed her to the correct marshrutka stop.

As they parted to say goodbye, everyone kissed everyone on both cheeks, as was the custom. Na had grown up with half of this tradition in the diaspora, with a kiss on the cheek that often veered into the mouth area, which she hated; the wet, sharp kisses of her relatives invading her personal space. As an adult she'd grown out of it, and she now appreciated the practice, which, compared to the American hug, seemed more continental and sophisticated, two soft cheeks in succession, slipping next to each other delicately, a blurry glance of a face in between. Na attempted to kiss each person, but as her marshrutka arrived, she was approached by Medzig, a large, round, and very sweaty man. In a split-second decision, she shook his hand instead. Everyone laughed at this formality—none of the Armenians had shied from the social duty of kissing everyone equally. Na knew it was impolite, but she couldn't help it, even though she liked Medzig as much as the other amiable strangers.

She turned around to say goodbye as she boarded the marshrutka, but the group was walking down the street, their backs toward her. The only one looking her way was Seyran. She then realized that she had been so concerned about avoiding Medzig that she hadn't kissed Seyran. He now waved to her, his head awkwardly tilted to one side, still smiling.

JOURNAL: SEPTEMBER 10, 2009
ASTORIA

Last night I left a baby on a rock.

Unlike the others, this baby wasn't very detailed—it didn't drool or coo or make jerky movements or ever-changing expressions. In fact, it wasn't much different from a doll except that it was heavy, straining my arms as I held it to my chest. I was with friends when I was called away to do something, I'm not sure what, maybe row a canoe or put on a skit. So I laid the baby down on a rock. It was a flat boulder, like the kind people sit on in Central Park, in between patches of grass. Inevitably, the moment arrived when I realized what I had done, so I rushed back to retrieve the baby only to find that it was gone. I was beside myself with guilt. *How? How could I have left a baby? On a rock?* I rushed around, trying to locate the lost baby, returning to the rock again and again, hoping someone would put it back where they found it, but relief came only when I woke up.

I've never felt my life would be incomplete without a child. I'm not entirely opposed to having a kid; it's just that I only want to pursue the idea if the right conditions arise, i.e., a loving partner who will take equal responsibility to parent. I'm not going to be like my mother or grandmother, unsatisfied with life. So if the right situation doesn't come along, no big deal.

But why, for years, have I been frantically searching for babies—which I've abandoned on airplanes, in art museums, libraries, and movie theaters? This time, leaving behind the baby on a rock—in the wide-open air, on such a hard surface, and among millions of people—felt particularly irresponsible, and the accompanying panic was painfully real.

I witnessed a similar scene a few days ago, but I don't think that was the emotional trigger. I think it's Seyran. Today he wants me to take photos of him to send to his parents. I guess they have been asking him for pictures, but he has avoided sending any because they would hate his hair grown past his shoulders and his full Jesus beard. It's so crazy that they think men's hair shouldn't cover their ears, but that's Armenia for you. Seyran hasn't cut his hair since we arrived, so two years now! And I can't remember when he started growing the beard. It's black with a sunburst of brown underneath his lip, thick and wiry, dense as a woolen carpet. He resembles a Byzantine-era king depicted in profile in bas-relief on an ancient church, with an angular beard covered in swirling curls.

To me he looks beautiful, but last week Seyran woke from a nap and scared a baby to tears.

My friend Nora was visiting with her son Raffi right as Seyran woke up to go to work on the graveyard shift. We were playing with the baby on the floor, and I was noticing the clumps of dust clinging to the edges of the oriental rug when Seyran silently appeared, standing in the doorway. He was sleepy in his shorts and tank— black hair covering his whole body, shoulders, chest, and legs. Raffi was instantly frightened by the sight of this apparition, perhaps the closest he'd ever come to a monster, though he had met Seyran—clean-shaven with much shorter hair—six months before. When Raffi was just a few months old, Seyran had played with him joyfully, cradling him in his arms and singing to him. Back then, Nora told me how much she loved visiting us as it reminded her of being in Armenia. Seyran had played the host, roasting fish and vegetables in the oven, serving tea with sweets. But now he was groggy and uncharacteristically cold to the child, who whimpered as he backed himself into a corner of the room. His mom explained that this man was Seyran, no one to be afraid of, but Seyran strangely did little to assuage the baby. "I think it's your long hair," my friend said. "He's never acted this way before with anyone." She asked Seyran how he was doing, perhaps to change the tone. Seyran shrugged and sullenly slumped away.

After Nora and Raffi went home, Seyran said he couldn't believe how big the baby was, now nine months old. "How can you call someone a friend when you haven't seen her for months?" he asked me. I gave him the answer that I always do, that friendship is less of a priority to people in New York, but he hadn't asked the question to hear an answer. It obviously troubled him that the baby was now so big and that Nora hadn't turned out to be like the kinds of friends we had in Yerevan, who had time to socialize regularly. "You didn't have to be rude to her just because she didn't meet your expectations," I told him.

"There is no point in talking about my life with a friend who is not really a friend," he said. I could understand his loneliness, but his ire didn't feel fair. I've been trying to give him the sense of belonging he provided me when I first arrived in Yerevan. But he doesn't want my middle-aged friends. To compensate, I've been spending more time with him and, ironically enough, not seeing my friends as much.

A couple of days later, we took a long walk around Astoria. We wound up and down the side streets of old turn-of-the-century homes covered in aluminum siding next to chains of brick houses built before the Depression. Then we visited a bunch of shops: Chinese, Korean, Greek, and Indonesian. He couldn't experience this ethnic diversity in Armenia, and it is the one thing that still gives him consolation after everything he left behind.

We made our way to Little Egypt for paklava when on a whim he decided to shave off his beard and all of his hair. A stylist in a small salon snipped off Seyran's eight-inch ponytail in one piece, claiming he would donate it to a charity that crafted wigs for women who had lost their hair from radiation treatments. I whispered to Seyran that the stylist would probably sell it, but Seyran didn't care. He had grown that hair as an expression of his freedom from the conformity of Armenia with all its corruption and hypocrisy. Now it was in a Ziploc bag, given away virtuously or for profit; we had no way of knowing.

As the buzzer made its way across his face and his head, hair gently sliding off his skin, I flipped through a magazine, getting lost in the wonder of the new first lady, Michelle Obama. A few minutes later I looked up, noticing a barefoot toddler, a little girl with dark curly hair, wearing a flowered top and diaper-heavy pink pants. She ambled toward me and stared my way, smiling sweetly. I couldn't help smiling back. She giggled as the other stylist knelt down beside her, pretending to poke her in the tummy.

"How old is she?" I asked.

"Isn't she yours?" the stylist replied.

I shook my head. We looked around the room. There were no other customers.

The conversation caught Seyran's attention, and he peered at us out of the corner of his eye. Another woman who was sweeping up his hair from the floor peeked out the door, where the sky was spreading dusk over the neighborhood. No possible moms were out on the block lined with hookah bars, mostly populated by men who smoked the pipe.

Eventually, while the stylist played with her, the sweeping woman called the police, though they suspected that the mother was at the mosque up the street and had lost track of the child. It had happened before. Still, they speculated what would happen if no one came to claim her. "Don't make me take her," one of them joked. "All I got in my fridge is a can of Red Bull."

I thought about bringing the little girl home for a minute. Here we were, Seyran and I, a straight-passing couple with a home and a kitchen full of food. Of all the characters in the salon to take care of a baby until the situation was sorted out, we appeared to be the most conventional option. A few months after we had met, after I'd accepted that he was more than a fling, I entertained the thought that we might have a kid someday, along with all the other happy projections into the future one makes at the start of a new relationship. But as our troubles have mounted, I've abandoned that idea.

I felt a finger poke my shoulder and there was Seyran, bald, with no beard, clean-shaven and shiny.

✧

Today he wants me to take photos of him because his look is now acceptable to his parents. I tell him that I am about to go to yoga, but I can do it afterward. No, he wants to do it now. So I grab my camera and snap one of him.

"No, stop," he commands. "I want to take some outside with my bike." This strikes me as incredibly cute. I smile, and he says, "Fuck you, I'm doing it for my parents."

"I'm not laughing *at* you," I defend myself.

He snaps. "Forget it, I don't need your help." He bounds down the stairs and takes the photos on his own, presumably using the self-timer. When he comes back in, he has trouble transferring the images to his computer. I offer to put them on mine and email them to him. "No, I told you. I don't want any help from you."

"What's wrong?"

"You should know."

"You're being passive aggressive."

"What does that mean?"

Without a way to translate, I scour my mind for the reason for his feelings. Perhaps it's because his behavior makes no sense that I look for answers within myself. Or perhaps I don't want to accept that he is simply a jerk. It's true that I've been working a lot lately and am more stressed than usual, with less time to pay attention to him. Maybe this is what's troubling him.

As I leave for yoga, I apologize if I've done something wrong. He says, "You don't understand. It's your attitude the last few days. When I'm unhappy or stressed, I don't put it onto you, but you do this to me." I'm not sure how I have put my stress onto him; it's not like I'm complaining a lot or demanding that he grade my papers. And it doesn't occur to him that he is now putting his feelings onto me. Rather than get into a blame game, I tell him, "Well, maybe you could give me some space when I am stressed."

He looks at me with resignation and says, "Never mind."

When I come home from yoga, I ask if he wants something to eat. He declines since he'll be leaving for work soon. I proceed to make green beans with bulghur in the rice cooker. As I am chopping, he takes some chickpeas out of a container in the fridge and starts popping them raw into his mouth. "I thought you weren't hungry," I say to him, and he says, "You're cooking these things, and it makes me hungry."

"Well, put that away and eat this."

"I don't want to eat with you," he says. He is naked, and with his bald head he looks like a big baby.

"Well, leave then!" I snap. "You're making me feel worse when I'm trying to be nice!"

"You're not nice to me," he says.

We keep going back and forth like this; it's almost like our dialogue is scripted and I have to recite my part, like one of those dreams when you're in a play and you proceed with the scene even though it's going terribly wrong. We have played out the same bad act so many times that it feels like it has carved a new groove in my brain. Or perhaps it has always been there to begin with.

While he's in the shower, I follow the neural pathway and ask if he wants me to scrub his back. He says no. A few moments later, I return to the bathroom and ask if he needs a towel. He is already wrapped in one and says, "You don't give me a towel when I need it, and then you try to give me one when I don't need it."

I burst out laughing. He is a caricature, a gluttonous king, like the bas-relief at Zvartnots. Nothing pleases him; nothing I do is right. I must draw so much of my self-worth from helping him that when he manipulates me like this, when he takes away my opportunity to care for him, I completely lose it. It's sad and absurd at once. I weep in frustration, laughing and crying at the same time.

He went to work a little while ago. Now, alone in my bed, I am thinking about the toddler in the salon. "This always happens," I remember the stylist complaining at the barber shop. "Why can't they watch their kids?" The child didn't seem aware that she had lost her mother; she was discovering a whole new world, smiling and giggling with glee. Eventually, the mosque let out, and the stylist brought the little girl outside to see if she would be claimed.

Dusk made way to night as a small crowd of people gathered in front of the salon. Suddenly, I heard a wail. There was the mother, in a black flowered headscarf. She scooped up the baby into her arms, her oval face wracked with grief, eyebrows arched in pain. According to a henna-bearded man standing next to her, the child had wandered off, and the mother had been searching for her throughout the mosque, then on the street until she arrived at the salon. I expected her to be relieved, the way I had felt when I woke from my nightmare. Instead, she was beside herself, sobbing uncontrollably, mourning the loss of what could have been.

3. OUTSIDE IN

Moving through the City >>> In Yerevan, there are cranes everywhere. I'm not talking birds; those would be delightful. These are building cranes, foreboding behemoths, lurking behind the facades of dead homes. Busy raising huge edifices above crumbling hovels of old brick and corrugated tin, the cranes loom overhead as I traverse the city by foot, cab, bus, or marshrutka. Buildings that I saw as skeletons last year are now completed: smooth, shiny, new, and ugly. The city is undergoing a transformation as I navigate the surface of the streets in a state of mystification.

Meanwhile, below the ground, by the metro stations and the pedestrian passageways beneath major intersections, there is a labyrinthine network of stands and booths. Everywhere you turn, something is for sale: fried bread, cell phone holders, chintzy underwear, graph paper pads, and stacks and stacks of used books. I cannot figure out how all these vendors are making a living. Who is buying faded, moldy tomes in Russian and English of *Alice in Wonderland*, the poems of Pushkin, and ESL textbooks from 1982?

Amid the contrasts I am finding it difficult to get around the city. There are no signals for pedestrians to cross the street, so you must be careful to move with the bulk of the herd, otherwise you're screwed. Yerevan drivers are nearly homicidal, seeming to speed up as they approach pedestrians in a crosswalk. Riding on a marshrutka feels safer, but I am awkward with the etiquette. It's not always clear where to wedge my body if every seat is filled, or how to crouch or slouch so as not to tip over into someone's lap. The first time on board, I waited nervously with my coin in my hand until the driver approached the corner where I wanted to debark, and I yelled "Ganganek!" which I'd learned from my guidebook. The van stopped, but everyone turned around to look at me funny. *Ganganek* is probably not the equivalent of "stop here" but "stop forsooth!"

Learning the language hasn't been fluid for me. At home I construct questions on paper and say them out loud. Then when I'm in public and announce the string of words, I realize I haven't accounted for the need to understand the answer. It's like being a bad actor who can memorize lines but cannot be present on stage to respond. I stammer one word here and there, praying the Armenians will get the gist. Often they do, but I operate in some airless space, hoping no one will yell at me. I try my best to listen, but I think much gets lost in the Eastern Armenian pronunciation of words that sound very different from the Western Armenian I grew up with. The Armenians sometimes become impatient and repeat the same word over and over again, which I repeat back to them, not having any idea what it means.

One night, a man in a taxi called his mother and told me to speak to her in English. I was annoyed because I thought I had mastered how to explain in Armenian the way back to my place. "Tigran Mets and Yervand Kochar are two different streets," she said in halting English. "I know," I snapped, "I'm going to where they meet!" (Tigran Mets was an emperor in the first century BC, and Yervand Kochar was an artist in the twentieth century; they likely never did meet.) I was reminded of the time, over a month ago, when I snapped at an Asian woman who could not speak English. She was working at the copy place in Flushing, Queens, where I made course packets for my students. A few important pages were missing, and I found myself uncharacteristically haughty. "Do you speak English?" I demanded. *No*, she shook her head. "Then how can you understand me?" She called her daughter on her cell phone to help. When the girl kept asking me questions, I snapped, "Hold on! Listen to me!" Now on the other side of the language gap, I am confronted by my previous impatience.

Communicating poorly with the cab driver and taking the wrong marshrutka are much more disturbing than they should be, but I must base a huge chunk of my identity on performing tasks efficiently. Traveling effortlessly on the subway in New York, I can come up with several contingency plans within seconds if a train is shut down. Proud to have built up my independence after many years of sorting through painful realizations, I have become undone by Yerevan, which has exposed the fear beneath my carefully constructed sense of control.

Yesterday, I had hoped to catch a free bus from Republic Square that would take me to Tsitsernakaberd, a.k.a. the Genocide memorial, to a diaspora conference. I was the only person who stood waiting at the designated spot outside the Marriott while well-heeled foreigners sipped coffee at the hotel's tony sidewalk café. I waited for an hour before giving up. I felt like a failure, but as I walked home, I noticed the police had cut off all traffic in and out of Republic Square; the bus probably couldn't get through, a factor completely out of my control.

Apparently, someone had decided that rush hour was the perfect time to rehearse for the celebration of fifteen years of independence. I stood and watched as a convoy of trucks roared into the square, carrying an endless stream of soldiers. The Azerbaijani government has been making threats to reignite the war over Nagorno-Karabakh, and so I wondered who exactly was guarding the border. These soldiers were packed into tight spaces, dressed in green, their thousands of black eyes gazing out shyly from beneath their caps. Thin as twigs, they looked like you could break them in two over your knee. Armenian national insecurity can't be camouflaged by all those skinny little soldiers carted into the shiny square to celebrate the glory of hard-won independence.

How fortuitous that they appeared at the moment when I was reminded of my tiny existence: my incredible fear to misspeak the simplest of sentences, my well-intended plans waylaid.

STORY: SEPTEMBER, 2006
YEREVAN

When Na entered the dark auditorium, Cameron Diaz's frizzy-haired heroine was stumbling across the screen in Spike Jonze's *Being John Malkovich*. As she took a seat, the lights came up, and a lecturer with a cockney accent began pontificating on the clip for a lecture at the National Gallery of Armenia, "Postmodernism and the Individual." Na realized that she had gotten the time wrong, but she sat down and tried to figure out what this professor from the UK was discussing, something about antiheroes.

The audience was sparse as it was 4 p.m. on a Friday afternoon, but Na was relieved to be out of the apartment, where she had been retreating to rest, read, and crochet for long hours, recovering from jet lag. In between dealing with bouts of exhaustion, Na went outside only to wrangle with people at the visa office, the embassy, and the university, trying to obtain her resident visa in rooms where practically no one spoke English. She found herself saying *passport* with an Armenian accent, hoping it would help convey her message, to no avail. When a few people in one office insisted that Na prove her credentials by showing them her graduate diploma from an American university, she was beside herself, imagining the framed, elaborately signed and stamped certificate packed into a cardboard box in a low-price storage unit in Brooklyn. "I didn't bring my diploma to Armenia!" she exclaimed, giving up and walking out. (She had never imagined her immigrant students in New York packing their diplomas to bring to the U.S., where authorities would immediately deem them worthless.) She then called and left messages for her contact at the U.S. embassy, an administrator born and raised in Yerevan, who had given her an orientation a few days before in an office decorated with photos of Condoleezza, Bush, and Cheney.

Na observed that the administrator seemed to change personalities depending on the language she was speaking. In English, she was formal and emotionless, ticking through the official rundown of what Na's position at the university would be as a representative of U.S. academia. Witnessing her speak on the phone in Armenian, Na noticed her pitch switch to a singsong as she called university officials "jan"—dear one. Na figured English was for work, and Armenian was the language of home, friends, and family. In seeing the staffer move fluidly between languages at work, Na wondered which personality of the diplomat was more real.

When the woman told Na that she could bring her students to use the library at the embassy, that it was open to anyone, Na filed this information away and added an embassy library visit to her syllabus. Later she would regret subjecting her students—their eyes wide, their bodies stiff and surprised—to the security detail at the imposing gated complex on the outskirts of town, resigning herself to the fact that it did teach them something new about the U.S., even if it was ugly.

Now the film scholar from the UK was commenting on *The Matrix*, and Na wondered why she was discussing only U.S. films. Sitting a few rows up from her was Mardi, who raised his hand and asked a similar question. Na recalled the conversation she'd had with Beatris at dinner after the previous lecture when Mardi had complained that Armenians didn't protest, prompting a heated debate. According to Beatris, Mardi was a troublemaker and had alienated most of his peers; she explained that they had once been friends, but they'd drifted apart the year before, something to do with representation to show work in Europe. Na didn't sense that Mardi was egotistical or petty, given his strong philosophical convictions; rather, she figured people resented Mardi's confrontational nature. She could imagine him insisting to Beatris that she would be exploited in Europe. To Na he had only been kind. Just the other day, he and Gharib had called and asked, "Should we be worried about you?" when she had said she was too tired to socialize with them.

As the conversation continued in English and Armenian, she noticed Seyran, the young man she had met at the previous lecture who had treated her like a rock star. He was leaning back in his chair so that his head was resting at the top of the seat, his face turned in profile to hear the speaker. Na noticed his thick, long eyelashes above the line of his nose. This sparked something in her. *He's really cute*, Na noted. In the months before her trip, she had found herself attracted to a string of younger men who had crossed her path. She was excited by these feelings but also found them curious. She felt a similar ambivalence toward her attraction to Seyran.

After the film, as discussions continued among the audience members, she tried to catch Mardi's eye with a wave. He either didn't see her or was avoiding her, and she became insecure for a moment that he knew she had gone out with his ex-friend Beatris. Wishing to avoid a confrontation, she slipped out quietly.

In the hallway she ran into Seyran, and he flashed her a wide smile of recognition. Hands in his pockets, he seemed more relaxed than when he had silently sat next to her at the restaurant the previous week. They followed the crowd to a tiny elevator. Na had been noticing lately the grandness of Soviet-planned public spaces, like the square in front of the museum, seemingly designed to prove the moral superiority of communism. In contrast, the elevators were so small as to be nonexistent, as if the architect couldn't be bothered to think about the humanity that would occupy such a space. Or maybe it was a covert form of protest, to remind people of each other's humanness.

Just yesterday, Na had been in a similar elevator on her way to look at an apartment nearby—Mardi had introduced her to the landlord the previous week, insisting she'd be cold in that big apartment in the wintertime. The apartment had an amazing view of the city and a great location, but Na felt it was haunted. The dingy wallpaper looked tea-stained, and the living room was crowded with two twin beds with flimsy mattresses and an old crib. Na didn't see how she could make it livable. When she rode the tiny elevator back down the nine floors with the landlord, he emitted terrible body odor and told her the rent was fifty dollars higher than what Mardi had quoted. Shaking her head, she blurted out, "Che!"

Now in the small space with Seyran and two strangers, she realized that elevators might be the only public place where people came so close that they breathed in each other's existence. Na wondered what pheromones she was picking up from Seyran or wafting to him. When they hit the ground floor, he was careful to usher her out politely before the two strangers. They strolled outside into the sunny day, up Abovyan Street.

"I read interview of you," Seyran told her. He was referring to the interview that Amal had done with her the year before in the women's journal, the one that Digeen Sargsyan had read. "You are bisexual?" he asked.

"Yes," she said, nodding her head. Na was surprised by such a question out of the blue, but on the other hand, it was refreshing for someone to ask her openly and specifically about being queer, a topic most people either evaded or were oblivious to.

"It is hard for homosexuals here," he said. Na wondered if he was gay and half expected him to say as much. Instead, he shared, "I have homosexual friend. They have hard times." She nodded, straining her ear around his heavy accent, hoping for a clue into his interest in her.

Seyran asked her about her experience in Armenia so far, and she told him of her troubles learning the language. Moussi had given her the number of a woman who taught Armenian to foreign students at the university, but Na was reluctant to hire her as she didn't know English.

"I know friend, she's a good teacher. She can help you." By now they were at Na's destination, an internet café where she could send more emails about her visa. "If you need any help, please, I can help you," he said.

Na took out her notepad and wrote her name, phone number, and email. "Okay, let me know about your friend, the teacher. And if you hear about any kind of poetry event, please let me know." It occurred to Na that she was in the process of giving a young, cute guy her number, a circumstance she couldn't recall doing very much in her life. She felt ambivalent about it, telling herself that he was too young and possibly gay and that she was merely making an effort to meet more people anyway. *I need to start setting up interviews, after all,* she rationalized. *Here's a friendly guy offering his help. Why not take it?*

A feeble American antihero struggling with language, jet lag, and her sense of self in a postmodern and deconstructed Armenia, Na gave Seyran the warmest, biggest smile she could summon as she handed him her number. She watched his face widen into a smile, his brightest one yet, with a breath of excitement behind it. As they parted, she looked back at him. He seemed to leap away gleefully.

A few days later, Na received an email from Seyran:

> *barev natalee,*
>
> *i like so much connecting and speak with you*
>
> *you make my brain sing*
>
> *one day we can write poems together*
>
> *I want to learn you like a book*
>
> *and i can make you Armenian tea*

Na smiled. Here was the clue she'd been hoping for. Seyran was wooing her with a poem. She also shook her head; *poor guy.* Na thought he was clearly misguided, a college kid misplacing his interest on her, an older woman in her late thirties. Though she enjoyed the attention, Na told herself that she wouldn't pursue him.

JOURNAL: OCTOBER 12, 2009
ASTORIA

Justin visited from Philly for a few days. It was nice to see my old friend, but unfortunately, Seyran screwed it up.

We were all watching this crazy Jane Campion movie last night. In a way, that film sums up my predicament. Harvey Keitel is trying and failing to deprogram Kate Winslet from a cult that she joined in India. Instead, he has sex with her, which doesn't seem an appropriate way to treat someone with trust issues and a distorted sense of self. It's confusing, because Winslet's character seems powerless, yet she uses all her abilities to manipulate Keitel, who is so unsympathetic and creepy with his late nineties soul patch. I am not sure who to sympathize with: Keitel, who loses himself while dealing with a disturbed, deluded, and fiercely intelligent young person; or Winslet, who feels unfairly trapped by her circumstances. I don't think I like either of them.

Seyran chose the film, *Holy Smoke,* and projected it onto the white wall of his empty room. It was uncomfortable, lying on the floor with my back against the wall and a pillow under my butt. When we moved in, I was glad he took the living room since he'd slept on other people's couches for so long—here was a room of his own. I also figured it would be better to settle in separate bedrooms in terms of a possible future breakup so I could kick him out and find a roommate. But I didn't realize he would waste so much space. It's been a year, and all he has in there is a bookshelf and not even a bed, just a tatami mat on the floor.

Besides the full-size bed where we periodically have sex, my smaller room contains a dresser, side tables, books, and art. The previous tenant had installed a lot of extra shelves with a nautical motif. At the rear of the apartment, my room, with its built-in desk and bookshelves clustered by the windows, is like the stern of a ship: I'm always looking backward from where I've come.

When we were watching the film, Seyran took the opportunity to poke fun at Justin whenever a gay character appeared onscreen, making some dumb comment. "Justin, do you like him?" Or "Justin, do you like the film because you are gay, and it's a gay film?" At first Justin chuckled a little, but apparently it really bothered him, because this morning when I called to see if he had caught his train, he told me how upset he was with Seyran's comments.

I was surprised, given that Seyran is bisexual; I expected Justin might understand that teasing was a way for Seyran, coming from a homophobic, repressive country, to break his silence on queerness. I also couldn't believe that my friend, as a privileged American, would feel threatened by the shenanigans of an immature immigrant half his age. But then that would suggest that I also shouldn't be upset by the stupid things Seyran says. But I always am. I just try to forget them.

I wasn't going to tell Seyran about the phone call, fearing that he would never associate with Justin again, but he asked if Justin had a good time, so I told him he was hurt. Seyran didn't seem to care about Justin's feelings, and unlike most people who would have probably reached out to explain themselves, apologize, and show goodwill, he was defensive, claiming that whenever he makes fun of my brother for being gay, he doesn't get upset. This made me pause. Maybe my brother, like me, is so used to dealing with our crazy relatives that he also brushes Seyran off.

Justin said to me on the phone, "If Seyran wants to make friends, he'll have to be nice to people." Coincidentally, Seyran said today, "Do you realize I haven't made any friends in the two years I have lived in New York?" It's not true; he has work buddies plus a guy who recruited him to be in his band, though they don't play much anymore.

Seyran rarely expresses feelings of failure. Normally he would claim that there is something wrong with the city or something wrong with me for bringing him here. Today he was making a sad observation about himself.

I recalled to him that it had taken me about two years to make friends when I first moved to New York. "Yes, but you knew the language," he told me. But he isn't illiterate like I was in Yerevan, since he had been speaking English with me for a year before we moved. When we first arrived, he had a particular fear of talking on the phone. It was funny when he didn't want to call for Chinese food, since the people who took the orders didn't speak English any better than him. And he sometimes served as a translator for me with recent immigrants, understanding more clearly the new English that they spoke.

I guess such daily interactions with strangers are different from the language mastery needed for friendship. "You knew my friends," I told him.

"Yes, but we never connected." Sadly, most of my friends don't understand Seyran through his heavy accent, and some can't even say his name correctly even after hearing me pronounce it innumerable times. I wonder if they are prejudiced toward an immigrant. Since they are much older and going through midlife crises, none of them seem to care what he is going through. I felt similarly alienated as a new visitor among people with full lives in Armenia. But I was older and knew my stay was temporary. And I had someone who rescued me from that fate—Seyran. I have tried to be the same for him, but it isn't working. Seyran likes to be the one in control, the expert showing a lost soul around town to meet all his friends and acquaintances. He can't do that now, and he assumes that if he can't connect with my friends, it is their fault, so he has stopped socializing with them. Now he is making fun of them to their faces.

I'm worried that all my friends are going to leave me. I haven't been telling them my troubles with Seyran because I am afraid they will totally abandon me. But now, because he is being a jerk to them, they'll abandon me anyway.

It's ironic, I realize, that I have fractured myself: one life with Seyran and one with my friends. But I suppose it is what I am used to from my childhood—living in an Armenian world with my family while experiencing an American life at school and among my friends. To not be fully understood anywhere became too painful, so I accepted the duality.

Now my two worlds are in direct conflict, but I don't want to be in the middle. Justin should speak to Seyran directly. And I can't break up with Seyran because my friends don't like him; I have to do it because *I* don't like him.

I also don't have to put up with his bullshit. I'm going to tell him not to make fun of my brother and my friends. *A little playful teasing is okay, but not all the time. Please be conscious of other people's feelings.*

I can't believe I have to say things like this. He's just too immature sometimes.

META-WRITING:

When I was in Armenia, the city was being built, and it was also being torn down.

The first time I discovered this, Gharib and Mardi were showing me Yerevan on my first visit. We were in the center, on a side street behind Republic Square, when we came across a beautiful century-old home. The family who lived inside, who had owned it for generations, was being turned out. The walls were being demolished to reveal the layers of wallpaper and the dishes inside of the built-in cabinets. The family spoke to Gharib, who plotted ways to summon a camera crew to the scene. He made calls on his cell phone to contact the people he knew in the media.

Mardi explained that no one could live in the fancy new buildings going up around town. "The government is corrupt and wants to make a city for the rich," Gharib interjected, his chin away from his phone. "Foreigners, diasporans come and move into them. The local population is moving outside from the center." A year later, I was shocked when I visited the National Gallery and peered out from its windows to see the decrepit homes with thin tin roofs behind the shining facades of the main square and, like war apparatus, scores of cranes dragging pink tufa stone up from the earth where it had been resting peacefully.

The owners of the torn-down home had been distraught. They weren't crying or hysterical, but they looked tired with glassy eyes. Wearing old sweaters, they gestured at the house. Gharib informed them that his friend would come by soon, but they didn't seem empowered by the news. They weren't yet giving up, but they didn't seem to have much hope.

Reliving my relationship through these fractured pieces of writing, I feel dismayed that I abandoned my friend Justin to Seyran's destruction. I've always believed writing can reveal truth to make change, like Gharib calling his journalist friends to shine a light on the homeowners' plight. But this assumes the writer is honest. The system of my personhood was breaking down. Unlike the residents of Yerevan losing their home, I simply did not see it.

STORY: SEPTEMBER, 2006
YEREVAN

On the phone, Seyran told Na the name of the metro station they were to meet at, Yeritasardakan, which translated to "Youth" since it was near the university. Na walked to the station rather than getting on the metro, wary of taking on yet another new transaction involving language. At the appointed time, she showed up outside the station wearing a white tank top with big black polka dots. She saw him from afar wearing a striped blue polo shirt with its collar standing erect. Smiling as usual, he waved to get Na's attention. He had styled his hair so that he didn't look so much like Napoleon as Elvis, with his bangs gelled away from his face. As she approached him, she noticed that he looked at her boobs quite obviously, then smiled in a pleased, self-satisfied way that reminded her of an asshole frat boy. She recoiled at the crass gesture, in stark contradiction to the sweet email he had penned about writing poems and making her tea, but she took it in as a piece of information about this curious creature. Though she had decided not to pursue Seyran, the reality was that she was lonely.

They had a plan to go to two concerts: one by his friend at the Komitas Chamber Music House nearby, and the other to see her friend, a diasporan rock singer at Naregatsi Art Institute, a longer walk away. Na and Seyran had time to kill before the first concert, so they walked and talked. It wasn't so easy to do with the erratic drivers who hated to stop, swerve, or slow down for pedestrians. Seyran's heavy accent and limited grasp of English, and Na's even worse Armenian skills, prevented any meaningful communication. Na brought out her dictionary and Seyran took it, but he declined looking up a word he was having trouble remembering. Instead, he held the book closed in one hand and turned his other up toward the sky, looking toward the heavens as if waiting for the word to land in the palm of his hand. Na admired his faith and patience to take space to speak. When they crossed the street, he put his arm out in front of her in an instinctive protective gesture against the on-slaught of cars, and Na warmed toward him.

As they continued down Abovyan, she asked him where he lived, which set him off on a long explanation about the couches and floors upon which he crashed. He lived with a series of friends and relatives because he didn't get along with his parents.

Rather than asking about this conflict, she stated, "That must be tiring, moving from place to place." Her large apartment wasn't working out too well. When she went to bed, she could hear someone hammering nearby, undertaking a home improvement project every night at 11:15. When she did manage to sleep, some sort of bug would bite her and wake her up, leaving itchy welts that troubled her for days. Still, the thought of packing everything up and moving was overwhelming.

"It's okay, I can live like this. I'm only twenty-one," he said.

He's definitely too young, Na thought, as if she hadn't already told herself not to pursue him.

When they reached Hraparak, aka Republic Square, they turned around and walked back up Abovyan to the Chamber Music House, a narrow building made of concrete slabs wedged together at soaring angles. They sat in red velvet-cushioned chairs and looked up at the stage. Seyran's friend Kristapor, a violinist, performed a duet with a female cellist from France, a lovely classical arrangement. Kristapor was a slightly overweight man with a full head of bushy brown hair and large round eyes, wearing neatly pressed black clothes. He couldn't have been playing for more than a few minutes when Seyran whispered gleefully in Na's ear, "He's bisexual."

Na was struck with insecurity. She assumed that in a highly homophobic place "bisexual" really meant "gay" as a way for some men to protect themselves. Separated from a support network, she defaulted to old stereotypes that bisexuality was a lie or a pit stop to being gay, ironically enough. It wasn't hard for her to then feel sorry for herself. *I am so lonely that I am seeking out the attention of a twenty-one-year-old sexually ambiguous kid.* She teared up a bit.

After the concert Seyran led Na backstage, and Kristapor was so excited and happy to see Seyran. He ruffled his hair and kissed him on both cheeks. It seemed they were lovers. Na felt happy for them and relieved to gain some clarity on Seyran's status.

They exited the concert hall and walked through the park that circled Yerevan, and Na saw that cafés had been built on this strip of green, too. They made their way to Naregatsi Art Institute, founded by a diasporan businessman. Vehine, a friend of a friend of Na's from Detroit, had assembled a rock trio and was singing classic hits. Na and Seyran sat in the back of the small but modern concert hall, and Seyran criticized Vehine the entire time: "She can't sing! You like this?" Na agreed that Vehine wasn't a tremendously talented singer; there wasn't much power to her voice, and she sang noticeably off-key during one song. But there was something about Seyran's intolerance of a mediocre performance, especially by a woman, that made Na cringe. "It's fine; she's a friend of mine," Na answered emphatically.

Afterward, Na and Seyran ran into Moussi, who was entering the front door as they were exiting. He stopped short and gave them an astonished look. As they greeted each other, he appraised Seyran, surveying his appearance up and down, almost with disgust. Moussi had been out with Beatris, Na, Seyran, and the others for khachapuri after the lecture the week before, so Na wondered why he would be so surprised to see them together now. Na's friend in New York who had introduced her to Moussi had told her that though he was married with a child, he was gay. If Na hadn't already known, she would have guessed he was queer by his expressive demeanor and dapper appearance. His reaction to her and Seyran now set off suspicion. Did he think Seyran was pretending to be straight to take advantage of her?

There were many stories in the Armenian American community about a diasporan marrying an Armenian, bringing them to the States, and then divorcing them when it became clear the Armenian had used the diasporan to get out. Na thought the stories likely had truth to them, though they always cast both parties in a terrible light: the Spiurkahye as a cuckold and the Armenian as a schemer. Just the other day, Na had spurned the advances of a young clerk at an internet café who had bought her a Coke and invited her to talk to him the second he learned she was American. So she knew there was truth to the stereotype and was wary that Seyran fit it, whatever his sexual orientation.

As the audience filtered away, and Vehine approached the group, Moussi's disposition became friendly, and he asked if they would like to go out for a drink. They were in a jovial mood as they walked down the street, deciding where to go. Suddenly, Vehine tripped on her heel and stumbled toward the ground. Almost instantaneously Seyran was at her side, offering his arm.

Na was astounded by the speed with which he had responded. Moussi, who had been walking right next to Vehine, hadn't even flinched. To Na, Seyran's action seemed to indicate a selfless sensitivity.

The group went to a low-key outdoor café and drank from bottles of Kilikia, a local beer. They made small talk about the Eurovision singing contest. Someone found a magazine left at a nearby table, and there was a photo

of a half-naked man in it. In an envious, self-conscious way, Seyran lamented, "He has no hair on his body."

As it was getting late, they walked across the grounds of the massive diasporan cathedral, hulking above them with its conical dome and cool, sandy-col-
ored walls. Now laughing and jubilant, the group wanted to walk Na back to
her apartment, but Seyran insisted on taking her alone, asking Moussi to accompany Vehine home. It was a maneuver, it seemed clear, and Na was piqued
by it, still not ready to let go of Seyran's attention toward her. She was nervous,
too. The word *bisexual* whispered in her ear, Kristapor's ruffling of his hair,
his critique of Vehine contrasted with his immediate rescue, Moussi's leering
look, and the self-consciousness that Seyran expressed about his body—all of it
confused her. The bottom line, she thought, was that he was too young for her
to be having any feelings at all. But Na had not had sex in a long time, and no
one had been interested in her in just as long a time. Her body felt vulnerable.

They walked into Na's expansive apartment, which was bright by the kitchen
but dark toward the far walls. In this space, Seyran seemed to Na like a small
wild animal, a squirrel wandering into captivity. Na offered the squirrel tea.
She showed him her new iPod and played a few songs for him. But he wouldn't
sit down. He asked if she was tired. Not really thinking, she told him yes.

She had been tired for a week, tired all the time; it was her default setting.
The concept of keeping her physical constitution to herself so as not to burden
people was something that she had only recently become aware of. Her mother had been very attentive to her physical needs when she was a child, which
continued to the present, so Na had always automatically assumed that other
people were interested in them as well.

"Oh, you're tired," Seyran said. "I'll go now."

And he was out the door.

She couldn't believe it. *What just happened?* She thought of Moussi's look, as if
they were disgusting, as if he knew Seyran wanted something from her, and
she from him. *How can I want anything from such a perplexing person?*

She got on her computer and wrote a screed in her journal about how
pathetic she was, how much she had given up on love, eventually resulting

in a long column of statements of "I hate myself," and "I wish I were dead." She was troubled that she was attracted to a guy who was possibly gay and that this seemed to be a pattern after her crush on Mardi last year. Thinking in polarized terms about her sexuality—that she either had gay relationships or straight relationships—she worried that being attracted to gay men meant that she wasn't doing heterosexuality right; perhaps she wasn't bisexual but really gay and should seek out a woman, not to mention mental help.

The last person Na had been with was a butch woman a couple of years before, but it had only lasted a few months—they got involved too fast, and the woman revealed herself to be an alcoholic before she dumped Na, the needy codependent. Though Na had been very attracted to her, the woman said they weren't compatible sexually, which left Na crestfallen, as if she had done being gay wrong, too. Before that, she had been with a man for three years, someone she had thought she would marry, but he was much older than her and wanted her to move with him to a small Midwestern city where she had no friends. She stayed with him a couple of months, and their relationship faltered. It was a painful breakup because he had been a kind, sensitive man, the first person she felt had truly loved her, and she still faced moments of regret, still wondered if he had really said what he had said, "I want you to take care of me full time and not write," or if she had misinterpreted that one sentence. Though logically she knew they were going their separate ways, she still punished herself, wondering if she were a selfish artist who would always be meant to suffer. Rather than realize that a loving man can turn out to be painfully sexist, she hoped that finding someone in Armenia would free her from her doubts, thereby absolving her of any possible wrongdoing.

Feeling disappointed and confused about Seyran, she beat herself up for being bisexual, as if it were a choice. She didn't allow herself to accept that there was nothing wrong with being attracted to men who expressed a feminine side. Nor did she recognize that most of the people she had been attracted to in the past possessed significant aspects of both genders. In truth, it wasn't a strange aberration for her to be drawn to Seyran in the gender fluidity he presented. Lacking such awareness, her shame silently extending its tentacles into the most vulnerable aspects of her identity, Na was very hard on herself. And she didn't know that this was one reason why Seyran was so drawn to *her*.

From her journal:

... the thing is, I feel incredibly sad for Seyran. He has to go to the army at the end of his studies, and he does not want to. (They will tear him apart.) He told me two people beat him up when he was in college because he had long hair. When we were walking down the street, a man stared—no, leered—at me. It was icky. When I told Seyran, he said, "Don't get upset or sad when people look at you this way. Maybe he was looking at *me* funny".

He laughs a lot, all the time. He has to laugh. It's a craziness. He's partially crazy, and I think maybe he needs someone to tell him in his life that he's okay. For some reason, I feel like that person is me.

It makes me so sad. That people can't just feel okay for who they are. That I can't.

I think this is going to be the opposite of what I wanted. I wanted to find love here and go toward closeness. I was feeling like I was ready to love someone. But I think this year is going to be about being an outsider and feeling lonely. Staying on the outside in order to write about it.

META-WRITING:

I've been thinking about interior and exterior spaces and how they not only exist in landscapes and cities—plazas, elevators, streets, and homes—but also in films, books, and bodies. You might think you're getting someone's innermost thoughts when you talk to them, when a narrator in a film speaks to you and the fourth wall is broken. Even in your own brain, you think you are fully inside of it. But truth is complex and takes many forms, and sometimes a truth seems like a lie, but it may be hidden or evolving. How do you explain a gay man who loves his wife and has created a life around a family? How do you explain a woman who is attracted to both genders and feels deep shame in uncharted territory? How do you explain a sexually ambiguous Armenian boy who uses people to survive? Some lies need to be torn down, some lies look like truth, some truths are multifaceted, and sometimes truth slowly reveals itself as the words are yet to be formed.

One night, a few months after Seyran teased Justin for being gay, I overheard Seyran speaking on the phone to his friend Kristapor, the violinist, who was now on tour in the U.S. with an Armenian orchestra. Seyran was giggling and speaking in Armenian for half an hour. At the end of the

conversation, he produced a kissing noise to say goodbye, which I had never heard from him before.
When he got off the phone, he strolled into the kitchen and announced that Kristapor had said that
before Seyran turned twenty-five (he was twenty-four then), he should come out of the closet.

I took the bait. "Are you gay?" I asked.

"Hello?" he said and gestured at his body in his briefs, lean from his compulsive yoga practice.

He didn't often joke like this about his sexuality—he usually felt insulted that I would ask, as if
I should know given what I had been through as his partner.

"I don't want to be with a gay guy," I told him. Being gay would mean there was no room for me,
and there was already so little left.

"But you have no choice until I get my green card," he said. Then came a more obvious joke:
"You always want to support gay people as an LGBT activist. Here is one way you can help."

Instead of telling the truth, he put on a performance to insult both my politics and my care for him.
I would never know what his sexuality really was: straight, gay, bisexual, or something else. In that
moment, he knowingly said exactly what I feared, which was the only truth that mattered to him.

❖

The day that I rode the elevator with the smelly landlord and declined to take his ninth-floor
apartment, I was in the center of the city, still new and seeking out the sights. There was a
thirteenth-century chapel nearby that I had read about: Katoghike. It was actually a remnant
of a large cathedral that had been demolished by the Soviets in the 1930s—the small chapel had
been saved due to the protests of international archaeologists. On the street, I found the alleyway
that led to the site, hidden behind apartment buildings on the corner of Abovyan (a poet) and
Sayat-Nova (another poet). It was a tiny structure, situated kitty-corner to an empty lot with only
a makeshift booth nearby. I bought a candle from the lady stationed inside and approached the
ancient stone structure with its telltale conical dome, its fourth wall torn away. Katoghike was so
small that the stands for candles were placed outside, under a canopy, so I lit my candle and set it
in the sand. Inside the chapel, there was room for only the altar and two pews, but I was the only
visitor. Though it was so small, I couldn't help but look up, take a deep breath in the calm it offered,
and realize the conflicted feelings that had been battling within my body for the last week. I cried
for a short while, a release.

Here I was, becoming undone in Yerevan, looking up for guidance in a structure that was
both interior and exterior at once. Yes, I needed to let go of the structures I had built for myself.
But there's no value in new buildings that shut people out and force them from their homes.

In remembering Katoghike, I understand that I could only find refuge in the truths that were revealed to me, the spaces that were open enough to let me in, and the remnants that were saved, protected, and cared for.

4. TRIANGLES

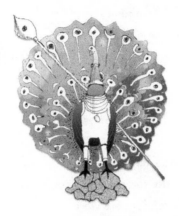

BLOG POST: SEPTEMBER 27, 2006
YEREVAN

Armenians Really Are Obsessed with Death >>> Armenia is beautiful in September. The skies are bright blue, filling lungs with dry heat during the day and cool air at night. It's still tourist season, and classes haven't started yet, so I booked a daylong trip with a tour company to the mountainous Lori region north of Yerevan. Our final destination? Sanahin and Haghpat, tenth-century Byzantine churches designated as UNESCO World Heritage sites. According to the UNESCO website, Sanahin and Haghpat "bear eloquent testimony to the highest achievement of Armenian architecture." I was hoping that such natural and human-made splendor would help me forget my recent troubles of adjusting to life in Yerevan. Instead, I found myself thinking a lot about death.

The tour guide stopped the van in the first village we encountered outside the city, explaining that the local inhabitants were the Yezidi, a minority in Armenia who practice a religion that's a combination of Christianity, Judaism, Islam, and Zoroastrianism. The guide's speech was mostly scripted as she informed our small group that the Yezidi worship God and Satan, and they build houses larger than their own to bury their dead. But then she editorialized, shaking her head in slow condescension as if the Yezidi were warped and ridiculous. As proof, she pointed out a typical structure, the size of a backyard shed and made of metal, simply ornamented with cut-out twists along the top.

Next on our death trip was the city of Spitak, the epicenter of the 1988 earthquake, which registered as 6.8, but the shoddy construction of many of the buildings caused most of the town to be wiped out, practically uninhabitable. Eighteen years later it still appeared to be in a state of recovery; everywhere I looked there were unfinished buildings. A temporary tin church built a few days after the quake was now a monument to those who had died, around twenty-five thousand souls.

We then passed through Vanadzor, Armenia's third-largest city, which had also been devastated by the earthquake. The guide informed us that around three hundred families still lived in temporary trailers here.

The road then wound along a cemetery for what seemed like several miles. I eventually realized that the gravestones were set within a long, narrow strip of land on the edge of a hillside, like a river winding next to the road. It was as if life and death were following the same path. I thought the tour guide was hypocritical for disparaging the Yezidi, for here were Armenians living with the dead, too, with their cemeteries, monuments, and "temporary" housing of eighteen years.

Not to mention their legends: we next drove by the green alpine village of Dsegh, dominated by a tall, rocky escarpment. The tour guide informed us that Dsegh was the setting of the famous poem *Anoush*, by Hovaness Toumanian, Armenia's most renowned poet. Unfamiliar with the work, I listened to the guide recount how Anoush's brother kills her lover and then Anoush jumps to her death from a cliff.

Finally, we reached Haghpat, spending an hour wandering around the grounds. It was a large, beautiful complex of churches and chapels. Cold dark stone, green trees, and grass, it felt cooler here than in the city. Intricately carved stone crosses and architecturally significant arches. Domes and red-tiled roofs, sometimes weeds growing in between. Big cisterns of wine buried by monks in the ground, now leaving empty holes among the floor stones. Tiny windows projecting beams of light. The sun cross, a symbol of eternity, and other motifs etched into the walls and columns. Heavy wooden doors, ornately carved. My favorite detail, high up on one of the exterior walls: a statue of the architect giving a model of the church to the priest, a tribute to the artist. This was the nurturing experience I had been seeking.

But I could only escape death for so long. At Sanahin, in a corner of the grounds, there appeared an eerie sight: a single lonely tombstone. As I approached, I saw it was a modern one, inscribed with a laser-etched group portrait of a mother, father, and two daughters. In the background, over their shoulders, an illustrated scene of a car falling into a canyon. The tour guide explained that the entire family had perished in the car accident just a few years before.

Sanahin and Haghpat are located on neighboring mountains, across a canyon. With one step, or a mistake at the wheel, life can change drastically or end in a second. In a place where recovery from an earthquake takes decades, and ancient sites are the main features of interest, where timelessness is part of everyday life, and loss and suffering are a constant reminder, it's not hard to understand how a legend would evolve of jumping from a cliff to one's death. A speedy demise could bring certainty; a sudden, painless death could provide a long-desired escape in a snap.

Diasporans are often accused of being obsessed with the Genocide, but I wonder if death has become such a prominent part of many Armenians' difficult lives—and for so many generations—that the relationship is intimate: death is treated like a family member, or desired like a lover.

JOURNAL: SEPTEMBER 22, 2006
YEREVAN

I wish I were dead.

I wish I were dead.

I wish I were dead.

I wish I were dead.

I wish I were dead.

I wish I were dead.

I wish I were dead.

I wish I were dead.

I wish I were dead.

I wish I were dead.

I wish I were dead.

I wish I were dead.

I wish I were dead.

I wish I were dead.

STORY: SEPTEMBER 23, 2006
YEREVAN

The morning after Na wrote in her journal that she wished she were dead because Seyran had abruptly left her apartment, she stepped inside a minivan to tour Sanahin and Haghpat. She would have canceled, but she had already paid for her nonrefundable ticket, and she had no other plans for the day. Once on board, she was joined by a couple of Armenian sisters from Iran, and a few moments later, by a big man, Na's age or a bit older, white and seemingly American, with a young Armenian woman who appeared to be in her twenties. Na sensed that he was a teacher and she was his student. She also thought that the girl was probably trying to land him to get out of Armenia, and that he was using her for sex. Na prayed that they wouldn't sit anywhere nearby, but unfortunately, they took the seat directly in front of her. The big white man was wearing a baseball cap, and Na could see through the gap in the seats that his hands were peeling and flaking. Otherwise, he would have been regarded as a hunk: tall, blond, blue-eyed, broad-shouldered. His girlfriend was thin with full breasts, her nose a fulcrum balancing her long face and, unlike most young Armenian women she had seen, short-haired. Brown locks with blond streaks. She wore jeans, sneakers, a T-shirt, and a pink hoodie. During the hours-long drive, Na watched the couple kiss and cuddle except for when she was scribbling in her notebook, still feeling irrationally ashamed about the night before: "This is torture. Why do I have to be seated directly behind these two when I just suffered a humiliating rejection?"

There were parts of the tour that could have pulled her out of her self-pity, like the stories of survival from the 1988 Spitak earthquake. It had happened near the end of the Soviet Union's reign, during Glasnost. Gorbachev made the unprecedented request for foreign aid to help Armenians who had lost their homes, loved ones, and livelihoods to the earthquake. For months before the disaster, Armenians had been engaged in mass protests demanding that the autonomous region of Nagorno-Karabakh join the Armenian Soviet Socialist Republic. It had been a mostly Armenian enclave when Stalin decided to place it within Azerbaijan's borders to divide and conquer, with one intent to appeal to Turkey, which he hoped to attract to the Soviet Union. In the ensuing decades, Armenians were increasingly oppressed in Nagorno-Karabakh. During the protests, Armenians in Azerbaijan were victims of pogroms and massacres, while Azerbaijanis were attacked and

oppressed within Armenia, too, which led to a forced exchange of the eth-
nicities between the two regions, not to mention the exodus of Azerbaijanis
from Karabakh. When the earthquake erupted, it was almost like the land
was expressing the social upheaval taking place. And yet, in the aftermath
of great tragedy, Armenians managed to declare their independence, fight a
war, and form a country.

After the group viewed Haghpat, they toured Alaverdi, a copper mining
town, and stopped for lunch. Na wound up sitting with the big white guy and
his sexy girlfriend at the restaurant. He told Na that he had been in Armenia for a year, teaching at one of the universities, and he gave Na unsolicited
advice on day-to-day living. He spoke to her in a conspiratorial way when he
made fun of the bad driving in Yerevan. Na recognized part of herself in him,
and she knew he recognized it, too: they were Americans. Na told him about
her writing, teaching, and educational background, keeping the conversation
professional. But perhaps because he was drinking vodka, he confessed to her
that he was interested in people with dualities. "I think people who take a
culture with them to a new place have a complex experience since they don't
strongly identify as either identity." He could have been talking about himself,
but Na wondered if he was trying to relate to what he imagined her experience
to be. She didn't uphold her end of the conversation to find out. Instead, she
clammed up and felt sorry for his girlfriend, who was nearly hidden by the
bulk of his body. Na didn't get a chance to talk to her, and he never brought
her into the conversation.

As they were departing the restaurant and making a pit stop in the women's
restroom, Na made a point to connect. The young woman told Na that she
was a student about to graduate. When Na asked her what she would do next,
she shrugged defensively. Na remembered her experience of being in a relationship with a much older boyfriend, feeling out of place among his friends
and their age-specific interests. Though Na knew she was projecting onto this
young woman, she felt sympathetic toward her. She wanted to tell her about
her writing workshop for women next summer but hesitated since it was so far
in the future and she barely knew the woman.

Na went back to the table and gulped down the untouched vodka in her glass, though she rarely if ever drank hard alcohol, never mind in the middle of the day. The booze started to dissolve the defenses she was trying to keep up around her confusing feelings for Seyran.

Afterward, she wandered alone around Sanahin and wept, the tears flowing more profusely when she lit a candle in the church. In this land where she had encountered symbols of death, she decided to light her candle to love. She realized that the big white man and the young woman had their own love story, and she could not judge whether he was taking advantage of her or she of him. In fact, she had no idea what their story was. So she lit a candle to have a love story of her own.

When Na made her way back to the bus, she ran into the big white man, and they boarded the van together. He helped her inside, taking her hand in a chivalrous gesture. As she made her way to her seat, he made a comment about how she could fit into that small space because she was so petite. She was piqued by the attention, though he was clearly tipsy, and mostly found the observation about her body creepy enough to disengage.

The three-hour ride back to Yerevan was long and uneventful, and when the van pulled into the city center, the big white man, the young woman, and Na disembarked at the same stop on Sayat-Nova by the Opera. Unprompted, the big white man wrote his email address on a piece of paper and gave it to Na, informing her that if she ever needed any advice, she could contact him. His girlfriend was impatient, looking away, not interacting with Na, telling him to hurry up. He told her in an annoyed tone to wait, as if he were dealing with an impatient child. Na told her that it was nice to meet her and shook her hand, and the girl closed her eyes slowly at Na, ostensibly to show kindness but really indicating that she didn't believe Na's goodwill. The man then took the paper back and wrote down his number, telling Na to call him if she ever needed any help with teaching. Na decided in the moment never to contact him.

It wasn't just that she was avoiding contact with a man who had given away his number in front of his girlfriend, with whom she imagined she shared solidarity as a woman. If these were truly her feelings, she might have said something to indicate her support for the young woman—like inform her of her workshop. In reality, Na was taking care of her younger self: she'd stood by once and watched as her own older boyfriend took the phone number of another woman right in front of her.

It had been after one of her ex's talks at the university, and Na watched from across the room as the woman approached him. Art insisted it was innocent, a professional networking thing, but Na told him she saw desire in the woman's body—the way she leaned her eager smile toward him in infatuation, like he was a star—and that he better not lead her on. She even joked with him when he was on his way to meet the woman for coffee that they would get married—and later, after he and Na broke up, they dated and eventually did marry within a year.

That's why Na was determined not to call a number that she was confusing with one that had once hurt her so much. She had no way of knowing that the couple might be suggesting her future rather than her past.

❖

Finding herself alone on a busy Yerevan street corner, Na took out her map and made her way to a place called Poplavok, an outdoor jazz club, where she was to meet Vehine. The two women found a table, ordered drinks and food, and Vehine asked Na about her walk home with Seyran the other night.

"At first I thought he was interested in me, but I also suspect he's gay," Na confessed, hoping Vehine might be able to shed some light on the matter.

"Okay, we need to talk. After you and Seyran left, Moussi told me how much he likes Seyran."

Na thought back to the moment when Moussi saw Seyran and her together at Naregatsi. *He wasn't looking at Seyran with disgust,* Na thought, *but desire. Or perhaps he was disgusted with Seyran for pursuing me.* She asked about Moussi's wife, and Vehine told her that they had an open marriage. Na wondered what it was like for Moussi's wife to have a family with a gay man in a homophobic country, then pondered what it was like for Moussi, for his life to be fractured.

As dusk enveloped Yerevan, the women's conversation was cut short by jazz musicians, who began to play. They were adept but not outstanding; their music relaxed Na, but it wasn't distinctive enough to release her from her ruminating mindset. Na realized that she had been awake since early morning, and she wanted to go home. She was about to leave when Moussi showed up, smiling and standing at their table. Not wanting to be rude, Na stayed to chat with him. He was very amenable as he told her about his work, but he was interrupted when Na's new cell phone suddenly rang. No one had called her on it yet, and she wasn't even sure the ringtone was hers. She picked it up and tried to make out the voice on the other end. It was Seyran. He asked where Na was, whom she was with, and if he could join them.

This is going to be fun, Na thought. She knew what it was like to witness gay guys cruise each other. When Seyran arrived a few moments later, he sat opposite Moussi, and Vehine and Na exchanged knowing, bemused looks.

But as the night and the conversation progressed, Na caught herself leaning closer to Seyran, as if protective of him. Moussi commented on a bracelet that Seyran was wearing—there was a flirtatious touch to it—but Seyran did not return the playful banter; it seemed that Seyran was not interested in Moussi but in Na.

Finally, Vehine said she was tired and needed to prepare for her flight home tomorrow. The group walked her to her apartment. Moussi was excited, practically skipping. While he and Vehine talked, Seyran said to Na, "After this, you come over my house, and I show you some things."

She saw this, finally, as the clearest affirmation of his pursuit of her. "Okay," she told him softly, and she felt lighthearted, like Moussi.

After they said their goodbyes to Vehine, Moussi asked Na and Seyran if they wanted to go to a disco. As they walked to the street and found a taxi, Moussi and Seyran entered into an extended negotiation in Armenian, with Moussi trying to persuade Seyran to go to the club. Seyran seemed adept at using his body language and the tone of his voice to convince someone that what they wanted was not actually what they wanted. *Here he is*, Na thought with admiration, *managing people nearly twice his age*. Eventually, Na and Seyran slipped into a cab, and Moussi trod away on foot—to his wife or to the club or to another lover, Na didn't know. She was interloping on yet another love story in process, basking for a moment in winning out over Moussi for Seyran's attention.

✿

It was a five-minute drive to Seyran's apartment, long enough to realize she had no idea where she was going or how she would get herself home. It was around 2 a.m., and she was exhausted. Her only option was to trust Seyran. He led her to a concrete block apartment building, not as nice as the one where she was staying, and they walked in complete darkness up a stairwell to the sounds of dogs barking in the distance.

The apartment was dim, lit by a bare light bulb in the middle of a long hallway. He led her to a nearby room, which was tiny and narrow. It contained a twin bed against one wall and an old upright piano against the other, only a foot apart. An outdated desktop computer dominated a small desk in the corner by the door. Na and Seyran sat by his computer, and he dialed up to get on the internet, connecting one cord to another cord that he threaded around the desk to plug into the computer. Once online, he played a Nirvana video.

She didn't evaluate the methods of his courtship. Instead, she disassociated from her desire and thought, *I am connecting with the youth culture in Armenia.*

Then he took out a bass guitar, sat on his bed, and played a Red Hot Chili Peppers song, "Otherside". Na watched him sing, seemingly in his own world, his eyes closed, a tattered quilt on his bed. The wallpaper's gold pattern faded behind him into shadow. When he was done with the song, she told him, "Seyran, you have a beautiful voice!" in a declarative tone. He giggled and blushed, and she felt like she could have been his professor or a friend of his mom.

Suddenly, he popped up and led her to the kitchen to have vodka and an apple. The light was dim in here, too, and there was no stove, just a propane gas tank to heat food upon. Na spotted a series of buckets on the counter, which indicated they didn't always have access to water in contrast to her place, which had an elaborate backup tank system. Though the apartment was neat and clean, it was run down. A poor but proud family lived here—enough money to survive, to buy food and essentials, but not to thrive.

Seyran took off his polo shirt to reveal a striped sleeveless shirt and hairy shoulders, suddenly resembling a gnome, Na thought, feeling ambivalent about this unexpected intimacy. And then she watched as he explained something, gesticulating with the apple-paring knife, letting his wrist bend backward. Na realized then that he could kill her, and no one would ever know. Maybe he was crazy. Na had no idea who he was, really.

They went back to his room, and he played more videos and songs on his bass guitar. He didn't play the piano, but they gazed at the Jim Morrison poster above it. And then Na was lying on the bed, and he was asking her why she was in Armenia. What was she really doing here? She tried her best to explain about fleeing the suffocating conservative political climate in the U.S. and wanting to learn Armenian, and he asked, "No, but why are you here really? You can tell me."

"I think I have something to give."

He was inching closer to her on the bed. His face was upside down from her as he spoke, and then she asked him to hold her hand. This led to him caressing her face. And then they kissed. They made out for what seemed to Na like a very long time. At one point, she found herself on top of him. She looked down into his face and said, "Seyran, aren't you gay?"

"I'm not gay," he said. "I'm bisexual. Like you."

Na finally understood the contradiction, why he seemed gay but had taken an interest in her and ogled her breasts: he was bisexual! She wanted to butt the heel of her hand against her forehead, but it would have wrecked the mood. *How did I not figure it out?* she thought.

They proceeded to have sex with Na on top. It was a relief, since Art had never allowed her to straddle him, claiming his hip was too bad. Something released in Na, and they went at it for a long time. He didn't come; he said it was because he had drunk too much. But Na came, and she was so loud that he asked her to be quiet so as not to wake the neighbors. She felt that it was the best sex she'd ever had.

In the aftermath, after Seyran fell asleep, Na wrestled with her blindness. She had been told that she was the first person in Armenia to publicly come out as bisexual—shouldn't she have recognized that in him? But it was difficult to ascertain what people were hiding about themselves versus what they did not yet know. There was so much hidden, so much silence as a function of survival in a homophobic society. She had mistakenly assumed Seyran was either gay or straight, and she hadn't imagined that, without the concepts in language, people would be able to identify as bi. With the utterance of two words—"I'm bisexual"— Seyran reiterated that the reality existed even if the signs weren't posted.

Na then moved on to another troubled thought: she knew that fucking a much younger person in a developing country was questionable. There was a danger of taking advantage of someone with less power, as she had suspected with the big white guy and his Armenian girlfriend. But the reversal in genders gave her an excuse to muffle her concerns. Ultimately, she wiped away all the confusion, intuition, doubt, concern, denial, and fear, which she had toggled between for the past twenty-four hours, because of the promise of sex. Not just any sex, but the type of sex that would mute her self-loathing, that would silence her wish to not exist because of what she thought of as her shameful being, the person who couldn't get homosexuality or heterosexuality right, who couldn't find a partner by her late thirties. Seyran told her that she was the most sexual woman he'd ever been with, his eyes wide. They were using his condoms, and Na suspected that this kid, as attractive and self-possessed as he was, probably had a lot of sex and that a one-night stand was typical for him. Two years without sex—Na thought she deserved it. And he was so hot. She couldn't quite believe it was happening.

Na slept with him in his twin bed but not very well. She wanted to leave, as soon as it was light, as soon as he woke up. She needed time to process all of this, to be by herself, to figure out what she was doing. But in the morning, he turned over and gave her the biggest smile yet, his lips crimson, his black stubble dotting his chiseled face, his eyes squinting at the morning light. He was so happy she was there. It seemed she should finally let go of her controlling impulse, to stay, to not run away. So she went back to sleep.

After they woke and dressed, they had tea, then she readied to leave. He walked Na to the train, guiding her through the concrete buildings and the dusty road of the quiet morning. As her mind wandered to the events from the past twenty-four hours, wondering what they meant, Seyran reached for her hand. They walked with their hands clasped lightly, and Na felt a sense of ease.

Remembering the candle she had lit at Sanahin, she thought that this was her love story.

LETTER: DECEMBER 14, 2009
ASTORIA

U.S. Citizenship and Immigration Services
Vermont Service Center
75 Lower Welden Street
St. Albans, VT 05479-0001

To Whom It May Concern:

Enclosed please find the documents requested in your letter from October 19, 2009.

We are enclosing documents of a shared bank account, which we opened when we arrived in America. Once Seyran found employment, we closed this account, and he opened his own account.

We've preferred to have our own separate bank accounts since we do not make a lot of money but each have our own expenses for our creative work—Seyran is a musician and Natalee is a writer. We are enclosing statements from our individual checking accounts that show these investments—for Seyran, musical equipment; for Natalee, her laptop. These statements also show purchases made near our homes in Woodside, NY (from September 2007 to October 2008) and Astoria, NY (from October 2008 to the present).

We do not have children, so we do not have birth certificates, school records, etc.

We do not own property. We are enclosing copies of the yearly leases for our current apartment, which have both our signatures. We have enclosed canceled checks to show that we have been sharing the rent on our previous and current apartment.

Also enclosed are photos of ourselves over the past two years with our friends and family and in our home, as well as photos of our marriage celebration with our families in Armenia. The date, location, and people appearing in each photo are listed next to each photo.

We are enclosing personal email correspondence between us over the last two years.

These documents show who we are: a loving, happily married couple who share various interests and a creative life together in New York. If you need any more information, please do not hesitate to contact us. If you like, you are also welcome to visit our home.

Sincerely,

Natalee and Seyran

JOURNAL: DECEMBER 9, 2009
ASTORIA

Last week, I went to a lawyer to figure out this stupid green card bullshit. I called the Queens Bar, and they gave me the name of an immigration lawyer: Esmerelda Quinones. Her office was in a two-story stone building, located in the heart of Latin Jackson Heights, among the Colombian cafeterias, fruit stands, and a Spanish-language movie theater. Her secretary made me pay in cash, and then I walked down a narrow hallway to her office fitted with a big cherry desk in front of a wall of diplomas and certificates. Wearing a suit jacket and rimless glasses, Esmerelda was robust and energetic. Almost immediately I knew she was a dyke. I felt put at ease by her gregarious nature, and I trusted her word. I wondered if she had many clients like me—an Ivy-League educated professional born in the U.S. As an adjunct I am probably in an income bracket adjacent to her immigrant clients. In fact, my salary and Seyran's are roughly the same.

I told Esmerelda how we had received a letter from USCIS with the claim that the papers we had sent them to remove the conditional status of Seyran's green card weren't adequate. They want us to continue to prove our marriage has been made "in good faith." Our joint tax returns aren't adequate. To the government, putting the utilities in both our names and having a joint savings account—which we don't have—would prove our love for each other. It's disturbing for a few reasons. Seyran will be deported if the U.S. government doesn't believe we're a real couple. It also feels like we're guilty until proven innocent—we're being told that not only are our tax forms not good enough, but that *we're* not good enough. I know I shouldn't take the government's letter so personally, but it strikes a nerve because I don't think we're good enough either.

It was helpful to get a reality check. In a friendly yet authoritative manner, Esmerelda instructed me to write a letter that explained our situation—why we don't have all the documents that they're asking for—and to print out all our bank and utility statements—every last one—to prove that we've been residing together in the same place all this time.

Seyran didn't come with me to meet Esmerelda because he thought it was a waste of time to consult with a lawyer. But when I came home and shared her advice, he heeded it. Over the weekend, we produced the endless amount of paperwork she suggested. Papers covered every surface: the kitchen table, my desk, and bed. They managed to stay out of his empty room, but we sat on the floor by his computer as we finished composing the letter and coordinated the documents with the items listed. It was his idea to invite the USCIS to our apartment. I can't imagine what I would do if an officer showed up at our home, but I am sure Seyran would find a way to entertain them.

When we were finally done with the letter, he went to yoga, which is like a wonder drug for him. He comes home so happy and loving. He holds my hand, kisses and caresses me. The other day he asked if we should get another tatami mat so that we can sleep together in his room. It seems this process with the documents is bringing us closer together, somehow, as stressful as it is.

But then tonight, as I was getting ready for bed, he asked, "So, are you ready for me to have someone over?"

I was enraged. I've been doing all this work to help him stay in the country— and he hits me with this again? I know his game. He wants to see my rage as further proof that I care for him. When I get upset, he feels better about himself, the stupid jerk. But I won't give him the satisfaction of provoking my feelings. I told him blankly, "Sure, invite whoever you want." I rummaged through my drawers, looking for my pajamas, which were already on my bed.

"Okay, great. But I'll have to change the sheets on the bed since the person likes your room better."

I looked at my bed, feeling disturbed. "Ha, ha," I laughed, playing along with his bluff. "That's a great idea."

Naturally, a part of me dies when he digs at me like this. I try my best not to feel it anymore.

It's not enough for me to help him stay in the U.S.; this doesn't adequately show my love. For some reason he's not fearful of the USCIS deciding we're phony. The stakes are greater for him, since they could deport him, and he would have to face the Armenian government for abandoning his army duties. My problem is that I don't think his misbehaving with me warrants this kind of a fate. Perhaps if I did, then he would stay in line and stop testing me like a child. But I don't want to be put in this position; I do not want this power. So I let him have power over me.

META-WRITING:

I didn't realize that when I played along, I was still being manipulated. The only way for my spirit to not be killed was to leave, which I didn't allow myself to do. Not wanting to be the person in power was another kind of denial. I wanted us to be equals. But not acknowledging the real story was a kind of suicide.

In the poem Anoush, by Hovaness Toumanian, written in 1892, the title character does not have a good life. Though she lives in the beautiful mountains of Lori, surrounded by streams and talking flowers, as well as a singing shepherd named Saro who is smitten with her, her mother is overprotective and shaming whenever she leaves their tent ("People will say, 'What kind of a girl is that: She goes to all the men and talks to them?'"). Her father is punitive and angry about her love for Saro ("Get out, you impudent, shameless wench!"). To see shame present in a work from the Armenian canon affirms what all Armenian women know—we are raised to be ashamed, whether we desire or not.

The most violent example of shame is the response of Anoush's homicidal, psychopathic, testosterone-engorged brother, Moussi. One day, Moussi and Saro are wrestling during a winter wedding celebration when Anoush catches Saro's eye. He is so excited to see her that he loses himself and pins Moussi to the ground, a faux pas. This is completely unacceptable to Moussi, and he threatens to kill Anoush for loving Saro. She pleads for her life, which Moussi grants, but she can't stop him from murdering her lover.

Anoush wanders aimlessly, stunned in grief, listening to the river Debed call her name, "Come, Anoush, come; Let me take you to your lover! Anoush, my child, Anoush, come home!"

In the translation I read, there is no cliff jumping, as far as I can ascertain. But there is an allusion to her reunion with Saro in death: "There fly out and come together the two stars of the dead lovers, their desires unfulfilled, and with yearning, tenderly they kiss each other in the azure vault, far away from this earth."

It's a truly tragic poem; everyone but the poet gives Anoush a hard time over Saro. And Anoush does not stand up for herself; she has absolutely no power, especially over the emotional rage of her brother. Caught in this twisted love triangle, it seems that the only answer to Anoush's troubles is suicide.

The real tragedy isn't her death, of course. Anoush lives to find love, but in her unashamed pursuit of it, she is presented with no other options in life.

❖

It's interesting that the Yezidi, who also lack options—and power—as a minority within a tiny country, live near the land of Anoush's life and death. At the time I visited, there wasn't a whole lot written about them, but it was well known that the Yezidi faced persecution because of their differing beliefs. Though many accounts claim that Yezidis have been living peaceably among Armenians since the 1850s, they have been subjected to misunderstanding and discrimination, without much government representation, since Armenia's independence from the Soviet Union. Part of this is related to Armenians' confusion of the Yezidi with Muslim Kurds, who basically left or were driven from Armenia after the Soviet breakup and the war with Azerbaijan. But part of it is the fact that they are a minority, and their religion seems alien to many Armenians.

The Yezidi do not praise Allah or God directly, nor do they praise Mohammed or Jesus. Rather, the Yezidi's highest deity is an angel in the form of a peacock, named Melek Tawus, whom God created along with six other archangels. When God went on to create a human, Adam, He was so proud of him that He told these seven angels to bow to Adam; Melek Tawus was the only one who defied God, refusing to bow to a mortal. God, like a manipulative boss, congratulated Melek Tawus and promoted him to rule over the earth. The Yezidi thus believe in a rebellious deity, someone who stood up to God in defense of the spiritual.

According to another account, the Yezidi worship evil with ceremonies to appease Melek Tawus. God doesn't need as much attention, for He is good; it's evil that we have to look out for. Whether this is an accurate account of the Yezidi religion or not, it seems like a pragmatic approach to life.

In Seyran I was drawn to a rebellious entity, perhaps like the Yezidi, to appease my own demons. It didn't matter if he was good or bad, if he had sympathetic reasons for his actions or not. He was trouble, a power I prioritized instead of accepting my own privilege.

5. ACTING OUT A RESCUE

After their first night together, Na and Seyran walked to the train station where they encountered the statue of Sassountsi Davit mounted on a horse. According to legend, Davit was an orphan descended from a lion, an exceedingly strong village boy who managed to single-handedly stave off the oppressive Egyptians by killing their powerful king. Davit and his horse were galloping away from the station, which had once brought people from every land. Now the only international route it offered was to Tbilisi, Georgia, only 108 miles away, but a fifteen-hour trip due to the outdated railroad infrastructure.

Yervand Kochar's bronze rendition of Davit on his horse captivated Na with its swirling hair and mane, burly thighs and front quarters, all motion. Davit held his sword with both hands horizontally behind him, ready to swing it forward to lop off someone's head. Below him was a cup, about eight inches in diameter, from which a trickle of water oozed, spilling a long brown smear of minerals by the horse's rear hoof.

"The cup holds the patience," Seyran explained to Na. "If it spills over, Davit fights." The statue was a message to anyone disembarking from the train station: *we are peaceful, but if you mess with us, we'll use our enormous strength, descended from the hardscrabble mountain villages, to decimate you.* "This was a fountain," Seyran told Na of the platform below the statue, "but now it's broken. People steal pipes to sell the metal."

"It doesn't look like Davit's cup will ever flow again," Na told him.

"Sometimes people steal the cup," he admitted, giggling.

Na and Seyran headed toward the metro, located under the train station, so she could return to her apartment, but now he had an inspiration. "Do you want to go to Etchmiadzin?" She stood looking at him, considering this proposal. Etchmiadzin was the seat of the Armenian Apostolic Church, the equivalent of the Vatican for Armenians. Na was not religious, but it was a site, and she wanted to see the sights. She also liked the feeling of her hand in his. "Yes," she said.

They took a marshrutka to an intersection near the Modern Art Museum of Yerevan that Na had tried and failed to find a couple of weeks before in an embarrassing mishap. Her guidebook listed the address at #7 Mesrop Mash-tots, but she could only find a strip mall at that location. Na had shyly asked passersby if they knew where it was, but they either didn't know, didn't want to deal with her, or couldn't understand her primitive Armenian. Finally, an old man approached and indicated that he would take her there. She followed him as he slowly plodded up Mesrop Mashtots, the building numbers getting higher. She let him know they were going the wrong way, and he responded by asking if Na wanted coffee. "No," she told him, and he kept going. She didn't know what to do but follow him a few more blocks until he stopped in front of a café and said, "Jashenk," *let's eat.* She noticed the man's worn-out shirt, bloodshot eyes, and alcohol on his breath. She felt stupid, a little more than a fat cat—a sheltered American—incapable of doing anything right. When she handed him a coin, saying thank you and goodbye, she was practically in tears.

Now Seyran found the correct marshrutka to take them to Etchmiadzin, and she was glad such a blunder was now relegated to memory. It was hot for September, and the crowded van was stifling. Na and Seyran stood very close to each other, hanging onto the sides of the seats. Seyran told Na, "This is a way that working people go. The government doesn't care about them and doesn't give enough marshrutka for them."

The trip through desolate-looking suburbs took about forty minutes to Etchmiadzin. When they arrived at the little city, once the capital of Armenia,

Seyran signaled for the stop and they jumped out. The complex of churches and chapels was behind a tall gate, the grounds manicured, and the main structures reminiscent of Sanahin and Haghpat, but better kept. Na read on a plaque that the cathedral had been built in 301 AD when St. Gregory the Illuminator converted the king (and thereby all Armenians) to Christianity. According to legend, Jesus told St. Gregory where to build the church; he'd had a vision of Christ striking the earth with a golden hammer in a ray of light. Inside, the dome was illuminated with a beautiful, detailed pattern of gold, red, and green. Seyran and Na looked at paintings, altars, and the Holy Lance—the tip of a sword that had pierced Christ's body while he was being crucified—nestled inside a gold reliquary. It occurred to Na that Christians celebrated pain with beauty.

They exited the cathedral and strolled among the grounds with other tourists, religious types, and priests in black robes as Seyran confessed to Na his feelings for men. The frank admission made her uncomfortable in such a religious environment, but also because she'd had sex with him and wanted him to be her love story. Seyran explained that he didn't want the kind of contact he had been having with men—brief sexual encounters. "It makes you a broken person," he said, "and lonely. I want to be in a relationship."

Na wanted to be in a relationship, too, but she was also trying to figure out Seyran's sexuality, recalling how he hadn't come the night before. As they were exiting the gate at Etchmiadzin, she asked, "If it were acceptable here, do you think you would be gay instead of bisexual?"

"No," he said, shaking his head. "I like women."

As they walked back to the bus stop, Seyran sang Nirvana songs, and Na listened instead of joining in. When she was younger, she had been the same way, breaking out into song to garner attention. Witnessing her former self in Seyran made him seem familiar. She remembered all the times she had been questioned by gay and straight people alike about her sexuality; it seemed someone was always trying to convince her to come over to their team. She felt she owed it to Seyran to give him the space to be bisexual in the same way she would have wanted.

The marshrutka back to Yerevan was even hotter than before, but it was slightly less crowded, and they were able to sit. As Na looked out the window, considering if she could accept Seyran's bisexuality, she started to freak out. *What am I doing? Who is this kid?* She remembered the drunk guy who had wanted a meal and wondered if she was being taken for another ride. She thought she needed to be by herself so that she could absorb the increasing flow of information that she had received in such a short period of time—it hadn't even been twenty-four hours since Seyran had joined the table at Poplavok.

"Where is Natalee?" Seyran suddenly asked. "I miss Natalee."

He was still holding her hand. Here was someone who simply wanted to be with her, to get to know her, it seemed. She didn't feel burdened by Seyran's plea for attention, but rather she was impressed that Seyran was not afraid to playfully point out her distant demeanor. When they got off the bus dripping with sweat, instead of taking her leave, she asked, "Do you want to come back to my place? We can take showers there."

As they took off their clothes and turned on the water in the diasporans' huge glassed-in shower stall, Seyran looked smitten, eyes wide and smiling. He jumped in even though the water hadn't warmed up yet. Shivering, he explained, "I like cold showers."

They eventually wound up naked in the bedroom, having sex. But Na was still tender from the previous night after having not been penetrated for so long, and now she was the one who couldn't come. When she told him to stop, he asked why.

"I need some time to get to know someone. To feel close."

"You're a typical Armenian girl," he joked. "You'll only let someone hold your hand after forty years."

She paused and looked at him.

"You don't think it's funny?"

Na thought about it. She had spent most of her twenties trying to figure out why she was so mortified by sex, mostly by analyzing the cues she had received from her family. So she did find it amusing that Armenian women were reputed to not let anyone near them until decades of betrothal had passed. *At least I'm not that bad*, she thought. The truth was that Na's younger self would have been angered by Seyran's dismissive joke. She now thought that because she had matured, and because she knew Seyran was young and didn't know any better, she could let his words slide right off her back like soft water.

JOURNAL: JANUARY 10, 2010
ASTORIA

A few days ago, Seyran walked into my room wearing a tight, blue, polyester long-sleeved shirt with a wide collar, reminiscent of Georg and Yortuk Festrunk, the "two wild and crazy guys" from *Saturday Night Live*.

"I think I'm going to wear this," he said, turning from side to side to examine his look in the full-length mirror in my room. He wore the shirt unbuttoned so that a lot of his chest hair was visible through the collar. The shirt was so tight that stray strands of hair poked through the fabric. "What do you think?"

We were about to go to the Queer Armenians of New York annual Christmas party. I usually love attending every year, but now I was nervous that all the men would hit on Seyran.

"Everyone will think, 'Poor Natalee married a gay guy from Armenia.'"

"Do you really think that?" Seyran asked, wrinkling his nose. He went back to his room and promptly changed into something else.

META-WRITING:

The story of returning to the old country to find a mate is not new. It was a practice originating after the Genocide. My great-uncle Dikran embarked on such an endeavor. As a young man, Dikran fought the Turks with General Andranik's battalion. After the Genocide, he escaped a prisoner-of-war camp, then went about rescuing his family members, including my grandmother, whom he found in an orphanage in Syria. He also found his two sisters-in-law living on the streets of Aleppo and reunited them with their husbands—his brothers—in America. Later, after he had settled in New York, Dikran traveled to an orphanage in Lebanon and plucked a young girl, Soorpuhi, from the dormitory to marry. She was roughly sixteen to eighteen years old, and he was in his late twenties or early thirties. They went on to build a happy Armenian American family together though they were poor working-class immigrants living in the tenements of New York City. They raised three children who became respected health professionals: two doctors and a nurse. I never knew Dikran, but according to family lore, he was extremely brave, and he must have been either very lucky or extraordinarily intuitive to pick the right bride with whom he would bring up their children to become such happy, successful adults.

I've always wondered what it was like for Soorpuhi to be rescued from the orphanage to marry an older man in America. What mixture of fear, hope, and confusion must she have experienced?

And what prompted Dikran to visit the orphanage looking for a wife? Could he not find an Armenian woman in the U.S. to marry—at least one whom he could relate to?

I should mention that Dikran was not a birth brother to my grandmother, but an orphan whom my great-grandmother breastfed and adopted into the family. Was rescue in Dikran's blood? Was rescue the way he understood family? Or did he do it because he thought he would only find love with another orphan like himself?

It seems pointless to compare myself to Dikran. First off, it's likely that he took a wife from the orphanage because it was one way for him to preserve his now nonexistent nation. At the time, it was common for Armenian men in the diaspora to find picture brides from the orphanages to perpetuate their Armenian identity—and culture and nation—through family. For many Armenian women survivors, family was a refuge, but it was also their only option.

Though I wanted to restore some of my cultural heritage lost to assimilation when I went to Yerevan, I wasn't looking to save the Armenian nation by being with Seyran. But perhaps something rang through me from the family legend: nostalgia for meeting that one tragic person to relate to. Here I was, reversing the cycle, a woman rescuing a man.

If you travel from a wealthy part of the world to a developing country today and happen to find a spouse, you are generally regarded as pathetic, sad, and lonely, an imperialistic pawn lacking self-awareness. Reading about such relationships online, I found this opinion from Dave Seminara, a member of the foreign service who worked as a consular officer in Macedonia, Trinidad, and Hungary: "The clichéd case involves Americans who for whatever reason—recently divorced, midlife crisis, etc.—move to or travel to a developing country and soon find that they are able to date members of the opposite sex who wouldn't give them the time of day in the United States ... When Americans overseas feel desirable, perhaps for the first time in their entire lives, many fail to see that poverty and desperation are what makes them popular."

When I read this, it stung. Being with Seyran made me feel desirable, it was true. But I was also dubious of his interest in me, constantly questioning it, wondering if he was taking advantage *of me. At some moments in Armenia, I was grateful that his presence in my life rescued me from myself; and at other times, I felt that I helped him much more than he did me.*

By the time I returned to New York, it wasn't that I had failed to see the unbalanced situation we were in. It was that I kept falling into a myth or fantasy, only to float to the surface of reality, gasping for breath. That moment of sudden clarity brought me a shame that aroused my fear and dread, that triggered my adrenaline.

I didn't know it at the time, but I was attracted to this dynamic more than anything.

STORY: LATE SEPTEMBER, 2006
YEREVAN

Na walked around the perimeter of the city center to the Cascade, one of the last monuments created by the Soviets. It was a series of white stone steps leading up a hill. On a clear day, the famed Mount Ararat would be plainly visible from the top, its gleaming white slopes looming from the other side of the city. As she ascended the stairs, Na admired the fountains and carvings—embellishments of Armenian motifs such as pomegranates, eagles, and infinity signs. Investing in the Cascade's completion after the Soviets had abandoned it, a wealthy diasporan was now populating the stairs with large sculptures and statues from his permanent collection. Most impressive were the fountains on every level, water shooting out of vases to feed flat pools.

Na was walking with Seyran's friend Hrair, whom she had met after Seyran and Na had taken a shower. Seyran helped Hrair at an office for a natural energy NGO, where the two guys worked on the office's computer networks. Hrair had enlisted his wife, Edita, a programmer, too, and now she and Seyran were working at the office. Hrair needed to walk their dog, so he invited Na along.

Na had enjoyed meeting Hrair and Edita, who were effusive and smiling, telling Na they were excited to practice English with her. With their unkempt hairstyles—hers a mass of mousy brown curls, his a tiny ponytail at the back of his neck—they reminded Na of American hippies from the seventies. She felt comfortable with this couple, in their late twenties, who seemed more easygoing than other Armenians she had met. Though they were nearly ten years younger than Na, they somehow seemed older, as if they were from another generation. She thought it may have been because they had lived through a major shift in society. Hrair and Edita had been teenagers when the Soviet Union broke up. They grew up speaking Russian and lived with the old paradigms. She was comforted to meet these friends of Seyran's, to discover that they were warm, good-hearted, and mature people.

Now Na and Hrair sat on the Cascade a few levels up from the street, halfway up the slope, among amorous couples, groups of teens, and young families. Hrair looked around and spoke very thoughtfully and nervously about being a man in Armenia: how he used to be a patriot, but his time in the army had changed him. Officers would regularly beat soldiers; hazing was out of control. "The Armenian army is very v-violent," he stuttered. As he looked toward the mountain, his hands, which were holding his dog's leash, were shaking.

Na looked at Hrair with concern, thinking about Seyran's upcoming army duty, and he paused for a moment. "Seyran was beaten by his parents, did you know?"

"No," she said.

"Please don't tell him I told you." Hrair went on to explain that Seyran's parents had called Edita and him on the phone to say that they were bad influences on their son. And yet, Hrair had taken Seyran under his wing to help him with his extra work, teaching him about computers, and paying him a little bit, too. They became close friends; often Edita and Hrair hosted Seyran in their home when he didn't have a place to sleep. "Seyran escaped his parents," Hrair said, "and now they are looking to blame us for it."

Though Seyran's abusive history seemed unlikely information to tell someone upon a first meeting, Na believed Hrair because of his earnest, sincere character. She took the story as a warning that his parents might call her soon, as if Hrair, Edita, and she were going to be working together in tandem toward Seyran's best interests, like foster parents with a social worker.

BLOG POST: OCTOBER 1, 2006
YEREVAN

Gender on the Streets >>> The hairdresser shaped Seyran's short dark hair with hair spray, a round brush, and a blow-dryer into a peacock's point—a faux mohawk. When I was walking down the street with him, people stopped to look and laugh. I asked Seyran if it was because Armenians are not regularly exposed to differences in appearance. He said no, that the people who laughed at him weren't thinking about him; instead, they simply lacked an interior life, so they were quick to react. Seyran has also told me that people think he's Persian. Because he looks different, people automatically assume he can't be Armenian. This is something another man told me, a bar owner from Beirut. Armenians automatically assume that if a man has long hair, he must not be from Armenia.

Seyran got the mohawk because he was singing with a punk band. One of the other band members told me at the show, "Seyran is going to get beat up tonight."

"Why?" I asked.

"Because of his hair."

"Someone drunk will try to prove something?"

"They don't have to be drunk. They just don't like it, so they'll beat him up."

But if you saw Seyran walking down the street in any suburb or small to mid-size American city, you probably wouldn't look twice: spiky hair, scraggly beard, jeans and sneakers.

Seyran has told me that he has been in altercations because of the way he looks. When he had long hair, a pack of macho students at his university beat him up. He tells me about the violent responses to his appearance in a disarming way, usually with the phrase, "I have problems," which he accompanies with hysterical laughter.

Seyran is twenty-one. The world he has grown up in is post-Soviet (he doesn't like that phrase because everyone uses it), and it seems to me he can't directly remember instances of Soviet repression. He simply wants to be free, to challenge authority, like any creative misfit anywhere. He laughs at how ridiculous the whole situation is, with a nonconformist glee. But in his giggle I sense desperation.

✤

Hrair says he doesn't like walking his dog, a very sweet black Lab, because of the other dogs on the streets. Not the homeless dogs, but the dogs with their owners, especially men, who have something to prove and try to provoke the canines to fight. I spent an evening speaking with Hrair about Armenia and what disappoints and disillusions him—mostly the way people treat each other, opting to be corrupt rather than to do the right thing. He had a peaceful, relaxed look: long hair, plaid shirt, and army-green hiking pants and boots. But his energy was quite frenetic; he spoke so quickly and with so much to say that he had trouble catching his breath a few times. But at the end of the evening, he surprised me by saying, "You are here a year; that's good. You will probably like it since you are a woman."

"What do you mean?" I asked.

"You won't get hassled the way a man does by other men and by the police. In fact, it's much easier for me when I am walking with my wife because men are less likely to trouble me."

✿

The women walk around Yerevan in stereotypically feminine outfits. They wear high heels and makeup; their clothing is embellished with embroidery and decorative straps. It's like I'm walking around in one continuous foreign-language-dubbed *Sex and the City* episode. The women clomp-clomp-clomp their heels against the cobblestone steps, balancing precariously above the earth, about to tumble. In contrast, I have been wearing sneakers and jeans nearly everywhere I go. But this week, for my first class at the university, I wore my first-day-of-class outfit: a sleeveless black-and-white checkered shift and black leather wedge-heeled boots. I normally think of this as a swanky outfit, but I noticed women giving my dress cutting stares as I walked down the street, so much so that I wondered if there was something wrong. I searched my reflection in plate glass windows to see what was amiss: a disgusting stain, a broken zipper, or even a hanging thread. But I didn't spot anything. In fact, I thought I looked pretty good.

I wonder if my experience is a more benign version of what Hrair experiences on the street as a man. It seems in terms of gender that we are all in competition. Who is doing masculinity right? Who is doing femininity right? Why are we even in this competition? I'm guessing it's because the structure of sexism is the means that people access and hold power in Armenia. Men can only achieve power by fighting other men, so it gets enacted on the streets. Women can only have power by mating with a man, and the primary way to do this is through their appearance, so beauty contests are performed on the streets.

People will tell you that traditional gender roles—man as provider in power, woman as nurturer/caregiver—are part of the natural order and the means through which the Armenian nation has survived and will continue to exist. They will tell you feminism is a disease imported from sick countries. So if you defy the concept that men are at the top and women are at the bottom, such as a woman working outside the home or a man wearing his hair long, then you are seen as an outsider, or worse, a grave threat to everyone's existence.

Not to say that there isn't cross-gender antagonism. It was surprising to hear that Hrair felt threatened as a man and that the presence of his wife protected him, because I often feel vulnerable as a woman walking alone. A few times, men have come right up to me, spoken to me in a suggestive way, and followed me in broad daylight. One even went so far as to grab my arm as we walked through a crowd in the light of midday; no one seemed to notice when I tore myself away from his grip. But this does not happen when I walk with someone else, man or woman. Same-gender friends, women or men, are often seen walking arm in arm down the street—not everyone is in competition. In their union, it looks like these paired individuals are trying to protect each other from the powers that be.

❖

After my first class at the university, Seyran asked me how it went, and I told him that it was a class of fifteen girls and one guy. "Are they chickens?" he asked. He had told me previously that this was the term given to girls (and sometimes boys) who attend school to study not because they want to learn but because they want to be seen. I'd also been warned by countless people that because of the Soviet model, most students in Armenia had not been encouraged to think for themselves or to offer subjective opinions. I was told that creative writing, especially creative nonfiction, would be completely foreign to them.

When I walked into the classroom, the girls were chirpy, and they seemed much younger than fourth-year students. They sat close to each other on benches—in some cases three to a bench—when there were plenty of seats for everyone. But when I asked them questions, they responded at once, trying to drown the others out—clearly thinking independently. Though their expertly applied makeup and cute outfits suggested the time, energy, and value they put on their appearance, they also looked at me with bright eyes and curiosity.

I answered Seyran, "Yes, some of them are chickens, but I think it's because no one expects much from them." I could see something opening up in them. They weren't merely appearance-based simulacra; they were girls—yes, giggly girls, but perhaps the giggle isn't too far in emotion from Seyran's defiant, desperate laugh.

STORY: SEPTEMBER 27, 2006
YEREVAN

While Seyran had his hair shaped into a mohawk at a salon, Na got her hair straightened. Sitting in the chair, she thought, *There are advantages to a bisexual boyfriend.* Not that Seyran was her boyfriend. It had only been two days since their long first date started at Poplavok and ended after her stroll with Hrair, when Seyran met up with her back at the office, walked her home, and borrowed thirty-five dram to take a marshrutka back to his parents' flat.

When they were done at the hair salon, Seyran and Na walked to Avant-Garde Folk Music Club for his rock concert. The building featured a dome on the first level that was the skylight for the subterranean concert hall. Na followed Seyran from lobby to hall, back and forth, as he did a sound check and greeted people who admired his haircut. There were a few bands playing, and most people were in their twenties.

Inside the dark cabaret-style room of tables and chairs, she met Hrair, Edita, and their friend Lalig, whom Seyran introduced as the Armenian-language tutor he had previously mentioned to Na. Lalig appeared to be the same age as Hrair and Edita. Her hair was long and straight, and she, too, had a more mature, grounded aura. She was a psychologist, and she spoke English well. Na thought that she would be a great tutor, and she took the woman's number.

Soon, Seyran's band started their set. He was the lead singer, backed by a guitarist, bassist, and drummer, with two young girls playing keyboards. They thrashed around, and Seyran jumped up and down, bobbing his head. Na was enthralled by their frenetic energy. There was nothing more exciting to her than seeing a date performing onstage, making a collective experience with an audience. Na thought that Seyran had an amazing stage presence—cocky and confident, like a real rock star. She took as many photos as she could, looking on in awe as he screamed and sang and shouted, as he bounced and danced around, sweating so much that his mohawk fell down.

After the concert, Na and Seyran went with Hrair, Edita, and Lalig back to the office to hang out, drink coffee, and eat chocolate pilfered from the NGO's fridge. They were having a joyful time talking about the bands, but Na caught Lalig looking at her funny a few times. When it was getting late, Lalig asked Na if she was taking a cab home. Seyran said no, and Lalig became irritated. "I was asking *her*," she said.

They all decided to leave at this point, gathered their things, and went out the door. Lalig and Seyran were having a conversation in Armenian, walking down the hallway, when all of a sudden he ran away, and Lalig took off after him, her long, straight hair swinging to and fro across her shoulders.

Na turned to ask Edita what was going on, when Edita ran after them with hardly a word. Na was left with Hrair, who said, "This is not good," remaining silent to Na's questions about what the hell had just happened. When they made it down the stairs and onto the street, Hrair ran off as well.

Na recognized the comic moment, but mostly she felt that her presence had caused an Armenian social circle to disperse like atoms, as if she were an American bomb.

She walked down the street in the direction of the runners. Suddenly Seyran appeared from an alley and grabbed her hand, and they walked in the other direction, toward her apartment.

"What happened?" Na asked.

"Lalig is crazy."

"Why?"

"Because of you. She is upset because I didn't tell her I have girlfriend." Na ignored for a moment that he had called her his girlfriend.

"Why would she care?"

"Lalig used to be my girlfriend." Na found this strange, given that he was trying to set up the two of them as tutor and student.

"She asked, 'Do you have a girlfriend?' Do I have to tell her everything?"

"How long has it been since you've broken up?" Na asked.

"One year, I think."

"How long were you together?"

"One year, I think."

Na was silent as they continued walking the dark streets. She suspected that he had said something to upset Lalig since he was being so defensive. She also realized that he had done the same thing to Lalig as he to her: he brought two women together without telling the other who they were. She was critical of the fact that Seyran lacked understanding toward someone he had once been in a long-term relationship with. Still, she didn't know Lalig or Seyran very well, and maybe Lalig was being overly sensitive. *It is none of my business anyway*, she thought, so she didn't question him further.

They continued to walk home. He was talking to her about the concert, and she was listening, and then he looked at Na in a strange way that made her laugh nervously.

Suddenly his energy shifted. He turned to her and asked, "You laugh at someone who looks at you with love?"

She didn't like the aggression in his voice. She knew she had done nothing wrong. She found it disturbing that he was talking about love so soon—and casting it with a threatening tone.

As quickly as the edge came into Seyran's voice, however, it disappeared, and he was his usual, jovial, scattered self as they walked home.

When they returned to her apartment, he slept in her bed, but they didn't have sex. As she drifted off to sleep, Hrair's warning of Seyran's abusive childhood came back to her, and in her dreams, she was back at the Cascade with its overflowing fountains. This time she listened to the drunk man on Mesrop Mashtots telling her in perfect English how he had been tortured in Afghanistan. As he spoke, she noted out of the corner of her eye a copper cup, like the one at Davit's horse's foot, this one streaming out like a fire hydrant opened wide onto NYC streets.

JOURNAL: JANUARY 10, 2010
ASTORIA

When we returned from visiting my family for Armenian Christmas, we finally received the letter that said Seyran's green card is going forward. They are taking the conditions off. He read the letter when he came home from work, sitting on my bed, wearing his hat and coat. I hugged him and he kissed me, a happy moment. We have come a long way for this, and now he is safe.

This means I can break up with him, I thought.

But the truth is that he is still my responsibility with just his green card, even if we divorce. If he goes on welfare or uses any public funds, I will have to pay the government back for whatever money they give him. I doubt that he will go on welfare, but the problem is that I don't think I will stop feeling emotionally responsible for him until someone officially tells me I'm not. And officially, he will only stop being my responsibility if he dies, moves back to Armenia, or secures his U.S. citizenship. If I break up with him, he won't be able to apply for citizenship for another three years.

But he can apply for his citizenship sooner, in six months, if we stay married. It might take another six months after that for him to become a citizen. Then, in one year, I would really be free.

I just don't know if I can wait that long.

❖

It turned out that Gharib and Mardi were at the Queer Armenians of New York Christmas party. For the past few years, since they moved here, Seyran has avoided them as much as possible. Now he was uncharacteristically warm, hugging and kissing them. "You will have to come over and visit sometime," he said. I couldn't believe it! Gharib was equally surprised; he turned to me and joked, "The yoga must be turning Seyran into an angel!" He told me how good Seyran looked—he'd lost a lot of weight over the last few months because of his yoga practice, and with his head shaved, his clear eyes and wide smile were even more dazzling.

At one point, I noticed that Mardi was subdued, not his usual gregarious self. By the food table, he asked me, "What are we doing here? Why do we have to meet each other here? It's artificial." He proceeded to wax philosophically, asking what was the point of socializing separately from other people. I told him that originally the group had been established so that queer Armenians could find each other and offer support for the misunderstanding and abuse we faced in our families and communities. Now after several years of bonding, we lacked a further purpose.

Mardi said he didn't like identity politics, the way it created labels to tell us how we should fit into the scheme of things in New York, in the world.

I sensed that he was also questioning his own life. After struggling financially for a while, working restaurant jobs that he could briefly tolerate, Mardi is now teaching video editing to high school students, and Gharib works remotely for a cross-cultural music conservatory in Yerevan, helping with fundraising. Their rent is low, and I suspect they have benefactors who help with their expenses from time to time. They asked me for money just once, and they promptly paid me back despite Seyran's claims that they were untrustworthy. They're also involved with an art center downtown affiliated with anarchists, socialists, and other radicals, and this gives them some satisfaction politically. But I know after two years of struggling in New York, they are disillusioned with American life: Mardi with the commercially driven film world, Gharib with his inability to find satisfying work as a consultant or singer.

When I next found myself talking to Gharib at the party, he asked, "Are you happy?"

"Not really. But Seyran has his green card now, and that's a relief."

"You have given him the best gift," Gharib said.

I nodded, smiling slightly.

"You are fighting?"

"Yes."

"Does he beat you?"

I laughed. "No, it's mostly verbal."

"Mardi and I are fighting all the time, always about to break up. But we can't afford to live apart."

I nodded. The same was true for me, a common NYC phenomenon.

"You know," Gharib said, "sometimes I feel our lives are like a movie. One day, we are complaining to you about life in Yerevan, and the next we are at a party for gay Armenians in an artists' loft in Brooklyn. Isn't it funny how things work out?" he asked, his voice registering at a higher range.

I reminded him how Seyran and I were so surprised when we arrived at my Greenpoint apartment three summers ago, only to discover they were staying a few blocks away from us. It was ironic karma that the people Seyran disliked the most were now calling us up and saying, "Hey, we live down the street. Aren't you going to visit us?" It was bizarre to see them in my American world, so close by, leaning out of the windows and calling to us down on the curb. Gharib reminded me that they had originally intended to go to Berlin, but Gharib couldn't get the visa in time. The German embassy had mixed him up with another Gharib Hovannisyan, born in the same month and year, who had violated his visa. He didn't know if he would ever be able to leave Armenia. Gharib wasn't able to meet Mardi in Berlin, but he came to NYC later, once the mix-up got straightened out, for a public policy internship, and Mardi eventually got a visa to the U.S.

As we reminisced, Gharib gave me reflexology, kneading the heel of my hand, pressing on my knuckles and nerves, because I was so cold in the underheated loft. Seyran appeared, standing next to him, and Gharib called him a Buddha. "But you can't be a Buddha because you are Armenian." He lovingly caressed and scrubbed Seyran's stubbly face with his hand. It was very cute as Gharib was so tall next to Seyran. For some reason, I have never felt threatened by his attention toward Seyran, perhaps because he is so dear to me, and I know he loves me, too.

We left the party and walked through the falling snow to the subway together. After we descended the stairs, Gharib and Mardi stood across the platform from us since we were going to Queens and they were going deeper into Brooklyn. Suddenly they started singing and synchronized their dancing, entertaining us from across the tracks. I don't remember the song, but it was very charming: tall Gharib with his scarf draped over his head, looking like a nomad, the usually sullen Mardi twirling around like a dervish. I found myself laughing so hard I was immobilized, transported back to Armenia, the land of orphans.

META-WRITING:

Sassountsi Davit's cup of patience was broken and would never overflow, but there he was, ready to fight for the Armenian people who were putting up with a fifteen-hour train ride that should really only take an hour and a half. Sometimes the warrior is not in sync with his people; sometimes patience is misplaced. After all, on the other side of town, water flowed throughout the

Cascade, but instead of being compelled to action, young couples felt soothed by the sound of the fountains after long days at jobs that didn't financially compensate them nearly enough.

Perhaps I am thinking of Soorpuhi, my great-aunt, all wrong. Perhaps she wasn't a poor refugee plucked from the orphanage by an Armenian American savior who gave her a better life. Perhaps other men had come looking for brides, and she had maneuvered herself to be chosen by the one she wanted. Perhaps when Dikran found her, she rescued him from a lonely life of bachelorhood. Perhaps she was rescuing herself. Perhaps they rescued each other, or perhaps no one was rescued at all.

6. REFLECTIONS OF A DEAD TWIN

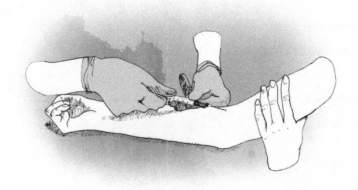

BLOG POST: OCTOBER 8, 2006
YEREVAN

100% Armenian Blood: A Theoretical Performance >>> The setting is Vernissage, a vast flea market/art fair nearby Republic Square where artisans sell their nostalgic wares, like delicately hand-carved wooden khachkars, ceramic pomegranates, and paintings of Mount Ararat.

Looming in the distance, in fact, is Ararat, a national symbol of Armenia. Though it can be seen from Yerevan, it is located across the border in Turkey. The mountain is a reminder of all that Armenians lost during the Genocide—countless homes, families, businesses, schools, and communities that were destroyed with the deaths of 1.5 million people and the dispersal of many others across the globe; a rich civilization and culture; and a history of autonomy. Ararat also confronts Armenians with their alienation from their Western side, aka Western Armenia, now Eastern Turkey, part of Armenia's historic homeland. It's like Armenia is a sad twin forced to gaze at the beautiful corpse of her sibling, captured behind bulletproof glass.

Situated between the stands for musical instruments, soap handcrafted from indigenous herbs, and old medical equipment, a thirtysomething woman in T-shirt and jeans is seated at a table. A tourniquet is wrapped around her upper arm, and a syringe saps red fluid from her vein into a tiny vial, several of which are already filled, ready for purchase. A person wearing a white lab coat standing beside her periodically replaces a full vial with an empty one. The woman's face is pallid. Fanned out below her are brochures explaining the prices, the authenticity, and the dire necessity of the product. The sign above the stand reads "100% Armenian Blood."

❖

During my first month here, I made a surprising discovery: some people don't think I'm Armenian.

They meet me, hear my name, see that I don't comprehend much, if not all, of the language they speak, watch me smile wanly, and ask me where I'm from. I usually say that I'm from New York in the hopes that it will signal I'm an Armenian from a capital of the diaspora, like others from Paris, Beirut, or LA.

I am then asked, "Duk hye ek?" Are you Armenian?

And I reply confidently, "Yes hye em." I am Armenian.

"Both mother and father are Armenian?"

"Yes. My grandparents came from Western Armenia, and my parents were born in America."

"And you're Armenian?" they ask. Something clearly does not compute.

"Yes, I'm Armenian."

"Huh." Suspicious glance, sorry smile, head nod—*you're not really Armenian*.

I suppose it's the combination of my Western apparel, American aura, and lack of native language that leads them to this judgment, and I shouldn't give it so much weight.

But I've spent much of my life explaining that I'm Armenian to Americans, who are curious about my appearance but oblivious to my ethnicity. Since childhood, I have been detailing the geographic location, learning the complicated history, and processing the generational trauma, so I somehow assumed that in the one place where people know where and what Armenia is, my ethnicity would not be questioned. Instead, I am told that I'm not who I think I am.

❖

We have been seeing each other for only a few weeks, but it's a running joke with Seyran now: "Hey, you really are Armenian girl."

One afternoon the phone rang while we were making out on my couch, and I went to answer it. It was my mother, so I spoke to her for a few minutes. When I returned and told him who it was, he smiled and chuckled, "Oh, you really are Armenian girl," and gave me a hug.

Today I wasn't feeling well, and I asked if he knew a place where I could get tan abour, or yogurt and wheat berry soup, known by its Russian name, *spas*, here. He said he didn't know, since he doesn't often eat at restaurants. "If we can't find it, we can make it," he said.

"You're right, I think I could," I said, imagining how to boil the wheat and the madzoon.

"Oh, now you *really* are Armenian girl."

"Do you have a problem with that?"

"Not with you," he said. The understanding was that he was initially drawn to me because I'm not very Armenian, so when I exhibit the traits, it's surprising.

"Even Hrair said this," Seyran went on.

"What, that I'm a real Armenian girl?"

"He said you don't seem like you are from New York."

When I was studying at college in Rhode Island, many people assumed I was from New York because of my black apparel and art major, though I had grown up only two towns away. I've lived in New York for seven years, but perhaps because I am now so shy with Armenians, it is hard for them to imagine me pushing through the crowds on the subway.

I suppose it's an asset, not appearing to be what you are, because then you can be anything, watching the reflections of what people imagine you to be, like the faint images of figures standing on opposite sides of a shiny plate glass window.

❖

In the Armenian communities in Iran, Maral told me, if an Armenian gets a promotion and is successful in the wider Iranian world, the Armenians say, disparagingly, that he or she is half Iranian. I was sitting in her gallery, sipping tea, ostensibly to help her with her English and she to help me with my Armenian; but more importantly I wanted to listen to her stories. Maral considers herself both diasporan *and* local Armenian since she came to Yerevan as a college student after growing up in Iran.

"They're not modern," she said of the name-calling Armenians. "They don't realize that you can't survive unless you become a part of the place."

"Do you think they see adapting to another country as a threat?"

"Yes, they want to protect their culture, to make sure they don't—" and she gestured with her hands, as if taking something from the other. "Lose it," I said, finishing her sentence.

As I left Maral's gallery and walked down Amiryan Street, I pondered why Armenians are still so afraid of losing their identity when they've been relocating to other parts of the world for much of their history. People still talk about protecting the language, protecting the culture, protecting the blood.

I suppose I feel this way, too; part of the reason I'm here is to find what was lost in me. It's upsetting to see that the West is already here—billboards, bottled Frappuccinos, gentrification—with its destructive, homogenizing effects of globalization.

So this is why I want to draw my blood from my body and sell it at Vernissage as a collective keepsake, a memento that tourists can take home with them from Hayastan. As my veins are tapped for my precious commodity, as I sell my blood for not nearly what it's worth, as more of my life is drained away, at least I'll know I'm Armenian.

STORY: LATE SEPTEMBER, 2006
YEREVAN

Na was at home in her cavernous apartment, preparing for her class at the university the next day, when the phone rang. It was Seyran. He told Na that he had called Lalig to see if she was all right after the night before, when Na felt like she was an American bomb causing everyone to disperse across Yerevan.

"I tell Lalig, 'I don't want you to feel pain, but I have to live.' And Lalig wanted me to say sorry for not telling her about me and you, so I did."

"That's kind of you," Na said.

"Vochinch," he said. "If someone asks me to do something to make them feel better, I do it."

Na found this reassuring since she had been wary of how insensitive he had seemed toward Lalig the night before.

Na then shared with Seyran how Moussi invited her to an art exhibition. She had told Moussi that she would love to see his work. He had then asked Na if Seyran would be joining her.

"I told him, 'No, probably not.' It seemed clear he was trying to find out if we are seeing each other," Na said.

"Armenians like to ask you about your private business," Seyran lamented.

Na thought this was strange, since Armenians seemed to value privacy; why would anyone overstep a boundary that they wanted to maintain for themselves? And did anyone hope to be told the truth? Or did they just want to demonstrate their knowledge through a suggestive question? It hadn't occurred to Na to ask Moussi if he liked Seyran or, for that matter, to ask Seyran about Moussi's crush on him.

"Don't people value privacy?" she asked Seyran.

"Yes, they do, but I think it makes them feel alone, so they ask."

Na thought about this. To keep your business to yourself would mean you could protect yourself from gossip and shame. But you would sacrifice opportunities to feel close to people. It would make sense to not reveal yourself and instead ask others to give you something of themselves.

And then Seyran asked a question: "Do you like being alone?"

"Sometimes," she said.

"What a stupid question," he muttered to himself.

"No, it's not. Do you like being alone?" she asked.

He said, "I like being with people. It doesn't matter who they are—girlfriend, friends, even people I don't like much."

This reminded Na of her life in New York, where she constantly arranged to meet with friends. If she read of an event that sounded even remotely interesting, she would mark it down as another opportunity to stave off loneliness. She knew that if she did not get enough human interaction, she would become depressed.

Na told Seyran about life in New York, about how hard it was to see friends because everyone was so busy. And then she told him how she had been hospitalized for five days a couple of months before she came to Armenia.

Even though her friends visited her, she felt terribly alone. Her parents, in their seventies, drove from Rhode Island to help her return to her Brooklyn apartment from the hospital. She watched them from her bed and thought, *This is not right. They should not be caring for me. I am supposed to care for them now.*

She'd come down with a crippling headache and hives. The doctors gave her a spinal tap and ruled out that she wasn't contagious—it turned out she'd had an allergic reaction to an antibiotic. When she was transferred out of her private room, she was placed with three or four elderly white women who seemed to have been there for ages. Na felt as if she had landed in a female version of *Waiting for Godot*. One thin, pale woman—ghostlike—disappearing in her gown and hospital bed, refused to speak to the rest, her glassy eyes staring into space whenever she was asked a question. Another, who seemed to be wealthy, was very scatterbrained, her hair a mess; a young Latina woman came to visit her, asking her to sign checks for the staff at her home. Still another, a chatty, chubby lady wearing glasses, younger and more alert than the others, announced that she didn't regret that she had never gotten married. She wasn't going to get hitched just for the sake of it; she would only do it for the right man.

The nurses avoided the room, it seemed. Na waited hours for a hospital staff person to come by, and as soon as one did, she begged to be moved. Na could not tolerate these aged ladies as they displayed their manias. It was irrational, but she felt like she was going to die with them, all alone, without her family or a partner. When she was transferred to a room with one other person, a working-class lesbian from Staten Island, she breathed a sigh of relief and thanked God.

Na didn't detail these stories of the hospital to Seyran, but she did mention how hard it had been to go through this experience alone, dependent on her parents' help. Afterward, she had headaches for two weeks because of the spinal tap. It was excruciating to sit up. All she could do was lie completely flat, waiting for her health to improve. Finally, she took an Amtrak to Providence, lying flat on the floor in front of her seat. Resting on the sofa on her parents' porch, among the trees and fresh air, she was able to recover. Being with family who loved her helped her to heal.

Na told Seyran how hard it was for her to be alone now. "I really miss my friends, and I'm so disoriented here. I don't understand people, what they say and how they act. The social codes are so confusing." She realized that much of her confusion stemmed from her interactions with him, but there was no one else to confess these feelings to, and she didn't think he understood her English anyway. He had asked, so she told him. She sobbed on the phone, letting go.

Na feared her emotions were too much and would scare Seyran, but he took in her sobs with sympathy, expressing that she could rely on him to be her friend. He asked her, "Do you remember the first time we met, when I said you could call me if you need anything?"

"Yes," she said softly.

"That is still true. Anything you need, you can ask me."

She had revealed a lot of her private life, and he only wanted to help. She didn't question why. Instead, she felt less alone.

JOURNAL: MARCH 26, 2010
ASTORIA

One morning last week, I woke up to discover that I couldn't access the internet. I went to Seyran's room to check his computer, not sure if the problem was our modem's connection or my laptop. I sat on the floor, opened his computer and then his browser—his computer was connected. Since I was there, I decided to check my email, and when I went to the website to log in, his email account was open. There were only three emails in his inbox, one from a woman named Veronica. He had never mentioned a friend named Veronica before.

The week before, however, he hadn't come home on Monday night. He said he was going to a party, and at another point he said he needed time to himself. That night I lay in bed, wondering whom he was lying in bed next to. I should have seen it coming. A few weeks before, he had reiterated that we should open up our relationship. Now he wants to invite people to our home. I told him no, that this was unacceptable, but that he could do whatever he wanted outside the apartment.

When he returned the next morning, he hugged and kissed me and held my hand. He wanted to make sure that I was okay, that the relationship wasn't threatened. I looked at him blankly and asked how the party was, and he laughed and said he hadn't gone to a party.

A few days later, we were in a supermarket in the organic aisle, and he picked me up and affectionately smooched me on the face. I giggled and smiled and thought maybe it was because I had given him his freedom on Monday night.

Now as I sat facing his computer screen, I wondered if Veronica was the person he had spent Monday night with, if she was the one making him so happy.

I read through the emails quickly, holding my breath, my heart pounding. She had sent him music, and he had listened to it before going to sleep. They called each other "sweetie" and signed their emails with, "kissing you" and "kisses." He had a plan to take her to Spa Castle, which we had visited twice together, once as recently as my birthday a couple of months ago. She had previously lived in Portland and didn't mind our rainy weather. He projected that when he turned thirty-five, she would be fifty-three. So she was the same age as me. If he was so desperate to explore other people, why not someone younger? He has always told me that his life with me has made him old.

I Googled Veronica and discovered that she is a painter. And more astonishing and weird: she looks like me. Glasses, long dark hair, no makeup, nerdy. The discovery was shocking. And yet, whenever I found myself forgetting about it, I couldn't help finding the whole thing comical when I remembered it again.

I decided I couldn't tell him that I knew; reading his emails was a violation. But I was so disturbed. *He's looking for a replacement? He has a mother complex? He is falling in love? He's simply confused?*

I was despondent for the rest of the day. Whenever I looked in the mirror, I saw her.

Though I tried to hide my feelings, Seyran sensed something was up the next day and asked, "What did you find out about me?"

I confessed, but it turned out he knew that I had read his email, using a program he had installed that runs surveillance on his home computer while he is at work. He seemed relieved when I admitted the truth. He said he would have read the email, too, if he were me, but jokingly chided me about it, pretending that he didn't want to leave me alone with his laptop.

He wanted to know what I thought of her. "She seems like a nice person," I told him. After all, she wasn't the problem.

"How was my English?" he asked.

I rolled my eyes and scoffed. "I'm not going to answer that."

"How did you feel?"

"Well, I was jealous. Here you are having a lovely exchange, and we're always making jokes about each other and calling one another names."

"No, that's all an act," he said. "I don't like her. I have been wanting to get rid of her."

I thought about how he had projected their ages into the future—something he had never done with us. "It's probably what you tell her about me."

"No," he laughed.

I don't know what the truth is, but it doesn't matter. My emotions have shifted, and I have started to let go of him; I don't care about answering his needs or carving out time for him. During the past week, I didn't panic about our sour relationship. I am finally allowing myself to let go. Something about seeing myself reflected in a similar woman has made me realize that when he pursues other people, he's not rejecting me but playing out a habitual pattern.

META-WRITING:

Perhaps this is obvious, but Seyran was sleeping around before I discovered Veronica.

He had always wanted to have an open relationship, and I didn't. The issue receded from our lives in Yerevan, but it emerged in New York about nine months after we arrived and then again every spring. For a long time, I tried to find reasons for it: he was young, he was unhappy in NYC, it was a form of escape. It was spring. But then I seriously tried to accept it; I read Opening Up: A Guide to Creating and Sustaining Open Relationships *by Tristan Taormino, which suggested the only way to proceed was for all involved to be conscientious, communicative, and respectful of feelings.*

At first, I asked him not to tell me about whom he was dating, and he agreed, but then he found ways to let me know without much pretense of hiding it. Later, when I told him I did want to know, he would conceal the fact that he was dating before finding a way to reveal that he had been deceiving me all along. Every time, I felt rejected. It eventually became clear he wanted an open relationship mostly to hurt me. He fed off my pained response.

I haven't included these details until now because I feared I would be judged negatively for not being able to break up with a complete creep. Admittedly, this is also a technique of fiction, of character and plot development—I am building the upward arc of exposition. But as a writer I don't have to tell the truth; I can soften the edges of what really happened, or make up some other story, or just stop writing. As a person, however, I'm tired of living like this, tying my self-worth to what I imagine are other people's perceptions, but is really my own shame.

STORY: LATE SEPTEMBER, 2006
YEREVAN

On a warm September evening, Na and Seyran walked into a hilly neighborhood she had never been to before and entered an old Armenian house, the kind with a carved wooden balcony looming over the street and a heavy wooden door with brass hinges. They were ushered inside by Hagop Baghramyan, an art historian and curator. He was in his late forties to early fifties, a tall, dark, bespectacled man with salt-and-pepper hair, wide dark eyes, the kind of eternal five o'clock shadow her own father had exhibited as a younger man, and sloping shoulders.

Na had been introduced to him a couple of times before at various cultural events, and it turned out that he and Seyran knew each other, too, which she learned about when they ran into Hagop the previous week at an art gallery opening. Seyran had been excited to see his old friend, overenthusiastically asking Hagop if he would let Na interview him. However, Hagop didn't speak much English, and though Na tried a few Armenian phrases, they couldn't communicate, so Seyran translated their conversation. Na noted that besides the language gap, Hagop seemed awkward. Seyran explained to Na later that Hagop could be antisocial. "Hagop has complexes," he said. Na prodded for more information until Seyran let her know that Hagop was gay, though he had been married for many years before his wife died.

Now Hagop seemed even more awkward as he brought Na and Seyran into his living room with rough wooden floors, large windows, and many modernist paintings on the walls. He showed Na a black-and-white photograph by the window, explaining to her in English about 3rd Floor, an artists' group that was active from 1987 to 1994, during the time of perestroika, glasnost, the collapse, and the war. He seemed a bit like Na's tour guide to Sanahin and Haghpat, as if he'd memorized the script. She wondered why he was informing her about the group. Hagop seemed to read her mind. "I am writing about 3rd Floor for next generation to learn." He told her about their performative and endurance-based work, which reminded Na of Fluxus in the U.S. and the UK; she wondered if Armenians were aware of this movement.

When she tried to say this in English, he couldn't understand. So she tried in her halting Armenian, but Hagop was impatient. "Natalee," he said, "You can speak it. Speak Armenian!" Na couldn't tell if he was trying to encourage her, but his tone came off as harsh, as if he mistrusted her. Instinctively, like when she was a child prompted to speak in Armenian school, she shook her head, confused. As they sat down to conduct the interview, Hagop asked Seyran to translate all of her speech to Armenian for him.

Though she had her notebook of interview questions in her bag, she felt reluctant to pull it out and formalize the situation. She was struggling for a way to begin when Seyran cut to the chase. "Why do you like Bush?" Seyran asked. Na smiled. One day, Seyran had told her "I like Bush," but he couldn't answer why. He admitted it was because Hagop had said as much.

Hagop lit a cigarette and pulled an ashtray on a wooden stand close to him. He explained, via Seyran, "I am against Muslim fundamentalism. Bush is fighting Muslim fundamentalists, and he is making the world and Armenia more safe."

Rather than listen to him, like a good interviewer, Na decided to argue with him, like a good Armenian. Na was concerned about an influential critic spreading such ideas to young people without debate.

She told Hagop, "Muslim fundamentalism isn't a threat to Armenia; Turkey and Azerbaijan are hostile, but they both have secular governments. And Armenia has good relations with Iran."

Hagop shook his head and said, "I don't want Muslim fundamentalism spreading to the rest of the world."

"I understand that," Na said, "but Bush is dangerous. He's spreading imperialism with a preemptive war on Iraq, and this exacerbates Muslim fundamentalism more than anything. In a way, Bush is a fundamentalist himself." She told him of the lack of freedom for gay people in the U.S. "They aren't allowed legal rights to care for each other. Bush got reelected in 2004 because he campaigned to Christians who are against gay marriage. This kind of scapegoating is immoral," she said.

Hagop responded that at least in the U.S., gays could fight for their rights. "In Iran, you can be killed for being gay." Na ceded him that point. But she wondered if his fixation on Muslim fundamentalism was really Islamophobia. She had encountered Armenians in the diaspora who pointed to the history of the Genocide, when Turkish Muslim perpetrators demonized Christian Armenians by calling them infidels, allowing them to live if they converted to Islam. Some

Armenians allowed their rage about the Genocide to blow up into an amorphous hatred of all Muslim people. But she hadn't yet seen this fear in Yerevan.

During the lull in the conversation, Hagop took a drag on his cigarette, then asked in English, "Natalee, why you only wrote about yourself?" Na now realized this interview was a complete wash. Being an argumentative Armenian was not the best approach. She explained to Hagop that she wrote about herself to break silences about the life of an Armenian bisexual woman, which was a political act.

After Seyran translated that last part, Hagop said, "I think the ideal marriage for me is with both a man and a woman." Sensing a sexist comment coming, Na said, "I don't believe in marriage. It's a limiting institution—it keeps couples isolated from others, it alienates single people, and it prevents people from forming families of their choice."

"And you would do away with it?"

"No, of course not. I just want there to be more options for everyone." At this point, Hagop smiled.

Seyran interjected, "Hagop wants to marry us!" Hagop and Na chortled at the playful remark. Then Hagop stood to bring his guests tea. While he was out of the room, Seyran whispered, "Hey, let's marry him. I really like him." Na shook her head, giggling.

Later, as they walked away from his home, Seyran told her that he and Hagop had been romantically involved. He said that for the few years when he was not living at home, he would visit Hagop four or five times a year. They had a relationship he couldn't quite explain—something that involved romantic love and sex, but Hagop was also a kind of father figure or mentor to him. Seyran went on to explain that he liked to hold and feel and kiss men, but he didn't want to fuck them. "I cannot go all the way. Something in me breaks, I cannot do penetration with a man. I don't think I am very gay," he said. Na imagined that while Seyran was exploring with boys, he went to Hagop periodically for emotional stability.

However, the news of his relationship with Hagop was a shock for Na to hear, given the age difference between them, even greater than hers. It also possibly explained Hagop's distance with Na. She wondered if Seyran had pursued the interview to gain approval of their relationship from Hagop. Na felt dismayed that he hadn't told her earlier, that she had walked into a situation in which she didn't have all the information, like what had happened with Lalig. Still, she was glad he had told her about him and Hagop at all. Most men in Armenia would probably have kept it a secret.

JOURNAL: MARCH 31, 2010
ASTORIA

Today we were chatting over Google, he from work and me at home, when all of a sudden Seyran sent me a command.

Seyran: Do the dishes

(This was strange, as he had left the sink full of dishes.)

Me: ?

Me: Are you going to do the dishes?

Seyran: No, you do the dishes

Me: Fuck you

Seyran: Do you want to split?

(My heart raced. *Yes, I want to break up,* I thought. *How does he know? I'm not going to tell him during a chat.*)

Me: I want to be friends, and friends are kind to each other

Seyran: You do half the dishes, and I will do the other half

(*Oh, he means splitting the dishes.*)

Me: Okay, that sounds fair

But he did not let the friend line drop. When he came home from work, he used it a few times, calling me "friend-y" at one point after stopping himself from saying, "sweetie."

This episode has made me paranoid that he has been reading the contents of my computer, including my journal and these very pages. If he can monitor his computer from afar, perhaps he can do the same with mine.

I suppose if I read his emails, he would feel entitled to read my stuff. But does that mean he is now acting in a certain way so that I will write about him? Or is he keeping things from me so that I won't include them?

Is he now controlling my writing?

META-WRITING:

When I was in the hospital room with the old women, I desperately wanted to flee, fearing I would end up like them. The woman who said she wasn't going to just marry any man—why couldn't I admire her, get to know her? I wasn't seeing her but an image I feared: a lonely, forgotten woman.

Similarly, Seyran had his own insecurities. In me he had someone who sacrificed time and energy to help him obtain his green card. But it wasn't enough. He intensified his manipulation, continually requesting to have casual sex with other partners at our apartment. It made me crazy. How could someone want this? *I would ask myself.* How much does he want me to not exist? *So I was relieved when he dropped that request and replaced it with a demand to have sex with whomever he wanted, whenever he wanted, in their apartment instead. It was classic manipulation: overdemand as a sham negotiation tactic to get what you want, couched as a lesser, more reasonable ask. It wasn't limited to sex—he was coercive even with minor tasks like doing his dishes. If he were secure, perhaps he wouldn't have had to rely so much on manipulation.*

And I kept finding reasons to fear him, which left me circling in my own crazy spiral. Not long after I discovered Veronica, I could only let go of so much angst before I reeled myself back in. Now I was paranoid he was monitoring my writing through my computer. I never asked him about it, though; he would have just said I was nuts. It's possible he had cut off my computer from the internet to trick me into viewing his emails from Veronica, an even more outlandish scenario, and yet it seemed entirely possible given his devious inclinations. Seyran was a destructive pest, yes, but I ballooned his ugly parts into a monster, like a distorted fun house mirror, a Medusa-like image that left me paralyzed.

❖

In 1988, a group of avant-garde artists, mostly male, entered the exhibition hall of the Artists' Union dressed as ghosts, with painted pale faces and ratty clothes. They took on different characters: some modeled themselves after heavy metal rock musicians like Black Sabbath and Kiss, others like aristocrats, soldiers, or the destitute—anyone in opposition to the Soviet regime. They titled the performance piece The Official Art Has Died/Hail to the Union of Artists from the Netherworld. *They strolled through the galleries silently as if the paintings of the Artists' Union, the official artwork of the Soviet state, were haunted by those who had been oppressed by it.*

The artists dubbed themselves 3rd Floor, since this was the part of the Artists' Union building that they occupied. Their first action was new in Yerevan, made possible by the freedoms of glasnost. It was groundbreaking, for it opened the doors for artists to critique the official party line and express their reality.

Nearly twenty years later, the artists' expression only went so far. Armenia was stuck with corrupt overlords whom no one seemed able to defy. Instead of being concerned by oligarchs using weapons of neoliberalism and capitalism, the negative effects of which were widely witnessed all over Yerevan—with their monopolies and real estate development and ability to co-opt the government—Hagop feared Muslim fundamentalism. Perhaps he'd been entranced by the beautiful dead twin across the border, too.

STORY: LATE SEPTEMBER, 2006
YEREVAN

While his parents were away for the weekend visiting their dacha in the village, Na and Seyran were making out on the sofa in his parents' apartment in the city. Getting overly excited, she told Seyran that she had to slow down. They talked for a while, a break in the foreplay. Na asked Seyran what he had thought of her before they met. Seyran had come to see her performance when she visited Armenia the year before. He said that he had read her poems and wanted to speak to her, but he was shy because of his poor English skills. But he liked the content of her writing. Then he said, "You're not bisexual, straight, or gay; you're just you."

It was at this point that Na wanted to tell him that she loved him, though it was absurdly too soon, after just a few weeks of "dating." Despite putting her in social situations that made her gravely uncomfortable, when they were alone, on their own, she felt accepted by him in a way that she hadn't experienced with anyone else. Because she accepted his bisexuality, he was able to give her the same. Na believed that this equality was resistant to the imbalance of their ages and the hierarchy of their countries in the world order. That night, Seyran seemed to echo what was going on inside of her. He told her, "I'm feeling something for you. I think you feel it, too."

7. FREE TO BE ARMENIAN

For Special People >>> Seyran was very quiet. It was the first time we were socializing with my friends, and everyone in the group was in their thirties, at least ten years older than him. On a tour through Hinanots, Gharib's family village, I was nervous, too. I held Seyran's hand, curious whether our unconventional age difference would go undetected as we walked a dirt road between mud brick walls and leafy trees now turning yellow. We passed by a just-married couple, bride and groom in their gown and tux, wending their way through the narrow street, stopping to greet neighbors at folding tables in each entryway for a toast of cognac in little gold-leafed glasses. Our new acquaintances Erin and Armine could have held hands, too, since women hold hands in Yerevan all the time, but they were short-haired lesbians, and maybe they didn't feel comfortable doing so during a heterosexual nuptial custom in this small village. Later, when we took another walk and there were fewer people about, I saw Erin and Armine link their fingers.

Gharib had called me early that morning to ask if I wanted to visit Hinanots with a few friends from Europe. As we became acquainted during the half-hour ride in the car from Yerevan, I discovered that Erin was from Belfast, and Armine was visiting her family for the first time in six years after studying in Liverpool, where she'd met Erin. Hoping to start a conversation on being queer and Armenian, I asked Armine if she was out to her family.

"I'm out to my friends but not family," Armine said.

Sensing her reticence, I asked, "Is that too personal to ask?"

"No," Armine said. She was in the front seat and turned around to smile at me.

"It's very American of you," Erin chimed in. I wanted to explain that I am normally not so inquisitive, but gay social circles seem more open; when I met Erin and Armine, who both spoke English, I thought, *Here's a chance for me to talk to a lesbian couple!* since it was nearly impossible for me to broach the language gap and ask the same question of a single, queer Armenian. The question would be culturally insensitive, and the answer would likely be, "No, of course not."

Gharib's 130-year-old ancestral home had low ceilings and lumpy straw beds, black-and-white photos of great-grandparents in dusty frames, and an oud and a doumbek decorated the wall beside a musty piano. It reminded me of old village homes once belonging to Armenians and now belonging to Turks that I had visited in Western Armenia, where my grandmother was from. I noticed other similar cultural features, like a tonir, a clay oven in the ground to bake bread, and a beautiful garden with a grape arbor in the back. We were drinking homemade vodka from grapes that had been fermenting in a tub nearby when I told Erin that it's been difficult to conduct interviews not only because of the language gap but also because of the cultural gap. I often sense that people are holding back their feelings from me. "It's hard to know what people really think," I told her.

"I find it's the exact opposite," she said, giving an example: she went to the opera with Armine, and the audience was expressing very loudly that it was incredibly lousy. "In the UK, people would never do that."

"Oh, yeah, I'm used to that," I said. "Armenians can be very loud and opinionated."

"But you seem rather different."

"I'm more reserved in public, but I'm pretty vocal with my family. What I find is that Armenians have trouble talking more intimately about their feelings."

"Yes," she said. "Why is that?"

In the past, I would have mentioned the Genocide. So much was inexpressible, so many feelings impossible, that it was easier to express rage or despair over trivialities than explain the deeper causes of emotional unrest. Somewhere along the line, through the generations, such a manner of dealing with feelings became a habit.

But most Hayastantsis seem to think that the Genocide is more the history of the diaspora, even if many here are the children and grandchildren of survivors. In reality, many diasporans have led comparatively cushy lives, so perhaps we have had more time to remember and advocate; in Armenia, everyone has just been trying to survive. So maybe centuries of accumulated oppression, or the unresolved war and closed borders, or never knowing which of your friends or family were party informants during Soviet times are all partially to blame for Hayastantsis loudly critiquing the opera but keeping their most tender feelings to themselves.

But I'm uncomfortable connecting psychological dynamics to cultural trauma, because it doesn't seem to be a practice among the locals. I don't know if it's because psychology is frowned upon or because giving people sympathy for their cultural loss seems absurd to Armenians, who live with their history—with the tonir and the vodka and the arbor and the oud.

"I have no idea," I told Erin.

❖

As Gharib took us on the tour of the village, he pointed out three churches lined on top of a cliff and told us of a local legend: three sisters were in love with the same prince, and rather than any of them risking heartbreak or betrayal, the two elder sisters wore dresses of different colors, red and apricot-colored, and jumped off the cliff. When the youngest sister found out about this inexplicable, unfathomable sacrifice, she did what anyone would do in these circumstances— she put on a dress, this one white, and threw herself over the cliff. As his penance, the prince built the three churches of colored stone corresponding to the dresses of the sisters.

I thought of Toumanian's poem about Anoush, whose brother killed her lover, causing her to jump off a cliff. "Why are there so many unrequited love stories in Armenian folklore?" I asked Gharib.

"Before Christianity, people married for love. After Christianity, they married for God and their families. So this created a conflict."

It sounded feasible to me. During pagan times, Armenians worshiped nature: mountains, trees, water, animals, sun, moon, and stars. Then they worshiped spirits, such as the Haralez (dogs who licked the wounds of dead soldiers to bring them to life) or Haverzahar (nymphs who protected women). Starting in the fifth century BC, Armenians worshiped gods and goddesses that were similar to the pantheons of Persian, Greek, and Roman gods. The most popular and powerful was Anahid, the Armenian version of Athena. Only one pagan temple still exists in Armenia: Garni, which was dedicated to Mihr, the god of the sun, and built by King Trdat in the first century. It survived because Garni was a getaway for the royals—they adapted it as a mansion. All the others were systematically destroyed by Trdat when he adopted Christianity as the national religion. When my students asked if they could take me somewhere, I chose Garni as an alternative to the plethora of ancient churches to choose from.

Many of my students write about their boyfriends or falling in love. In fact, they've written about love more than any other students I've had, perhaps because of the duty to family that's interwoven with their love lives, or perhaps because I give them free rein to write whatever they want—something they're mostly not used to doing in school, raised in the Soviet model. Whatever the reason, I felt compelled one day to give them chocolate, telling them that eating cacao creates the same chemicals in their brain as infatuation secretes, so it could free them from the drama of boys. They thought this was hilarious.

I'm really looking forward to our trip to Garni, to get outside of the classroom; I want to ask the students about their future plans—what kind of work they want to do, if they want to have children, etc. But I'm hesitant to enter this line of questioning because they might ask me about my personal life. Will they ask me if I have a husband, a boyfriend? What would I tell them?

In New York, I often come out to my students on the first day of class when I introduce myself since it's tied to my writing, but otherwise I tell my students very little about myself. Many are immigrants and live according to traditional or religious tenets—Jewish, Muslim, Catholic, Hindu, and Sikh; they wear yarmulkes, long skirts, headscarves, and turbans. Though they are respectful to me as their teacher, they normally wouldn't associate with me.

I tell my students I want them to write about their lives. I let them know they can write about anything and that we are in a safe space for them to express themselves. So shouldn't I be open and honest with them about my life? On the other hand, as a teacher, I don't want them to focus on me. I realize now that part of my fear of asking people questions is that they might ask the same of me.

Before we left the apartment to embark on the trip to Gharib's grandparents' village, Seyran warned me that he wouldn't be himself. In general, he has a lot of energy, sometimes veering toward manic. I assumed he was this lively with everyone, but he told me no; he's just more comfortable around me. It was still surprising to see him so quiet and reserved in the village. I suspected it was the age difference between him and the others. But it also could have been a protective maneuver since Seyran is an outlier in Armenian society; he might have been cloaking himself till he felt safe. When we were alone in the garden, he broke through his reserve and came to me to share his feelings: what and whom he liked and didn't like. He also said that Gharib had asked him if he was in love with me.

"It's none of your business," Seyran answered. "Do you always go around asking people if they are in love?"

"I ask special people," Gharib said. "Yes."

STORY: OCTOBER, 2006
YEREVAN

After a month in Yerevan, Na had not made much headway on her project to interview artists. After her discussion with Hagop, the art critic, she reconsidered conducting interviews via translation. So she sat down and made a list of people she could speak to in English. Tanya was first on the list. Na had met her in 2005 at the feminist conference. Tanya was an Armenian-Syrian-Canadian repat running a women's center on the university campus.

When Na called her, Tanya reported that the women's center had recently been shut down. While Tanya was away on a trip, a student at the center had initiated a discussion group on women's sexuality and sent out an email announcement that reached certain individuals in the university administration who found it unacceptable. Tanya said university officials had been positioning to shut down the center for a while now, and the email was the excuse they needed. The center staff slowly removed books and equipment from the space while Tanya searched for a new location off campus, where they would have more freedom to conduct outreach to women. "It's actually a positive thing—we won't be limited to only working with students on campus, and we won't have to keep to university hours." Na admired her upbeat attitude during crisis. Tanya spoke in a gentle, even tone, her slight accent apparent over the phone.

Na hung up the receiver and sighed. The news made her feel that she had to be vigilant as a teacher in presenting material. In prepping her course, she had already chosen passages on women's bodies and homosexuality.

A few hours later, Seyran called. He was with friends.

"Guess who I am here with?" he asked. "One of your students!" He was giggling uncontrollably. "Jhenya is in your class at the university!"

Na held her breath and scanned through the faces and names in her mind. Jhenya had sleek black hair that she wore in a bob and big, brown almond-shaped eyes. "I don't think it's funny," she said.

The professors at the Department of Romance Language Philology had been kind and welcoming to Na. In their forties and above, they wore boxy Soviet-era skirt suits and sensible trapezoidal-toed shoes in warm seventies-era tones: maroon, yellow ochre, burnt sienna. Na could imagine how well it would go over with the stately professors if they found out that she was canoodling with some student-aged punk. She had no reason to believe that Jhenya wouldn't gossip as everyone seemed to enjoy knowing other people's business. This was bad news coming right after Tanya's phone call.

Seyran was confused. Why didn't Na think this was a hilarious coincidence? Na told him, "Look, it's not good for my students to know about us. I could lose my job if someone from the university finds out!"

Seyran came over to Na's apartment to try to calm her down. Sitting on one of the mammoth velveteen-covered couches, he put his feet on the glass coffee table and sulked, his chin to his chest, his big eyes looking up at her while she stood in front of him, ranting about the tenuous position he had put her in by telling Jhenya about their relationship.

"Once one girl knows about us, they all will," she told him.

"No, my friends aren't like that," he insisted. "Jhenya won't tell. I told her you were upset and not to tell anyone."

"Oh, great. That means she definitely will."

"No, they aren't like everyone else. Jhenya and Stepan are my best friends."

He insisted that she should meet them; that once she got to know them, she would feel better.

The next night they all met at a lahmajun stand. Stepan, a bassist with a goofy grin and a brush of dirty-blond hair, was affectionate toward Seyran, roughhousing with him. Jhenya was nonthreatening as well, asking Na how she was liking it here and what she thought of the Department of Romance Language Philology. Jhenya spoke English very well, and Na found her manner friendly and respectful.

The conversation focused mostly on school. Jhenya didn't ask Na questions about her personal life, and Na didn't ask Jhenya about hers. Na was relieved.

But when Jhenya called Na on the phone a few days later to tell her that the trip her class had been planning to take to Garni was canceled, Na couldn't help but wonder if it had something to do with her liaison with Seyran. The fact that Jhenya was calling her, as a representative of the students, seemed telling.

"It's too foggy to go to Garni. It's a long trip, and it's not so safe to take in this weather," Jhenya said, her voice apologetic. "It has absolutely nothing to do with you."

Of course, it was that last line that convinced Na that it had everything to do with her.

JOURNAL: APRIL 5, 2010
ASTORIA

The other day, Seyran wanted to have sex with me.

"With a condom," I answered.

"But I haven't had sex with anyone." He had been insisting this ever since I found out about Veronica, my doppelganger, on his computer.

"You're lying."

"No, I'm not," he maintained.

"I can tell you're lying because you're not looking into my eyes."

"No, I haven't had sex with anyone ... " he said, looking at me. Then his eyes shifted away from my face and he continued, "without a condom."

He is so incapable of telling the truth, it's not even funny. Because I no longer trust him, I've secretly scheduled an HIV test so I can make sure I'm healthy. I don't know what I am hoping to find. If I have the disease, perhaps it will finally be the reason I need to let go of him. But then I will be faced with a lifelong sickness. What a wonderful situation to be in: between disease and deceit.

Part of me still believes that he wouldn't hurt me so much as to give me HIV after I saved him from army conscription. I don't want the story of our relationship to be so tainted.

I should have let him go a long time ago, and I am ashamed that I haven't. Most of my friends don't even know about my problems, and those who do have already advised me to break up with Seyran. Now things are even worse. There's no one for me to talk to since I don't want anyone to ask what's wrong with me—I don't know what I would answer.

STORY: OCTOBER, 2006
YEREVAN

"Natalee dear," Anahid Etchian said in her booming, broad voice with a pseudo-British accent. "It is not easy for us here, but we get on somehow." Her friend Sona, the quiet sidekick, nodded her head. They were both professors in the Department of Romance Language Philology. Sona had reddish-maroon hair, like the stain that wine leaves behind. Anahid, with her thick curly hair, wearing beautiful, chunky gemstone jewelry, looked to Na like a hippie professor from the seventies. Anahid loved Shakespeare, which explained the British spirit in her dramatic manner of speech, though she had never been to the UK. "Oh, Natalee, the students are so thrilled to meet you, as am I, and I do hope we will be friends," she had proclaimed, practically singing, upon first meeting Na. It didn't take long for Anahid to invite Na for coffee with Sona.

As the women sipped from their little dark cups, Anahid told Na about her family and career. She had two teenage daughters and an eight-year-old son. Unfortunately, her boy had come down with smallpox (Na didn't think people could contract this eighteenth-century disease and wondered if she might have meant chicken pox), and she was terribly worried about him, but she had to work. Her husband was an artist, a ceramicist who crafted exquisite museum-worthy creations. The family was living on her salary, so pitiful a pittance that she had to take on many private students to survive.

"But it isn't all bad, Natalee dear," she said. "You will get to see the real Armenian life while you are here." She told Na that she must come to her home during the Christmas holidays, and Na was grateful for the invitation.

Na wondered if they would ask her about her personal life, but they didn't, and Na was relieved. They were her contemporaries, mature women with husbands and families like the women Na had gone to college with. Na felt that they didn't need to know that she was dating a punk rocker and a poet who was a graduating senior at the State Engineering University of Armenia. Of course, it was possible that they already knew, but Na didn't consider this. Instead, she felt better thinking of herself as hidden from their view. Besides, there was an element of power in concealing herself, in bolstering her identity as an "other."

She would later conceal the dark elements of her relationship with Seyran from her friends in the U.S. in a similar way. It wasn't only due to shame and embarrassment but also a way to feel empowered. The thinking swirled around her mind like this: *You don't understand me, so you're not worthy of the special privilege of realizing my vulnerabilities.* It was a tactic Na had developed with her parents as an adolescent.

One night soon after her meeting with Anahid Etchian, Seyran was going through Na's clothes and came across a dress that he liked. It was pink, made of a knit material. He put it on and asked her to take photos of him. In one shot, Na positioned herself with the camera on the floor as he stood on the bed so she could see up his dress, peeking at his underwear, which was bright blue. With the stubble on his face and his big eyes, it was an enticing, beautiful shot. But whenever Na and Seyran later showed photos on Na's computer to friends, there was always the risk that they would accidentally open this file and everyone would see Seyran in a pink dress.

There was something exciting about living with a secret like that, so close to the surface, mixed in with all the posed, happy photos.

BLOG POST: OCTOBER 22, 2006
YEREVAN

Every Other Confessional Blog on the Internet >>> Before I came here, I was warned that Yerevan was a paradoxically sexualized place.

A woman who had been a Fulbrighter to Armenia a few years before emailed me, "People present very different public and private selves. The most matronly looking professional woman, married with children, will turn out to be a raging lesbian. And many gay men have wives, with whom they have an open relationship so they can have sex with men on the side. It's the strangest place in terms of sexuality, once you scratch the surface."

Now that I have contracted herpes, HPV, and CMV in the six short weeks since I arrived, I think it's fair to say that I have skimmed beneath the outer crust of Yerevan.

Something has fucked up my liver so badly that I've had to get a two-hour IV drip treatment for the past five days. Need I mention diarrhea, flu, and several neurotic episodes, most of which involve meeting Seyran at the European Medical Center every Friday to give him the bad news of my blood, urine, and pap tests. I've been going from appointment to appointment, trying not to freak out that either or both of us are diseased.

"Your decisions are making you depressed," Seyran said today. (He confuses the word *decisions* for *diseases*.)

Yes, I have scratched the surface, and I don't think I want to dig any deeper. But I will write about what's really going on with my diseases and hopefully, in the process, I will give you some idea of the medical system in Armenia, not to mention attitudes toward women's sexuality in general.

It all started when Seyran had sex with me without a condom. I didn't realize he was unprotected until afterward, and I immediately told him it was not okay. He said he'd never had sex without a condom before, but I felt uncomfortable and told him we should both get tested for HIV.

By that evening, it seemed I had contracted a yeast infection, and by the next day, it hurt to pee, so I figured I had a urinary tract infection.

When I went to the Youth Clinic on Vernissage, referred to me by a doctor listed in my embassy packet, I saw the sign indicating that it was an International Planned Parenthood clinic and that it was "client friendly." I met with a doctor and told her about the suspected UTI and that Seyran and I wanted to get tested for HIV. The doctor was a blond woman in her fifties. As she spoke with me in English, she would periodically pause and ask, "Do you understand?" As she queried me, I told her my age and that I was single, whereupon she announced with a huff, "Independent woman." She told me to lie down and immediately gave me an ultrasound and informed me that my cervix was infected and that what I had was serious. "Do you understand?" she said. *No, not really,* I thought. I looked at her inquisitively. She told me that she would give me a series of STD tests, theorizing that whatever I had Seyran would have, too. "Not necessarily," I said. We were different people with different sexual histories, ultimately, and who knows what did or didn't pass between us.

"Yes, not necessarily," she admitted. I didn't realize that this comment gave her further license to judge me: below the surface, apparently, it's an unchecked assumption that men are entitled to fuck multiple women, but women must stay monogamous to a single man.

Once on the examining table, I was not offered a drape. The nurse inserted the speculum and gave me a pap, but the doctor did not give me a pelvic exam. Instead, she left the room a couple of times, leaving the door open, my legs wide with the speculum inside me, as if I were a frog pinned to a board in a biology lab. It was the most unsettling gynecological exam I ever experienced. When I left, she told me she would be testing for herpes (which she repeated a few times), chlamydia, HIV, and gonorrhea. I gave blood and urine the next morning.

Over the next few days, I came down with flu symptoms. When I felt better, I went back to the clinic for my test results. There were three or four women in the waiting room, and the doctor was coming in and out as she saw patients. She noticed me and told me that all my results had come back negative.

"But I still have symptoms," I told her. For the past few days, I had been generally feeling uncomfortable down there. As I insisted to the doctor that I needed medicine for my condition—what I still assumed was a yeast infection or a UTI—the nurse was on the phone. She then interrupted our conversation to tell the doctor something. The doctor listened, turned to me, and blurted out, "You have herpes."

I stared at her.

"Do you understand?" she asked, as if she weren't in the waiting room announcing that I had a sexually transmitted disease. So much for a client-friendly, privacy-protecting International Planned Parenthood clinic. The doctor did not offer treatment, and I left in a daze, my head ringing with the word *herpes*.

❖

A few friends recommended the European Medical Center, which is clean, modern, and quiet. It is also very expensive by Armenian standards, but I've been able to afford it, paying out of pocket for my treatments, which have been many. Though the place is a striking contrast to the Youth Clinic, I've found that attitudes about sexuality are just as repressed.

The gynecologist, a mature, soothing woman who wore her black hair in bangs, with frosted pink lipstick that overstepped the boundaries of her lip line, was very calm and thorough, asking me a battery of questions on my medical history. When she asked me about my sexual activity, I told her there had been none the previous two years, but I had been active the past two months in Armenia.

I looked at her face for her response, and she smiled demurely. She gave me a pelvic exam and repeated the blood and urine tests. I had read online that flu-like symptoms, such as the head cold and fatigue I now felt, can accompany herpes, but the doctor told me that I had the flu. She told me to stay home and rest until I was better. When I went back the following week, the UTI was confirmed, as was a yeast infection. So was the herpes, unfortunately. More bad news: I also had HPV, and my liver function test results were four times higher than normal.

Ruling out hepatitis a week later, the gynecologist referred me to a general practitioner, a barrel-chested older man with white hair, blue eyes, a mustache, a red face, a smoker's raspy voice, and a big bandage on his left thumb. He asked me if I drank a lot and did not believe me when I told him I only had one or two drinks a week. He wanted to treat me for my liver through an IV drip of medicinal vitamins, which I would receive for two hours once a day for five days. He wanted to start that day.

I told him I would think about it, and I went outside to the waiting room to tell Seyran the news. When I returned, the doctor said, "Okay, now, you must be honest with me. Do you smoke crack?"

"No!" I said. "Never!" I was unaware there was crack activity in Armenia.

"Intravenous drugs?"

"No, I haven't done any drugs," I explained. "Just smoked a little marijuana," I admitted.

His eyes lit up. "I am telling you now, if you smoke marijuana while we give you this treatment, I am done with you." He wiped his hands together.

"No, I smoke marijuana once a year, if that. I've only smoked it once since I've been here." Seyran had picked some wild weed while we were in Gharib's family village. We had dried it, took out the seeds, and spent three days looking for rolling paper in tobacco shops (I was convinced the government was behind the lack of papers), but when we smoked it there was very little effect, and we threw it away.

"I saw that young man you are with. His eyes are red!"

"No!" I exclaimed.

"Look, I'm not police, you be honest with me."

I insisted to him I was telling the truth and left the clinic feeling like a criminal. I guess his suspicions were aroused by my American identity: I am a free woman, unmarried, independent, having sex on the second date, drug-addled, debauched, and diseased.

❖

So this is what I have been doing instead of my obligations to my Fulbright: being sick, freaking out, and dealing with doctors. During the weeks when we waited for my test results, Seyran and I looked up all my diseases online. On a Russian STD site, someone had posted a horrifying photo of a cauliflower-like growth colonizing some poor wretch's vagina. They called to mind something the doctor at the free clinic across town had suggested to Seyran when he got tested for herpes: that I had "mushrooms." I should mention that Seyran doesn't have blisters, and neither do I. His test came back negative: .89 out of a possible .9, which seems like a very tiny margin to me, and I have read that blood tests are not so accurate. I have also read that a lot of people with herpes don't develop the symptoms and can still pass on the disease, even while wearing a condom. I am not sure how coming to Armenia turned me into a font of STDs or who all these lucky people are, walking around completely oblivious to the disease they carry. It seems that Seyran may be one of them.

He keeps asking me, "Why you have so many decisions?"

META-WRITING:

At the time I wrote the above post, I had gotten to know more writers in Yerevan and had directed them to my blog. They were now telling me in typical blunt, Hayastantsi fashion that it was not very interesting. They preferred a more experimental style, written in jargon, spoken rather than literary—like the poems I had written in my twenties, newly freed from my parents' influence, needing to write my angst of sex and sexuality without punctuation.

Though it felt freeing to admit what was happening in my private life on my blog, and I was describing my misadventures at the health clinics to defy the status quo, I was also responding to the writers' criticism.

Meanwhile, my blog caused my friends back home to worry; they told me to leave Seyran, to get out of Armenia. I wrote them reassuring notes that I was fine. Strangely, Seyran didn't mind that I had published this post, probably because it supported his reputation as a rebel.

Amal, my translator friend who had grown up in Yerevan, emailed to say that my blog post had gone too far and that people who appreciated my openness would later betray me—smiling at me now but saying terrible things about me later. "Trust no one," she told me.

This mistrusting attitude was also made manifest in my English class at the university. We were discussing an essay by Bernard Cooper about a boy who feels that he is without gender. The writer describes himself as being at the age when boys and girls are indistinguishable from each other, as if he is floating in space, not readily identifying with any gender. Growing up in LA in the early fifties, he has a crush on—coincidentally—an Armenian girl, the smartest student in the class who raises her hand constantly. He soon realizes his crush isn't so much to be with her—but to be her. Alone in his room, he imitates her wriggling style of gaining the teacher's attention, and he plays in his parents' walk-in closet, trying on his dad's shoes, then his mom's heels.

I wondered what the students would think given the levels of sexism and homophobia in Armenia. They started by debating whether Cooper's behavior was "normal" or not. Most of the women said that the parents were at fault for not taking better care of their boy. They didn't understand why he didn't ask his mother about these "strange" feelings. But one girl, Lida, said that it was not unusual for little children to play with gender identity. "It is harmless," she explained. Lida was auburn-haired, and wore lots of makeup on her bright-blue eyes, the only student with short hair in the class.

Jhenya, Seyran's friend, went so far as to proclaim that homosexuality was normal. She said that among artists, it was not unusual to explore sexuality, to be open to everything. "I would like to explore myself through writing, too," she said.

Lida agreed, then added, "When I am going through a difficult time, I write about all my feelings, but then I immediately tear up the papers so that no one will be able to read them."

I couldn't contain myself: the thought of tearing up pages was sacrilege. "That's terrible!" I exclaimed.

Lida shrugged. "Life is hard, so it's better not to make it harder."

❖

I wanted to have a positive impact on the students, to inspire them to reverse the injustices they witnessed, but I wonder what they saw in me as a mentor—a single, child-free woman twice their age. Anahid Etchian once mentioned to me that the students had told her in a class discussion that I had lost my Armenian culture. But as far as I knew, they weren't aware that I was bisexual.

The students didn't deny that homosexuality existed, nor did they say it was a sin, but they did say that some people—special people, like artists—were freer to explore that part of themselves. For those queer girls among them—who studied together for four years, who called each other sister, who all lived with their families—that part would have to remain concealed, denied, unexplored, or unfulfilled. Expressing it would only make their lives harder.

They saw me as different from them, but even in my expressiveness, we were very much alike.

STORY: OCTOBER, 2006
YEREVAN

The Department of Romance Language Philology was having a big party for their fifteenth anniversary, coinciding with the fifteenth anniversary of the country itself. There were five sections within the school: Italian, Spanish, French, English, and German. Each section presented music, dance, and/or theater pertaining to each culture. The girls from the Italian department wore red, white, and green sashes, singing "Funiculi Funicula." Arranged in staged, staid groupings of two and three, they smiled discreetly as if appearing on Lawrence Welk. In contrast, the French department presented a heartthrob of a young man confidently crooning pop songs, as if performing on Eurovision; the girls screamed whenever he belted out a long note. The English department, under the direction of Anahid Etchian, presented the banquet scene from Macbeth when the ghost of Banquo appears. Though the students awkwardly struggled through the words, Na found it refreshing that young women were taking the lead, performing male roles.

The mammoth auditorium was filled with students, staff, and professors. Seyran had asked Na that morning if he could come with her, and she told him no; she didn't think it was a good idea for them to be seen together at the university among her colleagues.

A pair of child dancers, dressed in ballroom outfits, next performed the tango for the Spanish section. Na found it disturbing that the boy, about eight years old, was wearing a shirt made of sheer mesh. She had just suffered scorn from the Youth Clinic on Vernissage for being an "independent woman," and yet, here children were dancing in a sexual way that was not only condoned but also applauded. The next act, a troupe of flamenco dancers, a dozen young women dressed in black, moved their bodies dispassionately. Na was pondering this dissonance when she spotted Seyran walking into the auditorium, sauntering down the aisle with Stepan. He had gotten his hair cut, shaved on the sides and long on top, and he looked like a punk. Not a punk rocker but an actual ruffian. Suddenly, Seyran licked Stepan's ear, and Na was instantly appalled. She hoped that Anahid Etchian, sitting next to her, hadn't noticed where Na's eyes had traveled from the stage.

It was at this moment that Na decided to break up with Seyran. *Enough is enough.* She had asked him not to come to the performance, and he did anyway. Then there was the complication in their sex life, which was resulting in medical attention for Na.

It had all started because Seyran wanted to do it anally.

"I don't know," she told him. She'd never had anal sex before. Her two previous boyfriends, both much older than her, had been pretty tame. Exclusively missionary position.

"Please?" he asked. And he started sliding against Na. She thought it was the strangest sensation, like she was going to take a dump. But it didn't feel bad. Just different. Seyran described it as "stronger." She liked that it made her feel emotionally closer to him.

And then she realized he was not wearing a condom. She wasn't sure how that had happened. They had agreed to always use one. He pulled out right before coming and finished himself off. She lay in bed, sleepless, wondering why he would do this.

In the morning, he said he didn't think a condom was necessary since she couldn't get pregnant.

"But condoms also help prevent disease from spreading," she told him.

"I don't have disease. And anyway, you can't get disease from anal."

"Yes, you can!" she exclaimed. Na didn't know if he was playing dumb or what. She didn't like that he hadn't conferred with her about removing the condom, and she didn't know whether to believe him. She had heard stories of how men in Armenia refused to wear condoms and thus were responsible for spreading HIV to a large percentage of the female population. She managed to subside her fears and told Seyran the next day that they needed to get HIV tested if they were going to continue their sexual relationship.

Now, sitting in the auditorium, she decided that the next time she saw him privately, she would break it off.

In a couple of days, she was supposed to give a presentation in her department for a panel to commemorate the fifteenth anniversary, but when she went home to work on it, she was struck with fatigue. She decided to rest for a short while, and before she knew it, she had fallen asleep. When she awoke, she was freezing. She didn't know how to turn on the heat, so she put on a scarf and a hat.

The phone rang. It was Seyran, asking if he could come over.

"No," she told him, "I have work to do, and I want to be by myself."

"Please?" he asked.

"And I'm not feeling well. I need some space!"

She hung up the phone and fell back asleep.

The next thing she heard was the doorbell. When she got up, she felt stiff, and she made her way to the door, freezing. *Maybe I've caught a cold*, she thought.

It was Seyran. He took a long look at Na. She realized she must have appeared to be a mess, hunched over by the front door, wearing a beret and scarf.

"I think I'm sick," she told him. "It's so cold in here. Why did you come? I told you I wanted to be alone."

She fell on top of the bed, and he put his hand on her forehead. "You have fever," he said.

"No, I don't," she said, but she found the thermometer, which the State Department had advised her to bring in a first-aid kit, and it read 103. "Oh shit," she said.

Na lay in bed while Seyran washed the dishes in her sink. They had piled up over the last few days, and as she heard the water running, she felt relieved.

When he was done, he came into her bedroom with a tray holding jam and a pot of tea. "Why you don't want me to come over?" Seyran asked. "Who's gonna make tea for you when you're sick?"

Throughout the testing trials at the clinics, she was always on the verge of breaking up with him, weighing everything in her mind, waiting for the diseases to tell her what to do, for the diseases to make the decision.

When his herpes test results came back negative, she was confused. *Where did it come from?* She supposed it was possible that she had contracted herpes when she was involved with her last sexual partner, a woman, two years before. They hadn't had much sex in the short time they were together, but it also hadn't been safe.

When Na moved back to New York a year later, she went to her doctor and got tested for herpes. It came back negative, and she was never diagnosed with it again.

It seemed it wasn't only Seyran who had been dishonest. The Armenian medical establishment had been, too. The first clinic had lied to her to get a filthy American woman out of their midst, and the second had gouged her with expensive, unnecessary treatments. She had suspected as such, but now she knew more clearly why it was better to remain silent.

JOURNAL: MAY 10, 2010
ASTORIA

I hit another low. I was doing my best to not have sex with him, for my own protection, since my discovery of Veronica. And I even got HIV tested for my own sanity. I have set some boundaries for myself. But I still have to live with him.

Today he surprised me by showing up after my Weight Watchers meeting, requesting that we take a walk. I wanted to go home but ended up strolling around Astoria up to Titan, the Greek grocery store, to buy olives. I decided to take the opportunity to shop the nearby used furniture stores, and he helped me find a desk chair, then carried it back home for me.

When we came home, we went to our separate rooms. Then he unbelievably cleaned the toilet, tub, and sink. I do not know what inspired this, but I am pretty sure it is a first.

With the bathroom sparkling clean, I took a shower and got ready to meet some friends. I was getting dressed in my room when he propositioned me. He insisted that he had only had sex with a condom. He said if he had done it without, he wouldn't have sex with me. I relented and let him fuck me without a condom, asking him to pull out before he came. Well, he realized he was coming really quickly, made this odd face, pulled out, and his cum came with such force that it squirted into an arc, onto my face, and into my eye.

META-WRITING:

I wish I could say that I didn't see it coming.

But that pun stings a bit too much. This particular debasement seemed accidental but not any less shameful. It was like some spirit or ancestor asking me: Are you blind?

It can be infuriating to reread my journal entries. Though I know I can't change who I was then, I wish Na hadn't subjected herself to such indignities. At the same time, I can't be so condemning of how lost I was, paralyzed in Seyran's ever-widening web. Everyone probably gets entangled in a terrible relationship at least once in their life—even people who don't carry centuries of inherited trauma.

In that legend of the three girls in multicolored dresses killing themselves over a boy, I am struck by the fact that like Anoush, cultural mores dictate that women must sacrifice themselves for the romantic love of a man. This is why I gave my students chocolate as a substitute for love: better to avoid all this mess. But in such an equation, the spiritual side to love is lost.

In Hinanots, Gharib and Mardi had a vociferous argument in Armenian when we reached the site of one of the churches on the cliff. It bothered me that they were both so distressed, although I didn't know what it was about. Seyran was irked that I cared. "Why is it your business?"

"Because they're my friends," I told him. We were special people, after all.

A week or so before the trip to the village, Seyran and I went to a working-class restaurant for piroshkis. After we ordered, I went to the bathroom, and when I returned, Seyran announced that Gharib had just been there. "Did you tell him I was here? Where is he?"

"He left after he flirted with me." As we ate piroshkis, Seyran told me a story: he and Gharib had made a connection before Seyran and I met, back when Gharib gave Seyran a voice lesson. Nothing happened, Seyran said, but he admitted it felt good when Gharib put his hand on his belly to make him aware of his diaphragm. Seyran reported that when Gharib greeted him at the restaurant, he had winked and told Seyran, "You and I will have lots of sex." Looking back now, it's likely that Seyran invented part if not all of this story. Gharib told me later that they did actually have a voice lesson. Perhaps they had sex at that time ... but whether Gharib had been at the restaurant or said what he did? Seyran probably fabricated the story to portray himself as desirable. At the time, I was taking Seyran's word, and I could imagine Gharib saying such a thing in a place where people skimmed and scraped at the surface.

I've been pondering the other rumored story from this chapter: Gharib asking Seyran if we were in love. Seyran had said it was none of his business: "Do you always go around asking people if they are in love?"

"I ask special people," Gharib supposedly said. "Yes."

I do think Gharib asked him something about us. However, while Seyran was suggesting to me that Gharib wanted to pry into our intimate business and that he was seeking to protect our privacy, Seyran was really announcing his domain over his own interests. He might have added a flourish to make himself sound special to Gharib, but I choose to believe that Gharib was announcing that he loved and cared about us.

Here we were, artists and queer people, supposedly freer than the rest. And here was Seyran saying to Gharib, "I'm not going to make my life harder by opening up to you."

Of course, this was what he was doing with me all along.

8. ASK YOUR BODY

BLOG POST: NOVEMBER 26, 2006
YEREVAN

Why I Can't Speak Armenian >>> Digeen Madleen comes to my home twice a week to tutor me in Armenian. A professor from the university recommended by Moussi, she charges twenty dollars for each two-hour lesson. My friends tell me that she's soaking me because I'm American, but I can afford it. Though I wasn't sure at first if her lack of English would be a barrier, I have found that it forces me to be in the moment and grasp at all the possible words I know, or at least to flip through the dictionary to find them. But I'm thinking of letting Digeen Madleen go, because after two months of tutoring, I'm still not speaking Armenian.

It's true that I am learning vocabulary and Eastern Armenian grammar, and I understand enough of the language that I can follow Digeen Madleen's stories. During one lesson, she recounted a tragic tale about her best friend's uncle who was sent to Siberia and was beaten so badly that he was unable to have children when he returned. If that wasn't heartrending enough, I've also been made privy to the fact that her sister's ex-husband was an alcoholic, whom Digeen Madleen now believes to be a "narcoman." Perhaps to redirect the conversation, she has filled me in on her thoughts about cannibalism.

I tried not to look shocked as this petite woman in her sixties with a blond bob calmly gestured to sections of her arms as she recounted a recent news item about a French woman who was caught storing pieces of bodies in her freezer. Digeen Madleen placed the word for "man eater" on a list of compound nouns, which included "loud talker" and "flower lover." The lesson being that you can make up words in Armenian via common sense combinations, and they will most likely be actual words. It was a poetic, engaging activity in contrast to slogging through the subjunctive mood. However, "cannibal" doesn't pop up in conversation very often.

I can't blame my lack of fluency all on Digeen Madleen. The fact is, speaking has always been difficult for me as a shy, introverted person. One of the reasons I'm a writer is corrective—to take more time to get words down on paper, rearrange them, and express them the way I truly mean. When Digeen Madleen leaves my apartment, I feel the urgency to write sentences with the words she has taught because I need a blueprint of the written words in my mind to feel confident in speaking them aloud. But I find that I have little time during the day to absorb, practice, and contextualize this language.

The other problem is Seyran. Sometimes I force myself to speak only Armenian with him, but it never lasts more than two sentences because he insists on speaking in an incomprehensible mumble, which he says is his natural way of talking. When I complain, he drills me on vocabulary words. I usually know most of them (cat, car, plum, tree) except the dirty ones (dick, shit, masturbate). But then he keeps correcting my pronunciation of the consonants. Growing up with the simple Western sounds of *t* and *d, p* and *b,* I've now come to find out there are blended *td* and *pb* sounds in the Eastern pronunciation, and they cause me to sputter. Seyran repeats these consonants, staccato style, speaking like a mean teacher, very rarely praising me. He is usually very sweet and affectionate, but something about teaching obviously brings out the Soviet-style authoritarian instructors he's had over the years. Once he tried teaching me a song, then forced me to march around the room singing it while he played the guitar. When I told him this was ridiculous, he sat me down for a dictation, then screamed at me for not writing perfectly on the lines in my notebook, which reduced me to tears. Clearly, his teaching method does not work for me.

So I try to speak Armenian as much as I can when I am out and about, but these days, I am mostly out and about with Seyran, who does a lot of translating. Recently, I was at one of Seyran's concerts, and I saw a young, blond, blue-eyed boy with Nordic features sitting alone in the audience. I was tempted to ask him in English where he was from to include the lonely odar into Armenian society.

After the concert, we were introduced to the boy, who, lo and behold, held a conversation in Armenian with Seyran. It turned out he was Danish and was studying Armenian at the university.

Witnessing this exchange, our friend Edita asked me how my lessons were coming along. Sensing she was about to shame me, I told her, "I'm learning grammar and understanding more, but I can't speak. I don't get enough practice."

"Natalee," she laughed, "I haven't heard you say one sentence in Armenian."

This didn't seem fair. When I first met Edita, I attempted to say simple sentences with her. But as Seyran and I spent more time with her and her husband, Hrair, taking nightly walks around the city with their dog, they would switch back and forth between Armenian and English. For me to speak Armenian, I would have to insist no English be spoken, which would prevent me from answering questions thoughtfully in complex sentences. It would also cause me to sport a dumbfounded expression throughout the entire conversation.

There have likely been studies done on this, but from my experience it seems there are certain emotional and psychological qualities one needs, as an adult, to learn a language: you have to be willing to be stupid, you have to accept being misunderstood, and you have to give up how you identify yourself in the world. In other words, you have to give up control.

❖

One result of my failure to learn Armenian is that Seyran is acing spoken English. When we were first becoming acquainted, there were a couple of occasions when I had absolutely no idea what he was talking about. Now that we've been together a couple of months, we understand each other well—despite lingering quirks to his language—communicating readily in English about art, Armenia, and complex relationship issues.

When Digeen Madleen met him, she asked how he learned English, and I realized that I didn't know. He had mentioned that he learned from music lyrics (a song by Blur busted his brain, he said), but I assumed that he had studied it at the university.

It turns out that he attended a free class at the U.S. embassy, which met daily for a few weeks, but he went only two or three times a week.

It's true that Seyran is a self-educated type, teaching himself enough about computers to provide tech support for an NGO and learning enough guitar chords to play one song after another for hours. But learning a language is really hard. How can someone become fluent from studying lyrics and a few lessons? Seyran wants to understand the music he loves, he wants to know other realities not spoken in Armenian, and he wants to talk to me. So here's another element needed to learn a language: desire.

❁

As we were walking through Republic Square one day, Seyran told me that he doesn't translate Armenian to English in his mind. When he learns an English word, he tries to understand the meaning and connect it to its entity. "I'm like a child. When I see a tree, I don't think *dzar* and then translate it. I look at the tree and think *tree*."

Later, that very same day, we were attending a lecture by a German art critic who had curated an exhibit on immigration. He wasn't only explaining the art but verging into pretty intellectual territory, referencing Foucault and Benjamin, and I was strangely comforted that I can feel like an outsider even when English is spoken. As my attention drifted, I heard him discussing how difficult it is for people to learn new languages. By the time we are adults, he claimed, our identities have formed, along with ways of thinking that get encoded into language. But children, their brains like little sponges, can remain open to a new sensibility. He was echoing what Seyran had said earlier about looking at a tree and thinking of the word *tree*.

Afterward, a video artist of Greek descent, born in Germany, discussed the format of the film she was about to show on immigration and mobility. She discussed her grandparents' immigration from Turkey to Germany during the upheaval of World War I. Like my Armenian grandparents, they had been driven out by genocide. I took notes to keep up:

- Parts and pieces make up a language
- You can use words, but you can't communicate
- Reference fields
- Language code
- Everything new comes to you from stumbling
- Holocaust victims and perpetrators speak different languages
- A specific experience produces a different way of thinking and a different language

And then she said that it's very difficult for diasporans to communicate with those who have never left the homeland—their experiences have been so contrary that they have produced different vocabularies and even divergent ways of thinking.

YES! I thought. *Someone is finally speaking my reality!* I felt vindicated in my inability to speak Armenian.

Then I observed the Greek German video artist very carefully. She was stern and serious and barely smiled. She spoke English with a vague European accent, her skin was light, and her clothes were sleek and elegant. Like all the other European intellectuals who visited, she presented her work from an Apple laptop.

She's not Greek, I wrote in my notebook. Greeks to me were expressive, colorful, and traditional. It was a stereotype, sure. It was also close to what I think of as a typical Armenian woman.

And then I wondered if I looked like her. To Armenians, my ethnicity has been erased, obscured by my American assimilation. I wondered if her theory on the cultural rifts of language was an excuse for what could be seen as a loss of Greek identity.

During a cigarette break, I ran into Hankist, who had coordinated the event. She is an artist and critic who grew up in Armenia but has been living in Amsterdam for ten years. She, too, knows little English. She asked me how my Armenian lessons were going, and I told her, "Yes, sovoroom em, baitz chem khosoom. Yes portzoom em." *I am learning, but I am not speaking. I am trying.*

She told me, "Armenian is very hard."

"English is much harder," I said. Then I asked her, "Kanee lezooner keedes?" *How many languages do you know?*

"French, Russian, and Armenian."

I asked her why she learned French. The Armenian word is *Franceren,* very similar to Armenian—*Hyeren*—and English—*Angleren*—which I should have realized from Digeen Madleen's compound word lesson, but I still managed to butcher it, saying something like, "France-agan."

She said, "I learned French in shool," then she turned to an Armenian for assistance. "School," they corrected her.

"But I didn't learn until I live in France," she said. "I will learn English if I can live it." Then she told me, "Language is psychological and it is genetic."

I knew plenty about the psychological. But genetic? I wasn't so sure. "Baitz eem medzmairig yev medzhairig hye en." *But my grandparents were Armenian,* I tried to say. "Why aren't they helping me?" I asked in English. Hankist looked at me blankly. "Oknel," I said, ending on the Armenian word for "help." At this point, a bystander translated.

"I don't know," Hankist said. "Ask your body."

✣

The problem is there is a gap, a kink in the lineage. My grandparents were not from here, the Republic of Armenia. They were from the Ottoman Empire, so they spoke the Western version of the language. I cannot genetically learn Eastern Armenian because it is not the language of my ancestors. And there is no way for me to go back to the homeland that produced Western Armenian because it no longer exists.

One of my dreams was to learn Armenian—any Armenian—to find something in me that has been lost to assimilation. Isn't this desire enough?

Maybe I don't really want to do it. Maybe I am not capable of becoming more Armenian. Maybe this is as Armenian as I can get.

Maybe, as much as I describe the angst and the frustration, I really like this reality. I like holding on to words, I like control, I like my introverted nature. I like being in a place where I largely do not fit in.

But I would like to learn the reality here in Armenia that produced this language. Can I understand something without embodying it? Or am I not embodying it because Seyran is here?

I like the idea of bending the common perception of what's Armenian, to stretch and shape it, to make more room for others to be themselves. Can I bend it if I don't understand what Armenian is? Can I bend it with Seyran?

Can I be bent?

✣

Yerevan is like a bowl, a valley with mountains surrounding it. Recently, there has been little wind, so the smog has settled into the bowl. I've woken up the last few days with a sore throat. This morning in bed, Seyran turned over to face me, smiled, then turned over again and said, "Good night." I didn't know how to respond to this joke expressing his desire to go back to sleep. I could have said, "Bari keesher," good night, or "Bari arevod," good morning, but for some reason, I did not feel like scratching the words out of my groggy throat. There was no joke for me to make, nothing for me to say, so I hugged him instead.

STORY: EARLY NOVEMBER, 2006
YEREVAN

As Na and Seyran approached NPAK, a contemporary art center near Vernissage, they walked past *Melancholy*. Dali-esque in the fluidity of its forms, *Melan-*

choly depicts a torso with pieces missing from its head, appearing two-faced, its chest wide open with miniature buildings of a city inside, its giant hand resting at the base by its exposed genitalia. Na was surprised to discover this abstract work was by Yervand Kochar, the same sculptor who cast *Sassountsi Davit*.

When Seyran and Na went to Beatris's meeting for avant-garde writers at NPAK for the first time, they pretended they weren't together because they didn't want people gossiping. It was Seyran's idea, and Na agreed. They were trying to avoid exposure like that of *Melancholy*, his insides displayed for all to see.

Beatris introduced Na to everyone and found someone to translate the conversation. Medzig, the large man who had smashed a cup and his own chair at a recent event, volunteered. Though they had agreed not to sit next to each other during the meeting, Na still found it disturbing when Seyran ignored her afterward when everyone was socializing. She confided in Amal about it later in an email. Amal wrote that she was sure everyone knew about them, and she thought Seyran was being controlling. "What is he afraid of?" she asked.

When Beatris asked Na what she had been up to these last few weeks, she didn't know what to say. The next day when she spoke to Beatris on the phone, she let her know, "I didn't say anything when you asked what I've been doing because I have been with Seyran all this time."

"You didn't want to tell me this because you thought it would be boring?" Beatris didn't understand why she had kept the information from her. Apparently, it wasn't a confession. Amal was right: Beatris knew about the couple, even finding it dull that Na had done little but spend time with Seyran.

As she hung up the phone, Na considered this. It was true that Seyran spent much of their time together playing cover songs on the guitar and sitting at her computer to download porn.

At first Na found the porn disturbing, explaining to Seyran that porn took advantage of women and put them in dangerous situations. "No, they want to do it; they get paid," he claimed. "Anyway, I like the amateur porn."

"That's even worse!" Na said. "There are no controls on that!"

He explained his favorite type of porn was "upskirt," when guys try to catch photos of girls as they walk up the stairs. He also was fond of peeing videos:

when a hidden camera is installed in a bathroom, sometimes right in the toilet, at an angle that catches the origin of the stream of piss.

"That's a violation," Na said. "The women don't give their permission to be viewed like this."

"It is showing something we hide."

"Then why not watch boys peeing?"

He looked at Na like she was crazy. "I see that all the time!"

Seyran clearly didn't get the point she was making about gender inequality in porn, but she wondered about his explanation, nonetheless. Girls in Yerevan were so pristine looking; to see them piss was to take away their myth of purity and to realize the animal in them, the fleshy, hairy body part between their legs. And Na had to admit, when Seyran showed her a video of a bride peeing, somewhere in an Eastern European country, she was totally entranced. She had never even imagined a bride urinating. And did she have to go. She hitched up her big dress around herself, even needing a girlfriend's help, and squatted over a hole in the ground for what seemed like forever. Like the proverbial racehorse. Na loved the sanctity of marriage being brought down from its pedestal. She cackled, and Seyran looked on gleefully as Na let herself ignore the lack of the bride's consent, which guaranteed her loss of dignity—not only as a bride, but also as a human being.

JOURNAL: JUNE 14, 2010
ASTORIA

The other day, Seyran and I went to a halal Chinese food place on Broadway. As we ate, he said, "I don't know if you've noticed, but I have been conquering my desires for sex and material items." I looked at him. He has a brown birthmark on his neck that his parents tell him is shaped like a cross, though it looks more like a splotch to me. In Armenia, we always laughed at the irony. If anything, he was a Buddhist. But now he is a Hindu. Dining with the Muslims.

I told him that I realized he hadn't gone shopping in a while.

"I deleted all the porn from my computer," he said. "I am not even thinking about sex. So you can look to have your needs met elsewhere."

Not long ago, maybe six months ago, he read something that made him realize the desire to have sex with a lot of different people is a type of materialism. Still, he insisted on the open relationship idea. Now he is trying to conquer his desires. It's a pattern: he stopped drinking a long time ago, not for any reason, then stopped eating meat, then started doing yoga and became a vegan. We both think that he was already moving toward asceticism long before he realized why he was doing it. It was as if his body knew before his mind that this was the path he wanted to follow.

I was relieved that he's trying to conquer his sexual desire because then I won't have to worry about him having sex with other people anymore.

I forgot that this means that I won't get to have sex with him, either.

STORY: MID-NOVEMBER, 2006
YEREVAN

Upon entering the studio apartment, there was a small hallway that connected the only two rooms, the living room and a kitchen. A sofa unit took up one wall of the living room, and one part of it transformed into a full-size bed. Big glass cabinets lined the walls, containing dishes that the landlord forbade Na and Seyran to touch. There was a desk where Na could write and a coffee table where Seyran put his feet up.

To Na, the feng shui worked because glass doors opened from the hallway into the living room and onto the small balcony, which overlooked Mount Ararat. In the hallway there was a phone, a chair, cabinets, and a mirror. A small bathroom was at the end of the hallway.

It was a perfect, compact apartment for two.

The first night that she and Seyran slept there, the phone rang and Seyran answered it. His eyes widened and he handed the phone to Na. "Who was that man?" Na's mother practically shrieked.

"He's a friend," Na said. "He helped me move." It was the first mention she'd made of Seyran to her parents; she usually didn't share anything about her personal life with them until she was well into a relationship. Her mother tended to decry her choice in partners, and Na knew her mother would have plenty to say about Seyran being much younger.

The next night, she continued unpacking, and Seyran helped her move the furniture. They made a meal together on the electric plug-in burner—nothing fancy, just rice pilaf, which Na cooked with butter like her mother did. She'd always considered it a standard Armenian dish, but it was new to Seyran, and he gobbled it up in appreciation. He was excited by the appliances in the kitchen, including a food processor.

She never would have found the apartment without him. He called ads in the newspaper and asked all of his friends. In the process, he got into trouble when a realtor called him at his parents' house. His mother was alarmed that he was looking for an apartment after spending so many nights away from home; she knew he was in a relationship. But he brushed off the incident, claiming that she would have found out sooner or later. Though Na and Seyran hadn't formally decided to move in together, his mother's response made it clear to Na the need to have a space where they could be together. It seemed he would always be dealing with his parents' concerns.

In the days that followed, they settled into domesticity, buying groceries and making dinner, which seemed surprisingly conventional for a punk rocker to enjoy. Na felt that she was giving Seyran stability, a place where he could be himself.

Also, Na thought that the sex they were having in the new apartment was amazing. It kept getting better, and it was the best in her life. They had sex once a day, sometimes twice or three times. One day, she was standing on a chair to get something from a kitchen cabinet, and he picked her up and licked her belly, then went down on her on the kitchen table. Another time, she felt strangely aroused when he was playing a video game. Something about the tapping of his fingers was so irresistible to Na. She kept kissing him, and he kept resisting her to play the game, until he asked himself, "What am I doing?" They did it standing up against the wall.

Then there were the things he did with his fingers and thumbs. Na thought she was going to go insane when he fucked her with one finger in her anus and another on her clit. No one ever did things like this to her before. It made her wonder what was wrong with her previous partners. *Why were they so boring? Why was I so boring?* Seyran was a spontaneous, creative person, and her first younger partner. She thought she was being liberated. Or perhaps Seyran found a lot of sexual inspiration from watching porn.

She thought maybe porn was not so bad after all.

JOURNAL: JUNE 16, 2010
ASTORIA

I've been invited to go back to Armenia. Seyran can't come with me because the army is looking for him now, but he says he's okay with me going. I know it's odd, but we both figure it's better for me to go than neither of us. I'll be gone for six weeks, leaving early next month.

Gharib is giving me Armenian lessons to prepare for my trip since Seyran has proven incapable of teaching me anything over the last three years. In Yerevan, Gharib always claimed that if I spent just ten lessons with him, I would be able to speak, so now I am finally taking him up on this offer.

I'm always happy to see him, with his distinctive figure, tall and broad with long hair in a ponytail and a pyramid head, his nose leading him gracefully through the Whole Foods dining area. He sees me and waves, then kisses me on both cheeks as he sits down at the long communal table overlooking the grungy East Village streets, and I show him my old textbooks.

Gharib explains a grammatical concept to me that I never knew before: postpositions. On a piece of paper, he draws a table, and he diagrams *on, under, near, from, toward,* and then he writes down all the endings that must be added to nouns to indicate these positions. From this one lesson I realize he is a much better teacher than Digeen Madleen.

I still feel badly about when I let her go, at Christmas time, giving her a pen as a present. She knew, looking at that pen, that it was all over: no language necessary. I remember how she would come to my apartment when she was done with work, carrying a heavy, crinkly plastic bag filled with her textbooks. We had our lessons in the kitchen, so when she entered or exited the apartment, she would pass by the living room and look sideways at Seyran in his sweatpants sitting on the couch. I sensed she wanted to say something like,

"Watch out for this one." How she would have warned me in Armenian, I have no idea.

One day, Seyran overheard our lesson and told me Madleen was a terrible teacher. He thought she was giving me unnecessary information, teaching me formal, literary Armenian instead of regular spoken language. That's when he decided to give me those absurd lessons, yelling at me for not writing capital letters on the line perfectly.

Gharib is much kinder, though not any less absurd, in the Whole Foods store on Houston Street. For homework, he dictates a series of sentences for me to translate so that I can practice using post-positions with various nouns and pronouns:

1. Under that table you told me how much you loved me. That was my dream last night.
2. She is from New York but she hates noise and enjoys drinking tea with her lover.
3. I like that hairstyle but I don't like the way you talk to me.
4. You stupid idiots are sitting on the wrong place. Look at me and come to this room.
5. Your yellow hat makes me upset every time I see you. You know I don't like it. Please change yourself for me.

We are laughing hysterically by the end of this dictation. Gharib has channeled a stereotypical Armenian character—bossy, brash, megalomaniac. He once told me that when he and Mardi fought, it would invariably be in Armenian. Perhaps it's because the language shared their intimacy, but he seemed to be saying that Armenian was a language of strife. Some consonants, bombastically slung from the back of the throat, seem especially suited for communicating conflict, anger, and self-righteousness. In contrast, the consonants of English are softer and less percussive; more removed and distant. The Armenian word for language is *lezoo*, which also means *tongue*: Armenian is a more physical language than English. Madleen taught me the building blocks—the knee bone connected to the leg bone—and then she expressed vulnerabilities in her life to a listener who couldn't truly comprehend. With Seyran, in Yerevan, I shared a physical intimacy, but it did not help me to learn Armenian physically.

It's sad; I've never heard Armenian spoken to me to express love. Perhaps I would have learned it then ...

STORY: LATE NOVEMBER, 2006
YEREVAN

As the days became brisker, then colder, Na and Seyran continued their habit of taking nightly walks around the Yerevan circle. They often found themselves at the Cascade, which was now nearby the new apartment, but they sometimes took alternate routes, down near Vernissage. There was a crisp breeze one night when Na was glad to see the statue of Saint Vartan Mamikonian, who had tried and failed to liberate the Christian Armenians from the Zoroastrian Persians in the Battle of Avarayr, 451 AD. Yervand Kochar, who had designed *Sassountsi Davit* and *Melancholy*, and whom Na now mused might be her favorite Armenian artist, depicted Vartan on his horse, almost comically, the warrior flailing his outstretched arms as if about to surrender and fling down his sword. The pose was frenetic, energetic; so many feelings transmitted through the body—Kochar reminded her of a cross between Picasso and Van Gogh. The statue was notable in that Kochar had given the horse enormous balls, whereas Mamikonian's own balls were not visible. Perhaps it was Kochar's commentary on the leader's defeat? And yet, St. Vartan had planted a seed, as it were. Thirty-three years later, his nephew completed the insurrection that Vartan had initiated.

As they approached from the hindquarters, Seyran asked, "How would you feel if we had an open relationship?"

Na was quiet. "What do you mean?" she asked.

"How would you feel if we both have sex with other people?"

Again, she was quiet, then questioned, "Why would we do that?" She was perfectly happy having amazing sex with Seyran.

"What if I go to a concert, and I see a girl, and I want to have sex in the bathroom with her? Is that okay with you?" Before she could reply, he said, "Because it is okay with me if you want to do that."

"I don't think I want to have sex with a stranger in the bathroom. Not after all my health problems," she said tentatively.

"When you are all better?"

"Well, what if I have sex with someone again and again and again, and then I fall in love with him or her? How would you feel if I left you for that other person?" she asked.

"You don't have to leave. You can be in love with both of us. We can live all together."

"Well, maybe, I don't know."

"So it would be okay for me to have sex with a girl in the bathroom?"

Na smiled and let out a sigh. "The thing is, I understand why you would want to have that freedom. I like the idea of an open relationship. I just know my feelings would get in the way, and I would be jealous." Na remembered when she felt pressured to commit to a relationships with an older man, knowing that he expected her to be exclusive. Was she really that much in love with Seyran? Was Seyran saying he wasn't that much in love with her?

They were by the university now, and he broke into her thoughts. "Okay, never mind. I'm not going to have sex with a girl in the bathroom anyway. It's impossible here. And I can tell if it's hard for you to talk about it, then you will feel even worse if I do it."

As they continued to walk, Na realized that she didn't want to surrender, didn't want to flail her arms like St. Vartan on his horse with the enormous balls. She didn't want to have sex and explore love with other partners; she didn't even care about being with a woman. She wanted to have security and stability with just one person.

She told Seyran, "We could break up now, you know. We want different things."

"I don't wanna break up," he said. "I'm dependent on you. You made my life more free. And if we go to America, I will be protected from army."

She ignored for a moment the supposition that they would go to America together. "If we broke up, you would be harmed in the army?"

"No, my father can help me get into a lighter army." He meant an easier assignment: not near the border with Karabakh, where snipers on the other side periodically shot at soldiers. There was no guarantee his father, as the regional director of public records in a remote region, had that much clout, though.

Na broached the issue of going to the U.S. together. "It would be nice to think that we would stay together, and you would come with me to America. But it could be really hard for you. My immigrant students struggle with making a living and adjusting to the culture. They miss their homelands."

"Honey, I doubt that I would miss Armenia," he laughed. "We don't have to, but if we go there, I could work on computers. Or go to a real school to get a diploma. I am strong; I can even do hard jobs lifting things, anything to be protected from army." She looked at his broad shoulders, slightly hunched against his ears in the wind.

Na admitted her last reservation. "But in America, you will be even freer, and you won't want to be with me."

He had an immediate response. "I could have sex with a lot of people here, but I don't because I really like being with you."

Seyran's contradictory claims on the availability of sex zipped past Na as she looked at him. His hair was growing out from the bad haircut, and he looked calm, at ease with himself, for such a young man. She wanted some sort of security with someone, something. Some family. He seemed to appreciate stability, too, even as he was asking for openness—perhaps testing himself as well as Na.

So she met his eyes and asked, "You want to come to America to be with me?"

"Yes," he said.

They kissed. He hadn't said the words, but Na felt that he loved her and that he couldn't express it, but it was there, deep down. She thought of how he always came to her treatments at the European Medical Center. The first time, he was looking at the TV, trying to find cartoons, making jokes. She was terrified after her last experience in the hospital in New York, and she resigned herself to the fact that he wouldn't be able to give her what she needed right then. She held her breath and watched as the nurse put the needle in her arm. Seyran reached out and held her other hand, like he was adding a period at the end of a sentence, one she didn't think he was reading.

If they went to America, this year would be about getting him out of Armenia rather than about her doing the work she had planned—researching, reporting, and learning Armenian.

JOURNAL: JUNE 18, 2010
ASTORIA

Last week, Seyran and I went to downtown Flushing. He took me to a Hindu temple, and we had lunch at a little dosa place nearby. As we explored the streets, he kept holding my hand and hugging me. In these moments, I know he still loves me.

But then a friend came over briefly last week and told me afterward, as I walked him to the subway, that Seyran doesn't speak to me respectfully. I can't even tell. I scoured my brain for everything we did and said, and nothing stood out. Maybe I am in an abusive relationship and I don't even know it?

When Seyran is being a jerk, I tell him, "You're not being very yogi," and he becomes annoyed. He says he is a Hindu, which misses my point that spiritual people should strive to be kind. But he isn't spiritual—he is religious. Last night, we were taking a walk in our neighborhood, and he said that people were once only half a meter tall. I couldn't figure out what the hell he meant. "Not according to evolutionary theory," I said.

"It's been written in the Vedas, so I know it's true," he said. Now he was being a fundamentalist, and I didn't want to talk to him anymore.

We were on Northern Boulevard, a four-lane road with lots of traffic, car dealerships, and strip malls, with hardly any trees. Not many people walk down it, so it feels isolating. There are a bunch of big-box stores, and the sky always seems gray even when it is blue. It doesn't feel like we are in Queens or Armenia or anywhere, really.

It's funny because there is a Northern Boulevard in Yerevan, too. The Soviets had designed it into the city's circle, an extension that would cut from the park next to the Opera down to Republic Square. But they never built it. When we were living there, the oligarchs were evicting the poor people who lived on the alley to widen it to the size of a boulevard. Controversy continued when ugly condo buildings were erected, which no one in the city could afford. It is now a high street of fancy retailers. So it, too, occupies a liminal space—not part of the past or the present.

Perhaps that has always been our problem: we've never found a time or place where we can both be—we are always operating in a nether world where neither of us belong. Two misfits from two cultures, we couldn't create our own culture—or language—together.

And yet, there is something that's connected us—why else would we still be together? We were walking by an old-style chrome-rimmed diner, tucked between two parking lots. I realized I had never seen it open when I announced, "You know, no matter what happens between us, and how different we become, there is something that connects us. We have an unbreakable bond."

He pretended he was an uncomprehending immigrant. "What?" he asked, as the cars zoomed past us on Northern. "We are in bondage?"

META-WRITING:

I know it's ironic, claiming that I liked having control in relation to language and identity, and yet I let Seyran control me. I accepted his refusal to help me learn Armenian and allowed him to become an interpreter who wedged himself between me and everyone else. Likewise, in America, Seyran was letting go of sex and material items, but it seemed he was also trying to gain control over his life—his body—through a stringent belief system.

And then, we were each trying to control the other. When we met, I wanted to feel safety and security in a partner, something that takes time to acquire and is never truly guaranteed, especially when I wasn't secure in myself. And would this story have happened if Seyran believed he could survive the army? Or if the army, and Armenia, weren't so unstable?

I didn't realize how much we were both like that ugly statue Melancholy, lacking a strong inner core. Perhaps this was another reason for the miscommunication between homeland and diaspora that the Greek video artist had described. In Yerevan, I listened to the thrill in my body since there was no calm.

9. YOU SAY TRADITION, WE SAY CODEPENDENCE

Two Generations >>> "An Issue of Personal and Public Importance." This was the final assignment I gave to my students, asking them to revisit what they had written about their lives over the semester and to develop a personal essay to touch upon a social issue. (Possible themes included, "The role of conformism in religion," "Attachments to land and place," "The impact of war on families," etc.) When I asked one of my classes, Group 6, to brainstorm in writing on a possible topic, they were quietly focused for fifteen minutes.

Lilit, a blonde with big green eyes framed by mascara-heavy lashes, offered to share. A class clown, Lilit has an infectious grin with wide spaces between her teeth. Now, uncharacteristically serious, she said, "I want to write about 'working and making a living in Armenia.' It's very hard for people to find work, especially for the young people. They can't get enough money to pay for classes."

"Since this is a public university, do you get help from the government to pay your tuition?" I asked.

"No," the class answered.

"But what if you get good grades? Can you qualify for a scholarship?"

Lida, an auburn-haired girl, replied, "No, we can't compete with those who pay for the high grades."

My eyes widened at the concept. I was told that girls from wealthy families pay for high grades to qualify for scholarships, as if they're purchasing a membership at Costco. It's an egregious crime given that they obviously have less need for the scholarships compared to the young women from low-income families.

I teach two classes at the university with students at the same level—they're identified as Group 2 and Group 6. Jhenya, a friend of Seyran's who is in Group 6, filled me in that the girls in Group 2 were from wealthy families, whereas those from Group 6 were from less well-off families. The students were supposedly evaluated by their abilities, but in actuality, they were ranked by how much money they could bribe the school to get them into the higher groups.

A few days later, I went over the assignment with Group 2, i.e., the wealthy girls. Instead of writing quietly, they kept chattering. After I explained three times that they should start brainstorming the topic, a girl named Ella said, "But we don't know what we want to write about."

"You don't have to know right now," I told her. "That's the point of brainstorming." Ella gazed back at me with her wide, smiling, placid face, like a beauty queen. A buxom blonde, Ella had missed two thirds of the course because she had gotten married and had gone on her honeymoon. When she returned, she showed me pictures of her trip to Egypt: posing in a bathing suit by the Nile, relaxing in the hotel pool, visiting the pyramids with her linebacker-looking groom.

After I coaxed the women into writing for ten minutes, I asked if anyone wanted to share. One girl read what she had written about Nagorno-Karabakh. "It is a worry on every Armenian's mind," she read.

"Sometimes it's better not to talk about such things," Tacouhi said in response. She was Ella's sidekick, a demure girl with a wide nose and dirty-blond hair.

"How can we change things if we can't even talk about them?" Hannah piped up. Her eyes were a deep blue, and she wore her black hair in a romantic updo like a character from Jane Austen. The daughter of a brandy magnate, Hannah recently missed class to attend the release party of a new Cognac named after her. Regardless, she was the only one who challenged the typical thinking of society commonly expressed by other girls in class.

"None of us are in the government, so we can't change things," Tacouhi said.

"This is supposed to be a democracy; you're all meant to have some say in what goes on in this country," I reminded them.

"That's not the way it works," Melineh said. A tall spitfire of a girl, Melineh wore her dirty-blond locks in a flowing Farrah Fawcett hairdo. She had told me when we first met that she'd spent the previous year in New Orleans as an exchange student. "Everyone knows votes are bought, and everyone accepts it. If I were a minister, I would keep money for me and my family. Why not? Everyone else is doing it, and you can't change things when only a few people want change."

"*I* wouldn't vote for you," Hannah said in a low, accusatory voice.

"But how can there be change if people don't individually take responsibility?" I asked.

"People here are too afraid to change," Melineh claimed. "Things are better now, and they're content to sit back and enjoy it. They're used to the corruption. And the sad thing is that it's people in the villages who are really suffering. They're who I feel sorry for. They are living on subsistence farming. Even with all the help that's coming in from the diaspora, corrupt people take so much that it's not enough to help them."

Melineh continued to discuss people's general apathy: "I think it's because Armenians have had so many bad things happen to them historically, with the Genocide and the wars. They're surrounded by hostile countries, Turkey and Azerbaijan." She made a face then, scrunching her mouth. "And it's hard to feel like you have freedom."

I nodded my head, then said, "But there were mass protests here in 1991 over the conflicts in Nagorno-Karabakh, and Armenia was the first republic to break from the Soviet Union. Why isn't that enough for people to remember that they do have power?"

"Things were different in 1991," Hannah said. "There was hope then."

She repeated what Gharib had told me. When he had worked in the parliament of the new government in 1991, there was hope for the future because people wanted a different way of life, but now corruption has been institutionalized at every level of society.

Maybe it was easier for Armenians to protest against a colonizing, occupying Other than it is to now fight against themselves. Perhaps there is something hurtful in realizing the faults you see in your family, friends, neighbors, teachers, and coworkers reflected back at you.

I was trying to make this point to the class, but fucking Ella was gabbing away again. I had already twice reprimanded her and a few girls in the corner of the room for talking. Now I laid into them, raising my voice. Because of their disengagement, I told them, I would not give them credit for being here today. If they wanted to socialize, they should leave, since they were ruining the class for the rest of us.

Ella tried to make an excuse. "I don't want to hear it," I said, three times in a row, each time louder than the last.

But she spoke over me, having the audacity to raise her voice over mine.

"We're in a good mood today," she said, smiling.

This was her excuse? "I don't care," I told her.

Now, with time to reflect, I think Ella was telling me that their good mood wasn't common, so it precluded talking about serious issues, especially those they assumed they'd never be able to solve.

A tall brunette named Hasmik in Group 6, the poor girls' group, had approached me after class, handing me her brainstormed text because she didn't want to read it aloud. It was about her father, whom she barely knew because he had been working in Russia for the past several years. As I encouraged her to write about this important topic, since many Armenian families are similarly affected, her eyes teared up. Hasmik never turned in her essay; here was a problem *she* was powerless to change.

One group is diminished through deprivation, the other by distraction. The have-nots and the haves are not so different: as young women, they are lacking in support. The school has turned their backs on the economically disadvantaged Group 6 girls, and the sexist culture is neglecting the whole lot of them. No one wants these smart young women to care about their civic contributions to society but rather, to focus on their looks, their weddings, and their families. As they vie to have a decent life, will the societal institutions that need to be challenged ever change?

❖

After I graded final papers, I went to the university to turn in my course grades to my friend and colleague Anahid, who teaches the wealthy girls' class. She needed my grades to determine which of our students would qualify to take assessment exams.

I sat with Anahid in the common faculty office at the long conference table next to a bank of bright windows. As she looked at my gradebook and attendance records, she confirmed that three of her students had never attended my class. When I walked into her classroom to give her the grades earlier, one of these girls, whom I had never seen before, stared at me with such intense curiosity that I actually felt violated. Anahid told me that this girl attended only one third of her class sessions, but because she was the daughter of a bigwig at the university, Anahid would have to pass her or risk losing her job.

We wandered outside, and she confided her moral quandary since the student had done horribly on her qualifying quizzes. "The worst is when they don't ask for a passing grade, but for a good grade. A satisfactory grade won't get them

far in their specialization, after all. But a good grade will allow them to continue."
One of my students from Group 6 had similarly expressed in her final essay how
depressing it is that students who are promoted on their connections, and not
through hard work, still proceed to become teachers themselves.

"You would think that in a university, a place of reason, people would be
more sensitive to preventing extreme nepotism," I told her.

Anahid laughed. "You would think, but it's not the case. This kind of corruption
is ingrained in people's minds; it's part of our blood. Armenians are so dedicated to
their families, watching out only for them. I don't really understand it. I would *never*
think that my child was more deserving than anyone else. When I help my children
with their homework, I feel they are the same as my students. And I really think of
my students as my children. I am not sure that blood ties are stronger than intellectual ties. I'm really not. My students are my intellectual children. And that is why it
is so frustrating to not punish them or to not be able to demand of them the same
as I would of my children when they are doing poorly."

I nodded, wondering what she would think of gay people choosing their own
families. I still wasn't out to her.

"I tell you, Natalee. It will take two generations for this society to change."

I've heard this refrain before. "Two generations"—diasporans say it, locals say
it. Two generations would be about twenty-five years from now. The refrain makes
you feel like there's little you can do in your lifetime, in the present. It lets people
off the hook, suggesting that society must depend solely on the innocence of the
young to initiate cultural change. But to ensure that change could work, the elder
generation would have to take responsibility not to taint the younger generation
with old hurts, behaviors, and beliefs. The idea that it will take two generations for
society to change instead suggests that Armenia is a set of mentally ill, abusive
parents who simply need to step away from their children.

But who says the children will leave their parents?

It seems that family bonds are problematic in the case of change. Ultimately,
it is difficult to let go of family, no matter how much we are protected or hurt
by them.

STORY: LATE DECEMBER, 2006
YEREVAN

Soon after Na gave her lesson on individual lives and change, Ella and her lack-
ey, Tacouhi, invited Na to lunch after class, ostensibly to make up for their bad

behavior. They went to Doka Pizza, more of a smoky basement lounge than a pizzeria. It was a hangout for students during the day and one of the few restaurants open twenty-four hours in the neighborhood. Seyran and Na had been there a few times late at night, finding shady characters, worn-out prostitutes, and bulky mafia or government types furtively hunkering down over their pies.

The crust on the pizza was thick, and the students swathed it in catsup, a Yerevan custom. Na watched the girls eat politely, using a fork and knife, chewing carefully. She found herself speaking with her mouth partially full and felt rude, as if she were at a society luncheon requiring dainty deportment. It wasn't surprising to Na that these two girls would have refined manners, given that they came from wealthy families, even if they were dining in the sleazy basement of Doka Pizza.

Inevitably, the conversation turned to marriage. When Ella and Tacouhi asked Na why she wasn't married, she told them she hadn't met the right person yet and that she liked being single. She showed them the side of herself that she wanted to believe, rather than the woman who had once called a suicide hotline because she had despaired so much over her single status.

A year or so before she left for Armenia, Na had been depressed—all her close single friends had found partners, and she felt abandoned and flawed. Late one night, she cried over the phone to a suicide counselor, explaining that she wasn't going to off herself but that she just didn't want to exist anymore. The counselor listened and was sympathetic, but he eventually asked her to get off the phone in case someone who was *really* going to kill themselves needed to get through. She had to laugh. *You know things are bad when the suicide hotline rejects you.*

Ella and Tacouhi now scoffed at Na's embrace of singledom as if they knew she was bluffing. They told her she should get married and have a family. "Every woman should," they claimed. Na questioned whether to keep toeing the feminist line with these two, who must have powerful ties given the entitled manner they were talking with her, but she couldn't help herself. "Actually, studies have shown that women who get married don't live as long as single women. But married men live longer than single men. Obviously, marriage is better for men than women."

They laughed, telling Na she was crazy to not want to get married because of a study. She had been hoping they would be able to glean from this insight that marriage might not be all it was cracked up to be for women, but they had already been convinced by the myths of their wealthy families—and by the over-arching system at work in their country. Being married and having a family was the pinnacle of a woman's existence according to the official party line. They had been taught to believe that they would have less status without a man, who would be charged with protecting them.

✿

In the meantime, Seyran was asking Na to protect him from the army. His pals at the university had told him a bribe paid to a doctor for a medical excuse would cost two or three grand for three years, after which the army would come looking for him. Once he turned twenty-seven, however, he'd be home free. Seyran thus needed six years of protection, but if he wasn't in Armenia after three years, it wouldn't matter. He and his family didn't have the money, so Na decided to pay the hefty bribe; not factoring in the cost of perpetuating corruption, she felt it was worth it to protect someone she loved. They were also trying to determine how to get him a visa to return to New York with her.

"What if we break up before the New Year?" he recently asked. "Will you still pay for me?"

"Yes," she told him. Emotionally attached as she was, she would do her best to help him. But he must have sensed a breakup was imminent, that she was hitting the limits of the relationship. Na loved the domestic life they had made, but she was coming down with a case of cabin fever. In becoming dependent on him as a translator and proxy of Armenian society, she wasn't discovering or befriending others.

Even so, the next time her mother called and Seyran answered the phone, she didn't feel like covering it up anymore; it seemed the right time to announce that Seyran was her boyfriend, even if she was unsure of their future.

He handed Na the phone, and she sat in the armchair in the hallway, where they had the landline set up. After the niceties, Na's mother asked in a worried voice, "Is he living with you?"

"Yes, he is." She twisted the phone cord, gazing at the landlord's untouchable cabinets in the dark hallway.

"Does he have a job?" her mother asked.

"Yes. He's a computer specialist."

"And he can pay for himself?"

Na suppressed a sigh. "Yes," she said, trying to sound convincing. She paid the rent, but he chipped in what he could on shared expenses like food and utilities.

"Be careful," she warned Na. "You know, just because someone is Armenian doesn't mean they're good. There are bad Armenians, too."

Na didn't know when she had ever given the impression that she thought all Armenians were good, that she unconditionally loved Armenians, that she was the cheerleader of Armenians everywhere. Nevertheless, it was uncanny that her mother could exacerbate her own worries. She questioned whether her mother was affirming reality, as a concerned friend might, or if Na's fears stemmed from the overprotective, overly cautious, Westernized suspicions that she had inherited from her mother.

She and her family heard the stereotypes, perpetuated by friends who had visited the homeland years before: *Armenian men are too proud to take jobs they deem beneath them, so they sit in the square all day playing backgammon while their women work and take care of the family. Then they go have affairs. It's common at every level of society for a man to have a mistress.*

When she hung up the phone, Seyran asked, "What is someone called who wants to be with one person?"

"Monogamous," Na told him.

"I really love you, I am monogamous with you." He had made other pronouncements like this recently: "I don't know what you've done to me, but I am not even interested in other girls. I used to look at them all the time."

Part of Na believed him, and the other part thought he was giving her a standard line.

JOURNAL: JUNE 30, 2010
CUMBERLAND, RHODE ISLAND

We've been at my parents' house the past few days. I am leaving for Armenia soon, and we all felt it necessary to be together as a family before my six-week trip to Hayastan.

Tonight, we were all sitting in the living room, and Seyran got on a really silly matchmaking kick in a voice modeled after the title character in *Borat*, which we had watched in Armenia and he had found hysterically funny. I am not sure he fully gets the ironic satire of Sacha Baron Cohen's caricature of an oafish Kazakhstani man, devised to mock prejudiced Westerners. Now Seyran said to my brother, "Leo, I want Natalee to take nice picture of you to my aunts so that they can marry you, and you can bring them to America!" Seyran has two unmarried aunts, one slightly older and one slightly younger than me.

"Not interested," Leo said.

"What, they make meal for you, take care of you—you need the wife!"

It's ridiculous since my brother is gay, and Seyran was suggesting he would marry not one but both aunts. Nevertheless, there is some truth to the joke since Seyran has turned our marriage into a business agreement. When I complain, he'll say, "What? You get to be with a young attractive man for a few years."

Tonight, he extended the joke to my mother. Now he had a guy for her, his Uncle Gago. "Gago very handsome," Seyran continued in his Borat voice.

"What does he look like?" my mother asked, playing along.

"Oh, he has nice hair. Hair all over his body, but not on his head!"

My mother cackled. Seyran continued, "He have two teeth left, but not to worry! They are gold and in front of his mouth! And he have good job, too! Stable! He blow up old buildings and bridges! Oh, I almost forgot—he a good listener: he have 30 percent of his hearing!"

Everyone was laughing hysterically now. My mom wiped her tears away. "You know, old-timers used to arrange marriages this way."

Dad said, with a lecturing tone, "Seyran, you are married to Natalee, and she's nice and easygoing and smart—"

"And beautiful," Mom chimed in. "Oh, you have it made," she said. Now *she* was being a matchmaker.

"It's worked out well for you. But it's not like that for everyone who gets married," Dad said.

"Okay, then, I'll bring your picture to Armenia, too," Seyran joked.

I wondered what my dad was trying to say. My parents' marriage hasn't been great—they disagree frequently and are rarely affectionate. But they've always respected each other's contributions as parents and providers, and they've always been loyal to our family. As much as my father often drives her crazy, my mother has never taken a vacation separately from my father, and she doesn't understand how I can leave Seyran for such a long period of time. And yet, Mom and Dad spend evenings in adjacent sitting rooms, separated by a wall, each of them watching their own TV shows.

I find echoes of my parents' behavior in Seyran. My dad often acts childishly and disparages my mother in public. And my mother must always have her own way; she isn't much for compromise and rarely concedes that she is wrong. I don't know that I've ever heard her apologize to anyone.

So sometimes when I think of how impossible my relationship is with Seyran, I remember my parents. If they could make it work all these years, maybe I can, too. But this comparison ignores the fact that they have been faithful to each other.

Was this what my father was trying to get at, the point that he had been interrupted from making? That marriage might benefit Seyran, but not me?

I thought of my mother's laughter as Seyran invented the most ridiculous matches; it must have struck a chord. Though she chose my father, the question was whether they were mismatched. Nevertheless, it seems all they know to do is stay together.

STORY: LATE DECEMBER, 2006
YEREVAN

One ordinary day, Na and Seyran woke up late, had sex, then took a walk: a typical routine. They separated when Seyran went to his parents' house for a visit. When he returned, he was in a bad mood. Na pointed it out, but he would not admit it. "Do I have to be jumping around in order to be in a good mood?" he asked.

Na tried to give him space as he prepared for his band rehearsal. As he went out the door, he said, "We have this apartment. Why don't we invite someone over?"

Na asked, "What about Gharib and Mardi?"

He shrugged, opening the door. "Okay, it's better than nothing. Call them."

Na jumped on it, since he usually reacted so negatively if she even mentioned their names.

When Na called Gharib, he had good news: the soldiers whom he, Mardi, and some others had helped to defend through an NGO had been freed. He told her to meet him at Artbridge Café later, and he would tell her the news in detail. Then he and Mardi would come over to her apartment afterward.

When Seyran came home, she told him she had invited Gharib and Mardi over.

"What? Are you crazy?" he asked.

"You told me to call them!"

"I was kidding," he said. "You can't tell when I'm kidding?"

"No, I took you seriously," she told him. "What am I supposed to do? Uninvite them?"

"I don't want them to come over."

"Fine then—I'm going to meet Gharib at Artbridge."

"What for?"

"He's celebrating the release of these soldiers—"

"Oh, now he's so important. Gharib didn't do anything for them. And neither did Mardi!"

"But they've been working with other people and an NGO—"

"Fuck off," he said.

Na became very angry. She left in a huff, bundling up quickly and fleeing out the front door, down the dark stairs and out into the street.

Some of her anger dissipated as she walked down Abovyan, past all the shoppers and the workers heading home, trundling through the underground passages with the merchants and their old books for sale, their pantyhose and lighters, their greasy piroshkis.

As she entered the warm ambiance of Artbridge, with its wooden floors, walls, tables, and chairs, she found Gharib. His story of their recent victory took Na's mind off her domestic troubles. Gharib and Mardi had never served in the army because they had studied abroad during the years they were eligible to be conscripted. But they had friends who had been through the system and who told of how harrowing it had been, similar to Hrair's reports to Na. When a few soldiers were accused of murdering one of their fellow soldiers, Gharib investigated the case and found details suggesting that a superior officer had been involved. He also said there were many cases of soldier abuse and fatalities, far more than would be normal for such a small country not engaged in active combat. It resulted from extremely brutal hazing and a highly violent culture left over from the Soviet times, when ruling with an iron fist kept people in line.

Now the untrammeled power of officers was being hushed for fear that any kind of dissent would cause the army to weaken. Such perceived instability was frightening for many Armenian citizens when both borders were closed and a war could erupt at any moment with Azerbaijan over Nagorno-Karabakh. Na remembered Melineh, her student in class, echoing such a sentiment.

The good news was that Gharib, Mardi, and their group had held press conferences, issued media releases, and contacted international human rights organizations to put pressure on the case so that they would have a fair trial. It was heartening to know that change was possible, though it was clearly a risky business; Gharib joked about being killed just as his cousin walked in.

Gohar was a plain girl, heavy, a French-language specialist. As Na became acquainted with her, she expressed how she wished she could travel to France. But she felt indebted to her family, in particular her brother, whom she felt she had to care for.

"You really don't have to," Gharib admonished her. "Don't make him any food. Why do you have to cook for him?"

"I don't know—he expects it, and if I don't do it, my parents will be angry with me."

"So what? They're not here. What duty do you have?" He looked at Na. "Tell her," he said.

Na didn't know what to say. She understood the feeling of being beholden to someone for no good reason. Sure, in America, a sister being pressured by a family to take care of a grown, able-bodied brother wasn't so common. But there were other odd pressures felt between people. *Instead of tradition, we call it codependence,* Na thought. *When you can't stop a behavior you know is wrong, but it's your habit to care for others, and guilt is the primary motivator keeping it in place.* Na thought that Armenian women felt enormous guilt in their duty to their families, pressured to hold their relationships—and the nation—together. It was hard to break that thinking, even in unhealthy, unhappy situations.

In Na's silence, Gohar responded. "You're no better," she said, turning the tables on Gharib.

"You're right," he said.

"How so?" Na asked.

"I am sleeping in my family's living room, and I don't have a space of my own. I should move out, but they need me financially."

It was telling that this brave human rights activist also felt inured to his family. "You and Mardi could move in together," Na told him. She thought of how unhappy Mardi was living in the apartment with his mother.

"No, Mardi and I, we're not good." He pulled out a little pad of paper and showed Na a series of abstract line drawings he'd done to illustrate the methodology of being in a relationship. He laughed as he showed Na the meaning of a knotty little area: the root of Mardi's angst, interfering with the flow of love, a vague figure floating through space. He asked how she and Seyran were doing, and she told him they were in an argument, neglecting to mention that it was about him and Mardi. She said it wouldn't be good timing for him to come over after all.

By the time she got home from Artbridge, Seyran was putting on his coat, about to go to the store. Na asked if she could come with him, and he said, "I don't care." As they walked down the street, he asked if Gharib and Mardi were coming, and she told him no, then proceeded to inform him about their successful campaign with the soldiers.

"I'm not listening to you," he said, Na's iPod in his ears.

He can be such a child, Na thought. She stopped in her tracks and said, "I think it would be better if you went by yourself." She didn't understand what was going on, but she couldn't take the bad treatment. Rather than turn around, she waited for a response.

"I'm not coming home tonight," he said.

She didn't know what he meant and looked at him with pain in her eyes. Then she looked over his shoulder.

"Is that snow?" Na asked. She noticed it appearing lightly in the night sky.

He shrugged. With his hands in his pockets, he flapped open one arm at his elbow. It was an invitation for her to slip her arm through his.

Na wanted to walk through the Armenian snowflakes with him. The first snow of the year dissolved their ire.

They ambled to Urartu, the corner store, owned by an oligarch's brother. Seyran wanted to buy her some groceries—juice and bread and cookies—since Hrair had paid him today.

On the way back, the snow was beautiful, cloaking the dingy city and the angst between Na and Seyran.

Once they returned home, Na went to bed, and Seyran turned on the computer. When she woke up at 4 a.m., he was still there, illuminated by its screen in the dark. "You're just with me for my computer," she joked.

"No, for your iPod," he quipped.

When he slipped under the covers, the space where she felt he could be honest with her, she asked, "What's going on?"

"When I visited my parents this morning, my father said bad things about you." He was turned away from her, and she knew not to ask for more detail. But she had been right all along that he had been in a bad mood. She wondered why he couldn't have just told her—they could have avoided a lot of misunderstanding if he had. But mostly she felt relieved, as she had when she saw her first snowfall in Armenia, blanketing her state of mind.

JOURNAL: JULY 7, 2010
ASTORIA

Yesterday while we were doing the laundry, Seyran claimed that the subletter would get HIV from the sheets Kristapor had used while he was staying with us. Mind you, Kristapor doesn't have HIV; it's a stupid thing for Seyran to say. Nevertheless, I told him, "You can't get HIV that way." I was about to say, "You think you can get it through sleeping on sheets and not through having anal sex without a condom?" But then he said, "I got HIV from your brother's razor." He had used it last week when we were in Rhode Island.

"My brother doesn't have HIV," I said.

"He looks like he does. That's why he goes running so much."

"Okay, Grammy," I said, exasperated. "You sound just like my grandmother. She always made up crazy stories."

"Oh, I remind you of her? Is that why you like me?" Then he started to try to act like an old lady, a typical tatik doting on her granddaughter right there in the laundromat among the Latina moms and toddlers. It was bizarre and yet somehow a very accurate portrayal.

He also got superstitious like my grandmother when I told him my friend Nora would be dropping by with a few gifts for me to bring to friends in Armenia. He insisted that it was a bad idea, that she would give me bad energy before my trip because she was jealous and wished she could come. Clearly, he was projecting.

It was a very hot day, so hot that I closed all my windows and shades and turned on the ceiling fan. Seyran put on a tank top and underwear, came into my room to show me a photo, and when he left, Nora giggled. I hadn't even noticed. "Was he wearing only his underwear?" I said.

"Yes," she nodded her head.

He came back into my room and sat on my bed. I told him he was making Nora uncomfortable and that he should put on clothes.

"These are shorts," he claimed. "I wear them to yoga. Where is the bug spray?"

"In the closet," I told him.

"Go and get it," he said.

"What?"

"Go and get it," he said again.

"What's wrong with you?" I asked, opening the closet in the hallway. He didn't answer. I think that he feels emasculated that I am going to Armenia without him, and now he has to prove something in front of my friend. I felt sorry that I had invited her into this crazy home.

He insists that he doesn't want to go to Armenia, that he rather go to India. And he's happy that I'll see his family. But there are obviously many feelings he's not admitting. I feel guilty, especially that I will see his mom. How can I go there, to meet the family of the son I took away? They've been apart for three years.

META-WRITING:

He acted out, and I felt guilty about it. Over time it became more annoying, but no less confusing.

I sensed echoes of my parents' and grandparents' behavior in our relationship. Problems were never unpacked, processed, and discussed, but accusations and anger flew. It became worse over time, and it wasn't just him.

Why had he told me to invite Gharib and Mardi only to deny this request later? If he was honest when he said that his father's words had disturbed him, perhaps it was because they upset his sense of control over me. He saw Mardi and Gharib as a threat to my devoted attention toward his outsized place in my world, even more so when they were empowered and making positive change. But I overlooked his passive aggressive behavior: acting out on me, avoiding an explanation of his feelings, and threatening to leave that night.

In Astoria, I was in denial about the familial pattern of our relationship. I knew there were similarities, but I couldn't believe my family was sick like Seyran. I know—if I had seen him as sick, then why did I stay with him? Rather than admit the hurt from my upbringing and identify bad behavior from the past, my sense of shame allowed his worse behavior in the present.

And my guilt gave me a misplaced sense of purpose. I knew Seyran was missing his family. In another convoluted, twisted knot, I rationalized that love for his family was the source of his disrespect toward me.

BLOG POST: JANUARY 8, 2007
YEREVAN

Tradition, Duh >>> Before I met Seyran's parents for the first time, I had my hair straightened. We were at Tashir, a mall that everyone disparages as Western, overpriced, ugly, and stupid, but Seyran had heard there was a sale on a thermos he wanted to get for his father as a present. As we left the mall, Seyran sprung the idea of meeting his parents on me. I suspected he'd planned it all along and was only telling me now. Though I was nervous to meet them, it seemed I may as well get it over with.

"Before we go," he said, "we can go to a salon, and you can get your hair done."

"I don't think so," I replied.

"Why not?"

"You're saying I don't look good enough to meet your parents?"

"I think you're beautiful all the time," Seyran backpedaled, "but they are going to look at you different." He was flattering me, but I knew what he meant. To this day, my aunts finger my hair and question what I'm doing with it when I visit them. Upon further consideration, I decided it would be better to make this meeting— and my hair—go smoothly, so I went under the round brush and blow-dryer. At least Seyran wasn't asking me to dye my gray strands to detract from my age— only seven years younger than his mother.

I tried not to be nervous as we stood in the darkness outside their door. His mother answered it, smiling tentatively and peering at me in my big, black fur hat. I smiled back, took off the hat, swung my straight hair, and shook her hand. As we removed our coats, Seyran made a loud demonstration of saying, "This is my room," as if we'd never had sex in it when his parents were away at their dacha.

We entered the living room, and Seyran pointed out his father, a graying man in a sweater vest and flannel pants, and his brother, Robert, a gangly seventeen-year-old boy with arched eyebrows. Seyran's mother had set up a small table with five place settings in the living room by the sofa, and Seyran and I sat down. When she wasn't jumping up to retrieve things from the kitchen, she sat with us at the table, conversed with Seyran, and turned to me at certain points to smile. She was a pretty woman with dark hair and a confident, clear voice. I was staring at her eyes, practically the same as Seyran's, only nestled among crow's feet. She caught me staring, so I told Seyran, "You look like your mother."

He asked me, "Do I look like my father?"

It was hard to tell, since his dad was watching TV on the couch with his back to us, clearly disapproving. Seyran had told me he was forty-seven, but he looked about fifteen or twenty years older, overweight and balding. I wondered what in his life had aged him so. Drinking? Smoking? The stress of the Soviet years?

Seyran told me that his father had worked as a French translator until the Soviet reign, then worked for the government's department of public records. Now he is the head of a division in a remote region and comes home to Yerevan on the weekends. Seyran's mother was a computer programmer before she married. Seyran inherited her scientific mind. He received a college scholarship because he scored the highest in his class on the university entrance exams in physics. After studying French for thirteen years, his father's language, Seyran doesn't remember one word.

"You don't look as much as your father as you do your mother," I said. His father was reminding me of a portrait of an authoritarian patriarch one of my students had written. He didn't eat with us, only retrieving a beer from the table, and when Seyran presented him with the thermos, he didn't say thank you.

"My father speaks a little English," Seyran said as a cue, but his father did not take it. Instead, he spoke only to Robert. At one point, Seyran asked them what they were talking about, and they ignored him. In the tense silence, I noticed father and Robert were both wearing slippers, when *shwooosht*—the lights and TV went out, and we were trapped in darkness.

I heard Seyran's father say, "Don't vorry," in English, the only words he spoke that evening. We left by the time Seyran's brother found a candle to light.

As we walked down the stairs, I heard Seyran's mother ask if he was coming over the following night for New Year's Eve. No, he said, he was going to Zeytoon, where his aunts lived.

"Fucking stupid people," Seyran muttered on his way out. "I fucking hate them."

So much for my straightened hair smoothing things out.

✲

A couple of days before, Seyran had summoned me into the bathroom to talk about our New Year's plans while he showered.

"Look," he said, "We can go over to my aunts' house and keep them company, and they'll have lots of tasty things to eat. And then we don't have to be with my parents." He was rubbing his chest with a loofah and body wash.

"Okay," I told him. "And then what will we do afterward?" As I understood it, the tradition was that you had dinner with your family until midnight, and then everyone went to a big concert in Republic Square.

"We can go to sleep," he said. He was bending down now to get his feet.

"I want to check out the Square."

"Oh no," Seyran said, looking up at me. "That is the worst idea."

"Why?"

"Because it is all stupid, drunk people, and they set off bombs. [He meant firecrackers.] It can be very dangerous."

"Did something bad happen to you there?"

"No, I have never been, but I know it's bad, baby."

"I don't think it's dangerous," I said, recalling a friend who told me she had brought her young children.

"I don't care, do whatever you want. You're the one who cares about this stupid holiday," he suddenly exploded, like a firecracker. I rolled my eyes at him and prepared to go while he jumped out of the shower and dressed—we had plans to go food shopping since most of the stores would be closed during the week between December 31 and January 6, the day Armenians celebrate Christmas.

As we walked down Abovyan, I told him, "You don't get it; I'm not from here." I explained that I have never been to Times Square on New Year's Eve, and I would never want to go, but if someone were visiting and had their heart set on it, I would understand.

"Oh yeah, right. You are so traditional, the way you care so much about the holiday. You would get a tree and put it in the living room and get all kinds of presents," he continued.

Now he was being preposterous. Because I wanted to be a social anthropologist and observe what people were doing in the Square, I was accused of being a Christmas sycophant?

"I'm not traditional. That is so idiotic!" I yelled, swiping him with our empty canvas shopping bag, right in front of the Marriott.

"You're hysterical!" he accused.

We were at the bank now, so I took money from the ATM. And then we didn't speak as we walked down Tigran Mets to the food store. The silence gave me time to think about why Seyran would be so opposed to the Square.

For those who are nontraditional, who have been beaten and harassed for being the black sheep of their family, for looking different to strangers, for being targeted by the police, going to the Square meant putting yourself in harm's way. The holiday represents tradition, and the Square represents the government, both of which represent, on the whole, something very repressive and hurtful.

When I was in my early twenties, I rejected the Armenian community for what I saw as its adherence to convention and conformism. But at a certain point, I realized this was as absolute a position as those who unquestioningly embrace tradition. I was trying to explain to Seyran, as we walked past the freewheeling statue of Babajanyan playing the piano in front of the Opera on our way home, that I had rejected a part of myself when I distanced myself from all things Armenian, and denying one's identity can be as harmful, if not worse, than someone forcibly taking it from you.

At the end of the day, Seyran said, "I've been thinking about it. I'll go with you to the Square. It's too dangerous for you to go by yourself."

"It doesn't mean that much to me," I told him, "Let's see how the evening unfolds."

✧

On the way to Seyran's aunts' apartment, some kids were setting firecrackers alight and chucking them in the stairwells of the cement block buildings. "See, this is what you'll get in the Square," Seyran said. I had to admit, it was unnerving.

When we arrived, we saw both of his parents' coats on the bed. He said, "If I knew they were going to be here, I wouldn't have come."

And yet, his parents had transformed from the night before—smiling, laughing, festive.

Seyran told me later that his family liked me because I was kind, because I smiled. It wasn't much to know me by, but maybe it was enough, for now.

The dinner was delicious: ham, sausage, turkey, and basturma. The TV was broadcasting the events in the Square, and after midnight, when Seyran stood up to stretch his legs, he started dancing to the music as a joke. I'd never seen him dance traditionally before, only at the disco and onstage. One of his aunts stood up to dance with him, then his mother, who looked so cute in her pink sweater, jumping up and down.

Then he grabbed my hand.

I've had a block against Armenian dancing since my mother insisted I go to the mixers at the church as a teen, when I didn't know the steps. Inevitably, I wound up crying in the bathroom. Now I improvised the steps, twisting my outstretched arms the way I had seen others do, and no one seemed to care if I was doing it right or wrong. I was dancing with a family, feeling free.

I know that everyone would wish, no matter how nontraditional they are, no matter how much they want change, that they could have this—a sense of closeness, love, and liberation all at the same time.

II

10. DEALING

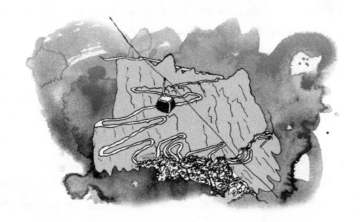

Leaving or Staying? >>> Many plaques festoon the apartment buildings of Yerevan, identifying famous or marginally notable people who once resided there. I didn't notice them when I lived here from 2006 to 2007. Now it seems I can't walk past a building that doesn't bear a plaque or even a bust. The building next door to mine features the bust of a bald man who was the first Olympic champion from Armenia. On Mashtots, I passed one building that was stacked with a dozen plaques, many belonging to artists. Even diaspora Armenians, like William Saroyan with his statue by the Cascade, have been honored. I wonder if I will ever be notable enough to have a plaque bearing my likeness on the building where I lived at Heratsi Poghots. Though Hayastantsis are known for being super critical and exclusionary, they can also lay claim to you, like family.

Maybe that's why my friend from the university, Anahid, thinks it's selfish for people to leave Armenia, to abandon it for Europe or elsewhere. It isn't that she is uncritical of Armenia; she is depressed about the faulty legal system and what she calls a fake democracy. And it isn't that she lacks the ability to leave, either, with her English skills and academic expertise. She confided in me that she has this overwhelming feeling that no harm could come to the country if she stays in Armenia—like it is a member of the family she is watching out for. For this reason, she told me, "Armenia is your country, too."

It was odd to hear this, when many people who were born here don't even feel that Armenia belongs to them. For example, a friend of Seyran's, on his way back to Europe for graduate school after studying there for his baccalaureate degree, said that he was aware of the losses he would face being apart from his family, and of the discrimination he would experience as an immigrant in Europe, but the last few years in Armenia had been very difficult. An energy expert, he had been pitching a plan to local investors on sustainable wind power. To his dismay, no one was interested in investing in it. Maybe in the future, the potential investors said, when current resources are depleted. For now, he said, people are content to receive any profits they can from sitting on a pipeline from Russia. Whatever benefits them in the immediate present is their primary motivation. "I really don't see a future for myself here," he said.

And yet, others feel that Yerevan could be a place for ideas to be exchanged. My friend Hrair spoke about Yerevan in the fifties and sixties when the repatriates arrived, before Brezhnev closed off the Republic. "This was a very nice time in Yerevan," he said. Armenians arriving from France, Iran, the U.S., and elsewhere brought their ideas, which were reflected in art, architecture, and film. He said he wanted to see this happen again, claiming that repatriates could bring change. In a way, he was describing himself.

When I had known him a few years ago, Hrair was anxious and unsettled, often complaining about the problems in Armenia. I was surprised at his transformation to happy, smiling, upbeat—even patriotic. "What happened to you?" I asked.

"I went into the world and gained perspective," he said. He lived in Switzerland, where he worked at a computer research group (and the salary was very bad), and the police often stopped him randomly. Without language or a network of family and friends, he was at a loss, and he increasingly appreciated Armenia. When he returned, it was with new energy to help his country, to keep developing a community of open-source computer specialists and developers. When I told him that Seyran wanted to translate yogic texts into Armenian, Hrair became excited by this possible contribution to Armenian society.

But when I talked to Kristapor, a musician, I gained another perspective. He has to travel in order to make a living, since the university where he teaches underpays him. He's a perpetual international nomad, teaching people about Armenia and bringing back what he learns from other countries. The problem is that it takes a toll, and he wishes he had other options. He would prefer to make a living here.

Which brings me back to the repatriates, who can return and leave at will. One repatriate from the U.S., a young woman, has created a sex education program for schoolchildren, which I never would have imagined in my wildest dreams. Another repatriate from Canada has raised about a hundred thousand dollars through Facebook to pay the health care costs of children in dire need of surgery and to provide training for artists to start small businesses.

Hrair asked if I would move here. I admire what the repatriates are achieving, but after a series of mishaps—like coming home to kill giant cockroaches, contracting food poisoning at a village khorovats, and having my wallet stolen at Vernissage—I still feel like the classic hapless tourist. And though this place inspires my writing, and I taught a successful writing workshop for women, my lack of Armenian language skills makes it difficult to spend significant time here. It seems too late for me to repatriate.

But is Armenia a home for me as Anahid suggested? When I picked flowers in the mountains with Seyran's mother, I enjoyed myself, but I wasn't having nostalgic feelings of "homeland." For me, as an Armenian, this word has often been linked to a drive in the diaspora for land reparations, to restore Eastern Anatolia as Western Armenia, which I find unrealistic. On the other hand, Armenians are entitled to have a homeland, just as everyone deserves to have a home. As someone adopted by Armenia, my experiences here are defined by loss—of language, identity, and culture. That doesn't mean I don't understand the urge to leave, or the need to stay, or the longing that results in both cases. Ultimately, I am happy that Armenia exists and that there is a place, though terribly flawed, where one can be Armenian.

Everyone should have a place where they can be.

META-WRITING:

On my trip to Armenia without Seyran, I went to his family's house in the mountains, where time passed slowly as we ate sunflower seeds on the back porch and watched the bull next door named Vlad (after Lenin) graze in his field. At the end of the summer, I visited again, and Vlad was gone. Seyran's father made the international snuffed-out sign, a finger drawn across his neck.

I met with Seyran's friends. In the three years that had passed, Stepan was still playing bass but drinking heavily; Archig had stopped playing with his band and gotten a day job, and Kristapor had entered a sham marriage with a woman and was already divorced. After Hrair returned to Yerevan, Edita left him and moved to Slovenia to marry a man she'd met online. She was now having a baby. "I'm happy for her," Hrair said, "and I understand why she left me—I was so anxious."

Through these experiences, I thought I was getting closer to understanding Seyran and his circumstances. But I kept wishing he was the one who was visiting.

This was made manifest most powerfully on the night before I was to return. I was outside the supermarket near the Yeritasartagan metro when I ran into a couple of Seyran's friends whom we had over for dinner right before we moved to the U.S.—an engineer and his wife. They were both such gentle and kind souls. Now she was visibly pregnant, and they were on the way to the market to buy milk. I almost wanted to apologize that it was me and not Seyran whom they were meeting in the street.

It was almost as if he had died, and I was seeing what his life was like without him.

Though this is a very personal response, it's not unlike what many diasporans experience when they visit Armenia. They confront not only the loss of all the Armenians who have left the country, but their own absence as well. They see what Armenia has been like without them.

I was seeing changes since I had been there last, but my eyes were for Seyran, too, who was now a diasporan. Every few days, I called him and reported what had changed. There were more cars, but they were better directed through the city, and they didn't threaten to run people over. The river in front of our old apartment building had disappeared—the city had paved it over with a road. Water was available at all hours in every building in the center. There were still aftershocks of the March 1, 2008, incident, when Armenians flooded the streets to protest the phony presidential election and were battered with state violence and mass arrests, resulting in the deaths of ten people. Friends told me what they thought had gone wrong and why protests would never work. People still felt desperate about corruption, perhaps even more so. People still wanted to leave.

I used to think Armenians were divided into two groups: diasporans and locals. Now I believe it's three overlapping categories that constantly observe each other through revolving doors: those who leave, those who stay, and those who return. While those who stay observe the returnees' admiration, it doesn't compel them to love their country more. Sometimes Armenians who are forced to leave can return to appreciate what they have lost, like Hrair. But later generations of diasporans return to adopt Armenia as their home, the way anyone anywhere finds that a place is important to them—or they treat Armenia like an exotic vacation, an option that distances themselves from their loss.

Seyran and I were dealing with loss in different ways. While I was trying to understand him through his friends and family on this trip, he was becoming even more detached. By the time I came back to New York, the link of our shared experiences in Armenia was broken.

JOURNAL: OCTOBER 17, 2010
ASTORIA

Seyran picked me up at the airport, wearing a new yellow-and-black striped shirt with a very low scoop V-neck, revealing his hairy chest. With his bald head, he looked like a queer Charlie Brown. He was late arriving to the baggage pickup area, and he rushed me into a cab in a fastidious fashion as if completing a chore.

He told me in the cab on the way home that my trip to Armenia made him realize feelings he had been suppressing—that Armenia wasn't such a stupid place and that he missed it. He also said that he liked the month on his own and that we should have more time apart.

"Things will change now—we will be different, we can spend time together, but I want to do my own thing."

I was relieved. He was finally letting go. We could finally move on.

But a day or so later, I felt odd. He was so earnest, doing the dishes, speaking kindly. Where was the charlatan? I kind of missed him—not the guy who kept hurting me, but the guy who was sarcastic and mischievous. It felt like I was living with a celibate monk. It didn't help that he had taken to wearing a large yellow-orange scarf from India as a sarong, flitting down the hall to the kitchen.

Suspicious of his emotional distance, I asked Seyran, "Did you have sex with someone while I was away?"

"Yes," he said. He was standing in my bedroom door, and I was looking up at him from my bed. I was hurt. We hadn't had sex for at least a month before I left.

"How many times?"

"Ten," he said. He told me later he thought it was a preposterous question. What was he supposed to say? But I had asked to ascertain how serious the liaison was.

"Did you do it here?" I asked. I imagined the worst, and I wanted to feel bad. No point in leaving out details. He said yes, then said no, though he had invited her here. He said she was just a regular girl.

"What do you mean by 'regular'?" I asked.

"She's not smart, she just works. And I don't know, it made me feel special to be able to show her things, even though I'm a dumb guy with a job. All I have is yoga."

Clearly, my trip to Yerevan had troubled him. He had had sex with a woman who was regular, not someone who had gone back to Armenia without him.

I told him we were growing apart, and we should give each other our freedom.

The next day, with the air cleared, I wondered if we would be all right. Maybe we would break up, maybe we would try the open relationship anew—I had no idea. But admitting our feelings had bridged the divide. We were sitting in the kitchen after dinner. He was playing his guitar, and I was singing an Elliott Smith song, "Pitseleh," with him. He was sitting down, and I touched his head, cupping my hand around his skull to feel his short hair.

He said, "I want to go for a bike ride. Am I allowed?"

"What is that supposed to mean?"

He didn't answer but got up to give me a peach when the doorbell rang. He ran to look out his bedroom window. "That's for me, Natalee. It's that girl." It was a surprise to him, and his eyes were wide, excited.

"Are you going to let her in here?" I asked. I was petrified, my heart slamming into my rib cage.

"No, I'm going with her."

He ran down the stairs and out the door. I stood for a moment, painfully stunned, then snuck into his room and looked out the window. She was young and Asian, her hair in a ponytail. He was looking at her, his head turned squarely, the same way that he would turn to me in bemused attention when we walked down the street in Yerevan—not at a slight angle, but perpendicular. She was facing him and appeared to be looking right up at his window. The room was dark, but I swore she saw me.

I tried not to think about what had just happened as I got ready for bed, then watched Jon Stewart under the covers. I even laughed at the jokes. I was able to sleep but woke up at 5:20 a.m. when his alarm sounded from his empty room. I went to turn it off, looked at his empty bed, and felt miserable. Like I didn't want to exist.

Not wanting to exist didn't seem like a healthy way to live, so I decided I had to leave. I didn't know where I would go or what to take with me, but I didn't want to be here when he returned. I wrote him a note that it was over, that I cared too much about myself to stay.

I didn't come home for two days. I stayed with friends and refused to tell him where I was; I didn't want to be found. It was too painful to be left by an unexpected ring of the doorbell, though now I wonder if he had planned it all along. In any case, he couldn't stand not knowing my location and kept texting me, demanding I reveal where I was staying. "Why should I tell you?" I asked. "Did you tell me where you were?" Really, he didn't care about my absence; he just wanted to know which of my friends knew the truth about him.

For those two days, I wandered between movie theaters, cafés, and parks. It didn't seem like such a bad place to be single, New York. Lots of people were sitting by themselves in the park and the cafés. Maybe I would be okay on my own. I had kind friends who took me in and let me sleep in their kid's bedroom.

Somehow, though, I did return to the apartment. I live here, after all, and I wasn't ready financially to move out.

Since then, life has gone on as usual, except that I have been telling him constantly that we are splitting up. I have been depressed, and I have been fine, and I have even had sex with him. I have taken walks with him, even spent time with him and my family. But I have been consistent in telling him we need to break up. I have even returned to therapy to help make this transition.

What has happened with Seyran? He has said he's stopped seeing this regular Asian girl. He continues to not apply for citizenship, which he has been eligible for since May, about five months ago. He claims he can't save seven hundred dollars for the application fee.

It's now been several weeks since the regular Asian girl rang our doorbell. I haven't been able to write in this journal till now: too many feelings to confront. But last weekend, I was standing at a bus stop in Williamsburg, Brooklyn, when who should ride by on his bike but Seyran. This was totally random as our apartment is three subway transfers or one long bus ride away. He was wearing strange clothes—his pants rolled up over hiking boots and a Nehru jacket I'd never seen before. I yelled his name, and he abruptly stopped in surprise, and the person on the bike behind him nearly rammed into him.

This slapstick scene would have been quite comical if the person on the bike hadn't been the regular Asian girl.

It's not as if he hasn't lied to me before, but catching him this time was a particular punch in the face. For as many lies as I have caught him in, there are many more that I haven't.

So I have decided to pay the seven hundred dollars and get him his citizenship. There was a price to get him out of the army to come be with me, and now there is a price to give him his citizenship and get him away from me.

I just want to get it over with.

STORY: JANUARY 4, 2007
YEREVAN

The morning after the New Year's Eve celebration with Seyran's family, Na woke with a stomachache and acid reflux in her throat. She thought it must have been that last toast of pomegranate wine. She took TUMS and the stomachache went away, but then the diarrhea hit. So she took medicine for that, too.

Seyran suggested they visit someone since it was a customary activity the day after New Year's. He considered a few friends before deciding to call his parents. His mother said she was reheating the turkey from yesterday and invited them over.

When Seyran and Na walked into the living room, they found a beautiful table with the turkey, fresh fruit on a platter, a yogurt-topped vegetable dish, and a thin-layered cake, with a bar of juices and Cognac in the corner. Na wasn't feeling up to eating, but she picked at some fruit so as not to appear rude.

Na gave Seyran's mother a gift: a pair of earrings along with a set of lavender shampoo and body lotion. She smiled and thanked Na, then disappeared into the next room and brought out a package of pale green pantyhose labeled "Melon". She also gave Seyran five thousand dram, around eighteen dollars.

It was a relaxed visit, very different from just two days before when they had been ignored until the lights went out. Though he had the TV on, Seyran's father engaged with the couple, flipping through channels and explaining the programming to Na. He eventually settled on the premiere of the Armenian version of *Deal or No Deal*. (The translation of the title was *Deal Gam No Deal*, written in Armenian script, Դիլ Կամ Նո Դիլ, which Na found very funny because it seemed to suggest that *deal* was a better-known English word than *or*.) Seyran's father told Na that the contestant won 7,580,000 dram, roughly 20,000 dollars. "But she could have won more," he told her.

At one point, Na went to the bathroom. Seyran told her later that while she was away, his father had asked why she was paying three thousand dollars to help him to get out of the army. Seyran explained that they were boyfriend and girlfriend. His father wasn't satisfied with this answer. Na was an American, and everyone knew Americans were stingy. Seyran said that Na was different. "You know how I am different from you? Well, she's different from other Americans."

When Na returned from the bathroom, Seyran was discussing his plans with his parents, explaining that he wanted to go to America. His father started asking about visas; he suggested it would be harder for Seyran to get a student visa and that the couple should get married if they were serious. As soon as possible—this month, after the holidays.

Na thought they were crazy. *They have just met me after suspecting the worst, their son has been with me for a little over three months, and they are telling us we should get married as soon as possible?* As she watched the conversation proceed, she felt like she had been planted into a TV show, the kind where an elaborate hoax has been set up to monitor an unwitting bystander's response. Or maybe they had been planning this scene all along. She didn't like thinking this way—mistrustful, like the typical miserly American Seyran's father had in mind. Na tried to find a reasonable explanation for the family's strange behavior. Maybe it was standard for Armenian parents to strategize around an opportunity when it presented itself for their children. They were simply watching out for their son.

Though Seyran and Na had discussed getting married for his visa before, talking about it with the family took it from the theoretical to the possible. His father asked if securing Seyran's visa took longer than expected, would Na be able to stay longer than August? Perhaps until October or November? Na shook her head; her job would start in September.

And then she thought about it. She could teach in the U.S. the following semester instead. Anahid at the university had told her she could help her pick up classes if she wanted to stay longer. Na told Seyran's father that she would be able to stay if she had to.

Seyran told her later that his father had been testing her to see if she really loved him, if she was the real deal. It didn't occur to Na to ask Seyran to pass such a test to prove his love.

When the couple left in a cab, the talk of marriage continued as the car rumbled over the bumpy backstreets. Seyran suggested they get hitched as soon as possible as insurance. He explained that if things didn't work out for them, they could always get divorced later, but it might look suspicious if they married too close to when they needed to leave.

Na had been saying all along that she wanted to see how their relationship progressed. They fought enough as it was, and there was a sizable age difference between them. Being married would still be a commitment, even if they were doing it for the document. She knew that it meant she would feel responsible for Seyran in the U.S., though he had been insisting she wouldn't be.

Once at home, Na prepared for bed while Seyran did research on the internet. He told her they would have to be interviewed at the U.S. embassy to prove they were a couple. As she nestled under the covers and fell asleep, she wondered what they would tell the embassy about Seyran's army service. She woke up at 4:30 a.m. with a bad stomachache and told Seyran her feelings.

"I'm willing to help you out of the army, that's important. But marriage will have to wait."

"But paying the bribe to get me out of army will only cover three years, not the whole six years I need protection. We should get married so that I can have something to do in America." Basically, he was saying that the two went together: paying the bribe and getting married to come to the U.S. would help him avoid the army entirely. "So you may as well not pay anything, and I'll go into the army and stay here."

To Na, this sounded like an ultimatum. "No," she said. "No!"

She ran to the bathroom and started throwing up. She vomited for a couple of hours until 5:30 or 6 in the morning. Seyran stood by her and held her hair back.

Na spent the following day resting, drinking tea, and trying to recover while Seyran worked on the computer. She grappled all day, in her mind, with whether she should stay with him or leave now.

That night, he came to her as she was sleeping and told her he had been thinking about it. "We don't have to get married. I don't want to do anything that makes you feel uncomfortable."

As she hugged him, she felt relieved. It seemed he truly cared about her, above and beyond anything having to do with their circumstances. He seemed like "the real deal."

META-WRITING:

Around the time when I ran into Seyran on his bike with the regular Asian girl, there were a few prominent stories of Armenians in the news. Across the U.S., a mafia network of Armenians had been caught in an elaborate, highly effective scheme, creating phantom doctors and phony clinics that had bilked Medicaid out of thirty-five million dollars. Their leader had significant ties to government figures in Armenia, including the current and former presidents Serzh Sargsyan and Robert Kocharyan. Three days later, a news story broke that an Armenian madame in Turkey had exploited eighteen prostitutes, who were all undocumented immigrants from Armenia and Georgia—a major human trafficking scandal.

That same day, the longest tramway in the world, 3.5 miles long, finished construction in Armenia, bringing passengers over a gorge up to Tatev, a ninth-century monastery poised atop a basalt plateau. It had been developed as part of a wide-scale plan to encourage tourism. And, weirdly, the world's largest chocolate bar was fabricated in Armenia that same month, weighing 4,410 kg, nearly five tons. Grand Candy had created the item to celebrate their ten-year anniversary.

Let us examine this collection of unseemly facts. In the first two cases, Armenians are living outside their nation, evading legal systems, and wreaking havoc on innocent victims in order to make money. In the latter two cases, Armenians are creating very big items within a very tiny country for monetary gain. It seems there are always deals to be had, whether in the diaspora or the homeland. To be fair, the tramway and chocolate bar could be seen as positive signs toward a sustainable economy. But they're both tainted: Grand Candy is owned by an oligarch, and the tramway project was funded partially by the World Bank. Villagers can travel on the tram once a day for free, but what is the point of that? If they need to get up to Tatev to sell food or knickknacks, they have to pay the other way to return home, and it's not cheap: three thousand dram or about eight dollars.

Here we have stories of dealing, at home and in the diaspora, with human lives devalued in the process. The worst stereotype of an Armenian is the wily, cheating merchant or middleman, motivated only by money, embodied most vividly in our current era by the Kardashian family. In reality, most Armenians are honest, law-abiding citizens, occupying a range of socieo-economic strata, demonstrating various mores regarding money, and vulnerable to the whims of exploitative world powers. If there's some seed of truth to the stereotype, then I can't help but wonder if the recent crimes and transactions suggest the kind of deals desperate people make against death. We are constantly reminded of our absence, whether living in our abandoned country or in an invisible diaspora. Armenians should be dead, so some of us resort to making risky wagers to survive, sensing we are owed, skirting on the edge of morality, feeling the thrill of getting away with something wrong.

When the news broke, two friends asked me if Seyran was involved with the Medicaid mafia. It seemed to point to their racism, but I also wondered why they didn't ask me if I knew any of the people involved. What were they sensing about Seyran?

While visiting Armenia without him, a part of me felt I deserved something from his family, his friends, and his life after all I had done for him and all that he had taken from me.

Without intending to, I had made a deal.

❖

On the Sunday before the Armenian news-a-thon, I saw Seyran with the regular Asian girl in Brooklyn as I was coming home from an Armenian Catholic church. I'd heard about its existence from a few people and wanted to investigate out of ethnographic curiosity, especially because it is located smack-dab in the middle of Williamsburg, a.k.a. hipsterville. Perhaps it was the excuse I needed to feed my soul.

The place was empty when I arrived. It was an old, large church with stained glass windows and paint peeling from some of the walls. Even in its decay, it was beautiful, with mosaics of gold tiles underneath each of the windows. It had been a non-Armenian Catholic church until recently, when the parish dwindled and the diocese closed its doors, only to rent it out to the Armenian Catholics. The story goes that Armenians broke off from the church in Rome in 451 AD over a rift whether Jesus was divine or a man or both, forming the Armenian Apostolic Church that dominates Armenian religious worship today. But a smattering of Armenians in various parts of the diaspora practiced Catholicism until the Armenian Catholic Church was formally established by Pope Benedict XIV in 1742.

As I waited for the service to start, I could hear the priest saying his prayers behind the altar. There was a pause, and then I heard him chatting and laughing with someone. I'd never witnessed a priest goofing off before.

A woman arrived not long after me and sat a few pews up, and then the service started. The organ played, a woman sang from the balcony, and the priest appeared in his finery, followed by a deacon shaking an incense dispenser. The service was very similar to the liturgy I had grown up with in the Armenian Apostolic church: same format, same songs. But in this huge church, the priest looked very small; though he possessed the usual authority, the empty space seemed to neutralize him. He wore big glasses and appeared to be about my age, late thirties or early forties.

Though a few more people stumbled in later, I felt sorry for the priest as he conducted the service, performing his ritual to a nearly empty space. I hoped the numbers of people didn't really matter—it wasn't like this was opening night on Broadway—but I wondered if the priest would do the service if we weren't here. I had read on the church's website that there were a thousand Armenian Catholics in NYC, but given the turnout, that number seemed inflated.

When the priest made the sign of the cross at me, I made it back at him; it seemed the least I could do. I wanted to ask, "How do you not get discouraged?" Here was someone confronting a lack of audience, and yet he did his job with more cheer than most priests.

At one point in the Badarak, when the most sad and beautiful song was being performed, we were instructed to kneel. I figured since I was in this position, and I hadn't prayed for a while, that I may as well ask God to help me find a way to break up with Seyran. I honestly didn't know what to do, and I cried as the music and the incense swirled around me.

Afterward at coffee hour in the basement, the priest entered and blessed the table. He then seemed preoccupied with his lay wear, a lovely woolen cloak, which the deacon hadn't tied to him properly.

What a prima donna, *I thought.*

When I was introduced to him, I discovered he was a Hayr Soorp—a celibate priest—and that he was new to the congregation.

"How do you like it here?" I asked.

"Eh, it's all right. Too cold. I miss my home." He had a slight accent, so I inquired where he was from.

"Haleb," he said. "Aleppo, Syria."

"Oh, I've always wanted to visit," I told him. "My grandmother lived there for a time."

"You should come with me," he said, "the next time I go back."

"Really?" I asked. I'd never been invited by a priest anywhere. They never seemed like regular

people, nor did they seem eager to dispel that myth.

"Yes, we'll eat and drink and party."

Now I was astonished. I looked at him as he tapped his paper coffee cup with mine. My gaydar wasn't reliable, but the alarms now sounded in my brain.

Not long after my visit, the Catholic Church decided to sell the Williamsburg church to developers to convert to apartments, and last I heard a studio there was renting for three thousand dollars. I don't know what happened to the priest—if he ever returned to Aleppo before the city was bombed to rubble.

Within an hour, I saw Seyran with the regular Asian girl at the bus stop, which compelled me to call Esmerelda Quinones, the immigration lawyer. She advised that once we applied for citizenship, Seyran would get it in four to five months.

I couldn't believe my prayers were being answered so soon. And in an empty church with a gay Armenian Syrian priest, his humanity reminding me to celebrate life, even while in displacement.

JOURNAL: NOVEMBER 6, 2010
ASTORIA

Last month, on the first day of Hrair's visit to New York, Seyran took him to Jackson Heights, and Hrair was not impressed. He said Jackson Heights was an "exploded" place with too many people, as if the asphalt had broken open and crowds were streaming through the streets like lava. Seyran and I love visiting this South Asian neighborhood because it transports us to another world, but Hrair wasn't interested. When Seyran took him to Patel Brothers, the big Indian supermarket, Hrair said it was filthy, like the stores in Yerevan during Soviet times. I had heard the stories of empty shelves and the bread turned black with mold. In contrast, Patel Brothers has one whole aisle filled with ten-pound bags of rice, and I have never noticed it cleaner or dirtier than your average NYC supermarket. I wondered what Hrair was seeing.

Hrair had been at a tech conference in Silicon Valley, then stopped by to see us on his way home. I had enjoyed visiting with him in Yerevan a few months ago, hearing how his mind had changed about Armenia. But now, visiting New York, he was very negative. Granted, he had a cold. But perhaps it was also his tour guide. Seyran took him to Starbucks, where Hrair witnessed Seyran's argument with the staff about putting a plastic lid on top of his cup. Then they went to a storied vegetarian restaurant, Angelica Kitchen, where Hrair couldn't order any meat.

Before Hrair arrived, Seyran had already been nervous in anticipation of Hrair's reaction to his embrace of yoga and a vegan diet. One night, we were sitting in Seyran's uncomfortable, empty bedroom, devoid of possessions, when Hrair challenged Seyran. "Why did you come here if you are rejecting American life? You have to consume to be American."

I said, "Are you kidding me? Every day he's consuming something."

Seyran said, "America isn't all about superficial people. There are nice people who are vegan and do yoga."

"But they're consumers," I told Hrair. "It can be expensive to be a vegan, to buy the food. And yoga classes cost at least fifteen dollars."

"So what? You spend that on a meal," Seyran claimed.

"Not every day, I don't."

I apologized to Hrair since we were fighting in front of him.

Seyran said, "Don't worry, he knows what you're like. When he goes back to Armenia, he will tell everyone that we have the opposite relationship—that you're the man and I'm the woman." Hrair smiled shyly, but the next day when we were alone in the kitchen, he confessed that he thought not eating meat had affected Seyran's hormones. "He has changed; his voice is higher."

I was standing at the counter, and he was sitting at the table. I turned around to look at him. Like the bottles of homemade kombucha Seyran had assembled atop our fridge, Hrair was offering dubious science. I remembered in Armenia that Seyran had been more macho in public, code switching to speak in a deeper voice. Here, in the land of the metrosexual, Seyran shows more of his feminine side, speaking with less force and carrying his beloved environmentally friendly tote bags around town.

"He has changed for the worse," Hrair continued.

I ignored his homophobia and confided in Hrair that I had fallen for Seyran in Armenia because he was a freedom-loving rebel seeking all forms of art. He used to find the most amazing films on the internet—horror films from Korea, comedy films from the Balkans—that I had never seen or heard of before. But then Seyran read a pamphlet by a guru who claimed one shouldn't play card games or watch films; one should instead be grounded in the real world and work in the garden or talk with friends. It's not that I'm against gardening and friendship. But why denigrate art? Instead of playing music with friends well into the night, he goes to bed at 9 p.m. so he can get up at 4:30 a.m. to practice yoga; instead of singing Radiohead songs, he chants Sanskrit. He has substituted art with religion.

In response to what I'd shared, Hrair said, "I told you I thought it would be good if he came back to Armenia, to translate the yoga texts. But now I don't think he would offer anything good."

I turned my head to gaze out the kitchen window. *Don't give up on him, too,* I thought. *He can't have both me and you giving up on him.*

After Hrair left, we filled out the application, assembled the papers, and sent in Seyran's citizenship package. I made a payment plan for him to remunerate me once a month on his payday. The deal is being done.

Yesterday, we celebrated Diwali, a Hindu festival of lights, by visiting Jackson Heights, eating dinner at an Indian restaurant, and watching people buy gold-and-silver-leafed sweets in the stores. We went into Patel Brothers, and I thought about Hrair's disgust for it. Sure, the floor was a little dirty from normal wear and tear. But the walls and ceiling were spick-and-span, beautiful even, with a blue sky and clouds painted above the produce section.

Even though he thinks he has radically changed, Seyran is like Hrair in his own way. All these years, Seyran hasn't been able to return to Armenia to embrace his culture, so he has replaced it, substituting one traditional culture with another.

We went to a small storefront window, and he bought paan. A leaf covered with spreads from little jars and sprinkled with spices, it's a medicinal sweet to chew on. He asked if I wanted one, and I said no. This cultural practice is a little too esoteric for me.

At the end of the night, he walked me to the subway, explaining that he was going somewhere else, but he wouldn't tell me where. As we were parting, he wanted to kiss. I said no way, but he maneuvered his head by my face and planted one on me anyway. I pushed him hard and called him an abush, tasting the sweet mint and fennel in my mouth as he walked away.

I went home, got some writing done, went to bed, and woke up after three hours of sleep. The moon was shining brightly outside. And then it hit me. It was "a moon day." This is a special day for him, spiritually, though all I can glean from it is that he spends the night outdoors—I imagine on a park bench or with some crazy cult. I didn't want to, but I found myself worrying about him.

I periodically imagine myself having to deal with his death. I suppose it's because some part of me wants him to die, but it's also a fear that I indulge in. How would I tell his parents he is gone? How could I live with myself for not protecting him from harm? It's ironic: I've always wanted to avoid feeling responsible for him, but here I am blaming myself for his imaginary death. One reason I never wanted to become a mother was because I knew I couldn't live with the terror of possibly losing a child. What have I done now but replace the possibility of one restrictive way of life with the reality of another?

It's 8 a.m. now, and he's not home. The sky is blue, and the clouds are moving fast, illuminated like the bright, pearly nacre of a seashell. Just like the ceiling at Patel Brothers, sheltering the unavoidably worn-out floor and all the diasporans trying to find their homeland in food, ritual, and one another.

11. ETHNIC CLEANSING

BLOG POST: FEBRUARY 2, 2007
YEREVAN

1954-____ >>> The week before he was killed, it was dismal in Yerevan. Snowy, cold, bleak. There were a few days when I woke up between 1 and 3 p.m. with nothing to do but read and buy food at Urartu, the corner market. I was hoping the winter malaise would be broken by traveling to Tbilisi with Seyran when I got the news. An article had been forwarded to my inbox, subject: "Turkish Armenian Writer Shot Dead." Though I had a feeling who it was, a shock jolted through me as I read that Hrant Dink had been gunned down in the street outside of his office at *Agos*, the Armenian paper he had founded in Istanbul.

I was disheartened that someone who had consistently opened dialogue in Turkey about the Armenian Genocide had been murdered so ruthlessly. Even though they faced charges in the highest courts for insulting Turkishness, Dink and other high-profile writers had been broaching the subject of the Genocide. Despite pushback and protest, academic conferences on the Genocide have been held over the past few years. Most notably, prominent Turkish citizens have been coming forward to announce that a grandparent was an Armenian Genocide survivor. Even if their ancestors had been renamed, converted, and cleansed, Turks have been learning that Armenia and Armenians are part of Turkish history, also sharing blood. All that good news now seemed to be dead with the image of Dink facedown on the concrete.

The next day, Seyran and I ran errands for our trip, then we stopped at his parents' apartment in the evening. His brother was watching CNN, and Dink's assassination was the leading story. Later, Seyran and I went to a concert, and a girl showed up with a sticker of Dink on her back. As Dink's assassination featured in the news globally and locally, we went about our business as planned.

Snow was drifting down as we boarded the marshrutka at the bus station the next morning. Seyran's mother had told us the roads were dangerous, and I found myself gripping his hand as we passed through snowy hills, the land and sky melding into a seamless whiteness. On one treacherous mountain bend, we were jolted from our seats, but once we made it past the cemetery in Vanadzor that winds next to the road, the ground was bare of snow, and the sun emerged.

It seemed that we had been living in a snow cloud. Yerevan was separated from the rest of the world by its elevation, a bowl-shaped city sunk into a high plateau. Emerging from this bubble, to the sun shining on the tin roofs of Georgian villages, brought me an awakening joy.

Once we disembarked in Tbilisi, we entered an eerie parallel universe. Upon finding the nearest subway station, we discovered that it looked exactly like the Yerevan metro, built in the same Soviet style and scale. Up above ground, I encountered people with noses and eyes outlined in striking shapes, like Armenians, but they were filled in with a lighter coloring. The Georgian language rang a close pitch in my ears, and the script on the signs, though unintelligible, echoed the Armenian alphabet's curves and swoops, both alphabets designed by the same Medieval linguist, Mesrop Mashtots. Going to Tbilisi was like opening a hidden door in your own home to discover a new room with the same scents and sounds.

Over the next twenty-four hours, I would realize that this room was much bigger, diverse, and cosmopolitan than Yerevan. The people's clothing didn't conform, the buildings weren't all made of the same stone. There were beautiful river views across bridges, sheer rock walls, and more ancient churches—and mosques and temples—than you could count. Old homes with latticework balconies still existed even as more contemporary architecture filled in the gaps. The restaurants ranged from East to West—Irish pubs, Sushi joints, Indian, Chinese, Spanish, Italian, Turkish.

Unlike in Yerevan, Tbilisi signs and posters are mostly in the native language, hardly any in English, and absolutely nothing printed in Russian. Ethnic enclaves in South Ossetia and Abkhazia have enlisted Russia's aid to break away from Georgia, so relations have not been cordial between the Georgian and Russian governments, but it wasn't until I read a newspaper that I realized they had been completely cut off from each other for a few months. Georgians had arrested four Russians for espionage at the end of September, so Putin imposed postal and transport sanctions. The Russian ambassador was only now returning to Tbilisi, but there were no flights, trains, or buses to Russia, with no way to send mail or get a visa to Russia. It turned out that Tbilisi was in its own bubble.

As Seyran spoke Russian to people, I worried that we might resemble Abkhazians or South Ossetians. A few people detected his Armenian accent, including a hotel clerk, a woman taking tickets in an amusement park, and a man selling sneakers at an outdoor market—they all turned out to be Armenian. I guess I shouldn't have been surprised. About half a million Armenians live in Georgia, around a hundred thousand in Tbilisi. During the nineteenth century, more Russians and Armenians lived in Tbilisi than Georgians. My friend Anahid at the university told me, "Armenians built that city!"

The most surprising response to Seyran's accent came from the guy at the sulfur baths. Seyran had just laid facedown on a ceramic-tiled table by the pool, when the guy, a large tank of a man in bathing trunks, dumped a bucket of water over him and asked if he were Azeri. Seyran told him no, he was Armenian. The man revealed that he was Azeri, then proceeded to converse in Armenian. It turned out that he had learned the language from his Armenian neighbors. We were in a section of town, he told Seyran, where Armenians, Azeris, Turks, and Kurds had long lived together peacefully. My mind was blown, realizing that their families had been friends before the conflict in Nagorno-Karabakh, maybe even before the Genocide. Perhaps they could form and keep close relationships in a city where they were outsiders, where the Georgian/Russian troubles in the present affected their daily lives more than land and history disputes across borders.

It was the day after Dink had been buried, and this man scrubbed my naked body with a nubby mitt. After a few days of tepid showers at the B&B and tromping around the filthiest parts of Tbilisi, my skin was rubbing off in gray bits. I was embarrassed, but the Azeri man didn't seem to care. He officiously tapped me with two fingers as a signal for me to flip over as he thoroughly scrubbed my shoulders, arms, and hands; my chest, breasts, legs, back, and butt. I giggled when he rubbed the underside of my feet and was only slightly miffed when his mitt brushed my clit. At one point, he filled up what looked like a pillowcase with soap and air, then squished it down onto my stomach, creating a cloud of soft suds. When the Azeri man rinsed me off and shook my hand, I felt relaxed, renewed.

The term ethnic cleansing is a euphemism for the dirtiest forms of human behavior—killing, mass displacement, repression of language, and erasure of culture. At the sulfur bath in Tbilisi, we repurposed the term for what it could really mean: honor, care, and intimacy among neighbors.

❖

Seyran picked up a photocopied picture of Hrant Dink, torn on the ground, as we marched into Hraparak with our backpacks. Under Dink's countenance was his date of birth, his date of death left blank: "1954–___"

"What does it mean?" he asked.

"They don't think he's dead?" I imagined people concocting conspiracy theories. "Or maybe that he is a martyr? His life cut short? Or that his memory will always live?"

Back at home, I checked the news online and learned there had been a massive demonstration in Yerevan the same day as the one in Istanbul. While we'd been away, I'd received emails from friends in the States mentioning the assassination. A picture of the demonstration in Istanbul was on the front page of *The New York Times*.

What was particularly surprising (and heartening) was the response of the Turkish media. Many columnists and journalists were outraged. Headlines read, "The Murderer Is a Traitor" (Hürriyet), "They Killed Our Brother" (BirGün), and "It Was Turkey that Was Shot Dead" (Milliyet). The sentiment was echoed in the protest signs: We are all Armenian. We are all Hrant. I didn't think I'd ever see such sentiment in Turkey: masses of people aligning themselves with the dreaded, maligned minority.

Hrant Dink's mission with *Agos* was to be a voice for Turkish Armenians within Turkey, but also the diaspora. Considering himself both Turkish and Armenian, he was critical not only of Turkish nationalism, but also of Armenian nationalism, especially the kind that he saw in the diaspora. He personally felt that he had transcended the Armenian rage against Turks and wanted to keep dialogue open between the two peoples, his newspaper acting as a mouthpiece. Dink led the way for more Armenians to find ways to mourn, to step away from their nationalistic self-defensive pose, armor down.

Which leads me to the Armenian mourning of Dink's death. As I read on about the demonstrations in Armenia, I noticed the use of the slogan. Although its chanting could be seen as an act of solidarity with the protesters in Istanbul, who were Armenian, Turkish, and Kurdish, "We are all Armenian. We are all Hrant," had quite a different meaning here.

Tanya, one of the directors of the Center for Armenian Women, told me that marchers trekked to the Genocide memorial at Tsitsernakaberd and placed flowers at the wall where the word Malatya was etched. It seemed both an act of mourning and politics, the two conflated. Yes, Dink had been born in Malatya, but he claimed Istanbul as his home. He was being equated with a victim of the Genocide, a term that he recognized as historical as well as political.

When I asked my student, Jhenya, about the demonstration and march, she said it was a waste of time. The Armenian government was using the opportunity to attract attention to the Genocide. I asked her if anyone she knew went to the demonstrations, and she said no, in a tone of voice that suggested, of course not.

Gharib had a more measured response. "No, I did not go to the demonstrations. Because there is a man that they have jailed for saying something against the government here." He was referring to Jirair Sefilian, a Karabakh war veteran and widely known hero who had spoken out that certain areas in the buffer zone around Karabakh should not be returned to Azerbaijan; he referred to those in power as "illegal authorities." Soon after, Sefilian and eight other members of his opposition group were taken into custody, their homes searched. Gharib thought it was hypocritical to call out Turkey when the Armenian government wasn't any better, arresting people for their opposing views. Now, suddenly, the same Armenian nationalists who had reviled Dink for speaking out against the bill in France that would have made it a crime to deny the Armenian Genocide (because he believed it limited free speech) were now demonstrating in his name.

The next morning, I woke up depressed. I couldn't move, I didn't want to get up out of bed, I was testy with Seyran, I didn't want to write, I didn't want to call Gharib and Mardi with whom I had made plans. What was the point? Here was a man who was working so hard, who had found his life's purpose in one area of the world. And yet his cause—even in his passing—was being misunderstood by his own people. As I work within a subset of a small community, in a bubble of queer, feminist progressive Armenianism, I question whether any of it will make a difference.

As the day progressed, I realized my despondency was at odds with Dink's vision. The reality was that the largest peaceful protest in Turkey's history was held, and the outraged response of Turkish society led to international awareness of the issues between Turks and Armenians. Already, many Turks were calling for the repeal of the anti-Turkishness code, and the Armenian deputy foreign minister was saying he was ready to negotiate opening the border between the two countries.

There is a story here about the ways we make and understand our societies, forming an insular sphere of identity, nationality, and ethnicity, but also how we must come to understand ourselves as a composite of truths. Though

Hrant Dink worked in one area of the world, he wasn't trapped in a bubble. His vision had a worldliness to it, an understanding of something larger, ideas like cells linked across borders and minds, cleaning old wounds and clearing away painful grievances.

STORY: JANUARY, 2007
TBILISI, GEORGIA

Na and Seyran shared a bathroom with a guy across the hall, a young and very tall strawberry-blond man whom Na called "the American" and Seyran named "the Russian." They were the only guests on the top floor of Hotel Havlabar, a B&B in Tbilisi's Old Town. It was the off-season, so they had received a good rate from the owner, a single mother. Their large wood-paneled room was situated atop a beautiful winding staircase, underneath the eaves, with small windows overlooking the city. Na and Seyran didn't interact with the guy across the hall for three days as they explored the museums, shops, streets, and neighborhoods. But when they returned each night to the B&B, Seyran would joke that the Russian across the hall wanted to have sex with them. Na rolled her eyes and hoped the guy wasn't gay. One night, she listened closely while Seyran went to the bathroom for the door across the hall to open or close.

A few days before they left for Tbilisi, before the assassination of Hrant Dink, Seyran had come home to their apartment and announced, "Na, I have to tell you something, but I don't know if I should." She was sitting in the kitchen while a plumber fixed the leaky pipe underneath the sink. Seyran was smiling but cagey, his cheeks flushed. In his hands he held an orange box of pastries from Croissant, the new French bakery across the street. Seyran saw the plumber and excused himself, rushing into the bathroom. Na could hear the water running. He was brushing his teeth and spitting water profusely into the sink.

Earlier that day, they had taken a walk holding hands; it was an unseasonably warm afternoon in the midst of a freezing cold week, and Na had taken off her gloves to feel the pleasure of their fingers touching once again in the outdoors. Then Na went home to write, and Seyran went to the British Council to check out videos from their library. Once the plumber left, Seyran sat down with Na at the kitchen table to tell her his story.

On the way to the British Council, he ran into a boy he knew, so he stopped to talk to him. The boy flirted with Seyran, then propositioned him. They went to a hallway in an apartment building, but someone walked by, so they left to find another place. As they were seeking out private spots to make out, Seyran was wondering if Na would be hurt, but he wasn't sure. He was also afraid of what would happen if they were caught. They finally found a hidden place in the staircase of an apartment building where they kissed for three or four minutes. With all their clothes on, including their coats. And the boy came.

Na had seen this boy before, a very skinny thing who wore flamboyant, fanciful clothes: long scarves and a black peacoat with a wide collar and cinched waist. Na thought he must have been hard up if he had come only from kissing—then she doubted it. She asked Seyran if they'd had sex. "No," he insisted.

"A blow job?" she asked, citing how he had washed out his mouth.

"No, we just kissed."

"Did you rub up against him?"

"No, but he rubbed against me."

"So did you like anything about it?"

"I liked squeezing his ass."

Na held her breath and furrowed her eyebrows deeper.

"I didn't like kissing him that much, but I liked him better than other guys."

"Than who?" Na asked.

"Moussi," he said.

But he never was involved with Moussi. Na remembered Seyran's diplomatic negotiation with Moussi that night she had first gone home with him. Would Seyran have taken that much care with Moussi if there hadn't already been something between them? It would explain why Moussi had looked at them with disgust at Vehine's concert. The reality was that she had no idea what Seyran meant—maybe he'd even seen Moussi after he and Na had hooked up. Na ate the French pastries from the orange box as she toggled between the safety of her denial and the reality of her fears.

Seyran interrupted her silence: "You're the only one I can tell about it."

Na thought of their day in Etchmiadzin, the morning after they'd first had sex, and how she had asked him if he'd be gay if it were safe in Armenia.

"I think I'm losing you," she said.

He saw the look on her face and hugged her. "No, I love only you," he said. "I'm never going to do it again. Not if it makes you feel this way. It's not worth it. I did it to see what it would be like."

Na didn't entertain the thought that he was saying these things because he didn't want to lose out on escaping the army. She also hadn't yet detected a pattern of him pushing her in one direction, only to backtrack when her emotions were piqued. She simply believed he felt badly about hurting her.

She took a deep breath, suddenly realizing something. "It's good you did it," she told him. "If you didn't, you'd always be wondering what it would have been like."

"I don't want to see this guy again," he said. "I love you and only want to be with you,"

Na tried to keep this expression of devotion in mind as she waited for Seyran to come back from the bathroom in Tbilisi. She heard chatter in the hallway and held her breath. Soon Seyran traipsed back into the room, giggling. He had spoken to the man across the hall, who turned out to be neither Russian nor American but Scottish.

"Can I invite him in?"

"Sure," Na said, trying her best not to be paranoid.

The man, named Thom, wearing olive corduroys and a brown sweater vest, was polite and friendly. He explained that he was working at the hotel, helping out with their website. Thom was in Georgia for a few months, but he had been traveling on his own for over a year. He had bicycled across China, Thailand, Laos, Kyrgyzstan, and Azerbaijan. Next, he was about to travel through Turkey, then Croatia, on his way back home. Na didn't get the sense that he was gay.

Seyran was excited he was from the UK, the birthplace of Radiohead. "I really want to go there!" Seyran said.

"Why?" Thom asked. He looked doubtful.

"Everyone in the UK has a band," Seyran said, smiling.

Thom didn't laugh condescendingly, as many people might have. "Not everyone, but there is a lot of music. I don't know though, it's all so commercial." He was reluctant to go back to Scotland, he said. "I'd like to do organic farming when I return, try to bring back some of what I've learned about Eastern life." He said that in the West, people were so busy working to buy things that they didn't enjoy their lives.

Seyran wondered aloud if it was because they had too much. He told Thom that systems administrators were paid only three to four hundred dollars a month at Lycos's Armenian branch, but in the UK they were paid ten, sometimes fifteen times more. Hrair would later tell Na from his own experience that the tech professionals in both Europe and Armenia would be considered middle class, but their buying power and quality of life weren't comparable. Young IT couples in Yerevan could afford to move out from their families' homes and rent an apartment on their own, and they could purchase cameras and laptops. But they didn't have access to health insurance since it didn't widely exist. And they couldn't buy a car, with so few imports, or an apartment, which were exorbitantly expensive, priced for foreigners.

"Doesn't it bother you?" Thom asked.

"Of course, it's a messed-up system," Seyran replied. Na was astonished, not only that Seyran knew this information, but also by how he was speaking. He was usually apolitical.

When Thom criticized the sons of the owner of Hotel Havlabar for never participating in the cleanup after meals, refusing to bring their dirty dishes to the kitchen, Seyran chimed in, "Armenian society is patriarchal like that, too. It makes me so angry." Na looked at him. Though he'd done her dishes when she was down with the flu, and he had been pretty good about sharing the cleaning when they first moved in together, now there were always sinkfuls of dirty dishes—if Na didn't do them, he certainly wouldn't. It was obvious to her that he wanted to impress Thom, but she didn't know why. Maybe he was out of his element—the first time outside of Armenia, trying to measure up to a very tall white man. Or maybe he really *did* want to have sex with him.

Na and Seyran spent a few evenings exploring the city with Thom, including their last night at a Spanish restaurant. He told them over glasses of sangria that he was happy to have their company. His friend who had lived in their room had moved out a month before, leaving him lonely. She was an American who had been married to a Georgian man, but it didn't work out because of the cultural differences—he couldn't accept her independent Western ways. After six months, she split up with him and wound up at Hotel Havlabar.

Na worried as he told this story that she was walking into a similar trap. But the woman had found a way out, and she supposed that she would, too, if necessary. Besides, Seyran wasn't some sexist old-country villain, Na told herself. He was a weird mix of things: a boy, a man, an artist, a tech nerd, a son, a lover. Bisexual, gay, and straight. A rebel and a survivor. Mostly, he was a question mark.

META-WRITING:

Leaving Armenia and going to Tbilisi—getting out of the bubble—was a window into our relationship. We were forced to operate as a team with only each other for support. Language shifted, and then we shifted. Now I understand how much of what we had experienced was a preview of our future life in the U.S.: All he wanted to do was shop, and I wanted to go to museums. Unfortunately, I didn't see Seyran's behavior with Thom—his political presentation shaped by what he perceived Thom to be—as a warning flag. Instead, I relished having new experiences with Seyran. It was a way for us to reconnect after his infidelity with the skinny boy, another opportunity for me to get distracted from my concerns.

After Seyran told me about kissing the boy, we had sex. I wanted to know that he still loved me. I kept imagining Seyran with the skinny boy in the hallway squeezing his ass, which was kind of hot, but also disturbing. Seyran came, but I didn't, so as he fingered me, I imagined being with a woman, something that I used to do while having boring sex with a man, but hadn't done with Seyran until now. I think I wanted to reconnect with my gay side now that he had.

Afterward, we did our laundry at his mother's place to prepare for our trip. She made dinner while we sorted our lights and darks, added soap, waited for the cycle, then packed the wet clothes in bags to hang up to dry in our hallway at home.

I'm not sure what I was thinking, bringing my dirty underwear over to Seyran's parents' house and pretending that everything was normal. Yes, of course, I was in denial. But I might have thought of it as trying to let go, like Dink releasing his Armenian rage.

It was in Tbilisi, the night that we got drunk with Thom, that Seyran asked me if I would marry him. I don't remember how he asked it, where we were, or what we said. There was no ring, no getting down on one knee. I just know that I agreed to it, and by the time we were back in Yerevan, it had been decided. It wasn't so much a romantic idea but a practical one. Ever since he told me on New Year's Day that he didn't want to do anything that would make me uncomfortable, including getting married, we had been discussing the options of getting him a student visa or a tourist visa, but we realized both options held too many uncertainties. Marrying seemed like the surefire way to go. In Tbilisi, in our own compact orb, it seemed we belonged together. I was used to him—even if I didn't understand him, I couldn't imagine my life without all the questions his presence posed.

JOURNAL: DECEMBER 1, 2010
ASTORIA

We had sex. For the first time in months. It was good; I came.

While I'm living with him, I may as well have sex, right?

I had been away for a week, visiting my family for Thanksgiving, but he didn't want to go with me. When I returned, the house was clean. My standards are so low now that I'm attracted to him if he washes the dishes.

Anyway, he called me the next day, and we decided to meet in Flushing for dinner. We went to an Asian food court in the mall. I ordered hand-pulled noodles, and we shared them with stinky tofu and scallion pancake. He was being sweet, and when we were walking back to the subway, holding hands, he told me that he wasn't friends with someone he had met at the yoga studio anymore because she wanted to have sex with him.

"Why didn't you have sex with her?" I asked.

"I didn't want to," he said.

My shrink thought it had to do with me, suggesting that Seyran was choosing our connection over others, but I didn't think so. Today I was telling her how things seem to be improving with Seyran, but that I am keeping my guard up. I want to protect what I resolved back in October when I saw him with the regular Asian girl on their bicycles—to get him his citizenship and split up.

My therapist is also encouraging me to explore my own interests as a way to put myself first. So after our session, I went to a women's writing salon, run by a colleague from grad school. Even though I empathize with the sexism these women are battling in their careers, I have mixed feelings about the group because it is usually upper-class, predominantly white, very privileged. As we went around the room introducing ourselves, I felt it was something of a competition, a measuring up, and I couldn't help feeling less-than. Tonight I was interested in the speaker, however, so I decided to check it out again.

Before the talk, people were socializing around a food table, and I found myself meeting a white woman with a slight twang of a southern accent. Her name was Carrie, and she was based in Delhi, India. "I followed my husband," she explained.

"You must be having culture shock, coming back here," I told her.

"I just moved to India two weeks ago, so it's the other way around. I'm back in New York for a gig I'd booked long ago." It turned out she was a performance artist, which made me hope that she wasn't like the other snobby ladies. We briefly exchanged notes about our work, and then a third woman approached, whose name I couldn't remember.

"You're friends with Elif," I said, referring to a Turkish woman I had met at the salon before.

"Yes, and you're Armenian," was her reply. I didn't take this as an unusual marker for me, since it was significant that Elif and I had connected despite our estranged cultures.

And then Carrie asked me, "So you're Armanian?" She pronounced it to rhyme with "Jordanian," with a long a, instead of a long e as it's spelled and usually pronounced in English. I've always found this way of pronouncing the word troubling, though the long e sound isn't Armenologically correct, either, as Armenians pronounce it with a short e, as in *let*. Not to mention that *Armenian* is derived from a French word. Armenians call themselves Hye.

"My parents live in LA and have good friends who are Armanian."

And? "That's nice," I said.

"They've been going back there," she said.

"Armeenia is wonderful, but it can be a difficult place for people to visit," I told her. I was thinking of the culture clash in India that she had described.

Our conversation continued to stumble along when she suddenly announced,

"Armenians are very clannish. They don't want to socialize with anyone else, and they marry only each other."

I looked at her. Here was a prompt to say, "What?" or "Why are you telling me this?" or "Not all Armenians are like this," or "There are reasons, historically and sociologically, that new immigrant groups have been insular in hostile environments," or "Judging by this this room, it appears that white women are very clannish and socialize only with each other." But instead, I was stumped. The salon started, and I sat in my chair fuming, unable to listen. I left at the break.

When I came home, the apartment was dark. I figured Seyran was in bed, so I quietly took off my shoes in the hallway, went to my bedroom, and turned on my computer. It was 10:14. Seyran had emailed me at 10:13.

> *Hi sweetie,*
> *I'm not coming home tonight, I'm staying at a friends house.*
> *Wishing you gentle sleep,*
> *Seyran*

And so, I was right to not let my guard down.

I burst into tears.

It is too hard, living in NYC, trying to survive spiritually, intellectually, artistically, and financially, and living with Seyran, whom I am supposed to be breaking up with but just had sex with, and he isn't a New Yorker at all, and he isn't Armenian at all, and I don't understand him at all, and no one understands what I am trying to understand, either.

I'm upset that I let my guard down, even if it was partially up.

I wondered why he fucked me. *Because he's attracted to someone else? Is this why he cleaned the apartment?* To stop my mind from looping, I went to bed at 10:30. But then I kept getting up to write Seyran emails that said, "I hate you," "Don't come home," "I used to think people were fundamentally good, but I don't anymore because of you." I sounded crazy, so I kept the emails in my draft folder. This enraged me even more, so I went to his room, grabbed his crap, and threw all of it down the stairs. Admittedly, there wasn't much to throw: the rugs, his shoes, his pillow, and blanket. I saw it all there strewn on the stairs, looking like the work of a disturbed person. I went back to bed, but my heart was beating so hard, I decided to clean it all up.

Somehow, I fell asleep. The next morning, I was at my computer writing and elaborating on all of the above when he came into my room, trying to kiss me, and I recoiled. I told him I was upset that he hadn't come home last night.

"What," he said, "I emailed to let you know!"

He wanted me to make a plan with him for the day. Last night, I had vowed to myself not to spend any more time with him. But he wanted to eat and do the laundry, and I had no other plans. Stupidly, I rationalized that I did indeed need to do these things. And I guess I needed answers, I couldn't let go. I blame my therapist for planting a seed. Why couldn't she affirm me, why couldn't she just tell me to step away?

As we walked to Sunnyside to find lunch, I told him about the white women's salon from last night, wondering what he would think about me not saying anything to challenge a stereotype of Armenians.

"She was a stupid woman. What does it matter?" he asked.

We went to a new Thai restaurant. It was a nice place, but as we were sitting down, he said that he didn't have any money and that I would have to pay. This set me off. He sensed it and told me to smile, so I let him have it.

"I can't stand being with a person who takes advantage of me, not coming home all night so I don't know where he is. It makes me doubt everything: that you cleaned the house and had sex with me not because of me, but because of someone else."

"That's crazy. You're making up stories."

"Whatever. I'm going home. No free lunch for you." I walked out the door, leaving the menu unopened, and he followed. As we walked home, I queried him.

"So where were you when you didn't come home all night?"

"Let it go, Natalee. Drop it," he said.

"Why won't you tell me?"

"I told you, I need to feel free. You get to go and do whatever you want, and I want to do that, too." He was referring to my trip to visit my family for Thanksgiving, but he hadn't even wanted to come with me.

So I struck back. "Like you haven't done whatever you want already? And who says that I'm so free? Last time I checked, paying for everything, including your citizenship, isn't exactly doing whatever I want."

We walked home in silence, and as soon as we arrived, he jumped into the shower while I continued to fume. I stood outside his door. "You're so fucked up because you come from a fucked-up society. You're taking advantage of me, and you lie so much you don't even know the difference between truth and lying anymore." I stormed off to the kitchen.

He came out of the bathroom, towel around his waist. "You're generalizing, too. The same as that white woman. Why did you get so upset when she told you about Armenians? How are you any different?"

I was stumped. I didn't know how I was different.

I knew he was deflecting responsibility as usual, but he happened to be right: thinking he is fucked up and feeling guilty for not helping him are rooted in the same prejudice. I don't see him as capable enough to take care of himself, and I am attracted to our codependent closed loop because I have never seen us as being part of the same world. His appeal has always been that of the other: unknown, mysterious, alien—and Armenian.

12. SORRY ABOUT THE VIOLENCE

BLOG POST: MARCH 5, 2007
YEREVAN

A Cup of Sugar? >>> He screamed for about ten seconds straight. Not a word; a scream. *"AAAAAAAAAAH!"*

I had heard loud voices emanating through the floor a couple of times before, but not like this. Heavy objects were being thrown, knocked to the floor, violence steadily escalating. Seyran and I agreed: someone was being beaten, and it sounded like the woman.

"So what should we do? Call the police?"

"Baby, the police won't come."

"Let's go up there."

"He's a maniac, he'll go crazy."

"We could get the neighbors together. They must hear it, too."

At that moment, we heard someone coming up the stairs. Seyran watched through the peephole as our next-door neighbors went inside their apartment, barely inclining their heads toward the sound of domestic insanity above.

I paced around. "I'm going to see Tanya tomorrow. I'll ask her what to do."

"You don't have a brain to think yourself?" Seyran asked, his sudden attack startling me.

"Yes, I can think for myself." I stopped, looked directly at him, voice hardening. "But I don't know about resources here. Do you know what to do about domestic violence?"

"What's domestic violence?" he asked.

It's a calm, clear-minded legal term for when someone in your family kicks the shit out of you.

"It's when people get beat up in their homes," I said.

"Yes, I know about it," he said.

I didn't ask how; I already knew he'd been on the other end of a beating. My voice softened. "So is there a shelter here? In the U.S., there are places women can go to get help."

"They don't have that in Armenia."

I paced around the living room as we continued to discuss what we could or couldn't do, and then I suddenly opened the door and went up the stairs. I thought I would know what to do once I got there. We knew the man; we once paid his gas bill by mistake, and he'd been amiable about paying us back. I hoped that when I saw the man, and he saw me, he would realize what he was doing and would stop.

But Seyran grabbed me before I could get past the fourth step and pulled me back into our apartment.

"Natalee, what are you doing? You crazy? He's a maniac, he could hurt you."

So I took a deep breath and stayed in the apartment, waiting for the sounds to stop.

✣

It turns out that there *is* a domestic violence women's shelter in Yerevan. A couple of days later, Tanya gave me a card with their hotline and a booklet about the shelter. She said there was room for six women, and it was almost always full. If you called them, they'd advise you on when to make your escape, feed you and your kids, give you counseling, and get you a lawyer if you need a divorce. She said they did good work, contrasting it to another shelter, now closed, that aimed to return abused women to their husbands. The abusive husband was typically advised that his wife was nervous and needed to take a break; his problems were not addressed.

Later that day, Seyran and I were walking out of our building to go to the post office when a young woman walked up the stairs carrying a baby. She wore a baseball cap, hair in a ponytail, head down. I mouthed to Seyran, "Is that her?" He nodded.

When we reached the bottom of the stairs, I told him that I would go back and give her the number and pamphlet for the shelter.

"Don't do that," he told me. "It will upset her."

"It's going to upset her more than being beaten up?" I snapped.

I marched up the stairs, only to suddenly feel scared and stupid. What was I going to tell her when I met her? Maybe she had already made it to her apartment and her husband was home.

When I came back down to the street, I told Seyran that I would give it to her later.

"She doesn't need that number. She can go to her family if she needs help," he suggested.

"You think she's going to tell her family?" I asked.

"She may not be getting beaten," he tried again.

"No, they might only be arguing, but just in case she is, she'll have the number. And I'll feel better," I said. I didn't want any harm to come to her because I had failed to act.

"Even if you give it to her and she is getting beaten, she probably won't use it."

"How do you know?"

"Because she's Armenian. An Armenian woman won't go to that place."

"Then how do you explain the shelter always being filled with Armenian women?"

We arrived at the PO at this point. They had left a notice at our door to retrieve a package, and I couldn't go by myself because I didn't know the two to four sentences needed to ask for it or how to fill out the slip of paper they required.

On the way back home, Seyran said, "You don't know what you are doing—this is Armenia, not America. Instead of giving her the number, go up there and talk to her."

"But I can't speak Armenian," I protested.

"I think she might know English. You can talk to her, bring her chocolate, ask her how you can help."

"I don't want to get involved like that. I just want to give her the phone number." I couldn't understand why he was against giving a phone number to someone who might need it.

At home, I sat next to him on the sofa by his perch in front of the computer and showed him the booklet Tanya had given me, thinking we could go upstairs together.

"This isn't a good place," he said. "They get money from the government."

"No, they get money from a Swedish women's nongovernmental organization." I pointed to their logo.

"You don't know if it's a good place."

"No, but it's the only shelter in Armenia, and Tanya knows the woman who runs it." I'd had enough of his pushback. I stood up and walked toward the door. "I'm not listening to you anymore. I thought we could do this together, I thought you could help me, but you're the same as any other Armenian; you don't want to change anything."

I marched up the stairs, bringing a cup with me to have the pretense of asking for sugar. I lingered outside the door, listening to hear his voice, when I noticed the peephole darkening. Someone was looking out. I rang the buzzer; it was him.

"Do you have sugar?" I asked in Armenian. I held out the cup.

He called to his wife and opened the door wider. He was smiling, perfectly friendly.

"No," she called from the other room, "very little." I couldn't see her.

"You have sugar," he insisted from over his shoulder.

"No, we don't."

As they were debating whether they had sugar, I looked at the baby, a girl of about one and a half, standing in a white, dingy onesie, looking up at me strangely. I did not smile at her and say hello, like I normally would with children this age. Instead, I looked at her with concern. Such a little thing.

"I'm sorry," I said in Armenian, and I went back down the stairs.

Seyran was waiting inside the door, where he had been listening, and he was laughing. "You asked for sugar?"

I hated him for laughing at something that was serious. I put on my jacket and ran out the door, my adrenaline rushing, and he followed. I was so livid that I pushed him, saying, "I want to be alone now." His smile disappeared as he wordlessly turned around.

I immediately felt terrible, so I ran after him, catching up to him across the street. We walked along quietly, then talked about our day, choosing not to speak about the couple upstairs.

I never gave her the number. For a while I thought I would slip it under her door, but Seyran said the man might take his anger out on her if he found it, and I feared he was right.

That was a couple of weeks ago, and we haven't heard fighting since then. The other day, she knocked on our door when she was locked out of the house with her other child, a little boy of five or six, so we invited her in to wait until her husband returned. Perhaps she was coming to us since I had made contact before. She spoke to Seyran since she, in fact, didn't know English. I noted that she seemed emotionally stable. She was very tall and looked strong; I thought she could take her husband in a fight or at least hold her own.

I'd like to think my presence made a difference, that it forced the man to realize others were watching, but that seems hopeful at best and selfish at worst. In any case, the woman seems braver than I; perhaps she was checking us out to see if we could be of any help.

Now that the troubles have subsided, I have been wondering why I wasn't concerned about her children but focused only on her. Seyran and I had never discussed the safety of the children. It was always "he and she." Perhaps we saw the couple as our shadows.

Not having Seyran's support to intervene deeply troubled me. I didn't have enough language to proceed on my own, and it made me feel alone and powerless. I felt that if something happened to the woman, I would have only myself to blame. Perhaps it's because a part of me worries that I am not being responsible for myself.

META-WRITING:

I am surprised by what I posted on the blog in 2007. As I became more dependent on the relationship, the more I lost my self-esteem. I needed an outlet to process, inevitably revealing my struggles online to my imagined audience in America.

When I went to Yerevan in 2010, I went even further, describing to the women in my workshop what I was physically experiencing in my relationship:

> ... I'm not sure when he first picked me up. Off the ground. It was a playful gesture, early in our relationship, but I was aghast. Um, no, I thought. Put me down. That's not right. I was a grown woman, and this lifting was being done without my consent ...
>
> ... After a while, I thought maybe it wasn't a bad idea to lose a sense of control periodically, even if I were a woman. When he wrestled with his friend, I saw how he liked to be picked up off the ground, so I stopped protesting so much.
>
> ... I don't remember when I first hit him, but it happened within the first

few months that we lived in New York ... He was still picking me up, but it
became less playful and more controlling in the middle of arguments. Then
he sat on top of me or pinned down my hands so that I could not move. One
time he sat on my face, and I suffocated against his underwear ...

... He never hit me, but I hit him. I had experience with it from childhood,
a behavior lying dormant all these years. I lashed out at him with my fists
because he had picked me up and whirled me around and sat on top of me; a
physical vocabulary was already part of our language. This was no excuse; I
hated when I couldn't control my emotions and worried about the results ...

*I did a reading of this text with the workshop in Yerevan, published it, then went on to use parts
of it in a performance in Milan, Italy. Though I had friends in New York in whom I could confide
at the time, I chose to never say a word to them about what I was going through. It was easier to
reveal the violence I had experienced later on to the public in Armenia (and Italy). It was a complete
reversal of how I had felt with my blog three years earlier.*

*The odd thing was that whenever and wherever I revealed our history with violence, I always
ran it by Seyran, and he always approved it.*

JOURNAL: DECEMBER 10, 2010
ASTORIA

Seyran has a ritual of calling his parents on Skype on Saturday mornings. There is
no set time, and he never tells me when he's about to call them, but he expects me
to be available to chat. This morning, I was descending the stairs of our apartment
in my down coat and woolen hat—I was on my way to rehearsal—when he ran into
the hallway with his laptop, his parents on the screen.

We were standing underneath the skylight at the top of the stairs. He asked
me to say hello, so I blew his parents a kiss. Laughing, he slapped me on the top
of my head. Trying to divert attention away from his shenanigans, I told them it
was very cold. His mother asked, "Why isn't Seyran dressed warmly?" I told her
no, I meant that it was cold outside.

Just then, Seyran said something in Armenian, then told me to repeat it to
his parents. It was a long sentence, and I didn't understand it, and I didn't know
how I would be able to say it.

"No," I told him.

"Yes, just say it," he said, repeating it over my shoulder.

"What does it mean?" I asked, but he wouldn't tell me and insisted that I say it. I didn't like how he was being so controlling, so I ignored him, smiled, and asked his parents, "How is Aragats?"—the mountain where I visited them in the summer, where we picked flowers to make his mom's special tea.

"C'mon, say it!" Seyran whispered. His mom must have seen something in my face and asked if I was sad. Seyran looked at me inquisitively, and I started to cry. He turned the computer away. "What's wrong with you?" he asked.

I trundled down the stairs and made it out the door, waving back at the computer screen.

Nothing horrible had happened, so I wasn't sure why I had cried. It was probably the pressure to speak Armenian, which is a sore spot from childhood, feeling coerced to perform something I can't do or be. I took a deep breath and walked to the studio ten blocks away.

My rehearsal went well. I can't believe I am being commissioned to do this piece for a gallery in Milan. The curator was looking for an Armenian performance artist, and my name came up. I haven't done a performance in a while and find memorization difficult—I'd rather read—so I've created a crown of wire to mount a scroll of paper on my head. The scroll contains a story about the time in Yerevan when Seyran and I could hear the couple upstairs fighting. The other part of the performance involves stories about the violence between me and Seyran, which I perform inside of a makeshift broom-and-bedsheets tent with revolving family photos projected onto the walls. Going through the motions, figuring out the choreography and all the pieces of text and image, is somehow a comfort even if the topic is difficult.

Seyran came to meet me for lunch when I was done. As we were walking down the street to the bus stop, he asked, "Why did you cry when you were talking to my parents?"

"Because I didn't know what you wanted me to say, and it upset me."

"You're not supposed to get depressed when you talk to them."

"I was happy to talk to them, but you kept wanting me to say something, and I didn't know what it was. If someone did that to you, you wouldn't do it."

"If you did that to me, I would say the joke," he said.

A joke? I thought. *He wanted me to tell them a joke?*

"I'm never calling my parents again when you're home," he said.

He was obviously upset, so I tried to speak to him as evenly and as kindly as I could. "I'm sorry, I didn't want to be a puppet. I still don't know what the joke was. What is it?"

"I'm not telling you," he said.

Perhaps it was because I had been working on a piece about violence, or perhaps it was because I had reached the end of my rope, but I exploded in rage. "FUCK YOU!" I yelled. "I WANT TO BE IN ON THE JOKE!"

The streets are usually desolate in this part of Queens where industrial buildings infringe upon a low-income immigrant neighborhood. A guy happened to be walking by at the time, so Seyran laughed and said I was crazy. He couldn't lose face with a woman in front of a man, even a stranger.

We abruptly separated, splitting off like opposing magnets. I made my way home and started writing in my journal. Not five minutes later, he came home, clattering around in the kitchen, making something to eat.

The next few hours were a crazy blur. I didn't know what to do with myself, so I lay on my bed, trying to have my interior space. I was thinking of my grandmother, whom I had referenced in the performance:

> My father never hit me, and he never hit my mother ... he would only hit
> my brother because he wanted to "make a man" out of him, so I figured
> my father had been beaten like this by his own father. I wonder if my
> grandfather hit my grandmother, too. No, he was too aware that she had
> survived a genocide in her childhood. She'd seen enough violence for one
> lifetime — or maybe twenty. This violence she spewed upon her family,
> yelling, screaming, saying cruel things. Like me, she was a small woman
> from whom no one would expect such behavior. Perhaps I should have been
> wondering all this time if she had hit him.

I am failing with this disturbed relationship. I am supposed to move on from this troubled pattern.

At some point, Seyran came into my room and ordered me out of bed.

"Wipe the table," he commanded me. I stood there, lacking the energy to tell him not to order me around. "Wipe the table, Natalee," he repeated, as if I were a child. Emotionally bereft, I complied: I wiped the table and sat down. He spooned aloo gobi that he had cooked onto a plate in front of me. Then he stood on the chair across from me and squatted down on his haunches in front of his own plate, and he used his fingers to eat. He was only in his underwear, so he was really a sight— all this bright-yellow food dripping down his fingers and covering his bloated lips, his furry chest.

"You look gross," I told him. I went to my room and grabbed my camera to take a picture of him squatting on his chair in his underpants. He laughed and immediately stood up. He didn't want other people to see him like this—just me. "You look like an animal," I told him.

He grabbed a fork and retreated to his room.

He never eats in his room. So I felt bad for lashing out at him. "Thank you for the food," I said to the curtain hanging in the doorway. No response. Indian music was playing.

"Sorry I yelled at you on the street."

I tried to tell him again why the incident with his parents upset me so, but he played the Indian music louder. I went to lie down in my room and cried again.

It was his turn to circle back. He stood in my doorway and said in a determined tone, "You keep protecting yourself from me, but this is coming from you. I don't want to hurt you, so it has nothing to do with me. I feel sorry for you that you keep doing it. I'm sorry, I won't make a joke with you with my parents again. That's all I have to say."

He was right, I did protect myself from him. I was right to do so, when he didn't treat me respectfully—when he didn't come home at night but expected me to be available for him. Even when he slapped me on the head when I least expected it.

"So what was the joke?" I asked him.

"That is all I have to say," he repeated. "Do you want to do the laundry now?"

Any reasonable person would have said no and given up on this insane dance. But I was beyond reason, still crying, pulled in too many directions. Through my fractured mind, he looked like he was moving closer to normalcy than I was, and I wanted to regain my bearings.

After putting the wash in at the laundromat on the corner, we walked to Little Egypt for a falafel, but then he revealed he had to be somewhere soon. There wasn't enough time for him to dry and fold and get the laundry home. I was going to be stuck with it. I railed at him for using me, sneering that this was why I protected myself from him.

"Why don't you come with me?" he interjected.

"Where?"

"To pooja."

"No way!" I told him.

"Why not?"

"Are you going out afterward?"

"Yes, so?"

"Are you meeting someone?"

"No," he said, shaking his head.

I knew it wasn't a good idea to go with him. But I couldn't help it—the writer in me emerged, seeking answers. I wanted to see this place where he has been practicing yoga every day and that inspired his performance at the kitchen table earlier. We took the wet laundry home and got on the subway.

The studio was in Soho on Broome Street and was very lovely with bright yellow walls, white-stenciled wooden window motifs, and shrines to Hindu gods. Hanuman the monkey god appeared in a series of framed prints along the top edge of every wall.

The ceremony had already started: an Indian guru in a red robe was pouring water over Ganesh. Then milk. His young son, about eight or nine years old, periodically left his backpack and homework sprawled in the corner of the room and handed him the ingredients to prepare the shrine. We sat on the shiny hardwood floor with about fifteen other people and sang, accompanied by a man on a sitar. The chanting reminded me of the Badarak, and I realized Seyran hadn't really experienced it since most worship in the Armenian Church had been snuffed out by the Soviets. Perhaps the pooja was his first religious practice.

Near the end of the evening, we marched around the space behind the statue of Ganesh, which was now bedecked with flowers and herbs and perched atop a stretcher. We made three rounds of the studio, and then the Indian man sprinkled holy water into our hands with a spoon. I put it on my face, but Seyran said I was to drink it. He said it would help to heal me. I did feel calmer by the end of the experience, by the colors and the chanting, by watching the process of devotion. By the ritual.

On my way home, alone, on the subway, with Seyran off to who knows where, I thought about my performance and why I need to make a ritual out of my personal life. As much as I want to end this relationship, it fuels my writing. What would I create if I didn't endure such destruction?

STORY: MARCH, 2007
YEREVAN

The performance artist from England wrapped himself in two flags. One was the Armenian flag and the other was the Union Jack, both of which he wove around his loins, gyrating his hips. He spoke directly to the audience, asking why there were no Jews in Armenia, what were Armenians smoking themselves to death for, and where were the gay people? When the minister of culture shut down the second and last night of the performance, she issued a statement that the British performance artist "may treat the British flag as he likes. He can drop it on the floor, step on it, chew it, or swallow it, but it is unacceptable and punishable by law to treat the Armenian flag that way."

The minister's words and action caused a furor among the avant-garde artists, who saw it as censorship. Mardi, Gharib, and a few other artists drafted a letter of petition. When Na received it in her email, she noticed there weren't many signatures. She wondered if Mardi's confrontational nature was the issue, if he'd alienated one too many people. They may have also had an issue with the British performance artist: who was he to criticize Armenians after visiting for a week? Without seeing the performance, it was hard for Na to contextualize the lack of response to Mardi's petition.

In any case, Seyran refused to sign it, and when Na made plans to meet with Mardi to learn more, Seyran was adamant that he wouldn't join her.

Seyran even tried to dissuade Na from seeing Mardi by claiming that Mardi was using her. Na didn't see any evidence that this was true. It's not like her signature would have a particular impact. Rather, she wondered if Seyran was worried that *he* was the one using her. She thought he probably wasn't aware enough, projecting his insecurities onto Mardi instead.

"I like Mardi," she said. "He's politically minded, and he says interesting things. I don't mind that he's a little unpredictable."

"Honey, it's worse than that. Kristapor told me one night they stayed at his friend's house, and when the friend came home, they had been fighting with knives, and their clothes were ripped."

"I don't believe it." To Na this claim sounded like scurrilous gossip.

"Yes, it's true. Besides, Mardi's crazy, and I'm crazy, and you can only have one crazy person in your life," Seyran joked.

Na shook her head. "I haven't seen either of them in a while. You don't have to come if you don't want."

They were standing outside their building on Heratsi Poghots when Gharib pulled up in a taxi. When he implored Seyran to come too, Seyran gave in, probably to keep watch on Na.

On the way, Gharib informed Seyran and Na that Shant, one of the intellectuals in their circle, had written a nasty letter to Mardi, calling him a fascist on the Armenian Activists online discussion group. Gharib said, "It is a purely personal attack and completely uncalled for."

They picked up another person on the way, Arsineh, a sociologist. She was a small woman in her thirties, wearing chunky hipster glasses. She had a quiet manner of speaking, which Na found comforting as they settled into the living room of the house where Mardi and Gharib were staying. Since they couldn't afford rent, and they needed space to be together, they took the opportunity to house-sit whenever it arose. The style of the home was eclectic, befitting the owner, a filmmaker who was away in Europe. Artwork covered every surface of the walls, which were painted in vivid colors of crimson and cerulean. The group greeted Mardi, who was preparing dolma in the kitchen nearby, and Na was content to be in their warm company. But then Mardi overheard something Arsineh said to Gharib, and he came out of the kitchen with a dish towel over his shoulder, spoon in hand, with a red face barking something in Armenian at Arsineh. She answered him, and he went ballistic, yelling at her even louder, screaming at her at the top of his lungs. Na had seen his ire at community artists' meetings before, but this response was off the charts.

Na asked Seyran what was going on. It seemed that Arsineh was commenting on the nasty letter from Shant, suggesting that it was in response to Mardi's language, offensive to the people he was trying to reach. The argument soon escalated, with both Gharib and Mardi screaming at Arsineh. Seyran gave Na an "I told you so" look, and Na now felt stupid. She announced, in English, "Your screaming is violent and disturbing."

Gharib turned to her and apologized while Mardi continued to harangue Arsineh. "Maybe it would be better if we were at least yelling in English so you could understand what was going on," Gharib said. Na chuckled and nodded. All she could take in was the sound of their voices, the angry expressions on their faces. Arsineh would say something calmly, and then one or both of them would rant at her. A couple of times, Arsineh lost her cool, raising her voice, too. In the midst of it, Seyran played the guitar to calm everyone down. As their hosts brought out the dolma and lavash, Na asked Arsineh, "Doesn't it bother you when they're yelling at you like that?"

"Yes!" she exclaimed.

Mardi returned with a plate of olives. "Why don't you ask me why I am yelling at her?"

"Because you're upset," Na told him, shrugging him off.

When the argument wouldn't cease, Na nodded her head toward the door and said to Seyran, "Let's go."

As they put on their jackets, Gharib explained their reaction. "It's so hard to believe that people who you assumed thought the same way you did, educated people, are saying that maybe it's good to have nationalists to keep Armenia from disappearing. That they're afraid of Turkey and Azerbaijan. And that maybe it was a good idea to have the war for Karabakh."

As Na and Seyran were saying their goodbyes at the door, Mardi said, "Sorry about the violence."

❖

A few days later, Na and Seyran ran into Gharib. It was late, but they invited Gharib back to their place.

"Vonc es?" Na asked Gharib as they walked. *How are you?*

"Oh, I was depressed today. And I feel lonely. It takes so much effort to explain my thoughts to people who should otherwise understand me."

His feeling of isolation reminded Na of how she had responded when Seyran wouldn't join her cause to rescue the woman upstairs from domestic violence.

When they arrived at the apartment, Na made rice pilaf, a comfort food from her childhood, cooked by her mother and grandmother, which Eastern Armenians treated as an exotic delicacy. As they ate the salty, buttery rice, the starchy scent steaming their faces, Gharib apologized for the day of yelling. He explained just how violent Shant's words had been towards Mardi.

He went on to say, "It's too bad the artists' response to the minister of culture's action was not unified. Several writers and artists wrote articles and appeared on TV, but no one came together to discuss and illuminate the issue."

Na asked, "Do you think it's hard for people to be unified when unity was mandated for so long by the government?"

"Maybe," Gharib said. "But people have to forget those times and do what's right now."

Na now considered that Mardi and Gharib might have been the most sane people in Armenia. They were responding with rage, which was normal in this place that limited them, and their frustration stemmed from the confusion of why people were afraid to act. But people were interpreting frustration as intolerance, like the government they were fighting against.

"I think the people who are fighters—the outcasts, the weirdos, the intellectuals, the artists—have a strong instinct to rebel against everyone and everything, so it is very hard to find compatriots to trust, to join together," Na said.

"Ha. Yes. You are even describing me and Mardi."

Na looked at Seyran, who by now had finished his rice and taken out his guitar. He was playing a tune he had discovered recently, of Spanish inflection, and he stared into space as he played. Na wondered if Mardi and Gharib's rage at seemingly inactive intellectuals was their only frustration. Were they also frustrated with themselves? She thought that if it were only directed at the lack of a political response, they would have found a way to deal with it besides yelling. But maybe we were not ready to stop yelling yet.

META-WRITING:

I did not make a mistake in that last sentence, switching from third person to the first, we instead of they. The ugliness in our personal lives correlated to our lack of collective liberation. We all wanted to be understood so badly, so much so that we would scream and yell, huff and puff and get upset, demanding what our story should be. What would our personal lives look like if we stopped trying to control our loved ones' stories? In this book, the "Story" narrative written in third person has helped me to gain objective distance, but it is also an artifice that makes my truth feel locked in print, as if I'm somehow safer from judgment.

Likewise, with the blog and performance, I wanted to tell people what was going on, and I didn't want to tell people what was going on. In Milan, I told the story of domestic violence permeating my relationship with Seyran from inside a tent made of brooms and sheets. On the walls of the tent, I showed various images: my grandmother glaring at the camera, Seyran hugging me tightly from behind, and random photos culled from the internet of Armenian families. I periodically emerged from the tent reading from the scroll on my head, and I wandered around with the paper obstructing my view, finding my way, pushing at imaginary predators, hitting my butt with a wooden hanger, until I found myself beating a yorghan with a stick, laughing hysterically. I needed to do something physical as I brought out my private stories into the open to create a ritual.

Finally, I projected a recent video of a woman telling her sister's story of being beaten to death in her home. Zaruhi Petrosyan's husband and mother-in-law beat her up repeatedly. They battered her with frying pans. They strangled her with their bare hands, leaving thumbprint-shaped bruises on her neck. At her autopsy, doctors discovered that her fingers and knees were broken and her skull was crushed. When they discovered that neighbors had reported the crime to the police, the family tried to cover up their handiwork by throwing her body down the stairs so it would look like she had fallen.

Her husband had told her that because she was an orphan, no one would care about her; he said that he had a friend high up in the police force. The police ignored Zaruhi's many reports of abuse; they even falsified their report, claiming they spoke to her at 2 a.m. when the hospital recorded her time of death as 1 a.m.

This poor girl was tortured since she married in 2008. Once, she left her husband for two weeks and stayed with her only relative, her sister, and the whole time he called and threatened to kill her if she did not come home. And the police decided it was necessary to cover it up. Let's protect a psychopath because he is a man.

There have been countless stories like Zaruhi's, but she was the one victim of domestic violence that caught the public's attention. Perhaps because she was an orphan. Perhaps because she was beaten not only by her husband but by her mother-in-law. Society didn't have to exclusively condemn a husband for such violence but could also blame a woman. Previously, Armenia had a hard time owning up to its record on domestic abuse. This case marked progress, though it was tragic Zaruhi Petrosyan had to die so brutally for the truth to emerge.

Tanya once surmised to me that Armenia doesn't have a record of mass shooters exterminating people in public, or serial killers systematically butchering strangers to store in their freezers. Because we speak to each other so harshly, we let everything come out. There's always someone around to receive your rage. Neighbors don't do anything when they hear a woman's cries because it happens behind closed doors, within the family unit. The government is not motivated to stop it. Why take responsibility for the incredible pressures that poor living conditions and unfulfilled lives have put on families? Let them lash out at each other instead of tearing the corrupt government down. They even use the same language of shame with journalists and NGOs: don't tell the Europeans or the Americans about human rights violations, or we won't receive foreign investment. *How is this different from telling a woman not to contact the authorities about being abused lest your family look bad to others? Suffering for the good of your family, your country.*

Though I thought I could see the problems of society, I was also subject to those problems, as well as being vulnerable to my own madness. Instead of realizing that hurt was coming to me from the relationship, I believed I had taken it on so that I could write about it. However, it was only through writing about it that I could attempt to understand the complex mess it entailed.

I think about the moment when I cried while speaking to Seyran's parents. His mother could see our accumulating stress, the point when our troubles were revealed. It wasn't the picture Seyran wanted to project to his parents.

We never discussed whatever had happened to him as a child, even when I inserted these details into my performance:

> He has scars on his arms and face, and I am not sure where they came from. I asked when we were first getting to know each other, and I half-remember his stories about an apple knife slipping to explain the shiny, hairless gash in his forearm and roughhousing with his brother for the deep, narrow marks on his face. In New York, he got an eye piercing by the one near his eyebrow, covering it up.

I sensed that I should never pry. When he said I should give the woman upstairs chocolate and ask if she needed help, was it because I had not made it clear to him that I would listen and help him? Was it evident that I just wanted a simple fix, to give her the number and move on, and that I was wrapped up in my own American version of reality? After all, he was performing a persona he thought I would like. When he didn't affirm my reality, I was deeply disturbed. I was so upset with him for not wanting to give her the phone number of the shelter, but perhaps he couldn't imagine the shelter, an official entity, coming to her aid, when such a possibility hadn't been available to him when he had been abused by his family.

Meanwhile, Seyran didn't mind me writing about our violence on my blog and again in the women's workshop, perhaps because I was taking the blame for it: he was the one who had been abused as a child, but now he could appear powerful and I could be humiliated. A part of me hoped he would stop once I exposed the behavior. But maybe my writing about him gave him an excuse to not open up to me—why would he, when I would project his vulnerabilities to the world? Running the work by him gave him control, and perhaps his familial history with abuse was far worse than anything I could represent or imagine.

One last excerpt from my performance:

> I am visiting his family in Yerevan, three years after we moved to New York. His father has a knife, and he is pretending to throw it at his mother. Then there is the playful head push or the grabbing of her ear. She does not do anything like this to him. She pushes him away and announces that he must have been drinking.

I was reading what I saw as clues, and it never occurred to me that I should say something to his father, to his mother, or to him. I felt safer putting details like these into a performance rather than taking action. An audience watched and did not hold me responsible for my decision, providing tacit approval. Action would have entailed that I end the relationship. But I felt responsible for Seyran's emotional and physical abuse. Why?

I suppose when you grow up feeling responsible for the results of genocide, you feel responsible for just about anything. I felt responsible for losing my culture and heritage when the process of assimilation was already long in force, for two generations before I was born. I felt double guilt for losing my culture and for not wanting it back. As a child, America constantly sent messages that to be Armenian, to be brown and ethnic and foreign, was dirty and wrong, a weakness. As an adult, those layers slid against each other, obscuring some realities while clarifying others. I felt responsible for Seyran because I felt responsible for my family's history projected onto him.

When I couldn't speak Armenian to help my neighbor, when I couldn't repeat a joke in Armenian, I felt the disgrace of my failed identity—to help others, to be Armenian. It compounded over time, exacerbated by emotional abuse, and exploded into a snarl of emotion without warning. I became enraged and undone.

Even though I didn't leave him, my performance was not inconsequential. Something inside me shifted so that I eventually gained agency. Owning my family history with violence made a difference. Or it could be that silence must be transformed to language before it arrives at action, as Audre Lorde suggests.

A few days after we went to the pooja, while we were having dinner, Seyran said suddenly, "I have to go shave my sideburns now."

"What?" He didn't have sideburns as he shaved his face and entire head, monk style.

"That's what I told you to tell my parents the other day."

I imagined myself in my coat and hat, appearing on his parents' computer screen and announcing these plans with my stilted, recited Armenian. It was so absurd I laughed out loud.

"See?" he said.

It could have been an inside joke, or a belittling of my independence as masculine and unbecoming, but I didn't bother figuring it out. Seyran was putting on a performance of eating on his haunches, engaging in ritual to provoke me and to escape himself. He needed me to deliver the lines he couldn't say to his parents.

The next time Seyran's parents called and he told me what to say in Armenian, I said it, and they laughed. I saw the delight on their smiling faces, his father's knowing grin, his mother's startled giggle, distorted by the pixels of the computer screen. This time, the joke was more revealing. Seyran told me later that his father had called him a cabbagehead. In my halting Armenian, I had replied, "Like father, like son."

13. WOMEN'S MONTH

BLOG POST: *NEVER PUBLISHED.* MARCH 29, 2007
YEREVAN

Na: There Are No Gendered Pronouns in Armenian >>> The hairs on my chin are like pins, he told me. Sticking into his back when I hold him in bed, they grow at the edge of my lower-left jaw, on the underside, with a few stragglers down my neck. When I prop my head in my hand, I can feel them, rubbing against my thumb, not an unpleasurable sensation. But when they grow too noticeable, about an eighth of an inch, I remove them. My aunt bought me a magnified compact mirror so that I can avoid pulling out the finer ones, which, if plucked, will grow back thick and coarse. Apparently I have not mastered the technique, because a hearty new crop keeps coming in. Now there are perhaps twenty to thirty strands.

Seyran can't stand them. "Girls aren't supposed to have beards," he says. Truth be told, I am not exactly in love with them and have considered getting electrolysis, which is cheap and accessible here. But my chin hairs aren't something I think about too much, a problem for the back burner. Since I have been negligent in plucking them, Seyran has been mentioning them frequently, with great disdain, to the point that I am driven to write about the issue.

What is it about women having a little facial hair that unsettles men so much? Seyran calls me a boy. When I remind him that I wear matching outfits, put on earrings, and style my long hair in various arrangements, he balks, claiming that I'm not taking care of myself as much as I should. "Can you make your skin look like people know that you are taking care of it?" I'm baffled by this concern, especially when most people think I'm ten years younger than my age. To his credit, Seyran doesn't care that I have put on a few pounds or that I don't dye my gray hair. Still, I keep asking him, why does he care about my appearance so much? Shouldn't he care more about my mind? My health? My happiness? Whether I'm making valuable contributions to society?

Meanwhile, he wears the same pair of jeans practically every day—and a pretty rabiz pair at that—with the leather outline of a guy's head stitched along the front of one leg. Though I've told him that I don't favor these pants, I have not launched a lobbying campaign for their removal. I am not saying that I am more virtuous than Seyran, or even more mature. But as I have mentioned in previous posts, Seyran has been subject to people's judgments based on his appearance, and he is aware of the strict gender conformity of the city. So his disdain for my chin hairs and pores seems hypocritical. The divide of the genders is too strong here, perhaps even for a critical, questioning, intelligent person.

I can't blame it all on Armenia since sexism is a universal plague. Many men—straight, gay, and bi—have unexamined expectations of women's appearance. Not to get too Freudian, but women ultimately remind men of their mothers, who likely disappointed them as infants. When boys become men with their supposed superiority instilled, they think they have the right to judge all women's looks to their personal standards. Admittedly, gender constructs are a dictum that men have to conform to as well, but if women don't appear as expected, they upset the gender hierarchy, which men are invested in as the empowered class. When the media reinforces objectified images of women, men further buy into the sexist system. Here, ads for alcohol are directed at men and almost always use women's submissive, airbrushed bodies. Even for someone like Seyran who has advanced critical faculties, appearance is governed by a male sense of entitlement that women must please them on all levels.

To this end, Seyran has been suggesting that we do procedures together. The other day, we stepped into a discount store, looking at creams, scrubs, and moisturizers, and he found some face cream from Thailand, a thousand dram. I passed on it, but after we went to the next shop, he asked if I would go back by myself and get it for him. I returned and read the box: it contained ginseng and pearl powder and would soften as well as whiten. It came in a pretty, pink plastic compact with a gold pattern raised on the top, and the instructions in several languages explained how to apply it at night before bed or to use it as makeup foundation. I found his request odd, but I got it for him, figuring that he must have really wanted it.

It was ironic not just because he had been criticizing my supposedly mascu-line chin hairs. Earlier that evening, we had been to Beatris's writers' meeting, which discussed the publication of Seyran and Archig's lurid lyrics in her latest literary journal. Many bookstores had returned the journal because words like *dick* and *fuck* appeared in the titles. To quote one song: "I don't want to fuck you. I want to fuck cake. I don't want to lick you. I want to lick your friend. Take me to your neighbor, I'm gonna lick her cake. Give me all your money, I'm leaving you again."

Reactions varied: one man said they were meaningless trash. Another said they were the masterpieces of the entire journal for they used words and ex-pressions that people don't read in Armenian. No one said they were macho and sexist.

Beatris said they had a throwaway, spontaneous feeling, which you don't often see in printed Armenian language. She said that she had been trying to destroy lan-guage, that she knew all the rules and how to break them, but she was now jealous that these two young guys had done it so simply, honestly, and brilliantly.

I bristled at Beatris's response. Though I appreciate the freedom of ex-pression and absurdity in the lyrics, I don't cull much else from them. They seem dismissive of women, but it could be that I am not understanding the cultural references or context. Beatris has received a lot of attention for the use of jargon in her poetry, using this manner of vocabulary to shock an elite circle of readers. I wondered if she was saying that she had been overthinking her word choices. Something about this felt very familiar. Writers like Kerouac, Bukowski, and Hunter S. Thompson are rewarded for their hypermasculinity, even when it verges into absurdist, sexist nonsense, valued over the carefully chosen words of women ...

META-WRITING:

I need to interrupt this blog post to emphasize that it wasn't ever published. There are a few reasons, which will become evident, and one of them is truly ugly.

But the initial reason was that I couldn't publicly admit my criticism of Seyran's lyrics. It's easy to see in the blog that I was rationalizing his sexism. I always had an excuse for the misogynist ways he treated me—usually that he was young or Armenian. And I continued to believe that he was a sensitive, politically progressive person. As I grew aware that he wasn't who I had originally thought he was, I became ashamed that I had chosen such a partner.

It was March, Women's History Month. Its most relevant date, March 8, aka International Women's Day, had been initiated circa 1910 when socialist women in the U.S. and Europe sought to bring awareness to the rights of working women. During Soviet times, it was championed as a day to celebrate laborers. Everyone gets the day off in Armenia; it's a national holiday. But it has also devolved into a version of Valentine's Day, when men give gifts and flowers to women. Thus, as I struggled to square my values with my reality, I witnessed how an effort to honor women's power was replaced with frivolity.

STORY: MARCH, 2007
YEREVAN

On Maria's first day visiting Armenia, Na confessed to her friend some of her worries about Seyran while they toured the countryside in an old bus.

Na had already been on a few trips with this company, which brought locals to various spots within a day's journey from Yerevan. The clientele weren't foreigners but mostly middle-class locals who worked at the international tech firms, who had new disposable incomes and fancy cameras but not necessarily automobiles. It was a friendly affair, with the tour leader asking everyone to introduce themselves. Na knew enough Armenian to say her name and profession, and she did the same for Maria. Her friend's presence made her realize she wasn't completely incompetent at speaking Armenian.

As the bus traversed the rocky, unpaved roads, Na told Maria that Seyran had given her a sense of safety and a place in the community, and that she worried about the relationship not working in the U.S. given the problems they were already having—between their age difference and finances. She stopped short of telling Maria about the skinny boy Seyran had groped (or whatever he had done with him), explaining instead that she had arrived at a pivotal point when she had to decide if she would indeed marry him and bring him to the U.S. They were standing by Azat Reservoir, a desolate moon landscape, when Maria asked Na how she would feel if she left Armenia without Seyran. Would she feel guilty if she did?

Thinking out loud, Na told her, "Whether I bring him with me to New York or I leave him behind, my heart will be broken."

"That's so sad," Maria said. But Na had never thought of these choices as sad. Rather, they were simply a matter of the options available to her.

Maria was also in a difficult place, recovering from a breakup with a long-time partner. Before she arrived, she had emailed Na to say that she'd been dealing with the crisis by drinking, smoking, and cruising guys. As much as Na was happy Maria was visiting, she was nervous, not knowing what to expect from an odar friend under duress who seemed to be in Armenia to escape. While visiting the pit where St. Gregory the Illuminator had been thrown by King Trdat for fourteen years for being a Christian, Na told Maria the legend of the king turning into a boar. "A boar?! Give me a break!" Maria scoffed, and Na found herself looking around, making sure no pious Armenians would be offended.

The next two weeks involved more touring. According to the Armenian custom of hospitality, Na and Seyran put everything aside for their guest. They took her to Etchmiadzin, wandering through a few ancient churches, where she was only somewhat impressed. She perked up at Parajanov's museum. And she seemed to appreciate dinner at Seyran's parents', his mother serving small sparrows that Seyran's father had hunted. She didn't like the Persian hookah bar. But she was fascinated by the dead animals hanging in the butcher shop by Shuka Number 2. They took her to Garni, the only pagan temple left in Armenia, overlooking a gorge. When Seyran tried to engage her in discussing music, she became annoyed. "Look, I can't talk about music all day." But she enjoyed having lebni and young walnuts at a little restaurant nearby. On these expeditions, the next trip was planned, as if the current one wasn't good enough: Maria wanted to go to Jermuk, she wanted to go to Tbilisi, she wanted to go somewhere to have a vacation experience.

After a week or so, Na was worn out by playing the host. She noticed herself evaluating the success of each trip through Maria's eyes, even though she knew Maria's discontent likely stemmed from the desperate state she was in over her breakup. Regardless, she was hurt that Maria was morphing into a disgruntled American tourist. She was reminded of her student who had written an essay that questioned selfless hospitality, pointing out that making such sacrifices can become a burden that no one will ever admit, for there is an element of trying too hard to prove that Armenia is so wonderful. Hosting becomes not only a drain on time and energy but a psychic burden as well.

She imagined her return to the States: Would any of her other non-Armenian friends appreciate what she had come to learn from the people and the culture? Though she could have seen it as a worthwhile task to share Armenia with them, right now she didn't want to face those who might not understand, who would render her homeland invisible.

✳

One evening close to the end of Maria's trip, on Women's Day, Na and Seyran took her to Shamrock, a new Irish pub. It was a small dive where they ran into their friends, including Seyran's brother. When they introduced him to Maria, he said he'd seen her the day before smoking on Abovyan Street. It was probably because Maria was a visually vivid figure—in her fake fur vest and large bug-eyed sunglasses, she was cut out from the streets of Brooklyn and pasted incongruously among the high-heeled and pencil-skirted women of Yerevan.

"That's so funny!" Maria announced.

"You know, it's not surprising that he remembered you smoking," Na said. "Women generally don't smoke on the streets here because it's seen as wanton."

"Bfft!" Maria announced, her beer spewing from her mouth. "That's so backward!"

Na laughed in agreement. But secretly, part of her liked informing Maria that she had made a faux pas. Though she knew it was a ridiculous standard that Maria could not have known about, her schadenfreude at Maria's displacement could not be denied. At the same time, Na was disillusioned that she had adopted this attitude. Apparently, it wasn't only language that she had absorbed, but the culture of disdaining "the other," too.

At this moment, Seyran was poking Na's shoulder, demanding money for him and his brother to buy beer. "Bitch, give us dram," he said.

"I don't like how you're talking to me," Na replied, taken aback. She realized he was drunk, but he was misguided in flouting the customs of Women's Day by being a dick to her.

"Okay, fine then. Stay with your stupid friend," he sneered under his breath.

Maria and Na spent the rest of the evening discussing what was wrong with Seyran, surmising that he was jealous of the attention Na had been paying to Maria. The women eventually wandered home and were drinking tea when Seyran showed up a few hours later, completely drunk. He was holding a bouquet of rancid flowers that he had picked up off the street and threw them across the living room at Na. They hit her on the side of the head.

"Happy Women's Day," he said.

If Maria hadn't been there, Na would have thrown the putrid flowers right back at him, right in his face. Instead, she felt exposed. No one had seen the degree of Seyran's juvenile behavior toward Na before, and she couldn't separate it from herself: it was like his twisted, childish bouquet toss represented who she was as a person. She didn't consider how little he must have thought of her, or that she didn't deserve such treatment. The next morning, Maria told her, "When he did that, I felt really bad for you."

Na didn't know how to respond. She didn't want anyone feeling pity for her, least of all a friend.

JOURNAL: JANUARY 17, 2011
ASTORIA

When I wasn't rehearsing during my trip to Milan, I walked around the city, going to museums and churches—I saw *The Last Supper*—and at night I stayed in, reading and eating pasta at the apartment where I had been put up by the gallery since I didn't feel comfortable going out alone. The time I went to a café for breakfast in the Galleria, the oldest mall in the world, I felt awkward sitting alone with my cappuccino and brioche among the parties of tourists. I had every intention of eating out, looking up restaurants in guidebooks, stumbling upon countless places, only to peer inside and lose my composure, avoiding the scene of white tablecloths and waiters in formal waist jackets. But when I entered an Eritrean restaurant, dark with red walls and heavy curtains, it felt like home. The immigrant owner behind the counter took good care of me. It occurs to me now that this was the type of place Seyran was drawn to when we first arrived in

Queens. We gladly sampled food from Chinese, Tibetan, Nepalese, and Filipino immigrants at their humble establishments.

On my last night, my hosts from the gallery took me to an authentic Venetian restaurant, a Milan insider's secret. The gnocchi was soft and cheesy, sharp and slightly sticky, my teeth sinking so pleasurably into such delicious sustenance. It was so orally gratifying, verging on the sexual. Even the pasta I bought in the supermarket and made in the apartment tasted better than the pasta in the U.S. I would wolf it down, muttering, "Mm-hmm," as I ate. I hadn't had sex in a long time, and this was how my bodily pleasure manifested.

On one of the last days of my trip, I chatted with Seyran over Gmail, and he asked me if I'd had sex with a random stranger. It's all he wishes for me, but it doesn't have anything to do with what I want. If I should feel attracted to someone, his urging seems to jinx it, making me feel unwanted in general. I told him that his question made me feel bad, and—surprise!—he apologized.

When I came back from Milan and he welcomed me at home with dinner, we both had sex on the brain. It was strange to feel attracted to him, even with all the hurt he has caused me. We went into my bedroom, and he flipped me over, pulled down my pants, and played with my butt, squeezing it to and fro—a new technique. I told him I didn't care for it, and then he went inside me. I felt the backs of his forearms, and his muscles were so well defined, like stones up against his bones. His eyes went back into his head. It was very, very fast, faster than he had ever done it.

As we lingered in bed afterward, he said something about inviting lovers to the house as he had in the past. I didn't say anything, so he imitated me saying no, then continued to talk to himself. "Why?" he asked.

"It's too much," his imitation of me said.

I interrupted him. "You can have sex partners over after I move out."

"Oh, you're moving out?"

"Yes."

"When?"

"When you get your citizenship."

"You haven't told me this before."

"Yes, I have."

"So when will that be?"

"Probably within the next month. Soon. I'm scared, but it's the right thing to do," I said, partially to gauge his response.

"It's not scary," he said. "But do whatever you want."

"Will you stay here?"

"No, I'll go to Brooklyn," he said.

He hopped into the shower because, as it turned out, he was going out, I suppose to see one of the people whom he wanted to invite to the apartment. He said, "We can both move to Brooklyn."

I told him I was tired of living in New York, but I didn't know where I would go.

As he was stepping out of the shower, he said, "You seem confused and lost."

I didn't think that I was, but I filed his comment away until I was reminded of it the following night, at a party at Gharib and Mardi's apartment. Gharib had invited a bunch of people at the last minute to celebrate Mardi's birthday. I arrived about five minutes after everyone had yelled, "Surprise!"

Gharib asked me how things were going, and I told him my timeline: Seyran gets citizenship, and I move out. He nodded approvingly, but he worried for Seyran. "He's young and playing now. I'm glad he found yoga, but I think he's going through a phase. In Armenia, with his family, being gay and punk was his rebellion. Now he's rebelling against you with this veganism and religious practice. When you leave," he said, "Seyran won't have anything to rebel against, and he'll be lost." It was ironic wording, given what Seyran had said to me the night before.

"It's good you'll move on," Gharib continued.

"I'm so tired," I told him.

"You need to find a new apartment—and a new lover!"

We laughed in a commiserating way. My relationship with Seyran paralleled his and Mardi's. I felt he was one of the few people I could confide in, who understood what I was going through.

The usual set of friends and acquaintances were at the party, but there was also an Armenian woman with a Dorothy Hamill bowl cut and thick eyebrows. She was from Yerevan. I was asking her what she was doing here in my bad Armenian when

Gharib approached, animatedly telling me her story. "She had been out of work for two years, depressed, not sure what to do with her life. She was home in bed one day watching the news on TV when it was announced that it was the last day to apply for the green card lottery. She got on a marshrutka and went down to the embassy and applied. She never thought she would win, and look, here she is! With a new life!" I shook my head, dumbfounded. "Can you imagine?" he asked, one of his favorite phrases. The woman has to be about ten years older than me—starting her life over at fifty-three. She was a friend of a neighbor of Gharib's parents. Now she is living with them in their shotgun apartment in Bed-Stuy until she finds a job and an apartment.

When Gharib and I were by ourselves, he told me that she didn't know about his and Mardi's relationship. It's hard for me to remember that there are people for whom homosexuality is completely taboo. I know it's not entirely her fault, given that she's from a land of homophobia, but it makes me angry that Gharib and Mardi must hide themselves from this woman when they are opening their home to help her.

Seyran and I may not have to contend with such issues, but I identify with Mardi and Gharib because I am in the closet about my abusive relationship.

META-WRITING:

If I hadn't done that performance in Milan, I don't think I would have referred to what I was going through as abuse. As I divulged in the performance, Seyran would restrain me in various ways: sitting on top of me or pinning me down so I couldn't move. I discounted this as abuse because I felt guilty about my own actions in response. When he said something that would enrage me, yelling wasn't enough since he did not hear me, so I resorted to hitting him. I felt absolutely horrible that I would enact violence on a survivor of violence. It was what ultimately drove me to therapy.

Lara's office was on the Upper West Side. I saw her for a few months in the spring and summer of 2008, before we moved to Astoria. I told her the history of the relationship: how he had helped me in Armenia but now I couldn't seem to help him here, and how it was thus painful to see Seyran removing himself from my life, refusing to spend time with my friends. One day, after I left her office and walked through Central Park, a lovely passage on a midsummer day, Seyran called to tell me that he had just been on a date.

I'd caught him once before—he came home later than usual one night, all dressed up, and when I looked through his pockets while he was sleeping, I found a receipt for a Turkish restaurant in Sunnyside.

When I'd confronted him, he'd said it was someone he'd met on the internet, an isolated incident.

Now on the phone my heart stopped, though I thought maybe he was joking. Why would he call to tell me he'd been on a date? "You were?" I asked.

"Yes. I was just walking with her in Jackson Heights," he continued. "Guess who we ran into?"

I was silent, not sure what he was asking.

"Maria!" I knew my friend went to Jackson Heights regularly to see a chiropractor. I didn't know what to say, partially in shock that he was telling me this story.

Seyran interrupted the silence. "You're in Manhattan? Can you bring me something to eat?"

I ignored the non sequitur, my heart beating in my throat. "Have you been seeing other girls?" I asked.

"Yes,"

"Do you like them?"

"It's better than nothing," he said.

I interpreted the "nothing" as me. Shell-shocked, I tried my best to stay away from home as long as possible, ambling around Queens, walking through the planned community of Sunnyside Gardens with its shady trees. I had grown up in a neighborhood with big suburban lawns, and the kids playing outside could hear my parents' arguing voices echoing across the vast yards. I didn't know why they yelled so much, but it always embarrassed me since I would never hear anyone else's family losing their shit.

When I finally went home after dark to our apartment in Woodside, Seyran was sleeping. I woke him up and told him how hurt I was. The only reason he could give me for his phone call was that he had thought it was too unreal that he had run into Maria, and I was the only person who could possibly understand the irony.

I yelled at him. "I'm spending all this time and money talking about you in therapy, trying to help our relationship, and you're screwing it all up."

"You're crazy! Me seeing other people helps our relationship."

"Fuck you. I'm going to visit my parents and leave you alone for the weekend."

His eyes widened, and for a split second, his face twisted into tears. It was the strangest look I had ever seen on his face. I had unlocked a secret: the infant didn't want to be abandoned by his mother.

Just as Seyran had tightly hidden away his pain, I couldn't ask Maria about her encounter with Seyran in Jackson Heights. (It would take many years before I could—and she told me she had no memory of running into Seyran while he was on a date.) I didn't want my friend feeling sorry for me again. I wanted to be perceived as the type of person who had a normal relationship—even though it was already abundantly clear that I didn't.

STORY: MARCH, 2007
YEREVAN

Stepan and Jhenya broke up during Women's History Month. Na was disappointed; sure, Jhenya was smart, sleek, sophisticated, and ambitious, and Stepan was goofy, happy-go-lucky, and content in the present, but she thought they balanced each other out.

One night, Na came home in the aftermath of the breakup to find Stepan in the living room with Seyran, and all their shoes in the hallway were lined up perfectly.

"What happened here?" Na asked as she took off her boots.

Stepan smiled sheepishly. Without Jhenya, Na now had to rely on Seyran for translation.

"Stepan has complexes. He does this in everyone's house."

"Line up their shoes?"

"Yes."

"Oh, I never noticed it before." She shrugged and said, "Merci!" to Stepan.

That night, the three of them went for a long walk, then had Stepan over for dinner. When it became too late for a marshrutka, Stepan slept on the couch. The next morning, a Sunday, they all went to the old run-down amusement park at the top of the city, where the statue of Mother Armenia guards the entire city. Na thought it was interesting that they had put a woman up there, transforming her into an erect phallic symbol. With the sword across her body, she formed a cross. Someone wanted to remind Armenians of religion and patriarchal tradition, as if they didn't get enough of that messaging.

At the end of the day, they were walking back to the apartment from the marshrutka stop at the Opera when Stepan decided that he would go home. Na kissed his cheek and said goodbye, and then Seyran tried to convince Stepan to come home with them, but he declined and hopped aboard his marshrutka, sliding the van's door shut. As they walked away up Mashtots, past William Saroyan's dark, heavy statue, Seyran was angry that Na hadn't insisted that Stepan stay with them. Didn't Na know Stepan was going through a breakup and he didn't want to be alone? "Stepan left because of you," he accused as if Na had been rude.

Na tried not to give herself a hard time about it. They had been with Stepan for twenty-four hours, and he hadn't seemed hurt or forlorn as he jumped aboard the van. She told Seyran that they had spent a lot of time with Stepan and that she needed to have some time alone with him.

"Yes, you should pay more attention to me," he said.

Na was irked. She sensed that he was lashing out, so she tried to remain calm. "How do you want me to pay more attention?" she asked. "I didn't know that he would stay overnight and spend the day with us. How can I give you attention when your friend is around?"

"Well, you're the one who started it when you brought Maria here." She had stayed for two weeks on the sofa in their kitchen and left a few days before. So that was the reason for his outburst.

When they arrived back at the apartment, Seyran turned on Na's computer and dialed up the internet. She was unnerved that he was shutting her out while they were having an important conversation. So she impulsively pulled out the computer cord and punched some pillows.

"You're crazy," he said. "You need to be more stable."

Na was fed up. He was using her money, her computer, and now her emotions. During sex, he had told her he didn't want her to be "active"—their sex changed from dynamic and exciting to the same old male-dominated positions of her youth. He was reading her emails over her shoulder, downloading porn onto her computer, and telling her that her poems were stupid and classical.

It was time to break up with him. In bed, she wrote by hand in her journal, imagining how she would return to America alone. "Maybe I need to get used to the idea. Instead of imagining him coming back with me, I can imagine myself going back alone, to the same apartment, and quietly taking care of myself."

BLOG POST: *NEVER PUBLISHED.* MARCH 29, 2007
YEREVAN

Na: There Are No Gendered Pronouns in Armenian, Cont'd. >>> After Beatris's meeting to discuss Seyran and Archig's lyrics, and our purchase of the Thai face cream, we went home to discover the phone ringing. It was my friend Maria, calling to tell me about her trip home—she had met a guy on the airplane, a musician whom Seyran vaguely knew. Seyran overheard my side of the conversation and wanted to know what we were discussing, but Maria preferred I not tell him so that nothing would get back to the guy. I complied with her request and brushed Seyran off; I closed the French doors and sat in the hallway while continuing to talk on the phone. As I listened to her story, I could see Seyran putting his hands in his pants—it soon became clear he was masturbating. I ignored him, but after he finished, he opened the French door and smeared some of his semen on my face, over my mouth. I was disgusted; I couldn't talk on the phone like this. I made an excuse to Maria, ran to the bathroom, and washed my face.

Probably because I was in denial, my emotional reaction was delayed, about ten minutes. I made tea, and as the water was boiling, it came to me. He had violated me. He couldn't stand me talking to Maria without him, so he had acted like an infant, putting bodily fluids on my face.

I stomped into the living room, flinging open the door. "What the fuck is wrong with you?"

"It's good for your skin," he claimed.

"I'm not going for that stupid joke," I told him. "You did it to disrespect me. You got so much affirmation for your stupid lyrics that you think you can do anything."

"You think they're stupid?"

I didn't want to be derailed by that argument, so I told him that his violation was unacceptable.

It makes me think that since independence, the new "freedom" is about the male prerogative to do whatever the fuck they want to women. Yeah, they have to go into the army. But there are no women in the government. Beatris told me that it hadn't been unusual for women to hold powerful positions during Soviet times, but they had been propped up by an ideological system. Once the system collapsed, the intellectuals, seeking freedom, abandoned the country, and the oligarchs seized power by reinstating traditional Armenian roles. Women ended up doing the jobs men did not want, simultaneously taking care of the family. Meanwhile, the men sauntered off into the square to play chess and tavloo. And I now spend my time arguing about things I never thought I would have to—about my appearance, about cleaning the house.

That very morning, when I found yet another sinkful of dishes, I had given Seyran my feminist speech about how my mother and grandmother had been compromised their entire lives by limitations put on women. My upbringing had led me to intellectual pursuits, not homemaking.

Seyran had asked me, "Why do you have to get upset? You have to teach me about feminism, I don't know it. I'm only 21."

I wondered if he was pretending to be stupid. Initially, I was drawn to his freedom because it is hard to come by in this repressed place, but now his liberation seems to mean my repression. I don't want to have to teach him; I want him to understand basic human decency.

I thought about pronouns in Armenian—there's no *he*, *she*, or *it*, only one pronoun for everyone and everything: *na*. This aspect of the language suggests that at some point Armenians held a fundamental understanding of the equality of the sexes and genders, the universality of humans and their placement in the world among other beings—a striking contrast to their current cultural misogyny.

That night, I didn't speak to him for the rest of the evening and I went to bed angry. Seyran woke me later as he was getting under the sheets. He smiled and peered into my face; I noticed in the darkness that he was wearing the Thai face cream. I smeared some away from his eye, hoping my acceptance of his gender nonconforming behavior would strike a chord.

STORY: MARCH, 2007
YEREVAN

As Na was writing the above blog post, which she never published, Seyran came home after being interviewed on the radio for the poems that he had published in Beatris's journal. They were causing a stir for their "indecency." Na hadn't listened to it (in Armenian) but took her time condemning his actions in her writing. When he walked through the door, he asked if he could check his email.

"I want to see if I got an email from a girl I asked to meet."

The night before, he had been chatting with three different girls on Na's computer. Na hadn't been upset then because she figured it was friendly. Now that she learned he was planning to meet one of them, she blurted out, "I wanna break up."

She couldn't quite believe she had said it, but she meant it. Everything shifted. The air. His eyes.

He turned away from her and took out his backpack and put some of his things in it, asking, "Can I have the laptop?" as if it were all a joke.

"No!" she exclaimed.

"Can I fuck you until you go to America?"

Na ignored him, went to the kitchen, and cried. He followed her.

"You can go fuck that girl you're meeting."

"Is that what you're upset about? Look, I'm only meeting her because you paid more attention to Maria than me."

Na calmed down, now that he was admitting his feelings. "Being jealous of my friends is really problematic."

"I don't like Maria. I am not jealous when you spend time with your other friends." But the fact was Na didn't have many friends.

"It doesn't matter. We're not compatible. You don't want me to be 'active' in bed anymore, and that's another problem."

"Well, what do you want? You have all the money, and it's getting to me. It's one way I can have some power."

"Whatever," Na said. She had to go to the university for a meeting, so she walked down the stairs of the building and into the city, unable to think about much else. Afterward, she went to NPAK for Beatris's writers' meeting and then to dinner with the group at the diner next door.

Seyran showed up as she was slurping some spas. Something about him had changed—he took a chair and accepted whatever food was given to him by the others. He was shy and humble as he had been when they'd first met. Afterward, as they greeted each other and walked home, he held her hand and said, "When I saw you in the diner, I thought, 'There's my baby. I don't want to break up.'" She knew what he meant. And she figured he'd shown enough self-awareness through a near-breakup that she decided to stay with him.

META-WRITING:

I often thought of going to Armenia as an experiment. What happens when you put a diasporan Armenian in her homeland?

Maria said she could understand why I would get involved with someone, to feel the safety of a partner in a troubled place. And yet, the partner turned out to be dangerous.

I've been doing some reading on narcissistic personality disorder. Shame is at its root. A child growing up in a strict or abusive environment doesn't have the safety or a support system to express vulnerability. When they are neglected by a parent, they are thus forced to blame themselves in a shame spiral, something they try to avoid at all costs in the future. Seyran abused me emotionally and physically, then twisted things around so that I was to blame, so that he wouldn't have to admit or deal with his feelings. It was my fault Stepan left, it was my fault Maria came to Yerevan and that I spent time with her, it was my fault I had money, it was my fault I hadn't taught him about feminism.

But it wasn't only Seyran—my own reluctance to feel shame, to avoid misunderstanding among my friends, to admit I was in a dysfunctional relationship, was intolerable to me. Thus, the conditions were set for him to push me to my limits, then reel me back when the attention I gave him was threatened.

And, of course, shame is common currency in Armenian society, in Armenia and the diaspora. Ask most Armenians, no matter how little of the language they know, and they will recognize the word for shame, amot. We're ashamed that we have sex, urges, desires. Ashamed that we're even alive. We are obsessed with the past, reliving our stories of trauma over and over again, writing countless memoirs and novels bringing us back in time to when heads were cut off and babies were carved out of bellies and women were forced to dance naked before they were burned to death, trying and failing to piece all these impossibilities together, so that it will all make sense, so that we, ourselves, will make sense; but in fact, there is no sense to the violence the perpetrators enacted upon us—nor the denial they insist upon. And then we feel shame about that.

Well before I met Seyran, the conditions were set for my abuse. The cycle repeated in various ways, but it was essentially the same, whether he smeared cum on my face, called to tell me he had been on a date when he ran into Maria, or had degrading sex with me when I returned from Milan. He frequently referenced having sex with other people. Initially, seeing other people gave him a sense of self; as time went on, he gained a feeling of power since I always responded with strong emotions. It didn't even matter if he hooked up with others; he could suggest it or lie about it, and the news would have the same effect on me. My humiliation broke whatever shame he experienced for feeling weak.

But when I came back from Milan, my response was muted, and I told him my plans to leave him. He attempted to gaslight me as "confused and lost," but I didn't fall for it. Over time, my eyes were opening, adjusting to the dim light of the closet I was in.

When Maria and I went on that bus trip into the countryside back in 2007, we visited the ruins of the medieval city of Dvin, once the capital of Armenia, dating back to the fifth century. No buildings from this city of a hundred thousand souls remain. We clambered over an excavation site, an empty open field with strings demarcating where the buildings once stood, now reduced to small hills. I had never seen an archaeological site so unguarded. Everyone on the tour blithely picked out little shards of pottery that a specialist probably should have been excavating and piecing back together. These were ancient pots, after all. But there were so many shards, and there weren't nearly enough archaeologists to do the work, so the place was left vulnerable to souvenir seekers. It made me think that no one would be able to truly retrieve the past, to marvel at its beauty.

At the time, it seemed to me the pottery had been dug up from the ground only to be left strewn about, meaningless and wasted. Undoubtedly, it was a shame, but now I also believe there was beauty in every shard—in the shape, color, and texture of each broken and displaced piece.

14. ONE FOR THE EAVESDROPPER

BLOG POST: *NEVER PUBLISHED.* APRIL 20, 2007

YEREVAN

Hitched >>>

Friday, April 13: I straighten my hair, and Seyran shaves.

I buy a plain cotton dress with tiny little dots, gray and blue with touches of pink, and Seyran gets a white button-down shirt splashed with a peachy Art Deco blob.

We secure champagne and Raffaello—coconut-covered white candies with a crunchy hazelnut core.

Trivial details, they somehow seem important because we had a lot of trouble finding witnesses. The night before, several people had said no—too busy, had to work. We finally thought of Beatris and Nishan, who said yes. Beatris had introduced us on the sidewalk in front of Aragats Art Gallery in September. Her husband, Nishan, is a progressive journalist. We don't understand why we didn't think of them to begin with since they seem perfect for our antiauthoritarian legal union, which we cannot bear to acknowledge is a wedding.

When we arrive the next afternoon in Republic Square, Beatris jokes, "Where is your white dress? Well, at least you did your hair." Nishan shows up in his journalist's vest, carrying a bouquet of bright candy-colored daisies. When the four of us announce our presence in the small registration office with the sound of cellophane crinkling around the flowers, we receive strange looks, which seems odd, since people must get married here all the time. On second thought, maybe too few Armenians would pass up a party with Cognac and dancing in favor of a low-key city hall wedding in grim-looking Soviet-era offices. Or the social pressure to marry the old-fashioned way is too strong. There is still a tradition practiced called the red apple: if there are bloodstains on the wedding sheets, the groom's family brings the bride's family a bowl of red apples as proof of her virginity. Hence our attempt to thumb our noses at such customs by signing papers with a zaftig office lady sipping coffee from a tiny cup at her cluttered desk. Unfortunately, she informs us that we don't have all the necessary paperwork and turns us away. Our plan to fly in the face of tradition and marry on Friday the 13th is thus foiled.

As we stroll down the street to a Chinese restaurant, Beatris asks me what I really think about marriage, and I tell her I have mixed feelings. I love Seyran and he loves me, and we want to make a commitment to each other to ensure that we can stay together across borders and oceans. But I have known too many international gay couples who have struggled to stay together in the same nation. I don't like participating in a privilege reserved for straight people, an unjust institution.

But Beatris isn't asking for a political response. "No," she says, "What do you think about marriage for yourself, because you are bisexual?"

I shrug.

"For example, what if you fell in love with me?"

She is being provocative again. Nishan warns her about starting such a game. "Watch out, Natalee will write about this on her blog."

I ignore him and egg on Beatris. "I'll tell Seyran, 'I love Beatris. Do you think you could love her, too?'" A discussion on polyamory ensues, on the pros and cons, the possibilities and limitations of a family of adults. I tell Beatris and Nishan that I like the idea in theory, but it is hard enough to have a relationship with one person, never mind two or three. They laugh knowingly. By now, we are seated at the restaurant, with our champagne in glasses. Beatris toasts us, expressing how much Seyran and I mean to her. She says, "I wish everyone could be as free as you."

I am reminded of a moment earlier in the day when I was walking up the stairs to our building with the champagne, dress, and chocolates, taking a moment to appreciate how fly-by-the-seat-of-our-pants this all was. I could never understand why people bought into the fanfare and the lavish expense of a wedding ceremony. As Beatris toasts us for being free, it feels sweet to be recognized positively as a couple. I can't remember if anyone has said anything that nice about us before. We have lied to our families about our sizable age difference, claiming to his parents that I am younger and to mine that he is older. His parents don't trust me as an American and mine don't trust him as an Armenian. So I now understand the appeal of a public ceremony, with people in their best outfits making toasts, especially to unconventional couples who aren't always celebrated.

❖

Before I met Seyran, I had been scheming to have a singlehood ceremony. I conceived of it as a ritual in the woods to which I would invite my best friends, many acquaintances, and even a few relatives. Everyone would be asked to wander alone in the woods to honor solitude and individuality, and then I would do a solo performance about my hopes, dreams, and expectations of living by myself for the rest of my life. A friend referred to the idea as "getting married to yourself," but I looked at it as a celebration of both the beautiful and the challenging sides of being on your own. It also didn't seem fair that married people get to publicly rejoice in being joined to someone, but single people don't get to honor anything about their lives. And a single woman needs pots and pans and a nice set of dishes like anyone else.

Friends have offered to throw a party for me and Seyran once we get to the States, but we declined. The last thing I want to do is parade around my ability to get legally married in front of my friends, most of whom are queer and whose relationships should be honored by their families and by the state.

We could really use some housewares, though, so maybe we'll have a housewarming party. I'll perform a ritual to honor everyone, whatever state they are in—single, celibate, dating, married, widowed, divorced, or misanthropic. I'll read passages from Barbara Feldon's book, *Living Alone and Loving It* on the virtues of being a single woman. She played Agent 99 on *Get Smart* in the sixties, so we'll watch reruns of the program, the Cold War international spies making jokes. Taking inspiration from the fortune-telling tradition from Hampartsoum, aka the Ascension, we'll take off our rings and throw them into a pot of water with wildflowers, sing a song, and pull the rings out to tell people's love fortunes. Then we'll have a big orgy.

On second thought, I am too uptight for an orgy, so maybe instead we will feed each other cake or cherries. Okay, I might be too uptight for this, too. But we'll think of an act that will unite all the guests—for us to love and appreciate everyone, even if we are not married to them, sort of like children making valentines for everyone in their grade school class. Or when John and Yoko went on the Mike Douglas Show, calling up random numbers in the Philadelphia phone book and telling whoever picked up, "I love you."

It's hard to invent a new ritual when there are so many old ones still around, but I am sure we will think of something.

META-WRITING:

Around the time of the above blog post, my journal entries sound bipolar, fractured by wild emotional mood shifts.

One day I wrote scathing rants: "I feel as if everything in my life is compromised—my work, my friendships, my sense of self, my health—but I don't see Seyran giving up anything. It seems the worst he has to deal with is my moods, which are mostly caused by him." Then I made desperate wishes: "Okay, I don't know what to do. Pray that he does something nice for me soon so that I don't feel taken advantage of."

Though I felt threatened and damaged by the relationship, I married him, or tried to, on Friday, April 13. On that day in the morning, I wrote: "It's happening very quickly. We sort of thought we would get married on this day, but now we're making it happen. I'm excited and happy. I feel close to Seyran. Something feels right about it. I'm really happy he'll go with me to America … We're marrying in a way I feel comfortable with. He's someone I love very dearly."

We told ourselves we weren't really committing to each other for life. I was less interested in the fact that I was doing a favor for someone who made me insane, and more concerned with marrying in a way that didn't contradict my liberal values. And yet, I expressed a lot of love for him, as if we really were getting married.

When I read my journal entries from this time—panicked right before we got married and placid afterward—I feel disoriented. I've never known myself to cycle through emotions so rapidly. At the time, I thought my heightened moods resulted from all the pressure we were under. Now I also believe that my ability to think clearly had been compromised.

One day at the beginning of that month, I woke up feeling anxious—my period was three days late. My breasts had been hurting for days, and then suddenly the pain went away. This usually happened right before the blood started to flow. I knew it was unlikely that I was pregnant, that I was probably just anxious because of PMS, but I lost my shit with Seyran anyway.

I cried and complained to him, hysterically, "Why can't you wear condoms? What's the big deal? Why do you always have to broker a deal with me right when we're about to do it? No American boyfriend ever put me through this." I knew Armenian men were reputed to be condom-avoidant, but I didn't realize how much they felt entitled to go around with their cocks unsheathed, streaming semen any which way.

"What the fuck is wrong with you?" I screamed.

He was cool. "It will be okay," he said. "I pulled out before I came."

Needless to say, I was in a state. I somehow pulled myself together to face my class at the university. Afterward, I ran into Anahid Etchian, whom I hadn't seen in a while, so we chatted and caught up with each other. She offered to help me find a teaching job to stay in Armenia. I hadn't told her much about Seyran before, but since she was asking about my plans, I told her that we would be getting married soon.

"It's about time you got married," she said, as if she had been waiting to tell me. "And have children!"

I looked at her, my eyes widening in horror.

"You know, you can't go on forever without children, Natalee," she said. "The day will come when you won't be able to. And then where will you be?"

"But I don't want to have children," I told her.

"Of course you do," she said. I didn't mention my acute fear that I was pregnant at that very moment as she palavered on about the joys of children and a woman's incredible power to be a mother. Instead, I listened carefully to what everyone in Armenia believed about the definition of a woman, then walked home feeling awestruck by the timing of her speech.

I should give up, I thought. The universe wants me to be pregnant, no matter how much I resist. I can't keep fighting. I'm a woman; therefore, I get married and have babies. That's all there is to it.

I was approaching an intersection that was nearly impossible to cross, right before the bridge over the river to our building. The bridge led to a defunct aerial tramway, which had once carried a tiny orange car over a hill to a distant neighborhood. Stray dogs, scary yet pitiful, roamed aimlessly in the area. It was also a spot where the homeless came to dwell near the dumpsters in front of our building. One woman set up camp in a small triangle wedged between the two main roads. I could see her from our windows every morning and evening, and I wanted to help her but didn't know how. With cars zooming past and feral dogs roaming about, it didn't seem safe for her. She didn't look old, but she was dirty and appeared distressed, perhaps in need of mental health care.

As I crossed the intersection in this dangerous, unfriendly area, where the river, roads, bridges, trash, and dogs converged, I felt a self-centered sense of relief. Certainly, being pregnant with Seyran's child—when I had no desire to be a mother, when Seyran was only twenty-one with his whole life ahead of him, and while he was making me totally crazy—wouldn't be good. But it wouldn't be earthshakingly tragic compared to all the horrible things happening in the world, in this little country, even in this corner of the city.

When I got home, I went to the bathroom to pee. After I wiped myself, I saw blood on the toilet paper.

Unfortunately, realizing there were worse situations eventually carried over to how I felt

about marrying Seyran and bringing him to America: it wouldn't be the worst thing in the world. It

wouldn't even be as bad as being pregnant with his baby.

STORY: MID TO LATE APRIL, 2007
YEREVAN

On Monday, April 16, Seyran's father met Na and Seyran at ZAGS, an acronym that represented a string of Russian words, designating the civil acts registration office. Vartan was going to try to pull strings to expedite the application for the couple's Certificate of No Impediment, which stipulated that they were legally able to marry. They arrived at ZAGS an hour before it opened, so they walked around the neighborhood to pass the time. Around the block, they encountered a hunting shop, which featured a whole dead deer standing in the window. Na looked at its unbelievably slender legs, like saplings, marveling at how they could hold up such a bulky body. The animal, once a miracle, was now the lifeless spoil of unchecked masculinity. Seyran's father was preoccupied, gazing at all the knives in the display case.

Neither Seyran nor Na knew how Vartan did it, but he went into the chief of ZAGS's office, talked to him for ten minutes, didn't hand over a bribe (or so he said), and the couple were given a special form to fill out, requesting the clearance to legally marry in two weeks rather than the usual four. They needed the rush job to have time after they married to apply for a visa from the U.S. embassy. Na and Seyran were elated when Vartan handed them the form signed and stamped by the ZAGS chief.

Vartan had to rush off to work, so Seyran and Na brought all their required paperwork down one flight to the lady who had turned them away a few days before on Friday the 13th. Na noticed the coffee simmering in the jazzve on top of the little electrical heater in the corner of the room and imagined what it was like for the office women to wait for an eternal winter to pass, for the wedding season to start up. While Seyran filled out the paperwork in his neat, Soviet-education-system script, a bunch of different couples paraded in: one guy with huge ears and his fiancée with medium-sized ears. A blond Ukrainian woman, also appearing older than her husband-to-be. The lady behind the desk threw everyone's papers in an untidy pile. It made Na extremely nervous. When the lady looked away, Na made sure to slide their documents to a clear spot on her desk so that she wouldn't accidentally give them to someone else. Perhaps the couples were all the same to her—Na and Seyran and the blond Ukrainian lady and the skinny man with big ears. Just numbers and names, males and females.

After they passed the first hurdle in the process, they were in a good mood for the rest of the day, but it didn't last long—Seyran's father found out how old Na was. When he had walked through the door of the ZAGS chief's office, he looked down at her passport and saw her date of birth. Na thought it must not have bothered him too much since he convinced the chief to help his son marry her. Or maybe he had been too shocked to halt the proceedings. Most likely, he was simply on this train, imagining the best for his son, thinking that he couldn't jump off of it.

Later that evening, Vartan called Seyran to tell him that he was disappointed. It would be okay for Na to be several years older than him, but Na was practically twice his age. Still, Vartan said, it was Seyran's life, and he wasn't going to stop him from doing what he wanted to do.

As Seyran described the conversation to her, she interpreted it as a remarkable moment of tolerance, the likes of which she had never experienced. In her family, parents threatened to disown children if they married someone who didn't pass muster. Families shunned their queer children all the time—in the diaspora, in Armenia. It had happened to Seyran. He had recently told Na that when he had been beaten up at the university for having long hair, his parents suspected he was gay and kicked him out.

Na couldn't figure out what made his father willing to overlook her age: because he wanted Seyran to go to America, to have a better life, or to be codified as straight. But there was something else at play.

His father also told him on the phone that he should pay back all of the money he owed Na. Over the past several weeks, she had taken out a total of three thousand dollars from her bank in small installments (because a large withdrawal might look suspicious), which Vartan then used to bribe a doctor to state in writing that Seyran was medically unfit for his military duty. Perhaps now that Vartan knew Na's age, he felt there was something illicit about the way she had been financially supporting Seyran, in addition to buying his freedom. He had asked Seyran on a few different occasions how he felt about Na, and Seyran kept telling him that he loved her. Despite his son's professed feelings, or perhaps because of them, Vartan was now concerned that their relationship was more of a business transaction. He couldn't know for sure who was taking advantage of whom. But he didn't approve of their age difference, and he didn't want his son to owe her anything.

❖

And so the wedding train continued, barreling down the tracks. A couple of weeks later, Seyran's father drove the couple to Ashtarak, where Seyran was registered as a citizen from the three years he had lived there as a child. Na put on her dress and Seyran put on his white shirt. The ceremony would consist of going to the city hall to fill out paperwork and then to celebrate with dinner nearby. On the way, Seyran's father took them to the countryside, to a fourth-century church in ruins. There was a red khachkar of an unusual, bright color, where Vartan took their picture. They lit candles and drank water from a spring. Na sensed that Vartan wanted to perform a religious component to the wedding to bless it.

Next, they headed to Seyran's family's village house, and on the way Seyran's father told a story about a church in the distance, the Raven Church, so-called because of a legend in which a Raven warned people not to eat food tainted by an evil Snake.

A few moments later, Seyran's father slowed the car to a stop in the middle of the road. Na had no idea what he was up to. Was he going to rough her up now? Tell her not to mess up his son's life? Was he the Raven, ready to warn Seyran about Na's evil ways?

When Na and Seyran had attended a recent screening of the film *Camille*, starring Greta Garbo, she learned from Seyran that his parents' favorite book was *The Lady of the Camellias*, by Alexandre Dumas, which the film was based upon. The story is set in mid-nineteenth-century Paris and involves an honorable young man, Armand, who is in love with an older, not very honorable lady, Marguerite. One of the most heartbreaking scenes occurs when Armand's father visits the heroine privately, telling her to spare his son, that he'll be shunned by French society and miss out on important opportunities if he marries such a wanton woman. Marguerite doesn't know what to do; she agrees with the father—she is dishonorable, for she is in debt up to her eyeballs and has been known to engage in romantic dalliances with wealthy old geezers to pay the bills. (In the book, she is clearly a courtesan.) But she's so in love with Armand, and she knows that her fiancé won't accept a breakup. She painfully sacrifices her true feelings and coldly tells him she's bored with him. In the end, they are reunited after some more melodramatic scenes, just in time for her to die in his arms.

Dumas was an illegitimate son of a dressmaker (though he was later claimed by his famous father, Alexandre Dumas, senior), and he was teased and tortured by French society for it. He became involved with a woman like Marguerite and became a writer of tragic heroines. So the story was in his blood, a painful fantasy of his mother, of himself.

This kind of tragic story had always appealed to Na, from a very young age. She was drawn to love stories in which a woman was misjudged and reviled, when in fact she was brave and good-hearted. She didn't think she had a story like this in her blood, like Dumas. But perhaps the story of the Armenians echoed it since they had been misjudged and despised by the Turks—and still were. In a way, her upbringing echoed it as well. She hadn't felt understood by her family or her friends, occupying a space between being Armenian and being American. Though she had done much as an adult to reconcile her two sides, she conceived of Seyran—a young Armenian bisexual man—as the icing on the cake: understanding how virtuous she was, rescuing herself from a fate lost between identities.

"Listen," Seyran's father commanded in English, bringing Na back to the moment. He turned off the engine. Na waited for the speech telling her to stay away from his son, to take her filthy Western ways back to America. But all he said was, "Melody," his index finger pointing up. Then Na heard the sound of twittering birds and the incredible music that they were making. It was a lovely, peaceful moment, and her fear dissipated without another thought.

When they arrived at the village home, Seyran's father gave Na a tour. The house and its sizable garden were enclosed behind a wall. Vartan pointed out a walnut tree, a pear tree, and an apple tree, sprouting young green leaves, a few scattered with tiny blooms. In one corner of the property, there was a small swimming pool, adjacent to a terrace with a table underneath a grapevine arbor, next to a fireplace to cook khorovats. A bathroom was located nearby, replete with a little sauna that Vartan had recently built. He led Na to the main house, noting the plaque outside dated 1935 and the one-foot-thick walls, then outside again and up a flight of metal stairs where they entered a new addition with two modern, sunny rooms, with white walls and lace curtains covering the windows.

"I made this," he said in English, gesturing at the room.

Na was told that the home had belonged to his wife's family, that her parents had grown up here. Obviously, Vartan had put a lot of work into fixing it up. Na wondered if he was showing it to her because she was going to be part of the family now, or to illustrate that Seyran's family had value—that the scales between Na and Seyran weren't grossly unbalanced. It was probably due to both these intentions, but perhaps he was demonstrating for himself that he had done right by the people whom he was related to by marriage, because he had mixed feelings about the predicament he now found himself in, helping Seyran and Na to do the wrong thing in getting "hitched."

❖

The ceremony itself was uneventful: they went to a nondescript rectangular building in Ashtarak, a small town. They walked down a long hallway to yet another office with a heater in the corner. It was cold in Ashtarak in late April. The clerk handwrote their names in her record book. She handwrote the marriage license, too. Na looked at the woman's hands. No ring. She was a big woman, with short dark hair and a mustache. There was a table by the window covered with a beautiful array of sprawling ivy plants, which someone must have tended carefully every day as couples came in and out of her door. The woman was deeply ensconced in her chair, and Na couldn't imagine her getting up out of it to water the plants. But they grew in her presence, and she must have spent hours gazing at them. Na watched carefully as she recorded their dates of birth to see if judgment passed over her face. It didn't. When they signed their names, the woman smiled and congratulated them.

Next, Seyran's father took them to dine on khorovats at a motel next to the city hall, where the owners brought the meal into their room—roasted pork, cubes of white salty cheese, stacks of lavash cut into squares like napkins, fresh herbs, and vodka. Na got drunk and asked Seyran's father about his family. He told her there had been a rift because his mother didn't like his wife—he hadn't seen his mother in years. So he was like Dumas, too, emphasizing the value of a misunderstood woman. Though this was an unfortunate situation, Na appreciated learning this detail, thinking it was another clue to why he accepted Na: he didn't want to repeat what had happened to him. Na herself came from a family of Armenian in-laws disliking each other, and it was liberating to think that she had married into a family where this dynamic would not be passed on.

The wedding party didn't last long because Seyran's father had to go back to work. Na was so drunk that she didn't get upset that Vartan seemed uncomfortable, slightly sad. He dropped Na and Seyran off at the bus station, and they took a marshrutka home, falling asleep on each other's shoulders. Once at home, they had sex and then fell asleep again.

In the late afternoon, Na woke up before Seyran and made tea. As she sat at the kitchen table alone, musing upon her wedding, she told herself that she didn't mind that it had been an uneventful day. Her new father-in-law had raised enough questions in her mind to distract her from her fantasy of being a tragic, misunderstood woman, and she wasn't ready to think about the reality of what she had done.

JOURNAL: JANUARY, 2011
ASTORIA

The night of Mardi's birthday, I stayed late at his and Gharib's apartment and decided to sleep over on their couch since it would be an interminable trip from Bed-Stuy to Astoria at 2 a.m. The next morning, I went home when Seyran was at work. He called me twice during the day to find out where I was. I assured him that I had slept on Gharib and Mardi's couch.

He didn't show up at home till around 10:30 p.m. when I was in bed. He was in such a good mood but would not tell me why. He thought it was a weird tincture he had sampled at Whole Foods. I didn't ask where he had been. I was relaxed and calm, and he kept telling me how cute I was in my new pink-flowered flannel nightgown.

"Do you like me?" he asked.

"Yes," I told him. I wasn't going to indicate that his absence had bothered me.

He proceeded to tell me why he liked me. "You're calm and nice and cute," and blah-blah-blah. "So, what am I to you?" he asked.

"You're my roommate," I told him.

"You're my roommate and sex mate and playmate and nation mate and universe mate and primate. And I'm a fan of your boobs." Then he said, "Oh, I'll tell you the reason I'm so happy. I met my soul mate. Don't be mad. Can I tell you?"

He was acting like a little kid. "Yes," I said.

"Don't be mad."

Knowing that he was going to tell me about myself, I wasn't. Even if it had been someone else, I didn't care anymore.

"She let me have sex with her the other day. Her name is Natalee."

He seemed like a little boy, his stature diminished physically and mentally. At one point when he was cuddling with me in my bed, he playacted like he was sucking on my tits. "Mama," he said. "Can you hold me like I'm a baby?"

I wondered for a moment if he was high because he suddenly got up and asked me to come to his room. "Hey," he said seriously, "I was upset when you weren't home. Why didn't you tell me?" I explained the situation, that it had been too late to call, and I didn't have enough money to cab it. I did not mention how frequently he had done the same to me; why get into it?

He asked, "Why didn't you ask me where I was tonight? It doesn't matter? You don't care?"

"It doesn't matter," I said.

"Oh, okay, I like that," he claimed.

And yet, he still keeps asking me, "Do you love me? Do you like me?" I am not sure if he is insecure because I've told him that I'm leaving, or if he is hoping that I will say no, I don't love him, and he will be free from any attachment.

I have my own version of this. As much as he has hurt me and I want to leave, I'm also gripped by a fear that he'll get involved with someone younger, and that it will make me feel awful about myself, and that I will punish myself for it more than any hurt he can cause me.

Hey, Na, maybe you don't have to punish yourself. Maybe you could let go of that story.

Two nights ago, while I was hanging out in his room, before he went to sleep, Seyran said that he had read his horoscope online, an Indian Vedic version, and it said he would be wealthy later in life.

"Can you give me the money you owe me then?" I asked. I've never asked him to repay me the three thousand dollars, but if he's going to be wealthy, I think it's only fair I get remunerated, especially considering all the grief he has caused me.

"Can you die young so I don't have to pay you back?" he responded. "I have this money hanging over my head."

"I'm going to live a long time," I told him. "You only have to pay me back if it's easy for you, if you become so rich that it becomes like five dollars for you."

"Like that's ever going to happen," he said.

"I have faith in you. You're young and smart. You have a full life ahead of you. Who knows what will happen?"

"I want to have babies," he said.

"That's nice."

"You can't associate with my children, though," he said. "You can bring my children presents, but I won't let you play with them. You can be like their granny."

These statements would have hurt me before, but he was painting such a ridiculous scenario that I had to laugh. What kind of granny brings presents but isn't allowed to play with her grandchildren? Maybe his tatik, his father's mother? I never did meet her.

I stood up to leave, and he pulled me down to hug me.

"At last," he said, "you get my jokes. The flowers are blooming from the seeds I planted."

Last night, I got a message from him at 9:20 p.m. when I was on my way home from visiting friends:

> **Hi honey, I'm not coming home tonight. It's eclipse tomorrow and fool moon today. I love you. Seyran.**

When I came home from work tonight, he was making salad. I went to my room to grade papers, and he was angry that I did not help him. I pitched a fit: "I'm okay with you not coming home all night, but you can't even let me do what I need to do in my own home!"

"You're crazy," he said and continued cooking. After a few moments, he came and tickled me as I was lying on my bed, then hugged me and asked if I loved him.

"No," I told him, "not today."

That was when he showed me the scratch on his bald head. It looked like a fingernail scratch, about eight inches long.

"How did that happen?" I asked, but he wouldn't tell me. Perhaps a ritual involving sex or religion, maybe both? I can only imagine, the fool to his moon.

META-WRITING:

Traditional Armenian folk and fairy tales typically end like this: "Three apples fell from heaven: one for the storyteller, one for the listener, and one for the eavesdropper." Sometimes that third one alternates. It could be one for the person who takes the story to heart or one who shares the story with the world. Whatever the case, it seems the third apple symbolizes the wider implications of the story, beyond the parameters of the time and place in which it was created. The storyteller crafts a yarn for the listener, but the eavesdropper is so compelled by it, they stop to take it in while going about their day. The eavesdropper hears that story differently than the intended audience, finding a pearl of wisdom or a silence broken that changes their world or saves their life. And so, when a story is blessed by an apple for the eavesdropper or someone who took the story to heart or who told it to the world, the story has a life of its own, spreading beyond the storyteller.

Seyran was the storyteller, and I was his listener. In one moment he told me that I was his soul mate, and in the next that I was the fake granny of his future children. I was kind to him, expressing my faith in his ability to change, grow, and succeed without me, and he responded with a stupid joke made at my expense.

I thus also became the owner of the third apple. As the distanced eavesdropper, I rebuffed the love story, and I laughed at Seyran's cruelty in portraying me as a spurned, gift-toting tatik. But laughing also meant that I empathized with his self-loathing. It helped me see that I was carrying my own loathsome story about the pathetic older woman, jilted for someone younger—a version of the tragic, misunderstood woman I had originally thought Seyran had saved me from becoming. I had swallowed Seyran's apple seeds and let them grow inside me. But this story ultimately had a life beyond me as a listener, eavesdropper, or storyteller, the branches growing up my throat, emerging alongside the words from my mouth, blossoming beyond anybody's control.

15. US AND THEM

Same Old Thing >>> Judging by the lack of creativity in the parliamentary candidate posters I've seen on display around town, the upcoming election is little more than a formality: instead of votes deciding the candidates, bribes will. However, Europe is watching how fairly the election will be run as a barometer for how advanced Armenian democracy is, which determines how much entities like the Organization for Security and Co-operation in Europe (OSCE) will listen to Armenia when it comes to negotiating with Azerbaijan over Karabakh. A lot is at stake, so it's strange that the political parties aren't offering persuasive arguments in their platforms; every election poster I've seen depicts an Armenian guy in a suit sitting behind a desk. I am tempted to take a marker to them and write, *SAME OLD THING.*

People aren't voting for individuals but for political parties, which could explain the lack of originality in campaign media. Beatris told me that it's difficult to know how to vote on election day because some of the newer parties may collapse at the last minute and give their votes to a party you don't necessarily like. In fact, some of the newer parties are set up by the more powerful parties for this very reason. The smaller parties probably don't put much energy into their campaigns, and the larger parties thus dominate the scene.

The Republican Party of Armenia, a conservative party led by current prime minister Serzh Sargsyan, has held a couple of highly visible rallies. The first was last weekend, when they shut down several blocks on Mashtots. Buses filled with villagers were streaming into Yerevan and causing major traffic jams. At the rally, speakers blared with candidates' voices, but none of the villagers seemed to be listening. They were strolling around, checking each other out, having a pleasant day in the big city. The ambiance reminded me of the grounds of a large-scale rock concert when the crowd socializes in between the major acts. When I was having my Armenian lesson at the Cascade, a group of village men and school-children marched past and stared at me sitting on a park bench with my new tutor, Houry, a grad student at the linguistics university. Houry, who grew up in the mountains of the Lory region, said that most of the villagers probably didn't even know why they were there—the schoolchildren obviously not old enough to vote, their teachers paid off to require the students to attend.

The next day, the Prosperous Armenia Party, led by arm wrestling world champion and filthy rich guy Gagik Tsarukyan (a.k.a. Dodi Gago), held a concert and rally by the Opera, also bussing in scores of villagers, and the atmosphere was similar to the Republican Party rally. I've noticed a lot of Prosperous Armenia offices around town, and Houry affirmed my perception that Republicans and Prosperous will take most of the parliamentary seats since they are the largest, most powerful, and most connected. Dodi Gago has been giving away gifts of brandy and beer to poor people in the provinces as an enticement to vote for him.

Opposition parties have not been as vocal or visible, except for the Impeachment guys who drive around in their little cars with pictures of Kocharyan, Sargsyan, and Dodi Gago and scream, "Impeachment!" It's hard to imagine this anemic display leading to a viable party.

Maybe the problem is that there can never be true opposition in a place where everyone treats each other as family and people call each other brother and sister or auntie and uncle on the street. When you accept a bribe from someone from your own country, nation, or ethnicity, is it somehow more shameful than taking a bribe from someone more powerful, like a Russian official? We expect those with more power to try to take advantage of us, and if we can gain a foothold or critical mass, we can fight them. But when an Armenian, who knows what it means to be subjugated, offers a fellow compatriot a bribe, what should the compatriot do? Accept the bribe with shame? Rebuff it and reject them? How does one fight? In a tiny monoethnic nation, I am not quite sure there is an Us and Them.

❖

The day before the elections, I was at Beatris's writers' meeting at NPAK contemplating Us and Them in a slightly different way. A coalition of European artists was in town for a cultural exchange with the progressive Armenian writers. Perhaps seeing me as a conduit to the Westerners, Nishan asked me to give my impressions of contemporary art in Armenia. I declined since I don't know much about contemporary art in general. However, one of the European artists pressed me, asking for a comparison of art in New York to what I had seen in Armenia. All that came to mind was what I had noticed when I first arrived: "Armenian artists are constantly referencing other work, old and new, mostly through the use of collage."

The translator, Medzig, looked at me incredulously as if to say, "What the fuck are you talking about?"

I nervously defended myself. "Well, I'm not saying *everyone* does it, but juxtaposing found material next to original work keeps coming up, in literature and film and art—there's definitely a trend." One of the European artists, a man with exceedingly blond hair, observed that he had noticed collage at the current exhibition at NPAK. Medzig cut him off to let him know that the European guy can't just walk into the Armenian Center for Contemporary Experimental Art one day and say what the situation is in Armenia. The blond European man swallowed his tongue.

After the discussion, we wound up at this weird place called Yerevan City Diner. Normally, we go to a cheap, smoky nondescript place for spas or borsch and dip bread in it, but it must have been closed (or deemed unfit for the European artists.) This diner was modeled after the 1950s cafés popular in LA, and the walls were covered with U.S. license plates, albums, and posters of fifties icons, including Miles Davis playing a trumpet.

In this environment of imported Western culture, Beatris explained how things haven't changed much for writers since Soviet times because European funding organizations tend to lump the Caucasus countries together to encourage them to dialogue with each other. It's not that anyone's against this, but it's an imposed mandate. Beatris said that during the Soviet-era there was a lot of talk about brotherhood, but underneath the official communication, ethnic tension simmered. She said you showed up at the conference but you didn't really dialogue with your Azerbaijani brothers and sisters while the Soviet authorities watched over you. Now OSCE seems to be performing a similar role in observing the elections.

Fifteen years after the collapse of the Soviet Union, defining what it means to be Armenian is still wrought with tension. Russia and the West jockey for influence and demand certain standards. These larger, wealthier powers are privileged enough to exist, no questions asked, while they place an onus on marginalized Armenia to explain itself. What I mean to say is that Armenians want you to tell them what you think of them, only to realize that they don't, because it turns out you actually know very little about Them, while they know everything about Us.

And, of course, the relationship between the colonizer and the colonized, the emperor and the serfs, is nothing new. The oppressors are internalized within the oppressed, same old thing ...

STORY: LATE MAY, 2007
YEREVAN

Na wasn't prepared for the pandemonium that ensued when she emailed her father, a few weeks before she and Seyran went to the city hall in Ashtarak, to tell him that she was *thinking* of marrying Seyran to help him get a visa. At that point, she had made up her mind and just wanted to emotionally prepare her parents for the inevitable. It was a difficult process, the phone ringing constantly in her apartment.

Na had many conversations with her parents, trying her best to explain that she was not thinking about this as a traditional marriage in sickness and in health. She told her father, "I think it's unrealistic to expect two people to stay together forever when they go through so many changes throughout their lives." She felt badly saying this since her parents would be celebrating their fiftieth wedding anniversary later that year. Did her father think she was disrespecting their union? He didn't say so. Na tried her best to convey that her marriage was a legal commitment she was making to help Seyran for the time being.

Naturally, her parents were worried that she was taking on too much by sponsoring Seyran. They enlisted various family members to convince her of such. One of her elderly aunts wept into the phone, so confident that only disaster would befall her niece since she had heard of so many examples of failed homeland-diaspora marriages. Another aunt told her, "Natalee, it's very hard for these immigrants to find a way of life here. In Watertown, I'm always seeing these out-of-work Armenian guys smoking on street corners!" Na gently told her aunt that she understood her concerns but that her partner was not at all like this stereotype.

Her family thought they knew everything about the situation, and Na thought she knew about every one of their fears.

When their emotional lobbying campaign failed to work, her parents suggested that she get advice from Raffi Hovannisian, the first foreign minister of Armenia, a born-in-America baby boomer, now a leader of the Heritage Party, whom they had recently met at a function in Providence, Rhode Island. Na knew that this friendly Armenian American was the closest her parents could conceive of a helpful third party, meeting him on some reception line. But the thought of consulting with a parliamentary candidate about her personal life a few weeks before the election was preposterous to Na, and she was sure her parents could hear her rolling her eyes over the international phone line. Their last request was that she wait to get married until after they visited Armenia. They'd booked their flight and would arrive in a few weeks.

Na felt that they needed to get married as soon as possible to process Seyran's visa in time, so she did not honor their request to wait. Her parents thus arrived just two weeks after Na and Seyran had tied the knot.

After picking up her parents at the airport and bringing them to their hotel, Na's mother, Stella, took a nap, while Na and Seyran brought her father, Tip, to change his money and to buy him a khachapuri at their favorite stand. He ate the cheese pastry, charcoal bits sticking around the edges of his mouth. To Na, he looked so vulnerable in his exhaustion and advanced age, now in his late seventies. Seemingly oblivious that Na's father was closer to the age of his grandfather, Seyran insisted they bring him to their apartment, where Seyran played songs for him. As Seyran strummed his guitar and sang, Na thought her normally cheerful father looked disoriented and withdrawn, like he was hiding an uncomfortable source of physical pain.

Later, after they had rested, Na and Seyran took her parents out to dinner and for a walk on the Cascade. On the way, they ran into friends who informed them of a protest in a park near the Opera to demand transparency in the upcoming parliamentary election. As much as she wanted to attend, Na had to take her parents back to the hotel, then get to bed early to teach in the morning. Seyran, however, went to the protest. He didn't come home until 5 a.m.

When she returned from class later in the afternoon, Seyran was just waking up. He told Na a story about meeting an idiosyncratic tiara-wearing singer, whose family had taken her daughters away from her, and who lived in an apartment with no water heater.

"I know her!" Na said. "That's Fimi!"

Fimi, whom Na had met on her last night in Yerevan on her first trip to Armenia. Fimi, the woman who had said she loved to be free, who only lived for love. Fimi, a.k.a. Mother Armenia.

Seyran recounted how Fimi had taken him back to her apartment and offered him wine. They spent the night reading poems and singing songs. She wanted him to have sex with her, he claimed, but he told Na that he hadn't.

So fixated on the sighting of this rare creature, Na didn't bother to question Seyran's possible infidelity. Instead, she was jealous that she had missed the opportunity to see Fimi. What would she say to Na about her life now? Did she still want to go to Europe? Why did she go to the protest?

Seyran described her magical qualities, her incredible creativity, her craziness. Na enjoyed seeing Fimi's light again, but she didn't pursue the apparition—instead, she left her romantic notion in place. So many of Na's hopes about life and love had been twisted over the past several months that she still held on to the tragic, beautiful figure of her homeland: Fimi, embracing a young son who was about to depart, sending him off by singing her pain.

BLOG POST: MAY 14, 2007
YEREVAN

Same Old Thing, Cont'd ... >>> In this climate of the upcoming parliamentary election, with OSCE observers lurking about, I have noticed that the dynamic of world hierarchical ignorance—"we know everything about you, but you know nothing about us"—veers into absurdity at times, with foreign exchanges verging on the farcical. For example, May 9th was a holiday celebrating the Battle of Shushi, which had led to the cease-fire over Karabakh, and it was also the day the Soviet Union beat the fascists during World War II. In the evening, Seyran and I went to his parents' for our weekly laundry and dinner visit. As we dined on lentil soup and dolma, his father turned on the television to watch the concert in Republic Square. Seyran's father told me that Russian singers would be performing Armenian songs. I was surprised to see the first act, a group of three scantily clad women dancing a set of provocative moves that suggested they were having sex with each other.

This is how to celebrate veterans' sacrifice? I thought. I'm all for liberal sexuality, but this sleazy act seemed a tad cheap for the occasion.

Seyran's father changed the channel, and we found a concert in Moscow, celebrating the same holiday, with non-lip-synching artists in non-form-fitting costumes. It soon became clear that the third- or fourth-rate Russian pop stars had been shipped to Armenia.

He switched back to the Yerevan concert, where the technicians played the wrong CD for their second song: men's voices emanated from the speakers. The gang of whores were unsure of what to do. But they were not humiliated in the slightest; rather, they strolled off the stage in a druggy daze, like it was completely normal. *Ho-hum, who cares about these lousy Armenian songs?*

Seyran and I went home around 10:30 p.m. to drop off our laundry, then took the same taxi to meet Mardi and Gharib at Miasin. We walked over to Tigran Mets, careful to avoid Republic Square. Gharib told me that the Impeachment people had met with four opposition parties, and they collectively decided that if the election results seem false, they would get together and protest in the streets.

And then the fireworks went off. It must have been sometime around midnight, and we were at Vernissage. Even though they were launched by the government, the fascists, we watched them, our necks arched and mouths agape, like George Romero's zombies.

It wasn't until two days later, when I was meeting with the interpreter for my upcoming writing workshop, that I discovered there had been a protest the night of May 9th at KGB headquarters. The interpreter also worked for a local news outlet; she told me the police used tear gas, truncheons, and brass knuckles with the small crowd, suggesting that there could be violence during the protests after the elections. It seemed odd to be talking about a creative nonfiction writing workshop for women when there could be a huge national explosion in the intervening days. What is the point of telling personal stories and individual memories in this violent environment?

When I had an introductory information session for the workshop, an Armenian woman from France asked something similar. "Should we be writing as Armenian women or as global women?" The question bothered many of the other women assembled, perhaps because it sounded like a nationalist or separatist agenda. But I heard the question differently. Should Armenian women be writing to the West? (The West doesn't care about Armenian women.) To the rest of the world? (Ditto.) Are they to write to men? (Armenian women know everything about Armenian men, but Armenian men know nothing about Armenian women.) To themselves? (Yes. Because Armenian women have had very little to read about themselves.)

Sixty percent of the people in Armenia are women. If they decided, they could actively change the situation here for the better—for children, the elderly, women, and men. But they don't have a voice. As the French Armenian woman said, "This country will not advance until the women are free."

Perhaps the elections won't be clean since they are being held to European standards, an artificial mandate. Gharib told me he would not be voting because the society is so corrupt that there is no point in participating. Then he cited Sarkozy, who purports to be for the people but vacations on a yacht the day after he wins the French presidential election. The Armenian Parliament is a copy of a European system of government, which is also dominated by men. I've only seen one woman on the Armenian election posters, and she is sitting with two guys at a table.

The next day, May 12th, was election day, and it was unusually quiet, like a holiday. Lots of stores and businesses were closed so that people could vote.

As Houry predicted, the Republicans came in first, followed by Prosperous Armenia. Two opposition parties made it into parliament: Country of Law (Orinats Yerkir) and Legacy, a.k.a. Heritage, the newly formed party of Raffi Hovannisian, a diasporan who had once been Armenia's foreign minister under the Ter-Petrosyan administration. It turned out that the European observers saw less corruption in recent years, which hurt the opposition parties' cause. Yet I heard many cases of bribes: just outside the polls, thugs from the big parties paid people to vote for their candidates. There was a protest in Republic Square, but I've heard very little about it. In an AP report, however, I did read this interesting statement from one of the protesters:

"They stole our votes again. The authorities are becoming more and more cynical with every passing year in their efforts to enrich themselves at the expense of simple people. I go to these radical rallies out of desperation." These words came from Narine Sahakian, identified as a fifty-two-year-old homemaker.

Perhaps to make change in Armenia, the issue isn't *Us* and *Them*, but *We*.

META-WRITING:

When I called the Russian third-rate pop stars a "gang of whores," I was unfairly judging the clothes they wore and how they expressed sexuality. But I was miffed that they didn't seem to care about honoring the sacrifice of others. Also, I didn't intend to cast aspersions on sex work, which is a valid profession. But getting paid by someone more powerful for something that you rather not give or that you give out of desperation is tantamount to prostitution. Like destitute villagers getting paid for their votes. Like Seyran continuing to be with me to escape the army.

One night in Queens, a year or two after we moved, we were walking down Steinway Street with one of my friends, a psychotherapist, and Seyran said something he had never told me before, which I'll never forget. He said that if he had known what his life would be like in the U.S., he would have joined the Armenian army. For a while after he arrived in NYC, he didn't know what was worse: the risk of being damaged for being different, or being in exile from everything you know and love—your friends, your family, your community, your culture. By now, it was clear to him that the second choice was worse.

Of course, he could have been making this up, projecting to my friend what he thought she wanted to hear. Perhaps he sensed she would view him more compassionately if she saw him as a victim of circumstance. Otherwise, if coming to America was the wrong choice, why not return and do his army service? He could have showed up when they looked for him after three years—but he didn't. It's also true that he didn't know exactly what he was giving up when he initially decided to be with me in America.

And what was my role with regard to prostitution? Had I known that offering Seyran safety in exchange for companionship would transform to trading my dignity for sex, I, too, would have made a different choice. If I had known how miserable we would both be, I would have left Armenia by myself.

But I didn't see any of us as prostitutes—not yet, anyway. I thought that Seyran would grow up, and I naively hoped that jumping through the corrupt bureaucratic hoops of our governments would eventually result in our happiness.

STORY: MAY, 2007
YEREVAN

The days during Na's parents' visit were filled with activity. Every morning, Na and Seyran snuck into the brunch buffet at her parents' hotel. Every evening, they dined at a different restaurant. In the interim, they visited various sites—

the Children's Art Museum, the Martiros Saryan House-Museum, the Sergei Parajanov Museum, the Matenadaran. Sometimes, they hung out in her parents' hotel room and talked. Seyran and her parents hit it off. Once, when Na was teaching her workshop, Seyran took them to Raffi's Persian restaurant and ordered the nargileh for them to smoke. He said he liked spending time with them because he was getting to know Na better. He was also wooing them the way that he had courted Na—even skipping out on his classes as he had done when she'd been sick in the fall. He was insuring his safe passage. She, too, wanted him to be accepted by her parents. Unknowingly, Na played into his campaign to convince her parents that he was a legitimate partner.

When her parents met Seyran's parents at the country house in the village, Na was nervous their age difference would be obvious. Her mother had fallen down about a month before the trip, and she still had trouble walking. Seyran's mother, Nazeni, noticed, offering her arm to help the older woman to walk in the garden. Na's parents had mentioned to her that Seyran's parents looked young when she had emailed them a photo. She didn't tell them that they were in their late forties. Luckily, Seyran's father, Vartan, looked older than his age in person, fifty or more.

When they were all seated around the picnic table making khorovats, Na's mother, Stella, pointed to an old woman, asking who she was. Seyran's great-aunt Tato was dressed in layers of fraying, pilly sweaters, a homemade apron over her skirt, and a kerchief tied over her bright-orange hair. She was Seyran's mother's aunt, and she preferred living in the village, where heat and running water were limited to one day a week, instead of her comfortable apartment in Yerevan. Never married, she was considered the black sheep of the family. It was hard to guess her age because she was so wizened, her wrinkles deep crevices like the cracks in a canyon.

"Im krocheh," Vartan joked—*my sister*—as he tended the skewers in the fireplace.

"Oh," Stella replied, nodding her head. She seemed to believe it. "How old is she?" There was an awkward pause. So she asked the question in Armenian, "Kanee daregan?" to Nazeni and not to Tato.

Vartan answered for his wife in Armenian, "Forty-six," Nazeni's age, and Stella laughed—she thought he was referring to ancient-looking Tato.

"You know, in Armenia, it's not polite to ask someone their age," Seyran explained.

"Oh, sorry!" Stella apologized. "I thought it was okay because she's an elder!" Tato did seem ageless. When Tato hugged Na or held her hand, it felt like the life force of the land was shooting through the conduit of Tato's body. She looked 102, but she could have been as young as 70. Regardless, Seyran's admonition to Stella curtailed any further talk of age. Na breathed a sigh of relief.

But then Vartan asked her parents in English, "Do you think people in Armenia look older than their age?" Na almost choked on a chunk of khorovats. She had no idea why Vartan was asking this. He was the only one with knowledge about their age difference after seeing her passport at ZAGS. Was he trying to give Na an embolism? Or sabotaging their future together? Perhaps he was trying to understand why Stella believed Tato was his sister. He could have just been curious, given that Na's parents were older than they appeared to be. Luckily, the conversation soon headed elsewhere as Tato asked if a lot of Americans take medicine for anxiety.

Once the fear of being found out wore off, Na could feel a sadness settle in. She attributed it to the Cognac, but it might have been Seyran taking so many pictures as proof of their marriage for their interview at the embassy. Or it might have been her parents giving toasts to Seyran and Na as if they really were newlyweds. The worst was when Na and Seyran took her parents on a walk around the village, stopping at a tiny church. It was not much more than a storage shed constructed of thin metal walls, adorned with a few posters of Mary and Jesus. As they were lighting candles at a stand filled with sand, her father said, "God bless Natalee and Seyran, that they have a long, happy life together." In truth, it was what she wanted, but she couldn't admit it because she knew it likely wouldn't happen.

As they walked back to the house, her father suggested the couple have a church wedding when they arrived in the States in a few months.

"That's not me," Na said.

"Think about it," her father replied.

Na thought it was a strange suggestion. Throughout her coming of age, her father seemed to understand her better than her mother, telling her how much he trusted her to do the right thing. Na had made it clear over the years how she felt about the Armenian Church's repression of women, with its male-only clergy dressed in robes and slippers. Perhaps he was worried that his daughter had been married too informally. The ceremony of the diaspora—with its high ritual of frankincense and soul-stirring music—represented the validity and stability that he wished for her.

Her mother seemed to think differently. The next day, Na and Seyran took her parents to Garni, a Roman temple and a prime tourist spot, where a woman from New Jersey struck up a conversation with Na, who then introduced the woman to her parents and Seyran. Na wasn't sure what to call him; to say he was her husband was legally correct, but it felt bizarre, like wearing a formal costume. Na's parents were standing right there, so she said it with as little emphasis as possible, in a rushed mumble, "Seyranmyhusband."

Na's mother chimed in, "She came to Armenia on a Fulbright, and she got a *bonus!*" gesturing toward Seyran with a higher-pitched emphasis on *bonus*.

Seyran found this hilarious, and it soon became a refrain that he imitated regularly, replicating the change in pitch on the word *bonus* to make it sound as ridiculous as possible. He thought it humorous that Na's mother saw him as little more than an added feature, a surprising delight, a trifling object given away for free with a major purchase. Na found her mother's expression odd but reasoned that it was echoing the laissez-faire attitude the couple had about marriage in general.

One night, they ran into Gharib and Mardi, who were smiling and happy to meet Na's parents. "What do you think of your new son-in-law?" Gharib asked gleefully. It turned out that Mardi and Gharib had told a lot of people the news, so Na and Seyran regularly encountered acquaintances who congratulated them. They found it strange, but Na surmised to Seyran that perhaps Gharib and Mardi were excited for them because they would like to get married themselves, but the possibility was denied to them. Still, Na found herself in awe when single, straight cronies and queer friends alike asked if she had changed her last name, as if she had suddenly abandoned her former life, as if they had been wanting and waiting all along for her to be something definite, something recognized. Na marveled at the strong mythology that surrounded the institution of marriage—practically everyone placed that cookie-cutter image onto the couple based on their own attachments to it.

As much as she resisted definition, Na couldn't deny that after all they had been through, all the trips to offices and meetings with family and impromptu congratulations in the street, it did feel like they were more formal as a couple.

She also reasoned it this way: though they didn't feel the bind of the traditional commitment of marriage, they were joined in the love that they had.

Regardless, Na performed such mental gymnastics so she didn't have to question what exactly she was giving away.

❖

A few weeks after her parents returned to the U.S., Na was talking to her mother when Stella asked at the end of the conversation, "Do you want to have a reception when you come home?"

"No," Na said.

She laughed. "You don't want to have a church wedding?" It was clear she was joking. Somehow, Na had been let off the hook.

"No," she said. "Do you want to have a fiftieth wedding anniversary party?"

"No," her mother said.

"Why not?" Na asked. She expected her mother would say how sad it was to be reminded of all the people their age and older who were now gone. Over the years, Na had often gazed at her parents' wedding album, at the black-and-white photos of the web of extended family. There weren't many relatives left, a sentiment her parents expressed a lot lately.

But all Stella said was, "For the same reason you don't."

Na was astounded. Was her mother saying she didn't feel that she was truly married to her father?

At one point during their "wedding party" in the village, Seyran and Na had sex. It was after everyone had become acquainted, made toasts, and taken photos, but before they went on their walk through the neighborhood to light candles in the church. In other words, it seemed that Na and Seyran were in the clear; they had convinced her parents that Seyran was a legitimate age-appropriate partner. They went to the room at the top of the stairs of the family home, the one that Seyran's father had built as an addition, retrieving some dishes for the party. Suddenly, Seyran was overcome with lust and pulled her pants down and fucked her from behind.

"This is why I love you," Seyran said as they were doing it. But she didn't know what he meant. It felt so illicit; maybe this was why it appealed to him. The freedom to fuck behind their parents' backs? Or was it because she had complied? He had won her, proven himself to her parents, with her help.

There was a stuffed bird in that room. Seyran's father had shot it. The crane was a harbinger of fortune, with their huge nests in the countryside, easy to spot on the tops of telephone poles. Not the American version, a cartoonish animal that brings a baby, but the Armenian one: a mystical, powerful symbol. A famous folk song, filled with longing, asks the crane to bring back news of relatives, lost to genocide or exile, when it returns from its migration. In Armenian, the word for crane is *groong*. Even its name has the sound of return, a circular word.

Na's parents had come to Armenia to make sure she was safe; otherwise, they never would have made the trip. They were Armenian American, born in the U.S. to parents who escaped persecution and genocide. Stella and Tip were raised during the Depression and came of age in the nineteen-fifties and assimilated to whiteness via their college diplomas and their professional careers, ascending to the middle class. In visiting this land, they were returning to a culturally-inherited space of loss, poverty, and despair that they had intended to transcend when they wed. And here was a child who had resulted from their union, who was in the process of tearing herself apart through the legal, emotional, and traditional aspects of marriage. While her pseudo-husband fucked her from behind, a dead crane watched over them in silence.

META-WRITING:

Over the years, I had traumatized my parents by coming out as bisexual multiple times—because they were in denial and kept forgetting. So before I met Seyran, I had always been under the impression that my parents' dream for me would have been to marry a man of Armenian descent. I had now anticipated their concerns about our differences in citizenship status and class, but I was surprised by just how much distress the news initially caused them.

Looking back now, I suppose it was because I was so contradictory. I had told them that Seyran and I were boyfriend and girlfriend, but why would I have made such a serious commitment to help someone if I didn't love him like a husband?

Perhaps it was also because they didn't have the happiest of marriages themselves.

One night when I was visiting them in Rhode Island while trying to break up with Seyran, my mother was attempting to use her new computer, and my dad was making fun of her. She complained about how he did this every time she sat down to learn how to use it, then she mentioned how he often belittled her intellectually and professionally. "I didn't let him come to arts council meetings when I was president because he'd criticize me afterward," she said.

"He must be insecure," I told my mom.

"He never grew up," she said.

"Perhaps he should have gone to psychotherapy."

My mother laughed. I find myself more sympathetic toward her these days. She had lost close family through death and estrangement shortly before she wed, then had to deal with an emotionally immature partner on whom she was financially dependent, and with whom she made a family, her main source of love and companionship.

At the same time, my father had married a woman who was traumatized by losing her mother at a young age, not to mention other hurts she might have witnessed in her own parents who had separated when she was three years old. His own mother was traumatized, a child survivor of the Genocide. Had he been drawn to the traumatic response in strong women?

My mother was fairer, lighter-skinned, and conventionally attractive. She was the more verbal one, more confident and charming. She was also loath to compromise, often had to have her own way, and rarely apologized if she hurt your feelings. She wouldn't talk through the pros and cons of a situation but organized conversations so that she was irrefutably correct whatever the scenario. I learned from a very young age that when I had a problem, she would try to help me solve it in a way that would benefit her—if I wanted to ride my bike with my friends, it was too dangerous, so

I should spend time with her visiting art museums instead, especially when she was at odds with my father. She didn't like me leaving her. Even when I told her the news of getting a Fulbright to Armenia, she initially said it was a terrible idea.

My parents' fights consisted of my father taking potshots at my mother in a futile attempt to gain ground on a woman who refused to compromise. It always seemed to me that love was combative: I watched my mother prepare for battle, storing up resentments and mistakes to use as weapons. She always defended herself, at the ready to prove her greater worth, and she possessed stamina to engage in fighting for long periods of time, no matter the needs of others.

So the narcissistic nexus was not one I was unfamiliar with. I just didn't have the words to identify it. My mother often twisted feminism into a story of "women good/men bad" to draw me into her battles with my father. She said that he expected her to only be a housewife, and she pointed at his angry outbursts as proof of his wrongdoing. Though she indubitably experienced a lack of choices in her life as a woman in the fifties, and I am sure my father had sexist expectations of her, I also remember that if or when she neglected some of her responsibilities in pursuit of her interests—she was often late to pick me up from events; the house was usually a mess—she would act in manipulative ways to defend herself, and he would respond in frustration.

The power switch was similarly flipped with me and Seyran, around the time I took him back after he smeared cum on my face. By the time he had met Fimi, he was married to an American, impressing her parents, and on his way out of the country. Not yet a diasporan but something other than an Armenian. He'd already been using sexism against me, and I had bought further into the myth of the pathetic unmarried woman.

One way the disenfranchised can find power is to use something they know about you that you might not even know about yourself—in my case, fear. I couldn't know whether or not Seyran had fucked Mother Armenia—or anyone else for that matter; I, on the other hand, was always honest with him. For much of our relationship, he knew everything about me, and I knew little about him.

But I can imagine: Seyran and Fimi cavort a few blocks from the futile protests, singing and giggling in the cold water flat, a concrete block apartment with mold on the ceiling, plaster peeling from the walls, water in buckets in the bathroom. Fimi has infused her humble home with glamor, draping silky fabrics over lamps, paper flowers tucked into the frames that hold photos of her girls. Wine in a plastic soda bottle is nearly gone, spilled onto the carpet on the floor as she lifts up her skirt and mounts Seyran, wide-eyed. She gyrates her hips and sings when she moans. Afterward, she gives him advice on how to serve his American wife.

Seyran often claimed that everyone wanted to fuck him. Sex was currency for him, but what did it mean? If he and Fimi did have sex, I imagine it wasn't good—Fimi drunk and stuck in her own reverie, Seyran attracted only to someone's attention toward him.

What would Fimi have told me if I had spent the evening with her instead? I'd rather not try to imagine. Instead, I draw inspiration from the example she showed me that first night when I had met her by the Opera. To keep on singing, even if you are in pain. Even if your children are taken from you.

Fimi was in pain—and she created something beautiful. Her life experiences may have influenced her art, and vice versa, but it wasn't cause and effect, as I had initially thought. Her singing wasn't an exchange of strife for art. I can't know why her children were taken from her, if she had been incompetent or dangerous, if she had given them up, if society or her family had punished her for her aspirations to sing or for her drive to be free. But the pain she experienced and the talent she nurtured existed at once, independently.

16. POWER PLAYS

BLOG POST: *NEVER PUBLISHED.* JUNE 21, 2007
YEREVAN

The Interview (Part I) >>>

Interviewer: What side of the bed does Natalee sleep on?

Seyran: The left side.

I: What kind of face cream does she use?

S: She brought a big bottle of moisturizer from America. I think it is called Keri.

I: What color is Natalee's toothbrush?

S: It's pink. And white.

I: She has two toothbrushes?

S: No, it has two colors on it.

I: What kind of cosmetics does she use on her face?

S: Not a lot. Brown lipstick and eye—what's it called?—liner.

I: When does she wear them?

S: For special occasions.

I: Does she color her hair?

S: No.

I: Has she ever colored her hair?

S: No.

I: She's natural then.

S: Yes, she is very natural.

Na: Wait, I hennaed my hair in college.

I: Oh, like women do in Armenia. No, don't tell them that. If they ask you, say no.

Every toiletry in our flat has been memorized, as well as the intricacies of our hygienic practices. We can cite the birthdays, including the year, of every in-law. Favorite color, food, song, film, book, place in Yerevan—all have been identified. I tell Seyran it's going to look bad if we know the answer to every question by heart as if it's a chemistry quiz. But he doesn't care. He is nervous, and he must do well on this exam.

We have paid an interviewer ten thousand dram (around thirty dollars) to drill us with questions, meeting her at the apartment she shares with her mother in a remote corner of Yerevan. We sit at a round dinner table covered with a linen tablecloth embroidered with swallows. Behind her is a china cabinet that I gaze at when I am bored. She is younger than me, in her early thirties, and she worked at the U.S. embassy as an interpreter at one point, I am not sure when. And I am not positive she has interpreted any of these green card interviews before. Seyran found her through one of his friends.

We've already practiced while on our walks, mainly based on common sense and my memory of the movie *Green Card* with Gerard Depardieu and Andie MacDowell. Sometimes we are anxious when we think of all the people who have been denied visas lately, and other times less anxious when I discover how many of my friends in the U.S. have successfully passed through a similar process.

Our interviewer says that I won't have a problem because I'm not nervous. But Seyran will. It's good that he is practicing answering questions in English with her. When she asks if I have siblings, and he explains, "She had one brother," she ribs him: "What do you mean 'had'? Did he die?" She likes to give him a hard time. Sometimes she seems like a couples' therapist since she has such a generic, inoffensive appearance, with her long hair, modest makeup, and nondescript black pants and purple blouse. But if she were a therapist, she'd be an unprofessional one since she is always on my side.

Interviewer: Now, you said Natalee likes to read. When does she read?

Seyran: At night, while I'm working on the computer.

I: What time do you go to bed?

S: At around 2 or 3 a.m.

I: Do you go to bed at the same time as Natalee?

S: No.

I: Do you think that's right?

Na: No, I think it's unhealthy. It bothers me that he stays up late working on the computer.

I: Who does the cooking?

S: Natalee mostly.

N: But he did it a lot when we first met. Now hardly ever.

I: It's always like that, Natalee jan. How much did your wedding rings cost?

S: Seven thousand dram for three rings. My friend made them.

I: Three? Why did you get three?

S: I had one made for my thumb.

I: Don't tell them that. It's weird. Don't tell them anything that will cause suspicion or make them ask more questions. Okay? What is the first thing you do when you wake up in the morning?

S: Turn on the computer.

I: You have so much work that you turn on the computer first thing in the morning?

S: No, I just like to check my email.

I: Do you think that's healthy?

N: Probably not, but I do the same thing.

I: Don't tell them that it's the first thing you do, okay? They'll think you are strange. Just tell them you go to the bathroom.

This last exchange depresses me to no end. It seems we don't just have to prove that we are a couple, but a normal couple, whatever that means. I can't help feeling that our interviewer derives a sick pleasure from learning about our personal lives. She knows our salaries, our total monthly income, and expenses. She has asked me why I don't work at the embassy (like they're going to ask me this?) and how much I pay my Armenian tutor per class (three thousand dram), which she deems as needless extortion of foreigners. "I'm glad you're getting out of Armenia," she scoffs. Most insidiously, when we discuss my family history and I tell her that my grandparents were Genocide survivors, she smiles and says, "Nice."

"What?"

"Not that it's nice that they went through the Genocide. The people at the embassy like the Genocide. They like any disaster. September 11th. Hurricane Katrina. They love hearing about the earthquake in 1988. They like when people struggle."

At least I'm getting a picture of how local Armenians view the Americans who work at the embassy. My friend Annie, whose kids are in the same playgroup with some of the diplomats' kids, told me that State Department staff assigned to the U.S. embassy in Armenia are considered to be in a "hardship position" because of the unresolved ceasefire in Karabakh, so they get paid more, enabling them to live in the most exclusive gated community in Yerevan. To average Armenians, these privileged Americans' interest in their tragic difficulties must seem sensationalistic and grisly.

But we didn't pay our interviewer to learn her psychological analysis of the embassy staff. This lady should be asking the most obvious questions to discern if we're a real couple, e.g., how did you meet? What was your wedding like? Why didn't you get married in a church? Why weren't your parents there? How can you have a relationship when there's a seventeen-year age difference between you?

The websites and chat rooms that Seyran consults advise to be as honest as possible. A white man marrying a Chinese woman should say he has always had an Asian fetish. Here's how I would confide to the consul, whom I imagine to be a beefy Midwestern white man wearing a blue blazer: "I had been wanting to meet someone Armenian. But most of them are so traditional. Because he's young and more open-minded, Seyran accepts me for who I am as an independent woman." But our faux interviewer does not ask me such a question. She does ask Seyran why we are moving to New York as opposed to staying in Yerevan. Seyran explains that we have discussed it, and I have offered to live here in Armenia, but he doesn't want my career to suffer.

His coach says, "Good! You must seem like you are sacrificing, that you are doing everything for her because you love her. But you need to pause, sigh, and then say, 'Because I love her.'"

She makes him repeat the answer a few times—big sigh, "because I love her"—insisting that he say it with emotion and certainty, like a final answer on *Who Wants to Be a Millionaire*. (There's an Armenian version that is quite popular.) When he says it, the line sounds phony. My feelings would be hurt except that it's not like him to tell strangers that he loves me ...

META-WRITING:

When he rehearsed the line with our coach, he only looked at her, never at me. There was a moment during this exchange when he sounded so stilted, she forced him to delve deeper.

"Seriously, you tell me, why do you love her?" she asked.

"Na is the only person who accepts and understands me," he said sincerely.

In the moment I believed him. I felt that he revealed more of himself to me than to anyone else. It was well before I discovered just how much he kept from me, of course.

Once, he almost let the truth come out. Around the time of the above blog post, I told Seyran I worried for our future if we couldn't get him a visa.

He became irritated with me. "If I don't get a visa, you should go back to America and we'll try again later."

"If you don't get a visa, I'll stay and wait with you," I said.

"No. You can't do that."

"Why not?"

"I won't be with you if you stay here." Clearly, he'd thought about what he would do if I left.

I looked at him. "What? You mean you're going to stay with me if you get a visa, but you won't if you don't?"

He backtracked. "No, I will be with you. I just meant that I don't want you to stay with me. Don't you want to publish your book about your family history? You should go back and do that."

I wasn't fully convinced by this explanation, but I couldn't allow myself to question it further. His quick save made it into the sessions with our coach, and it became part of our narrative: he was sacrificing, giving up his life to be with me so that I could publish my book. The story was crafted by our coach to counter the most obvious narrative that the embassy would suspect, that he was marrying me to get out of Armenia.

With her set ideas of how couples should appear, our interviewer struck me as judgmental, her eyes narrowing as we answered her questions. Seyran had gone to her a few times on his own before I met her. I now wonder what he had told her about me. Here was a nice yet older American woman who thought she was helping him. Had he told her that he was duping not just the U.S. government but me, too?

A warning bell should have gone off when I saw her training him to say that he loved me. But I was too preoccupied with her. I questioned whether she was qualified to counsel us on a green card interview, and when she suggested my tutor was bilking me, I suspected her, especially since she was charging three times more. When she criticized Seyran's behavior—going to bed late, turning on the computer first thing in the morning, getting a third ring—I was further miffed as if she were criticizing us collectively. Here, I thought, was the typical Armenian conformism about how the

world should be. Anyone could adopt and wield the criteria, even someone you wouldn't expect,
like a single woman in her thirties living with her mother on the outskirts of town. I found myself
triggered by her judgment, more suspicious of her than of Seyran.

Did it make her feel powerful, taking my money to help Seyran while also suggesting that he
was a fraud? Or did the circumstances simply force her into this unlikely position? When we left her
place for the last time, she hugged and kissed us and wished us the best.

STORY: MID-JUNE, 2007
YEREVAN

Na was cooking dinner for Amal, tasting the green beans in tomato sauce, when she realized that she needed lemons. Walking from the kitchen down the small hallway to the living room, she found Seyran watching TV and asked if he would go to the corner store for her.

"No, I'm tired," he said.

She looked at him skeptically. He had gotten up very late, so he'd had plenty of sleep.

"You're not doing anything. Can you please go get them for me?"

"Why should I? If you wanted them, you should have gotten them when you were out."

"I didn't think I would need them then."

"We can call Star Supermarket and get them delivered."

Na thought this was ridiculous. "That seems silly and a waste of money when you're perfectly able to get them, and you're not doing anything else." She knew she sounded like a mom talking to a teenager, but she couldn't stop. "It would be a big help to me if you could go down to the store and get them. Please?"

He ignored her. Something about this pushed her buttons, and she exploded, informing him that he was an asshole, that he never cooked or did the dishes, that he couldn't treat her like his mother, and that she wasn't going to give him any more money.

The last part must have riled him up because he said he would go to the store.

"But you have to sit with me for a while," he demanded. Na thought he must be feeling neglected by having to share Na with visitors, first Maria and then her parents. Lately, Na had also been spending time with Amal, back for the summer from the States, and Tanya, both with whom she was engaged in a writing project. The school year had ended, and Na was now leading the women's writing workshop at the Center for Armenian Women.

She told him she couldn't sit with him right at that very moment. "I'm cooking rice, and if I don't watch the pot, it will burn."

"As usual," he said.

"Fuck you," she said and stormed out of the room, back to the kitchen.

She thought of how he had been so kind to her parents while they were here and even to Maria when she had first arrived. He was always going out of his way to help people. Now she worried that his kindness was purely an act—that it had been fake with her, too.

He's always acting, Na thought as she stirred the beans. She thought of an event a few days before. They had been visiting his friend Archig who was recovering from surgery. The two competitive friends were sharing stories of people they knew, and Seyran mentioned that his ex-girlfriend Lalig was married and had just had a baby. Since they were in bull session mode, Seyran claimed he was really the father of Lalig's child. Na laughed with the boys. "Yeah, she got pregnant from when she had sex with you two years ago. That's hilarious."

"Oh no, the last time I had sex with Lalig was last July."

"Last July?" It was now mid-June. Na did the math in her head. The timing wasn't right for the baby to be his—not unless a baby could be six weeks late. But then Na continued to pull the thread: when they first met, he told her that he had broken up with Lalig about a year before. But now he was saying he had had sex with her in July, which was just two months before Na and Seyran met. Had he still been with Lalig in July? Or later? Had they overlapped? It was too much for her to fathom.

In front of Archig, Na broke through her polite facade. "Are you lying to me all the time?" she asked. Archig stopped laughing and clammed up, turning away, while Seyran stared at her. "Well? This relationship is a game to you?" she asked.

He hemmed and hawed and tried to explain, and Na figured that he hadn't fully thought through his braggadocio to Archig. As they changed the subject, she looked out the window, fuming, and they soon stood up to go.

Normally, she wouldn't break down in front of another person, but she was tired of pretending that everything was okay. When she had been doubtful of Seyran in their first few months together, she often found herself thinking that if he was really awful, someone would have warned her—Amal, Tanya, Gharib, Mardi, Beatris—someone. She now found herself thinking this again. Why couldn't someone—Archig, for example, sitting right there—tell Na that Seyran was no good? Perhaps they didn't know, or they didn't think that he was a problem. Maybe they couldn't believe Na didn't see it—or maybe they thought that she did see it but that she didn't care. Perhaps they didn't think it was their place, and they feared she would be offended and rebuff their friendship. In her worst, most paranoid moments, she suspected that the Armenians wouldn't rat out one of their own, even if they did care about her.

Now, as she cooked the beans and rice, Seyran sauntered into the kitchen and asked, "So what do you want?"

Na was cutting up a pepper and said, "A lemon."

"To put in your pussy?" he asked.

Her brain curdled with rage. She had no words.

So she screamed.

META-WRITING:

I let the rage come out through my mouth, for as loud and as long as I could, bouncing off the walls in a trill, through the window, down to the street. The scream separated me from my time and place, and yet it was all me.

Seyran put his hand on my back and laughed; he was so startled. I was still holding the knife. "Wow," he said. "Honey, that was so strong. Have you ever done that before?"

I had no idea what to say. I had a history of yelling with my family but not with anyone else. Though I sometimes yelled in anger, it was usually a word or two—not a crude, extended shriek. "I think so," I told him, shaking with emotion. It seemed he'd never imagined that I had anger inside of me.

He wasn't upset. It appeared to startle him, and he thought I was weird, but he didn't otherwise care.

I felt terrible, embarrassed by what had come out of me.

What I found strange at the time was that his demeanor had completely changed. He was kind to me after I screamed.

He was happy.

I thought most people would have condemned such behavior. I was relieved when he didn't distance himself from me. I didn't even remember that he'd asked if I wanted lemons in my pussy.

JOURNAL: MAY 5, 2011
NEW YORK CITY

At the front of the room, in the federal building where we were waiting for Seyran's citizenship interview, a TV was mounted from the ceiling, and the channel was tuned to NY1. It showed Obama laying a wreath at Ground Zero after he had killed Osama bin Laden. Seyran joked that everyone would be so happy that they'd hand out green cards left and right.

The room was vast and long, with teller windows, like at the bank or the DMV, situated on either end. Rows of hard pink chairs stretched out in between, arranged in several sections. The guard at the door, who had a Russian accent, told us to sit in the middle of the room under fluorescent lights, where people were crowded into chairs facing each other. When he wasn't looking, we moved to seats near a wall of windows where sunlight was streaming in.

The room was full of immigrants from every continent and color category: Asian, Black, Latino, Middle Eastern, Eastern European. A Jewish couple sat in front of us. The man in a yarmulke, with long curly forelocks, white shirt, and matching black vest and pants, tried to memorize the history questions. Seyran and I had been going over them since he received the letter about his appointment, only a month ago, and four months later than Esmerelda the immigration lawyer had predicted. I was so relieved when the letter arrived that I helped him every day so that he could nail the test. It has been a rough month, filled with fights and discussions about our plans to move on. And yet, every night, I sat by his tatami mat and went over the questions with him before he went to sleep. Within a week, he seemed to know the answers to most of the hundred questions. He had trouble with a few, though.

When I asked, "Who was Martin Luther King?" he insisted that he had freed the slaves, which I suppose has some truth to it. I corrected him even though I knew he was joking.

In his answer to, "Who is the speaker of the House of Representatives?" he would reply, "Joe Boner." He kept getting John Boehner, Joe Biden, and John Roberts mixed up. Who can blame him?

He had trouble with the names of our representatives, too. He looked up our representative in the House and found a photo of an old man with a flower in his lapel, but this was a mistake: our rep is Carolyn Maloney. Still, whenever I asked, "Who's your representative in the House?" he would answer, "The cute old man with the flower!" and smile brightly, like he was describing a puppy.

In the end, I think all the testing paid off. Last night, we prepared by getting his clothes and papers together. As he was shaving his beard and mustache, I questioned him one last time, and he got all the answers right, though he made all of the same jokes. Perhaps they helped him to remember. He left a funny mustache and pretended to be Borat.

He observed, "These are my last hours of being an immigrant."

"You'll still be an immigrant," I told him.

"Why?"

"Because you moved from somewhere else. It doesn't matter if you're naturalized. You'll be an American citizen, but it doesn't change the fact that you immigrated."

"Oh shit," he said. "That sucks!"

Now at the waiting room, we watched the other immigrants as they were called into the back offices. Every few minutes, a different person opened a door and called out a name. There was no loudspeaker in this huge room, so if you didn't hear your name, or they didn't say it correctly, you were screwed. A Latino-looking man sitting to our right was called, followed by a group of East Asian people behind us who had two lawyers accompanying them. I wondered why they needed the lawyers.

One thin, young Asian girl was wearing cut off shorts so short that I could see her black panties underneath. This irked me. The instructions explicitly state to dress respectfully. Another woman, tall and dark with black hair and light skin, resembling Diamanda Galás, was wearing a black see-through mesh top that fully displayed her black bra. *What is this, a night club?* I wondered if anyone got kicked out for dressing inappropriately. Last night when we were buying pants, Seyran wanted a white pair. "This is the federal government," I insisted. "Black, brown, navy blue, or gray *only*." He ended up choosing a gray linen pair.

"How can these people dress so slutty?" I now asked Seyran.

"No, it's a good idea," Seyran said. "It makes the other person nervous."

In my diligence to obey and fulfill every rule, I had not thought of a power play.

It goes to show how different we are. This past month, I agreed to his stipulation that we are just roommates, but it hasn't stopped him from walking around the house naked and propositioning me for sex. He even did it last night, claiming that it would relax him before his interview. I told him no, that it was impossible because I was not attracted to him anymore.

"Why not?" he asked.

I told him, "I stopped wanting to have sex with you because you've hurt me too many times."

STORY: MAY 5, 2011
NEW YORK CITY

In fact, there were a few nights in a row that Na felt he had harassed her. Once, he lay down next to her in her room and put his hand down her pants, claiming he felt something on her ass that he needed to look at. Another time, he wouldn't let her get up, pinning her arms down until she had to struggle free from her own bed.

The next day, she was taking a shower when he kicked open the bathroom door. When she went to her room to change, he opened the door on her. Na told him to get out, but he took a picture with his computer and joked that he would put it on the internet. Na was frazzled out of her wits, and she didn't want to use up her energy to scream at him.

She felt that it wouldn't matter if she told him he was harassing her; he would continue these antics, all the while claiming he was celibate. He came home from work one day and tried kissing her. When she pushed him away, he grabbed at her crotch. Clearly, this was assault. Na told him to stop, threatening that she was ready to call the landlord with her month's notice.

It had been his idea to be roommates, not only in word but in deed. Now that Na was satisfying that claim, he couldn't stand it. She'd been telling him for weeks that they would break up as soon as he got his citizenship. They had even planned when and how to get divorced. But the other night, he suggested they stay together for the perks. Na didn't think it was worth mentioning that getting sexually harassed in exchange for lower taxes wasn't really a fair trade-off.

The worst was when he insisted that Na tell him what she wanted in life because he could help her. Na told him that she didn't want anything. Then he asked, "What makes you unhappy?" She told him she didn't feel respected at work and didn't have enough time to write.

"What would be the difference if you had those things?" he asked.

"If I were respected at work, I would do a better job of teaching; if I had more time to write, I would be creative, which makes me happy and in turn helps others."

He said that Na should be happy just to teach her students. "Why do you care about the system and not the children?" he asked.

"Because the students want to get good jobs and do better than their parents. How can they learn from me if I can't even do this for myself? That's why I need to stand up for myself and fight for what's right."

"There's no such thing as right and wrong," he said.

"Sorry, I'm not going to accept injustice. The government takes advantage of workers, limits their opportunities to be educated, and of course the rich keep getting richer. It's even worse in Armenia, which is why you came here."

"You're being judgmental," he said, then asked, "Why do you need a lot of money?"

"I don't need a lot, just enough to take care of myself when I'm old."

"Why?"

"So I can be comfortable."

"You'll be comfortable, so what?"

"Isn't it better to be at peace than to be debased and suffering? Sorry, we have a fundamental disagreement. I can't talk to someone who doesn't believe in right and wrong." Na stormed out.

He followed her to her room, "Na, I'm trying to help you because of all the help you've given me. You seem to really need help right now. You're so angry."

"I'm angry because I have someone patronizing me and telling me I'm messed up," Na yelled.

He replied, "You eat well, and you have always had a good life, and you will continue to."

Na told him, "I'm not supposed to say your behavior is wrong because I can eat? I was fine before this talk. You made me angry. You're the one who is unhappy. You don't have money because you spend all of it the minute you get it. You don't have friends, and you never will because you never take responsibility for your actions. You come in here touching me, harassing me, and you have the nerve to tell me there's no such thing as right and wrong?"

"You were born here," he said, "and you have a good life; you've never been hungry. Nothing bad will happen to you. The government wants you to believe that you have to fight—but they don't actually fight you. They're only making you tired."

JOURNAL: MAY 5, 2011
NEW YORK CITY

But he is the one making me tired.

At that point in the waiting room, there was a poll on the TV screen: Do you feel safer now that Osama bin Laden is dead? At that very moment, a woman in a hijab entered door number 1. "She won't get it because she's Pakistani," Seyran said.

"I don't want to be American anymore," I told him.

They finally called Seyran's name at 8:23 a.m. When he came back out—it couldn't have been more than ten minutes later—he was smiling, but he looked at me funny as he walked across the room. When he was back in his seat, he showed me a form with boxes checked with red ink. It said that he'd passed his English and history test, but he needed to fill out form N-14. We had to go to the windows on the opposite side of the room and wait for someone to tell him what to do.

He told me it was a strange interview, that the woman was Russian and didn't speak English as well as him. She didn't want to see his papers, including bank statements and my pension, which names him as a beneficiary. Instead, she had said it was bad that we didn't have a joint bank account. But all it requested on the form was proof of residence and marital union. We have both: leases in both our names and all kinds of correspondence sent to our home.

"She said it was a new thing for New York," he said.

"We are dealing with the federal government, not New York," I explained. I didn't understand—was he lying again, or had she lied to him? At this point, it didn't matter as the result was the same: he didn't get his citizenship.

The Russian guard was watching for any use of cell phones, which was prohibited in the room, so I stepped out to go to the bathroom and look up form N-14 on my crappy phone with the slide-out keyboard. All I could figure out was that it was a request for additional information. Someone had posted in an online forum that we needed to show bank statements, credit card statements, health insurance policies—none of which we have. Someone else had advised that it would take several more months to sort out. Dejected, I returned to tell Seyran, who was talking to a random Asian woman who had just been given the same form. They both looked at me for answers. But my world had crashed, and I didn't feel like dealing with a stranger. I gave her the details as best as I could discern from my phone, but she didn't understand much English and eventually stood up and walked out of the room without waiting.

Seyran was angry. Not at the situation, or the government, or that hapless lady. He was upset with me for not being kinder to her. He said, "You're gonna get her deported because you wouldn't smile."

I glared at him. Thankfully, Seyran was finally called to the window. Again, it took less than ten minutes. When he returned, he showed me a list of items he had to bring in person on June 23 or his application would be rejected: documents that demonstrated our financial union from the past three years, most of which we didn't have.

276 | Nancy Agabian

I am tired. I have to take care of myself, and him, a person who is currently harassing Na.

When we went outside, I told him he would have to be the one to get a lawyer and find out what to do. He didn't say anything. I can't imagine that he'll ever take the lead on his own citizenship.

While Seyran stopped at an ATM to withdraw money, I cried quietly, standing off to the side on the sidewalk. I must have been crying more visibly than I realized because a white man passing by in a business suit and carrying a briefcase stopped to ask me if I was all right. I nodded, astonished. I have cried silently on the subway or in line at the grocery store many a time after fights with Seyran, and no one ever says anything.

Seyran was oblivious to the whole exchange. By now we were both late for work, so we said goodbye. Surprisingly, I held on to him as we hugged; I was so upset that my body involuntarily wanted comfort.

"What's your problem?" he asked as he pulled away.

I had thought I was going to be free from this cycle. I fear that it will never end, even if the government gives me what I want.

META-WRITING:

I had long disassociated my ashamed self as Na. She wasn't me. But the compartments were breaking down. I stood on the sidewalk and cried.

When Seyran told me that I didn't need to fight the government, that the system was a ploy to tire me out, he seemed to be talking about himself. I don't know if he realized that he was sending me a message to walk away, to step back, to disengage from him. But I couldn't imagine he would get his citizenship on his own. I couldn't walk away, even though he was abusing me.

Perhaps it was similar for the diplomats who were of a particular personality type, believing they were helping others, in a hardship position, wanting to find disasters that would give their life meaning. When you feel responsible for taking care of those less fortunate, a kind of mania is created: you believe you are more important, but then why do you feel lacking?

BLOG POST: *NEVER PUBLISHED.* JUNE 21, 2007
YEREVAN

The Interview (Part 2) >>> The wait was interminable at the consular section of the U.S. embassy in Yerevan. For a few hours, Seyran and I must have watched half a dozen Armenians plead their cases to the consul behind a glass window and through a microphone. Seyran and I were number 7; while waiting for our turn, we saw parties 1 through 6 have their visa applications heartlessly rejected.

The feeling of impending doom wasn't helped by the setting: the embassy is a huge fortress compound with only a few windows, so you can't help but feel you have entered the lair of The Man who is going to fuck you over big time. A few weeks ago, I visited the American Citizens Services section, where we got all our forms, and the consular section, where I dropped them off. These had been minor tasks compared to what we were going through today, but I still found them unsettling and paranoia-inducing. One consul told us that I didn't have to be very detailed with my job history, but Seyran had to account for every year because if he didn't it would seem as if he were lying. "And we don't like liars," he said with the same tone as a junior high school vice principal. He was wearing a tie with fish on it. As I made fun of him on the marshrutka back home, Seyran said he liked the consul because he had given straightforward answers, unlike the Armenian bureaucrats.

I was reminded of the Armenian clerk who had given me the forms and instructions a few weeks before. When I had asked for his name, he smiled sheepishly and declined, claiming that he could be known only as an assistant immigration officer. A moment later, I noticed he was wearing a name tag.

This gives you an idea of the three-card monte operation we are dealing with. It took us three visits to drop off all our paperwork because we had been told different requirements by various staff members. And no one called us back within a month, as we had been promised, for our interview. It is unclear whether they would have called us if we hadn't contacted them first. I can't decide if they are inept or if they are testing us.

The TV was playing Beyoncé and Justin Timberlake on the Armenian video channel. This is America: thighs and butts. I don't know if it's because I've been in Armenia for so long, but I am appalled at how much music videos resemble porn nowadays. There were little children in the waiting area, but no one asked the guard, in charge of the clicker, to change the channel. We were expected to accept the culture of American pop stars, the same way we had to admire the little images of the Statue of Liberty's face and the dome of the Capitol above each window in the consular section, 4 through 12. Only two of eight windows were in use. One was manned by the Armenian guy who would not tell me his name, and the other was shared by a consul and his translator. Seyran asked why there were so many windows. I had no answer. For when The Man anticipates a rush of visa processing? This U.S. embassy is reputedly the largest in the world after Japan's, supposedly for its proximity to Iran.

We had nothing to do but sit and be nervous. We each went to the bathroom a couple of times. Seyran wanted to talk and joke, but I preferred to play out my fantasies of what could go wrong in the interview. For example: we were planning to tell them we had gotten our wedding rings a couple of weeks ago, because our photo albums end then and all our pictures show us ringless, but the truth is that we only got them yesterday. What if they asked why there was no tan line on our ring fingers? "Because we haven't been in the sun much," Seyran said, as I continued to scrutinize all the answers we'd been producing and practicing this past week.

Eventually, the shell game playing out at the windows distracted me. Two elderly couples, a deaf guy who was livid at his mom, and two sets of young families with small children had all sidled up to the consul's window, only to be denied visas. One of the moms told the children to smile. Another little kid tiptoed to the counter, her hands reaching up to it, as she peered at the consul.

Seyran said the families were misinformed. They'd spent a lot of money, about two hundred dollars per person, to apply for the visas, but their reasons involved visiting family. It was better to have a short-term reason, like going for a conference that would help your work here in Armenia, he said.

In explaining his case, one dad went so far as to plead, "Consul jan," which we found hilarious. But we were watching from behind their backs, and when they turned around, I suddenly felt exposed. They could see our smugness while we eavesdropped on their moment of need. Who was to say we wouldn't go through the same kind of travesty when it was our turn?

I hated America for making me go through this. Who the hell do the Americans think they are, messing with people's lives? It takes feats of the imagination for me to construct a situation in which the embassy is not supposed to try us but to protect us. Since I am a United States citizen, I possess certain rights, and one of them is to bring my spouse, who is not a terrorist or a criminal, to America. I tried to remember that I was small, the world was vast, and this was just one moment among many other far more important moments happening on Earth.

I glanced across the room at the consul, sitting behind the glass. He looked about my age. He wore chunky glasses and a goatee, and he seemed to be rubbing his head an awful lot. It dawned on me that this would not be the most pleasant job to have. I couldn't imagine waking every morning to face scores of strangers who wanted something from you. It occurred to me that the consul was just as nervous, if not more so, than the people approaching him.

As the day dragged on, it eventually became apparent that Seyran and I were the last case the consul would be reviewing. When we appeared at his window, he was all smiles. He told us that I would go next door with him to be interviewed first, and then Seyran would follow when I was done.

I brought our photo album with me, and I sat down. He was sitting down, too, but there was a glass divider between us.

He asked how long I'd been in Armenia, and I told him ten months. He asked what I'd been doing here, and I told him that I was a Fulbrighter and that I was teaching. When I told him about the writing workshop, he said, "That sounds cool."

"It is cool," I said. Was the consul trying to be friends with me?

He asked how I met Seyran. I showed him the brochure of the lecture where we had met. He asked about our wedding ceremony and whether my parents had attended. I showed him photos from the album. I didn't talk too much about them because I was nervous. I was pointing out our family members, when suddenly I realized I couldn't find Seyran's brother, and I became flustered. It had never occurred to me before that he wasn't there. Then I remembered: he had taken the pictures.

The consul asked what side of the bed I slept on.

He asked if I spoke Armenian.

He asked if Seyran spoke English.

He asked what Seyran's job was.

Before he let me go, he asked if there was anything else I wanted to tell him. I showed him the letters of testimony from our friends. He skimmed through them, and I saw him smile. I had asked people to write in detail, to give a stranger an idea of what Seyran and I are like as a couple. In her testimony, my friend Annie calls me shy and gentle and Seyran a social butterfly. I wondered if the Consul was smiling at this or at the part where Annie describes our affection, when she once saw Seyran feeding me a strawberry at a pastry shop.

As I passed Seyran in the hallway, I whispered, "It's easy, he's nice."

Later, Seyran told me he had been sitting outside the door and had heard our entire conversation. The consul asked Seyran the same questions he had asked me, but Seyran had a lot more fun answering them. The two joked and laughed.

(Perplexed, I could hear them giggling from my seat outside the door.) When Seyran told him about our first date at a chamber music recital, the consul said, "That sounds romantic!" I would have been disappointed that we hadn't gotten to put all our ablutions and birthday information to the test if Seyran hadn't been so happy and relieved afterward.

The consul said that he would approve our application, just like that. I have a feeling he had already decided before we even sat down, that it was simply a formality, and that he was even looking forward to it. Later, Annie suggested that maybe he had been persuaded by our application and the interview convinced him. But the application isn't very extensive; it only lists my income and our ages. I have a sneaky suspicion that he has been reading my blog, that he already knew me before I sat down. Likewise, I have an uncanny feeling that I know him, as if I could easily run into him any night at a bar. It's not likely, given that he probably lives in a mansion near the other diplomatic workers.

Whatever the case, the whole experience renewed my faith in America. I know it's a small, stupid story, and maybe I should reserve my faith until after the war in Iraq ends, or when the educational system gets the investment it deserves, or when racism, sexism, and homophobia cease to exist. But it's reassuring to know there are people like you in the government who trust you to make the right decisions.

All this time, have I misjudged the U.S. government? Or have I misjudged myself?

17. I'LL TAKE YOUR PAIN AWAY

BLOG POST: JULY 23, 2007
YEREVAN

Book Chamber >>> I didn't question my parting gift of *Reading Lolita in Tehran* to my friend Anahid until I found myself apologizing for not having a present for my fellow colleague Sona. I am not really friends with Sona, but Anahid had invited her to come along with us to our end-of-the-school-year celebration. Because I had spotted Henry James in Anahid's bookcase when I visited her home at Christmastime, I thought she would find commonality in Nafisi imparting her love of Western literature to her students. But had I known Sona was joining us, I would have found her something special in the collection of books that I am leaving behind. Now I felt awkwardly empty-handed.

I met Anahid and Sona at Crepe de France near the university. Anahid had wanted to take me to the fancier Caucasus, but it was too far away from the Book Chamber, where I had to go directly after lunch. Amal had called unexpectedly that morning, alerting me that the national book registration officers needed my signature along with hers and Tanya's for the book we had written together, *Voch Mi Batsatrutyun*, or in English, *No Explaining*. The Book Chamber was open to the public for only two hours in the afternoon, and we needed to catalogue the title before bringing the manuscript to the printers the next day.

The sun was shining brightly, and Anahid requested a table by the window. She ordered a few orders of crepes, some with curds and others with mushrooms. I presented my gift to Anahid, telling Sona that if I had known she was joining us, I would have brought her a book as well. Sona told me not to worry, and then, in a way that seemed very much unlike her, she launched into a speech. "You know, Natalee, there are no great Armenian writers right now. It's because of the way our society is—we are not free. The mind needs freedom to write, for the mind to connect to the hand. But you have a free mind. You need to be our writer."

I was touched and taken aback. As far as I knew, Sona hadn't read my writing, so I was skeptical, especially of her assertion that there were no great Armenian writers. There was Beatris's crew, for starters. Apparently, Sona didn't know them. Or perhaps she did but deemed them less than great, or maybe she just didn't approve of their work.

I decided not to challenge Sona to skirt any possible conflict. "Okay," I told her bashfully. "But I don't write in Armenian."

"That's okay, you can be translated. Saroyan didn't write in Armenian, either, but he is considered an Armenian writer."

Anahid begged to differ. "He is an American writer," she clarified. "Of Armenian origin."

"Nevertheless, Natalee," Sona continued, "you should write your observations about Armenia. We Armenians need to see ourselves represented. We need to think critically about our predicament, and we need writers like you to prompt us."

The suggestion begged me to tell Sona that I have been attempting to do something like this right here on my blog, but I was having trouble admitting it.

To operate in the world, I have compartmentalized the people I know. Everyone does this to some degree. There are people we can be more of our true selves with, and there are others—family, coworkers, neighbors, etc.—whom we can't. As a writer, I know there are some people who can't handle that I write about sexuality, identity, and the Armenian family, but I still want them in my life, so I hide my writing from them.

Sona is telling me she wants me to be free, but I suspect I'm a little bit too free for her taste. *No Explaining* is a collaboratively written story about three women who live between languages, nations, and identities; our intersections cause other people much confusion. So, together, we have created a space to write to each other in three languages, embracing the idea that we cannot be understood easily.

In my portion of the book, I write about the plight of our young female students who are valued more for their appearance than their abilities; how I don't believe that a woman must have children to be whole; and about my scandalous history of being diagnosed with herpes—in other words, topics that I have chosen not to discuss openly with Sona and Anahid.

And yet, I now felt that Sona's insistence that I write with a free mind prompted me to tell her about our book, the reason that I had to leave early. But I couldn't bring myself to do it.

I suddenly stood up and told them that I must go. Anahid had ordered coffee and ice cream though she knew I was in a hurry. I watched as she poured her coffee over her ice cream. She insisted that I have some, so I gobbled down the vanilla, sweet and white, and slurped a bit of the coffee, black and sour, and she said, "Well, if you must ... " as I turned and ran out the door.

❖

Unbeknownst to me, I was about to deal with other problems of compartmentalization at the Book Chamber, located in an office building that I have walked by a million times without noticing. Once I found Tanya and Amal waiting for me out front, we entered a hallway that had the size and sound of a high school corridor. The offices were dingy, reminiscent of the government building in Ashtarak where Seyran and I had gotten married.

After we met with the director in his office, where we signed our names, we were sent to another office, a tiny one, in which three women were sitting at their desks eating ice cream. They offered us some, which we refused, and they asked us what we had written and where we were from. The woman filling out the register by hand said that Amal looked like she was from New York, while I looked like the one from Armenia. It's because Amal has short hair and a nose piercing and big cuffs on her jeans, and I was wearing a skirt and wedge shoes, my pseudo-feminine professor look. She didn't say anything about Tanya, in black, with her long blond hair, perhaps because she didn't have a firm idea of what Armenians from Canada by way of Syria look like. Amal laughed and said we were a three-headed dragon.

Off we went to another office until we landed at the card catalogue, the classification of literature section. Two women were sitting at desks across from each other, surrounded by piles of unfiled newspapers and publications. They were eating ice cream here, too—the frozen-novelty-on-a-stick variety. The woman helping us was confused because our book is in Armenian, English, and French and can't be classified as Armenian since it's not *entirely* in Armenian. Then her kid called on her cell phone, telling her that she was sick and wanted her to come home. The woman did all this while slurping the melting ice cream, trying to catch with her tongue the hard chocolate shell slipping off the stick in one plank.

She called around to a few of her colleagues while we waited for a determination. I looked over at the other woman, who didn't seem to have much to do. I imagined that she made very little money in this government job. A few moments later, she started complaining about her salary. Tanya whispered to me that she wanted to volunteer to work here for a week to see what their world was like.

Amal was now on the woman's cell phone to explain to a faceless Book Chamber colleague while Tanya translated for me. There was a question about which category the book should be assigned to. We wanted it listed under Armenian feminist literature, but there was no such listing in the big Soviet rule book they were consulting, so more troops were called in, more women emerged from the depths of the Book Chamber. A woman with chunky glasses suggested women's issues or women's movement. She was familiar with women's studies/gender studies as a discipline, but the idea of feminist literature was unfamiliar to her.

Finally, they decided to list it under Armenian Literature and Women's Literature.

As we walked back down the hall, a couple of hours after we had stepped inside, Amal said we had just had a post-Soviet experience. Though the country has been "free" for fifteen years, the library cannot break their dependency on the Soviet rule book to tell them how to construct the world, how to put writers and people and ideas in their proper places.

META-WRITING:

Just as I had trouble understanding that there hadn't been a single book classified as feminist in Armenia, it was hard for me to believe Sona's assertion that there was no great Armenian writer.

Don't get me wrong; I was flattered by her assertion that I was the one to set the Armenians free with my writing. But I think the more pertinent takeaway was that many things weren't said in Armenia. And when they were said, they most likely weren't listened to. At that time, it seemed some Armenians, like Sona, had lost hope in their ability to make a place for themselves—to speak out—so they put hope on people who looked like them, who held ancestral traces of them, but who weren't quite them.

I was also suspicious of Sona: How did she know my mind was free? Had she read my blog? Or was she testing me to see if I had a Western superiority complex? After all, I had just given Anahid Etchian a copy of Reading Lolita in Tehran.

I recognize from this suspicion that I was still tied to my insecurity. I often felt that I had to put people in boxes to operate in the world. And yet I was stuck in a box with Seyran, unsure of how to break out of it. When I compartmentalized people, I thought that I was protecting them from harm, but I didn't recognize that I had a limited view of what their pain was.

JOURNAL: MAY 23, 2011
ASTORIA

Last week, after his failed citizenship interview, I told Seyran that I couldn't help him anymore, that he would have to take over from now on to find his own legal aid.

"It doesn't matter. If they reject my application, they can't deport me; I'll have my green card for up to twenty years," he said.

I have to be responsible for this guy for twenty years? I thought with dread.

"I want you to get citizenship," I told him firmly. "It's better for both of us."

He agreed, but then he went on and on about why he didn't think he needed a lawyer, mostly having to do with their lack of knowledge. I tried to convince him otherwise, but he insisted that I listen to him and not interrupt.

When he was done, he said, "Okay, you can talk now, and I'll listen." As soon as I began speaking, he started snooping around my room, looking at my mail, then my books, anything to distract himself from listening to me. I hated him, leaning against my desk in his underpants. Eternally: in his underpants.

"YOU'RE NOT LISTENING!" I yelled. I grabbed a book out of his hands. "Repeat back what I just said." When it was clear he didn't know, he walked out of the room.

I followed him into the hallway, continuing to make my case for a lawyer. Just outside his room, in the brightness of the skylight, he turned around and stared at me, using his body to tower over me, his hairy plank of a chest leaning into me.

Something snapped. I punched him like I never had before. Three or four times, really hard. "I hate you! You're nothing but a motherfucker!" I screamed, the force of rage scratching my vocal cords.

He laughed. "You're waking up the neighbors," he said, bouncing into the bathroom.

My adrenaline was surging, so I pushed my way through the door and grabbed his arms and dug my nails into them. I could feel the soft fuzz of his hair cradling my fingers as I clawed into his skin.

"You're not kind," I said, gritting my teeth. "You're a tyrant. You're not kind to me at all; you're a child." Then I slapped his face.

He laughed.

When I slapped him, I thought he was going to hit me back. Why doesn't he hit me back? Because he cares about me? Because he was beaten, and he'll never do that to anyone? Or is it because he is torturing me slowly? Because he likes to feel superior over someone whom he has caused to lose their shit?

The next day, I felt badly about blowing up and apologized. Then I made an appointment to see Esmerelda Quinones and cleared the date with Seyran; he agreed to go.

But a couple of days before the meeting, he told me that he would go to yoga instead and that I could give him a report afterward.

I lost it. He goes to yoga every day; he couldn't miss one session? And what was I, his secretary? We were in a small sushi restaurant in Astoria, with young people seated around on all sides, a trendy place with black and green décor, the windows open to the street. We were waiting for the bill to come when he told me his plans.

"You're so stupid!" I yelled. If the people around me stirred, I didn't notice. But Seyran turned red and told me to shut up under his breath. We sat in silence as we paid the bill, then parted ways. I went home, walking the Astoria streets, the food carts and trucks, treeless sidewalks, young people walking and talking on their cell phones, all in my way. When I got home, I graded papers, but I was exhausted from my anger and fell asleep halfway through reading one of them. I awoke to Seyran sitting on the side of my bed, saying that we were always fighting, that I was never happy and always depressed.

"It's very simple," I told him. "If you want to make me happy, you can go to the meeting with the immigration lawyer."

"That probably won't help. You're always depressed."

This hit my last nerve. "So what? I have a lot of resources to deal with being depressed," I defended myself. "I go to yoga and meditation and therapy. I have a lot of friends. People like me, even if I get depressed."

And since it seemed clear that I had nothing left to lose, and he wasn't listening to reason, and I needed release, I said, "But you have no friends, and no one likes you."

He laughed.

"In fact, in Armenia, I never liked you. I always thought you were kind of a jerk, but I didn't know how to get rid of you."

He continued to laugh. He thought it was a joke—because this was the kind of cruel joke he always made. We were lying on my bed, and he grabbed my stuffed tiger as a puppet. "This bitch is going crazy," the tiger said via Seyran.

"No, I'm serious. People don't like you."

I knew I was getting to him because he made an excuse. "I'm young," he said, "and people don't try to get to know me."

I had finally found his weak spot buried beneath five years of bravado. I dug deeper.

"Once they get to know you, they don't like you," I said. "No one in your family even likes you. Why do you think they let you come to America?"

He laughed again, half-heartedly this time. The tiger was silent, a sad puppet.

"I should have left you in Armenia."

META-WRITING:

Seyran didn't talk to me for two days after that. He claimed that it wasn't just what I had said, but how I had said it. He said it sounded like I was giving a speech that I had long rehearsed in my mind to hurt his feelings. I laughed at him for making up such a silly story.

Those thoughts about people not liking him struck me anew when I said them aloud. It was like a switch had flipped and I was going with the current. Our system relied on me thinking he was wonderful and making excuses for him, like the kind he was making. I am sure Seyran knew he was hurting me with his words and actions, and he simply rationalized his behavior away. He never imagined that he could cause me so much pain to push me over the edge, to abandon myself and my values.

This moment was a turning point. Na had so fully compartmentalized, she was pushed beyond her feelings. She became another person when she told Seyran no one liked him. She didn't feel bad about it—it made her feel powerful.

Let me try that again. I became another person when I told Seyran no one liked him. In the narcissistic nexus, the narcissist tries to mirror their target, to entice them into a situation in which they lose their power. I'd fallen so far into the trap at this point that I was inflicting pain without remorse. When we first met, I cared for who I thought Seyran was. After many months of rationalization, when it was clear that he was a sham, I downgraded to survival mode. If I acted out or hurt him, I felt bad about it—my guilt was a way for him to lure me back in and control me. Now that it was obvious that he would never do anything to release me, I just wanted him to hurt so that I could break free. And when I saw that he hurt, I felt release, for a moment anyway. But hurting him would never save me, because now I was contributing to the web of hurt and manipulation that he'd built, keeping it in place and expanding it further. To save myself, I'd have to change something in me.

JOURNAL: MAY 25, 2011
ASTORIA

I noticed that Seyran has been speaking more Armenian than usual. He repeats one phrase in particular. It sounds like, "Ara lava, tsavet danem." He says it over and over again, in an antagonizing tone of voice, world-weary and nasal. It means something like, "Oh, so you think you can just go ahead and give me your pain?"

I heard this phrase frequently in Armenia. A couple of weeks ago, I went to a memorial for Mardi's mother, and I overheard one of his friends saying it to him, but he meant it in a kind way. I learned that *tsavet danem* literally means "your pain I take." *I will take your pain away. I will bear your pain for you. I love you so much, I don't want you to hurt, so I will hurt for you.* The expression seems to indicate the selflessness of the culture. Mardi's mother had died forty days before, and his friends had given him a hokihankist ceremony for her soul to rest.

It was a trying time for Mardi. Gharib had left him finally, to travel extensively in Europe, which made Mardi realize how vulnerable he was without Gharib. When his landlord undertook eviction proceedings, Mardi had to deal with it on his own, on top of finding work to support himself. And then his mother died suddenly. Mardi had trouble realizing she was gone. But he didn't want to go back to Yerevan for the funeral. "I don't want to see her that way," he told me. If he remained in the U.S., maybe she was somehow still alive, the way she had been in his mind. But I suppose one can only maintain that figment of the imagination for so long before your body tells you something different.

We witnessed Mardi's pain, and then he bore it: he went up to the priest at the service and stood in front of him as he said his prayer. Before that moment, I couldn't imagine Mardi believing in God or going to church. Now I watched his back slouch, grief gripping him.

Afterward, in the church basement during coffee hour, I gave Mardi a photo I had taken of his mother when I visited her last summer. She had been in so much physical pain from the problems with her spine, back, and hip, but she had put on a pretty pink outfit and lipstick and fed me chunks of sweet red watermelon. When she asked about Mardi, I told her he was happier than he had been in Armenia. She suddenly burst into tears. She missed him so much, she told me. I rubbed her back, though I knew it was probably hard for her to let me see her cry. I wished I had told her about Mardi more delicately, but my Armenian is so limited, I couldn't communicate nuance.

Mardi loved the photo and was grateful for it. But I wish I had told his mother, "Tsavet danem." I hesitated because it's one of those phrases I'm never sure I am using in the correct context, and it seemed important not to say the wrong thing to a woman in grief, facing the fact that she may not see her son again.

Often when Seyran says the phrase, he's making fun of a provincial Yerevantsi who throws around the term aggressively, like, "Fuck you, giving me your pain." He says it with the accent and the attitude. I think if Seyran could cry like Mardi's mother or grieve like Mardi, he would grow and become more human. Instead, he's become the stereotype of the brutish Armenian man he never wanted to be.

Perhaps one meaning of *tsavet danem* could be, "Let me take your pain away from you," as if removing a newly arrived package of hurts from the front door and dumping it in the trash. Seyran's pain arrives daily to our apartment. He doesn't even bother with it. I pick up the box, open it, and let the pain wear me out. But it's not mine to experience.

One problem with taking someone's pain away is that they don't get the chance to feel it, accept it, process it, or learn something about themselves.

STORY: JUNE, 2007, AND AUGUST, 2010
YEREVAN

In the women's workshop, Na is incredibly nervous. Everyone is very nice, but she is still anxious, her breathing shallow and her teaching stilted. She's working with a group of twelve women—young, old, short, tall, local, diasporan. They range widely in their politics. Twice a week, they sit in a circle on folding chairs in the library at the Center for Armenian Women, surrounded by books. Na introduces readings about corruption and war, tradition and family, and genocide. About inhabiting a female body. The participants speak multiple languages, and Na relies on an interpreter to moderate, so the conversations can be slow, but they still cover a lot of issues. They talk about the multiplicity of languages appropriate for different situations: how they speak at home and at work; for public writing and for intimate, interior, and personal expression. Then they talk about how there is no Armenian word for "pussy."

After the discussion about the lack of Armenian words for certain body parts, they all go out for a beer afterward. It's around this time that Na stops feeling nervous. She thinks she knows why: the Armenian women she had grown up with could be judgmental and combative, and she had never truly felt safe or accepted among her aunts and her mother. As she journals during the workshop, she realizes the women sitting beside her are not her family members.

One day, the women in the workshop decide to go outside and write together. Soon after, they decide to create a book together. They take on different roles: translator, proofreader, editor, layout, design, marketing. They bond in a multitude of ways over the two months that they work together. They become friends. Some of the women who are queer decide to form a collective.

One night before she goes to the workshop, Seyran invites Hagop the curator over for a visit. As she is leaving, Seyran tells her that he is going to have sex with Hagop. When she returns, Hagop is gone, and she asks how the visit was. "We had very nice sex," Seyran says.

Na treats it as a joke. She doesn't realize these kinds of statements are a form of abuse that will chip away at her and will spiral into something dangerous.

A few years later, Na will return to teach another workshop for women, only a few sessions long, specifically centered on the female body. In this workshop attended by women who are straight, gay, pregnant, old, and young, they will bond immediately. They will sit in the garden behind the center and talk about rites of passage: menstruation, marriage, family, love, sexuality, pregnancy, relationships, menopause, and death. One woman leads them in yoga, and they stretch toward the sky, toward each other. In the workshop, Na starts writing about the physical abuse in her relationship. Though no one else writes about such experiences, no one bats an eye when she reads the words aloud. Later, the whole group will read to an audience, including Na. A few people comment on what she wrote, indicating that they heard it, understood it, and appreciated it, and no one condemns her, her words traveling in time from the moment of abuse in her apartment—through her body—into the space underneath the grape arbor, amid the accepting energy of the group. She releases some of her shame.

On her last night in Yerevan, the women from this workshop come over to the apartment where she is staying and throw a party. They bring flowers. One woman was formerly a florist and shows Na how to strip a stem of leaves and arrange it in a vase. Another woman shows her how to make Armenian coffee. They drink wine and eat sweets and talk about writing, about life. They are celebrating creativity and their connections with each other. They take group photos by her arched Soviet window, feeling jubilant. Na doesn't think she has ever felt happier in her whole life.

This is what it means to take someone's pain away.

III

18. TIME WARPS

• •
•

T hree platoons of new soldiers marched around a field, their guns perched over their shoulders. Most of their families had traveled many kilometers to this remote alpine region to observe their boys in a final training exercise. During the initiation ceremony, each soldier swore their service and their lives to their country. Families in the designated viewing stand inched closer to the fence to snap pictures of their loved ones. These were people who didn't have connections and couldn't pay to get their kids out of the military: regular, hardworking folks.

Posted around the perimeter of the training field were flat, amateurish paintings of military heroes throughout history, from Dro (WWI and WWII) through Monte (The 1st Karabakh War), who fought for Armenian liberation. The ceremony was so theatrically staged that it didn't feel real until a platoon marched close by, and I could see how youthfully vulnerable the soldiers were, with acne and big brown eyes. They wore cheaply made boots, they ate bad food, they were treated like prisoners. And yet, here they were smiling shyly and proudly, transformed from sons into soldiers.

I remember this initiation ceremony in the summer of 2007 because it was the last time I saw Seyran's younger brother Robert before I returned to Armenia in 2010. In the interim, Robert had changed, which gave me insights into what I had done for Seyran—and what he had done to me.

When people are abused, time warps and breaks down. To get my bearings in this book, I tried to separate time into distinct sections and voices, the way I fractured my selves. But to tell the rest of the story, I've got to see it through a different lens, one that integrates my disparate experiences as one narrative.

"I am not afraid," Robert had told me about his army duty at a picnic at his family's village house a few months before the ceremony, just as Seyran and I were planning to leave Armenia. Seyran's brother was in his first year of college and could have deferred compulsory military duty until he graduated, as Seyran had done. But he wanted to get it out of the way, he said. Here was his older brother leaving Armenia to avoid the army, while Robert was willingly entering it.

I wondered if he was doing it in response to Seyran's escape. Was he taunting Seyran in competition? Proving himself? It didn't occur to me that he might have been making a sacrifice in the hopes that their family would avoid scrutiny over Seyran's phony medical exemption.

During the months of training that preceded the initiation ceremony, Seyran's parents kept in touch with Robert to protect him from harm. They checked on him every weekend and called as much as they could. Seyran and I visited him with his parents a couple of times, traveling in the car for a few hours over mountainous roads and meadows filled with flowers. We bought him better boots in Yerevan but found out on a subsequent visit that the officers wouldn't allow him to wear them. On one of these outings, we brought Robert to a restaurant composed of private cabins with screened windows, and he cheered up as we dined al fresco, on fish and lavash, cheese and herbs. He seemed happiest when he later helped Seyran's father dig up a tree from the woods to plant in the garden of the village house.

Now, after his initiation ceremony, the extended family held a picnic with three kinds of barbecued meat and a bounty of fruit and vegetables, cakes, and coffee. Sprawled on blankets spread over a clearing in a forested park, his aunts, cousins, and family friends ate and drank all day long. By dusk, Robert did not want to return to the base. He stood outside of the car, slumped his back against the door window, and peered down at the ground. I saw his head fall forward as he suddenly sobbed into his hands.

❖

When I returned to visit Armenia without Seyran a few years later, I spent time with Robert, who'd now been out of the army for a year. Strangely, he insisted on being my chaperone. Before I left New York, Seyran had told me that I could call his brother to pick me up and drive me anywhere I needed to go. I found this odd. Had Seyran made an arrangement with Robert? Or was Seyran thinking of his own brother as a willing chauffeur? Whatever the case, he accompanied me to the Stop Club to see Stepan's band play. I allowed him this once since it seemed he was now friends with Stepan, who had invited him. Afterward, Robert took it upon himself to walk me home, like a good brother-in-law. He asked if I wanted to go to a café, and we wound up at one of the places by the Opera.

Three years ago, he had been Seyran's awkward little brother. Now I thought I saw echoes of Seyran. We were chatting about the band when he suddenly told me that I spoke English poorly.

"What?"

"You not good speaker. I can tell."

"I think I'm pretty good. My students tell me they like the clear way that I speak."

"No, you don't understand me," he said dismissively, and he changed the subject. I was perplexed. How could a new speaker of English tell a lifelong speaker of English that she couldn't speak the language well?

Here was a similar pattern between the brothers: feeling insecure, taking it out on me, and when I responded, not acknowledging or apologizing for his misdeed. It was similar to a common refrain of Seyran's—"I'm just kidding" —after hurting anybody's feelings.

As the evening progressed, Robert kept laughing at inappropriate moments in the conversation, and it didn't seem that he had had that much to drink—another trait similar to Seyran's. The brothers looked a lot alike, too, with their angled cheekbones and Roman noses.

Robert showed me photos on his flip phone: a pretty girl in Belarus who he had met on a dating site, Seyran and me at our kitchen table in Astoria (which

Seyran had sent him), and Angelina Jolie wearing a T-shirt with Robert's face on it. At the latter, I let out a cackle.

Then Robert asked, "Do you want to see a Turkish man killed in Armenia?"

"No," I told him, taken aback.

He proceeded to show me anyway. It was a bloody body, his head all red and his chest opened up, with someone's foot on his arm. Robert said that the Turk had killed five Armenian soldiers at the Karabakh border. At this point, I realized the dead soldier was really an Azerbaijani—Armenians colloquially call Azerbaijanis Turks. In this way, Armenian time is fluid, our perpetrators conflated over eons.

I was taken aback by the image and chided Robert. "I told you I didn't want to see it."

He laughed.

It had only been a year since he had left the army. His father had been able to have him transferred to a safer base, farther from the border than the training camp where we had witnessed his graduation. Had Robert ever been stationed at the border to witness such violence? It's likely that someone had sent him the photo of the dead solider, like the other pictures he showed me in his phone.

When I told Seyran about the photo of the Azerbaijani soldier, he said the army had messed Robert up, in an accusatory way, as if it were Robert's fault. After all, Seyran had not chosen this path, and he seemed to suggest that he had been smart enough to avoid it. Clearly, Robert had wanted to shock me with the photo, perhaps because he had been forced to build up defenses so that he couldn't feel shock anymore—I was his proxy. But perhaps he wanted to display what he had sacrificed for his country. For Seyran. For me.

❖

After the party for Robert's army initiation, the family went to a mineral hot spring, and we all jumped in. I had no bathing suit—none of us did—so we all went in our underwear. I tried to not feel weird about it and to enjoy the warm water, but my panties were soggy, and the warm water was soft and slippery with minerals. Someone took a photo of us: Seyran and I appear only as heads, our bodies remaining beneath the surface of the water, and Seyran's aunts and parents are proudly standing up, their blocky bodies dripping wet.

We arrived back in Yerevan so late that night that we all slept at Seyran's aunts' apartment. For some reason I can't recall, Seyran and I were assigned his grandparents' old bedroom, where a photo, featuring them both in 1950s outfits, hung on the wall, while another framed portrait of his mom and sisters as teens was displayed on the dresser. It was strange to sleep within those walls, with their faces looking on, some of them ghosts, some of them sleeping in the next room. Were we going to do it in his grandparents' bed? I didn't want to, and I don't think we did. But in the middle of the night, I woke up feeling nauseous. It had to have been all the coffee, booze, and meat warmed up in my belly from soaking in the hot spring. Not to mention the emotional disturbance of Robert crying and now feeling awkward in their ancestors' cherished bedroom while Seyran's parents slept in the living room. Everything felt jumbled up: Seyran's parents were supposed to sleep here, not us. Seyran was supposed to go into the army, not Robert—at least not yet, anyway.

I threw up several times. Seyran didn't get up to see if I was all right. I suppose there was no point given that there were three people helping me, the sickly American princess. His mom held my hair from my face, and she rubbed my back the way my own mother used to do when I had been sick as a child. Seyran's aunts made me herbal tea, which I also threw up a couple of times before all the bad stuff was out and my stomach settled.

If Seyran had any troubled feelings from the events of that day, they didn't keep him up. Perhaps he slept them away. I don't remember him talking to me about Robert's decision.

What would have happened to Seyran if he had joined the army? What would he have lost or gained? Robert seemed desensitized by his experience. Seyran seemed desensitized in general, the scars on his body—the scratches in his face, the wide gash on his arm—visibly apparent, a faint reminder of his vulnerability. However the boys had been treated by their family as children, they responded very differently on the day of Robert's initiation: one cried, and the other kept sleeping. I didn't know Robert very well before he entered the army, so it was difficult to discern if the traits he later exhibited that reminded me of Seyran had already been instilled or if the army had somehow changed him to laugh instead of cry, to blame instead of admit. Perhaps both family and country were responsible.

The damage to Seyran had already been done. I thought I had saved him from the army, which probably would have compounded that damage. But from the moment I met him, it was already too late for me to save him—or myself—from abuse.

❖

Before I recount the worst of that abuse, here's another time warp to consider: our last night in Yerevan and our first day in our Astoria apartment. Transitions in time and place. From the outside what looks like moving on and moving up are in fact different vantage points of the same spiral. And yet, like an initiation ceremony, it's important to mark those times, to realize where we came from, what we were leaving behind, and where we were going, to get to the present.

On our last night in Yerevan, Seyran's entire family came to our apartment. I arrived late because there had been a party for me at the Center for Armenian Women. The women in the writing workshop had made a sweet scrapbook of images and messages so that I would remember our time together: "You're so special to me and my writing." "You helped me find a new side to myself." "Thank you for bringing us together." I was touched as I didn't know I had made an impact.

Not knowing when I would return, I was sad to leave, but one thought comforted me: Mardi and Gharib were already in New York. Before they left, I visited them in Mardi's mother's kitchen, and we joked about the jobs they would do once they got to New York City. "We can start a restaurant together," Mardi suggested, and we laughed hysterically at the thought of it. My goodbye was not a goodbye. I would be seeing my friends soon.

Seyran was having a very different experience. His mom and aunts had made dinner, and we all crowded around the table in our kitchen. Our flight was at 5 a.m., so we had stayed up all night to go to the airport. His aunts had to leave early to be at work in the morning. They hugged Seyran by the car, sobbing.

I don't remember saying goodbye to anyone in his family. I tried to not overshadow Seyran's goodbyes.

I remember being in the back seat of the car, Seyran speaking in Armenian to his parents in the front.

This is a mistake, I thought. I recorded it in my brain. It's one of the only details I remember clearly: "This is a mistake."

There wasn't anything I could do to stop the car, or at least I didn't think so. I'd bought his ticket, and he had his visa. This machine had long been in operation, and I couldn't turn back now. What would I say to his parents? I couldn't imagine any other outcome.

We were sitting on the floor in the airport, and he cried. I had never seen him cry before. He yelled at me not to look at him.

After landing in my Greenpoint apartment for a month, we moved to an immigrant neighborhood in Woodside, to a one-bedroom apartment with red shag carpeting on the ground floor of an industrial neighborhood, the best I could afford. Seyran found an IT job not three months later, and he worked the graveyard shift. We slept at different times of the day in a bedroom with a window overlooking the air shaft. Though the apartment was less than ideal and could barely compare to the studio with a balcony view of Ararat, Seyran was mostly happy and excited for the first few months.

I didn't journal much then. But in the spring, his mood turned, and in the frequency of my journal entries, I tried to make sense of the changes. Our living situation added stress: the elevated train rumbling loudly overhead, the depressed people climbing up and down the endless stairs of the train station. The angry Hasidic Jew who worked behind the bulletproof glass at the post office. The gloomy ruins of an old Episcopalian church, built at the turn of the century, that nearly burned down one winter night and was still boarded up several years later, the last time I passed through the neighborhood. The machine shops across the street, the Playbill factory with its churning motors and yelling foreman next door. The smells of garlic and onion that would waft down the air shaft with heated conversation at 2 a.m. when someone's husband came home from a late shift. The calling cards strewn on the front steps outside, left by our neighbors calling homes far away, across oceans. The bigoted Irish super posting offensive notices to "the Indian Bastards" in the building about separating the recycling.

When our one-year lease was up in September, I had already caught Seyran dating other women, and I tried to break up with him. I answered ads people posted looking for roommates, but they were all bleak situations. One skinny Goth guy had a photo studio in his room to upload images to the internet that he vowed weren't porn. A loquacious Korean American woman with a ponytail on top of her head offered a tiny room with a laundry list of rules, including how I needed to be scarce during her fiancé's visits. It didn't seem I could find a home. So I chose to stay with Seyran in a new move to Astoria, telling myself that I could always kick him out and find a roommate.

On the day of the move, we rented a U-Haul truck, and I drove it since Seyran didn't know how. His parents told him that they were nervous—women largely don't drive in Armenia. Truthfully, I didn't feel comfortable in such a big vehicle, either. But all was going fine until I parked the truck in the driveway of our new house, which was on an incline. I had my foot on the brake and put it in park, then opened my door and started to step out. At this point, Seyran was out of the truck and mounting the front steps. As I turned the keys to take them out of the ignition, the universe shifted. For some reason, the brakes gave way, and the truck rolled down the incline. I was half in, half out, and instinctively trying to stop the truck with my one leg on the ground, but it was impossible, and the door was open, about to jam on the side of the wall. I was nearly dragged out of the truck, but luckily it stopped after it broke through the garage door.

Seyran leaped to my side. "Honey, are you all right?" He hugged me. "Are you okay, what happened? I thought you were gonna die." I was stunned mute. He looked at me and hugged me again.

I was shocked by his response but also by my own. I hadn't expected that he cared about me that much.

I think of this moment whenever I consider all the pain I went through after we moved into that apartment. When I face my regrets. When I recognize all the times I almost stepped away. When I wonder what my life would have been like if we had never met.

I hadn't expected the brakes to fail—why would I? And I couldn't see that I was in danger. Instead, I was sure I could stop a fully loaded truck from crashing. Yet, somehow, I survived. I saw how messed up it was to be shocked that he could care for me as a human being.

If Seyran and I hadn't met, something else would have caused me to discover my weaknesses. But only living in Armenia could have made me so vulnerable to his wiles. And yet, only living in Armenia, confronting historical wounds in real time, could have made me this strong.

✿

A final time warp: I visited Karabakh when I lived in Armenia from 2006–07. Tanya invited me, which was kind and gracious of her, especially when she knew how critical I could be. It's been difficult to write my observations of such a controversial place when I was there for such a short time, and I couldn't know the extents of the sacrifice and trauma endured by the residents. I include this brief account with the acknowledgment that my frame of reference was limited.

When we arrived at Tanya's home in Shushi, a beautiful old wooden house with carved balconies like the kind I saw in Tbilisi, she told me the history: she'd bought it from a carpenter who had fixed it up, and he had bought it from a vodka distiller, who'd probably claimed it as a spoil of war, but she couldn't know for sure. She told me that she often wondered about the Azerbaijani family who last lived here—who they were and where they were now. As I walked around the town with her, encountering abandoned homes, an empty mosque, and half-empty apartment buildings, twelve years after the ceasefire, I could feel ghosts, like the ones that shook me years before when I'd visited homes that had once belonged to Armenians before the Genocide, abandoned decades before, in remote villages in Turkey. Intellectually, I knew they were different events, caused by different fears and powers. With the exception of those who were massacred in nearby Khojaly, the Azerbaijanis who were driven out of Shushi likely lived somewhere over the border. But Armenians lost their lives in the Genocide, and those who survived in diaspora lost their homes and families forever, their culture destroyed, a crime never acknowledged nor atoned. And Armenian ethnic cleansing had taken place in Shushi, too, in 1920, when the Armenian quarter was burnt down. Still, I couldn't shake the pit in my stomach, the pain behind my eyes: the haunted aura physically felt the same. I felt for all those who had been forsaken.

I finished writing the bulk of this book by 2016, two years before the Revolution would liberate Armenians from corruption and four years before what everyone feared would happen: Azerbaijan attacked Karabakh, displaced Armenians, and seized land. We watched in dismay as crowds of Azerbaijanis took to the streets in Baku in the middle of a pandemic to agitate for the attacks, rather than to protest their own corrupt leader who silenced their speech, imprisoned their journalists, and pilfered their money by buying up luxury properties in the UK via offshore accounts. They cheered as Armenian civilians were bombed by high tech Turkish drones and forests were burned by glowing fireworks of outlawed white phosphorus. Western leaders looked away from such strangely violent spectacles, shrugging their shoulders at the situation, equating "both sides" in favor of continued oil imports from Azerbaijan. As I write these words, Azerbaijan—a country with three times the population and three and a half times Armenia's military budget—continues to threaten Armenians remaining in what is left of Karabakh and even in Armenia proper. Armenian prisoners of war are still being held illegally by Azerbaijan.

Tanya lost her beautiful house in Shushi. Now it is an Azerbaijani's turn to imagine an Armenian family who has been displaced by violence.

I don't regret feeling empathy for the Azerbaijanis from Shushi when I visited that ancient mountain town. To hold onto our humanity, we must identify with those who suffer, even if they go on to hurt us, even if it makes us vulnerable. To find our strength, we have to acknowledge our weakness. As I would eventually learn, we can empathize with those who cause us harm while also drawing a line to defend ourselves.

19. RECOGNITION

• • •

As soon as Seyran and I arrived at the federal courthouse in downtown Brooklyn on a hot August day in 2011, we were separated. After we passed through metal detectors at the security checkpoint, where I relinquished my phone and camera, the guards pointed us in two directions: Seyran to the courtroom and me to the cafeteria. In the latter, I was confronted by a large flat-screen monitor, and I could see Seyran in the center of it, sitting in a bank of wooden benches, the camera filming him from above. The screen was frozen, and Seyran was smiling. He was wearing a black shirt and carrying a white bag with the strap across his chest. No one was sitting next to him, but when the screen thawed, twice as many people suddenly appeared seated beside him. It was weird to watch the time warp, almost as disorienting as the moment when he would transform from Armenian to U.S. citizen.

❧

Back in May, a few days after Seyran's application for citizenship had been rejected, I was trudging to the bathroom at 7:30 a.m. when I noticed he was lying in bed. He usually left home by 5 to make his yoga class before going to work. "What are you doing here?" I asked. "Were you laid off?" It was something I'd been afraid of since he didn't seem to take the job seriously anymore.

He laughed at me from under his blanket. Then, as he was getting ready, I asked again why he wasn't at work already.

"I got laid off," he confirmed. "They said I was hanging from a loose thread, and yesterday they said they'd had enough. That they would pay me for two weeks, but they wanted me gone."

I was in shock. This was my worst nightmare come true. Now I would have to pay the rent on my own and feel financially responsible for him until he got his fucking stupid citizenship, which we were not even sure he would get. Esmerelda's advice had been to inundate the USCIS with paperwork—every single bank statement, every single canceled rent check—just as we had done when we petitioned to get the conditions removed from his green card. But we hadn't assembled any materials yet. I could feel my panic rising.

"I don't understand," I said. "What did you do?"

"Well, Michael found out that I had been meeting his wife."

"So? You ran into her at Whole Foods." He had told me about it a few weeks ago, how she had talked to Seyran about their kids.

"No, I've been fucking her in a hotel room."

Boom, he dropped a bomb on me. Now I almost wanted him to be fired. At least I now knew just how sick he was. I was unable to breathe. All the times I'd found out he'd fucked around felt dropped on me at once, a shit ton of hurt, pain, and disbelief now compounded by financial uncertainty.

"Are you telling the truth? Or are you joking?"

"Michael wants me to come in," he said. "I think he's gonna kill me, I don't know. He told me to bring a change of clothes." He was putting his yoga clothes into a bag, which was a clue, but I could also believe he was depraved enough to screw the boss's wife—and that the boss would want to kill him. Fuck, I wanted to kill him half the time.

"I know it is playing with fire," he said. I wondered about the idioms he was using, like "hanging from a loose thread." They were out of the range of his lexicon, as if he was repeating what Michael had said to him.

He put his guitar in its case, claiming, "I'm going to play music outside to make money now that I won't have a job." I watched the guitar strapped to his back as he walked down the stairs.

I honestly didn't know what to believe. I went to work and let my interactions with students distract me. Not until 12:30 when I saw that he had called me from his work number did I feel relief. Later, I listened to the message he had left:

> *Hi Natalee,*
>
> *I was just wondering if you think I could become a writer. You know me well, even my abnormalities. Do you think if I learn new phrases with my Kindle that I will be able to become a writer? Well, I hope you are having a wonderful day and that your students are listening to you and not making up stories like me this morning.*

✿

Long before this experience, when I had first started to write in my early twenties, I went to see Annie Sprinkle perform her show *Post-Porn Modernist*. She told stories about her life as a sex worker and porn star, detailing the sexual empowerment she found as well as the abuse she suffered. The scene in which she reenacts her degradation was particularly disturbing for her to recount. I don't remember the content, but I recall her emotional difficulty in performing it. Afterward, she put on a robe and said, "The first ten times I did this little performance, I cried a lot. Then the next ten times, I got really angry. Now every time I do it, I feel less and less. Performance therapy, it really works."

The more I read this book, writing and revising it, the more I'm able to see the systems of abuse. For a long time, I never connected all the claims that Seyran made about having sex with other people as a pattern. I would simply become retraumatized while reading them, in their fractured sections. Now it's gotten to the point that when I reread this scene, I can't believe I couldn't see at the time that he had been joking, mocking my fear. But one of Seyran's weapons was uncertainty—I could never be sure what he was capable of—and he knew that upsetting my sense of control was a way to undo me. It was a weapon that had been cast long ago, reinforced by his antics and my fear. Every time he talked about having sex with other people, he exploded the ground from under me—at first like a grenade, and then with the force of a bomb. In fact, when I told trusted friends about these experiences, this was the most apt metaphor I could use. Seyran dropped another bomb; Seyran created chaos in my emotional life.

I've never lived through a war. The closest I came to one was 9/11, but I was living in Morningside Heights at the time and wasn't even aware of what had happened until the first tower fell. For days I woke up feeling hopeless, as I had when Hrant Dink had been assassinated. The Islamophobia and general mistrust of Middle Eastern people that followed weren't exactly a picnic. But there were no other attacks after September 11, no bombs to cause me to have PTSD.

My father shot automatic cannons in the Korean War. For many years, I have asked him how he felt about the destruction this caused, and he has never once expressed distress. He's not overtly patriotic, and he's not uncaring toward those who were affected. He seems to feel it was simply a job he had to do since it had been assigned to him. His mother was a child survivor of a genocide, so I've always wondered if he felt that the primary objective was to get through the experience alive. And yet, he never expressed anxiety about it.

Genetic scientists are now making claims that we store trauma in our genes, that it gets passed on through our DNA. Sometimes, the scientists say, genetic trauma skips a generation, impacting the grandchild of a survivor. I can't know the merits of these studies, but I can believe that some of us are somehow more physically predisposed to be affected by fear and anxiety.

I wonder why I've held on to that story by Annie Sprinkle, about healing from the abuse she suffered through telling her story repeatedly. When I first heard it, I had never been sexually abused. But it was likely my grandmother had been violated, because rape was a weapon of control by the gendarmes during the Genocide. If she hadn't been raped or assaulted, she surely would have witnessed such violence, as well as other attacks and violations against the unprotected line of deportees, women, children, and the elderly trudging through the desert.

Later in her life, as an elderly woman, she would accuse my aunts of having sex with the postman or the man who mowed their lawn. My father told me that she would accuse my grandfather of having affairs with other women.

During the Genocide, she was rescued for a few years by an Arab family who had taken her in as a servant. Had she experienced sexual abuse in that home as a ten- to twelve-year-old girl? Perhaps betrayal got cooked into her experience of survival, mixed in with all the other violence and loss.

I can't know exactly what got written into my genes. But Seyran was always identifying himself and other people through sex, whether he had fucked them or not. He clearly had "abnormalities" or pathologies as he occasionally admitted. And now he was trying to be a writer, joking about it, belittling the trauma he had caused me, and demeaning my source of strength as a form of telling lies.

The more I write, the more I see, the more I heal.

❖

As I watched the courtroom on the screen fill up with soon-to-be citizens, I looked around the waiting room populated by loved ones sitting around the tables. A woman with high strappy heels sat right in front of the TV monitor. By her flouncy dress and coloring, I guessed she was from South America. Tattoo on ankle, sunglasses on head. When she stood up to buy something to eat, she told a Black guy in a suit at the table behind her to save her chair. He nodded and put his head in his hands, then on the table. It was early—the ceremony was to start at 8:30, and it was 8:15 now.

I looked up at the screen to see a short, plump Black woman in a blue dress sitting down in front of Seyran. A moment later, two older Black women in skirt suits entered the cafeteria and sat next to me. One smelled very fragrant, like jasmine, maybe. I assumed the Black women were related to the Black woman on the screen. I wondered if Seyran could also smell jasmine emanating from the lady sitting in front of him.

At 8:30, a flood of people streamed into the cafeteria, their counterparts edging into the screen. *Who are all these people arriving after 8:30?* I thought. *Who are these latecomers to their own citizenship ceremony?*

On the screen, Seyran and a few others in the first row of seats stood up and moved forward. A lady was speaking on a monitor, but no sound emitted from the speakers. The woman was gesturing with her fingers to indicate a square. Seyran reached into his bag and pulled out a form.

In that moment, I decided that when the ceremony was over, I would hug him. Or maybe I would kiss him. I had kissed him on the cheek when we had separated at the courtroom door earlier, but his cheek was flaccid and limp.

We had worn our wedding rings. A few times, as we were walking down the street to the courthouse from the subway, Seyran announced, "Happy married couple," as if to remind me of our charade. Meanwhile, I was brainstorming endings—the kiss, the hug—because I wanted to feel that what I had done was positive, that there was some redeeming value to what I had endured. I wanted the ceremony to also be mine. It didn't matter who the person was that I had tried to save, that he would never admit his wrongdoing or my pain. I fruitlessly believed a hug or kiss would mean that I had somehow made a difference.

❖

A few days before, I had been lying on my bed talking on the phone to a friend when Seyran walked into my room. He lay down next to me for the last five minutes of my conversation. I was telling my friend about my recent time away, writing in Vermont and at a writing residency in Texas. I had been gone for most of the summer to get away from Seyran, with the hope that a physical separation would help me to make my permanent exit. At the end of June, he'd had his second citizenship interview, and a few days later, after we had brought in every document we possibly could, he received the letter about his citizenship ceremony. When I had come home from Texas a few days before, he told me he had met someone. For some reason, this time, it seemed serious, like a real girlfriend. So everything was in place for me to move on.

When I got off the phone, he was messing with me, first touching me, then squeezing my butt. I didn't mind the butt squeezing—he was pushing his fists into my tightened hamstrings, and it felt good, like a massage, rather than sexual. But then he started taking my pants off. "No," I told him. "I don't want to have sex."

"It will be a better massage this way." As he proceeded to pull my pants and underwear past my rear, his wallet fell out of his pocket, and he joked about putting his MetroCard in my ass. What kind of poem could he write about it? "I thought the doors would open, but you just farted." At this point he was straddling me, saying that if he used his new card, wrapped in plastic, it would be like a condom. And then I felt something tickle my ass. I turned around and saw he was sliding an old MetroCard, without the wrapper, in my ass crack. "Stop it!" I yelled.

He responded by squeezing my butt, rolling the cheeks like they were dough. He said he was loosening me up; he just wanted to look at my asshole. I don't know why I let him, why I figured he'd take a gander at my anus and stop. Maybe I was tired. Maybe I was in denial. Maybe I'd already said no a couple of times, and he didn't listen to me, he never stopped, he kept going, as he always did, chipping away at my resolve where he found my female indoctrination, my hesitancy to say no still ingrained at this late date. Suddenly, I felt something wet. He had put his tongue in my butt. "Stop it!" I yelled.

"Shush, it's just my finger." And then he spit right into my asshole and stuck his finger in. I felt a sharp pain, a hollowing in my stomach, a scratch inside me. Finally, I struggled free and pulled up my pants.

"Why are you doing this?"

"Because I want you to feel good."

I sat in my chair by my desk. "It's making me feel bad," I told him. "Why don't you do this to your new girlfriend?"

"Oh yeah, she's coming over later so you can meet her," he joked.

I didn't take the bait this time. "And you put that old MetroCard in my butt when it has germs on it," I said.

"Yeah, probably a lot of people have put it in their ass," he joked.

He wouldn't admit to what he'd done. He had heard me say no, but he hadn't stopped. I had left him for the summer and would leave him permanently within weeks. All he knew to do was degrade me.

He left the room to shower, ostensibly to prepare himself to meet his girlfriend.

❊

Back in the courtroom, at 9:25 a.m., people on the screen were waiting in line to turn in their forms. "This is going to take a long time," the fragrant lady next to me said. "It will take hours," the man sitting opposite said.

I wanted to tell them not to complain. *Things are much worse in Armenia, I thought. In other countries, the courts are rigged, elections are stolen, and there is no justice. You're waiting in an air-conditioned room, and you're complaining? What kind of loved one of an immigrant are you anyway?*

I didn't realize how angry I was.

On the screen, Seyran stood in line to turn in the form. It took an hour for him to do so. Then another hour for everyone else. By the end, a man was collecting remaining forms, running around the room like Donahue in his studio audience with a microphone.

So efficient, I thought.

It didn't really matter how the event unfolded. I was angry at everyone: family members sitting next to me, random Federal courtroom workers.

Everyone but the person I should have been the most angry at.

✥

While Seyran was in the shower, I was on the phone to another friend, this one visiting from out of town, with whom I was making plans to meet shortly. As I wrapped up the conversation, sitting at my desk, he came into my room naked. I felt a shove against my shoulder and saw it was him, with an erection. I turned away, but he proceeded to put my watch around his dick and my glasses above the watch. His dick was a nose. He said, "Kiss yourself," and laughed.

I had stopped his violation of me, and now he was violating my effects. He was turning me into his dick, degrading my whole identity. Confronted by the fact that I would be leaving him, Seyran was acting like an infant, a perverted one. I wanted to vomit. But I was still on the phone.

I didn't feel anything as I visited with my friend afterward. I told her that he was getting his citizenship, that I was leaving him, and that he had a girlfriend. I told her that it seemed he was moving on but then he would say things like I knew him better than anyone. I told her nothing of what he had done to me. All I said was that he was still trying to have sex with me. It didn't even occur to me to tell her what had happened. I stored it away, pushed it down.

It wasn't until I came home that I realized he had violated me. When I was going to bed, I received a text from him that he wasn't coming home. "See you tomorrow," he wrote. I texted back, "I won't be home tomorrow because I will not be assaulted by you anymore."

I recognized then that we had only been together for an hour. I had gotten off the phone with my first friend at 5:40, and I must have left the house at 6:25 to meet my other friend. Though I couldn't tell my friends what he had done, I knew enough to realize that the situation was dire: he had violated me twice in one hour.

Several years and drafts later, it's still hard for me to read this little passage, and I can feel my heart dissolving in my rib cage. But each time I've re-visited it, my heart has grown stronger and dissolves a little less.

❖

10:45 a.m.: the sound returned to the screen. A woman from the NYC Commission on Human Rights, which combats discrimination in employment, housing, and public accommodation, introduced herself to the people in the courtroom. I couldn't see her because she was off-screen, but I could hear that her voice was accented by the Bronx and tinged by the Caribbean. The woman handed out a newsletter to welcome the new citizens and spoke about a law that makes discrimination against the "protected classes" illegal. She explained that the "protected classes" are groups designated by race, color, national origin, gender, religion, and sexual orientation. She said, "You may think, *I'm a citizen now, I won't be discriminated against*. Well, guess what, you look the same as before, and you talk the same as before. It's easy for people to pick us out, even though we're no different from them. We're all equal: blood is the same color."

The official gave an example that landlords sometimes discriminate against people with children or against single people, failing to mention racism, the most obvious form of discrimination. Though I was somewhat impressed that someone was discussing the cold reality of American citizenship, I didn't care for the way the woman was speaking. Her tone was condescending, as if the new citizens were children.

She continued, "Those of us who are lawyers or who work in the system are also discriminated against because we know our rights. We want you to know your rights, too." *So that they'll be discriminated against for knowing them?* I thought. I waited for the official to complete the idea—that it was better to know the law in order to fight discrimination effectively—but she didn't.

She added that it was illegal to be discriminated against for being incarcerated. The Latino man sitting across from me denied this. "People don't want to give you a job if you've done time. Why else do they ask on job applications?" he asked. As if she had heard him from the other room, the woman answered, "You may not get a job if the crime relates to the job. Like, don't apply to Citibank for a job if you've robbed a bank." Laughter broke out in the cafeteria while the new citizens stared disbelievingly. Now she was talking to the new citizens as if they were criminals. *Who is this clown?* I thought.

Next, the woman discussed domestic violence and how it was important to report, too. I didn't understand why this was being included. *Aren't undocumented people more vulnerable to abuse?* I thought, assuming that those now with citizenship wouldn't be fearful to report to the police. I didn't connect the dots—that I was a citizen, and I was being abused, and I never would have reported Seyran to the police. I wasn't even able to describe what I was experiencing as abuse *to anyone.* It wasn't until that very moment that I wondered if I could be considered a victim of domestic violence.

Even with what he had done two days ago, my situation felt too complicated to unpack. Discussions of transformative justice hadn't reached me yet. *The Revolution Starts at Home,* the landmark anthology addressing intimate partner violence in immigrant, BIPOC, and social justice communities, had been published just the month before the citizenship ceremony, and I wouldn't encounter it for a few more years. If I had, I would have learned about other people like me who didn't want the system to dole out punishment to someone with less power in the system, like a green card holder fleeing a sadistic army. That other women like me who operated in queer and feminist communities, the people you would least expect to allow bad behavior from men, also experienced abuse in their relationships and felt ashamed about it. I might have considered who I could have told in my community who would have supported me and intervened, instead of assuming that everyone would think the worst of me. I would have learned that my screaming and punching, when I was pushed to the limit, wasn't an equivalent violence but a gradual and un-derstandable (albeit unfortunate) response to Seyran's constant gaslighting and emotional abuse.

I would have recognized that I was being abused—emotionally, sexually, physically—even if the web of identities Seyran and I inhabited were hard to pull apart. An Armenian American woman entering Armenia may still have privilege as an American, but she loses her status as a human being. The global system of sexism gave powers to Seyran that he freely took advantage of. He broke boundaries, and I let him, writing him off as a harmless kid. On the internet, he found porn that dehumanized girls and he read a guidebook on how to be dishonest to take advantage of women. In America, though I had more power as a U.S. citizen, I did not use this against him; in fact, my care for him and his situation, stemming from my identity as a queer Armenian woman, became what Seyran repeatedly abused. The more he took from me, the more he was empowered since there was nothing to check him: my shame and silence protected him.

The woman from the NYC Commission on Human Rights didn't warn the new citizens not to abuse other people. The assumption was that the immi-grant was the one who was weak, dependent on others. The one vulnerable to beating and rape.

The onscreen video periodically went silent and black, attempting to reboot.

The last thing I heard the woman say was, "If you don't understand En-glish, ask for an interpreter." *How can anyone who doesn't know English understand what you're saying?* I thought with rage. I was seeing the system that had pushed and pulled me through such strange charades, and I was livid. The only way for me to truly separate from Seyran was to make him a citizen. Thus, I was depen-dent on a flawed process to survive.

Then it happened: the people on the screen were shifting about and mov-ing around. A woman entered the cafeteria, announcing something in Span-ish. When I looked at him with a question on my face, the Latino guy translat-ed, "They're letting us in now."

❖

The day after he violated me and the day before the ceremony, I asked him why he did it. He deflected responsibility as usual. He said he thought I had liked it, that I was having a good time. "But I was saying no," I told him.

He replied that he felt sorry for me, an old lady who needed a thrill.

I told him how much it had hurt me.

He said that because of his parents, he learned to express love negatively, and this was why he was messed up. "You never should have touched me," he said.

"Why not?"

"Because look what happened."

"What happened?" I needed for him to say it—to say that he had violated me. Saying "You never should have touched me," put the blame on me for getting involved with him in the first place and, ultimately, for what he had done.

"I became an American."

It was another of his evasive jokes. Americans are violent, it's true, but he had been abusive before we set foot in New York City. What had America really done to him? It amplified his pain, which he further took out on me.

Beyond this example, I wonder if this is what America does to all of us? Amplifies our hurt, our lack, and when we are at our worst, or even not our best, we take it out on someone else?

❖

Those in the cafeteria crowded into the courtroom. The wood-paneled space had high ceilings, much grander than had appeared on the screen. Seyran saw me and smiled slightly. I stood to the side, just inside the entrance.

The judge entered and gave a speech about the American dream. His father had lost his family in the Holocaust, and now look—his son was a judge. The judge claimed that all the people who worked in the courthouse—all the judges— were the children and grandchildren of immigrants. *But the judges aren't immigrants,* I thought. *What kind of message is that sending? You don't count, but your children or grandchildren will? What if some people here don't have children? Will their hard work and sacrifice matter?*

A WPA mural along the top of the wall, originally in the dining hall at Ellis Island, seemed to answer my question. A Native American man lies on the ground on one end, and white people work their way across the country in pioneer wagons harvesting wheat, working on the railroad, mining coal. The only other person of color is a coolie in a wide straw hat, his face turned toward the ground. Later I discovered the name of the mural: *The Role of the Immigrant in the Industrial Development of America*.

The judge gave the oath, and everyone repeated it. Then they recited the pledge of allegiance. When each person's name was called out, they filed up to the bench to get their certificate. They didn't seem happy as they walked out of the courtroom. Some gazed at the certificate, most looked straight ahead.

Seyran took the certificate and strolled past me, virtually ignoring me, through the doorway. There was no hug. There was no thank you. We descended the stairs, and I retrieved my phone and camera.

✧

The next day, Seyran was fired.

I had seen it coming. He was never going in on time and always leaving early. I imagined he was as problematic to work with as he was to live with. Not taking responsibility for his actions.

He came home around 5 p.m., appearing at the kitchen door while I was cooking. He slowly walked toward me, stood in front of me at the sink, smiled and said, "I got fired today."

This time, I believed him. He was excited, the way he was when the regular Asian girl rang our doorbell. "Why?" I asked.

"My boss said, 'Personally, I love you, but we're reorganizing. And you don't seem happy here.'"

I thought of the joke he had made a few months before—that he was fucking his boss's wife.

"Did you beg for your job back?"

"Was I supposed to?"

"Well, do you want it?"

"No, I hate that job."

He was wearing a tight pink T-shirt with *Sammy's Spa* in white lettering (an item from the Salvation Army) and a pair of yoga shorts. He'd been going to work almost exclusively in his yoga clothes. He'd also been punching in for time that he wasn't there for, before he arrived and after he left, essentially stealing from the company. I asked him if these were likely reasons.

"No," he said, "Michael never checks the timecards, he doesn't care."

It was clear he was incapable of seeing the truth. I thought it was interesting timing that he had been fired the day after receiving citizenship. I wondered if Michael had been putting up with him the same way I had. Perhaps I wasn't the only one who inexplicably cared for Seyran despite his bad behavior or who felt responsible for him even though he wouldn't own his actions. Fundamentally, a job interview is a date, an opportunity to charm. Once he got in and ensured his employers' trust, he likely repeated familiar patterns.

Though I knew his patterns, I still didn't know him at all. I put up with him all these years because I believed he would eventually break free, that he would reveal himself to me. But he never could, and he never did. Two days before he became a citizen, he sexually assaulted me, but what troubled me now was that I had made someone a citizen, and I did not know who he was.

Before I went to live in Armenia for a year, I was unaware of the power I had to make someone else an American. I can't say that I even knew what being American meant to me. I had learned of the many sacrifices and circumstances that made for my own citizenship, but I didn't have an inkling of the lived emotion and struggle behind those migrations. I also didn't understand fully the odd spot I occupied in privilege as a third-generation Armenian American woman: darker in skin color and bolder in facial features, small in stature and continually mistaken for Latina, my racial identity frequently questioned—as an other—yet my grandparents and other Armenian refugees like them were deemed legally white in 1924, right before the U.S. restricted access to Asian immigrants. Much of my privilege had been guaranteed well before my birth.

So I never thought my country would fail me. I couldn't know that I'd become trapped as a woman married to an abusive green card holder. I know it could have been worse—America might have punished me for marrying Seyran and making him a citizen. But I don't only mean the government; I mean all the systems, communities, and relationships we find ourselves in. And I mean the America that I occupy with my body, the America that is me.

Writing this book has been a means for me to survive. I've recorded how Seyran enacted his pain onto me and how I couldn't leave. But it's also true that with all my failures, there were successes. With all the enabling, there was also confrontation. Accounting for accidents and expressing mistakes are part of what defines America—the way we strive through language and action to make a more just world, to refine our voices to enact fairness, even as we stumble and stumble and stumble again.

❖

After the citizenship ceremony, I saw my therapist and told her what had happened the day Seyran violated me. She was extremely angry. She said what he had done was wrong and that I should call the police if he ever did anything like it again. I was perplexed. Sure, I didn't feel safe in my own home. But why be angry about it? It was over, and he had his citizenship, and now all I had to do was move out. But she insisted that I set boundaries with Seyran, that I make it clear he couldn't come into my room without knocking, especially since I would still be there for nearly a month.

So I did it: when I went home, I wrote him an email telling him that I would give notice to our landlord on September 1 to move out on October 1. I told him that I didn't feel safe in my home, that he needed to knock and not come into my room naked, and that if he kept doing it, I would leave without notice.

When he came home that evening, he knocked on my door. I told him he could come in.

He said that my move-out date was fine. But he didn't understand the rest of the email. "Why are you making such a drama?" he asked.

"It's serious," I told him. "I don't feel safe here."

Again, I wanted him to admit that what he had done was wrong, but he wouldn't. "Ask yourself, would you want someone to do to you what you did to me?" He wouldn't ask himself. He kept avoiding the question. I asked how his yoga teacher would think of him if she saw him doing the things he had done to me.

He refused to answer. Instead he said, "You're just doing this because you went to therapy today. And you have your period."

I became so angry that I exploded, hitting him, kicking him, pounding him with my fists, the worst outburst yet.

"YOU'RE A MOTHERFUCKER!" I screamed. He was so sick as to fuck me, to fuck the one who cared about him, to fuck his mother.

He laughed as I hit him. "Oh, you like it?" I asked.

"Now you're being abusive," he said.

"I am just giving it back to you," I yelled.

I tried to hit his dick, the source of all the problems, but I missed and fell to the floor.

He ran into my room and curled up on my bed, giggling.

"You like this? You wanted this?" I asked.

He stood up and came toward me, raising his hand as if he were going to slap me. He froze there a moment, bluffing, then backed down.

I had somehow escaped to the hallway. Standing beneath the skylight, I felt blank at the front of my brain, like it was rotting. Intense stress, but more. A sickness. Madness? I had never plumbed to these depths before. Maybe I was looking into my void, where my persona so desperately needed to be affirmed. Why did I need him to understand me? Why was it so important that he admit that what he had done was wrong, that he apologize? Why couldn't I know he was fucked up and dispassionately tell him the rules without losing my shit?

I had been frozen during that last year, wondering how he could do such things. How could someone who had been abused turn around and hurt someone else—and not recognize it? How could someone who was treated as less than by society turn around and consider an entire gender less important than himself? It is a question for eternity, really, why any abused person turns around and abuses others. Perhaps for the narcissist, they develop their hard core of shame at such a young age that they can't find a means to heal to see what exactly they are doing and who they are hurting. This describes me, too—I couldn't fully see how I was hurting myself and how I was neglecting the friendships around me. I'd placed someone else's amorphous, fully denied pain in my center.

If I had been able to verbalize what I had been through and name it as abuse, I would have taken steps to defend myself and my needs a lot sooner. Instead, I had to skim the bounds of my sanity, recognize a ledge that I didn't want to cross, write it in my journal, and hold on to that moment. When a friend told me about a three-week sublet in Sunnyside, I finally packed up and moved out.

❖

The monitor in the cafeteria with its grainy video, its unreliable technology, did its job. It gave me a window into another space. It separated me. There are many separations in this story, many spaces between the threads of the web. Within the span of two days, he got his citizenship, and I was sexually violated. I put my stuff in storage and slept on friends' couches for a few weeks, I stayed in a sublet for a few weeks, I found an apartment in a few weeks.

Several years later, I was sitting in a café in Jackson Heights with my monthly peer writers' group. We had just arrived, were catching each other up, joyful and jubilant. Across the room, a face was smiling at me and a hand was waving. Good mood that I was in, I smiled and waved back before realizing who it was, then felt a rush of dread. The face, probably just twelve to fifteen feet away, now headed towards me. I froze.

Seyran stood by me as I listened to my friends' conversation and I did my best to ignore him. After a moment, he said, "Hi Natalee." He looked the same as I'd remembered, but he was wearing a black beret, worn in such a way that it resembled a shower cap.

"I don't want to talk to you," I said, and just as quickly as he appeared, he turned and walked out the door. He drifted in on a thread and a current quickly blew him away.

At that point, I hadn't seen him in a few years, the last time in February of 2015, when I blocked his number from my phone. After I moved out of the apartment in the summer of 2011, he was intermittently in touch with me, until I read a book on narcissistic personality disorder. Suddenly, so much of the behavior that I had experienced had a name—and I wasn't crazy.

I learned that other people found themselves stuck in such relationships—sometimes for decades, caught in a mutual web of shame. According to psychotherapists, most people with severe forms of the disorder are untreatable, their patterns long established.

Unsurprisingly, my attraction to Seyran had much earlier roots. Some of the descriptions of narcissists reminded me of my mother—her inability to apologize, her demands that everything be done her way. I knew other women my age who also had controlling, difficult, rigid mothers, and who had also come of age in the 1950s. I considered whether narcissists established their patterns of avoiding shame not just in terms of family dynamics but societal ones as well. Perhaps my mother had developed her rigidity to help her survive as a woman during limiting and repressive times. Perhaps Seyran had found the manipulative methods of narcissism useful tools to survive in Armenia.

People who are raised by narcissists often take on a codependent role in their adult relationships. It was clear to me, as I read, that something of the codependent role has narcissism baked into it as well—the conviction that the codependent can help the narcissist, for example. The codependent has a void of persona similar to the narcissist—while the narcissist creates an appealing mirage around this void, the codependent fills their void with the narcissistic mirage. As I read self-help books, I thought I might have been narcissistic in previous relationships. I wasn't very rigid, and I found emotional honesty with my partners, but I could be performative and charming, and in my pursuit of positive attention, I could be myopic and self-centered.

Though I loved Art, my previous boyfriend, I was overly dependent on his attention and affirmation, lacking self-esteem resources I had yet to build. To me, it seemed people could operate on a spectrum of narcissism. I thought Seyran, with his inability to process shame and his pattern of passing it on to me in deliberately hurtful ways, was at a more defined end of the spectrum. I could never understand why he couldn't leave me if he kept hurting me and wanted his freedom. But the hurt gave him fuel to feel self-worth. He would always seek my attention. According to the advice I read, I had to block Seyran out entirely to take care of myself.

How I wish I had known about this disorder not just while I was with him but after the breakup as well. After I moved out of the Astoria apartment, Seyran drove across the country with the woman he was seeing and lived in the Bay Area for six months. He called me practically every day. I had to tell him at some point that we needed to limit calls to every other day. Then I demanded once every two to three days, then once a week.

He lived a peripatetic life in the Bay Area, as far as I could tell. As soon as he arrived, the woman he had been dating broke up with him, and he shifted from place to place, making friends with a gay male couple, volunteering at a library to help kids read, living off unemployment from NY State, and eating at the local Hindu temple. I started filing the divorce papers once he told me he was returning to New York. The first time I saw him back in the city, he said he was experiencing his gay side and went to parties wearing lipstick. Eventually, he was dating another older woman, someone my age. He made sure to tell me, "She's smarter than you. She has a PhD." He moved into her apartment in an exclusive complex in Manhattan.

After that, I met him for coffee or a meal maybe once a month, then every three months. When I saw him, it brought up all the old feelings. One time, he convinced me to let him join me in attending a concert, and he acted in strange, annoying, and inappropriately sexual ways, writhing his body against the subway pole while speaking to my friend on our way home. I had broken up with him so that I didn't have to deal with this kind of shit anymore.

The last time I spoke to him on the phone was in 2015. He had called and asked to meet, and I had told him no. A couple of days later, I ran into him at the subway in my neighborhood. He was coming through the turnstile, the very same one that I was walking out from. He saw me, and his eyes lit up. "What are you doing here?" I asked.

"I came to get some lunch," he said. It was evening, so he had either been there all afternoon, skipping work, or he had misspoken because he was nervous.

"You want to hang out some time?" he asked.

"Mmm, not really," I told him.

"Okay," he said and walked through the turnstile. I noticed his stylish green backpack, brand new, expensive looking, bouncing through the station.

He called the next day and left a message asking to get together, and that's when I blocked his number.

For a few years it seemed I'd been able to lose him. The spaces in the web had widened to pull the threads apart. But then he popped up a few years later at that café, out of the blue, and the sight of him caused my breath to shorten and my fight or flight defenses to trigger—an even more panicked response than when he abused me. I felt physically ill the next day. What helped me recover was remembering that I had created a hard line when I blocked his number, when I said no.

I don't think I can ever accept Seyran's abuse. And I don't think I can ever forgive him, since he never apologized or atoned for the pain he had caused me—as a narcissist, he likely wasn't capable. More importantly, I forgive myself and the many dynamics beyond my control that created our situation. For now, after all these years, I can be kind to myself.

20. CHANGING THE STORY

•

• •

The waterbug, also known as a giant cockroach, was too big for me to smash. I trapped it under a glass jar, hoping the lack of oxygen would slowly kill it. It had been two days now. Day and night, I asked myself, *How can I watch this creature die a slow death?* But I didn't have the stamina to change the situation. For three days I had been washing clothes, putting them into plastic bags, sorting through every item I owned, and inspecting them for bedbugs. The apartment extermination would be the next morning, and I would have to be ready. There were only so many kinds of bugs I could deal with, only so much my nerves could handle.

I didn't mind the distraction after just returning from Armenia. It was my first return visit after the breakup four years before. It was a meaningful trip, so it had been challenging to return to my life in New York.

In the years after the divorce, I missed Armenia and kept wanting to return but could never figure out a time—too much money, too long a trip. But then I found myself wanting to finish this book, and it became imperative.

I arrived in July, 2015, a few days after Electric Yerevan ended. When the mismanaged electric company, owned by a Russian corporation, raised their rates by 16 percent, a small group protested in front of the Parliament Building's gates, sitting on the street, blocking traffic. The police fired high-power water cannons that scattered Armenian bodies down the length of the street, which amplified the rage and the crowds. For two weeks they occupied Bagh-ramyan Avenue, a main thoroughfare. Ten thousand people thronged the street each night.

Since 2007 when I left Armenia, there had been other grassroots protest efforts: against mining and gentrification, in support of soldiers and a domestic violence law, to restore pensions and to keep public transportation fees low. People had learned to enact their power to make progress.

I felt that I could make change, too. I accepted my lack of language rather than beating myself up for it. I enjoyed speaking my broken Armenian and allowing myself to listen. One night I was staying at a residency at an art school, and the new night watchman and I interacted. He was a tiny, thin, aging man, with big ears, named Manoog. I had been cooling off by dipping my feet in the small pool when he brought out a bowl of plums. We spoke our names, where we were from, how long I would be there, whom I knew and whom I didn't know. A few days later, a friend visited me, and he told her, "I know she's Armenian, but I can't understand what she's saying." I was crestfallen, but it didn't mean that I hadn't made a connection. Whenever I saw Manoog, we smiled at each other and exchanged barevs.

❖

Progress is slow when language and knowledge are absent. My friends in Armenia who had said it would take two generations to effect change were partially correct. In fact, it had only taken one generation—the one that was born after the collapse of the Soviet Union. As children, they weren't enmeshed in a culture of bribery and corruption. As this generation grew up, they developed a language of democracy and grassroots activism, gradually pushing back on the status quo. Once they gained momentum, their elders joined in.

There was one disturbing setback, however. In the aftermath of a parliamentary election in May 2012, when it looked like votes had once again been rigged, some nationalistic kids firebombed a gay-friendly bar. A few days later, a homophobic mob of young people attacked a diversity march organized in part by an LGBT group. I watched helplessly from afar as my friends in Yerevan became targets, including Gharib, who was back in Yerevan for a visit after touring around Europe. He had bravely given a television interview, making himself visible to homophobes. Other queer Armenian friends fled to Europe to seek asylum. It turned out the firebombing youths were later bailed out of prison by Tashnag and Republican parliament members. It had clearly been a ruse to distract people from the stolen election.

I wondered how queer people had fared during Electric Yerevan. I arrived a few days after some of the protesters' demands had been met and the demonstrations had disbanded. Amal was living with her girlfriend in an apartment near the protest site and had witnessed much of it. Nationalists were at the front of the barricades, followed by the queer and avant-garde activists, and then the people who had showed up to party stayed in the back. "The amazing thing was that so many people from all backgrounds showed up," Amal said. Tanya, now a mom to four children, also thought that something had shifted. She was tired after years of being attacked in the press for leading demonstrations in support of women's rights and initiating anti-gender-discrimination laws. But she wasn't taking it personally, and her own teenage daughter was out on the streets every night to protest. "The younger generation realizes they can make change," she said.

❖

In the four years between my breakup and my trip to Armenia in 2015, I experienced my own slow transformation of healing. I moved into my own apartment in Jackson Heights. I'd always lived with roommates or a partner, so I was nervous to live by myself. But I got used to it, and it allowed me to start a small business, teaching writing workshops in my living room. Even Gharib came to a few of them.

During the same four years, he was ping-ponging back and forth between Europe, Yerevan, and New York. I saw him in the spring of 2014 after he spent a year working in Paris, where he lost his green card, stolen from his wallet. He was stuck in NYC temporarily until he could get another.

On Easter Sunday, he came over for dinner and earnestly read my coffee grounds. There were just two spires dripping down from the mud in the bottom. He asked, "Does anyone in your family have a heart problem? Heart disease?"

"My grandmother," I told him.

"You were close to her?"

"Yes. She died of a blockage to her heart."

"And your heart? Any problems?"

"I called the paramedics one night last summer because my heart was beating so fast. I thought I was having a heart attack."

Mardi laughed. He found this totally ridiculous. He and Gharib weren't a couple anymore—they'd broken up a long time ago, living on different continents—but Mardi was ping-ponging too. He was in New York after traveling around the world so that he could keep his green card. He had just spent three months in Yerevan and by all accounts loved it. I couldn't believe it—what was up was down. But Mardi was still his same self, arguing vociferously about art and politics. After participating in Occupy Wall Street, he felt that fighting the system puts you in collusion with it. The best thing to do is stand apart from it to resist, to not take part at all, to put your energy into creating something new. He had spent the spring traveling around Europe, learning about farming and biodynamics. He was going to collect seeds while in the U.S. to surreptitiously bring back to Armenia so that he could teach others to stand outside the system, too.

Gharib looked like he was about to respond to Mardi's mockery of our tasseography session, but he thought better of it, took a breath, and continued reading my cup. "You are holding on to this story of your grandmother and her heart," he said. "It's not a bad story, but it's not your reality." I looked at his bearded face, his dark eyes. "You don't have to take it on anymore."

❖

Fast-forward a few months later, and I found myself on a mountaintop village with Mardi and Gharib in Armenia. At first, it was just me and Mardi in a large house overlooking a canyon. It was incredibly hot and amazingly beautiful, the village a magical place with three ancient churches with khachkars, eagles, bears, and intricate banners carved into the thirteenth-century stone walls. One was a simple outdoor altar where warriors could ride up on their horses to be blessed before riding off to battle, located on a gorgeous site in the middle of the long canyon beneath the wide sky, sunset, and stars—you could imagine that any human being looking upon it would feel its spiritual power.

Day after day, I did small things. I made coffee and sat on the porch overlooking the mountains; I picked apples with Mardi and cut them up to dry; I hiked with him over the mountain to another ancient church, where he excitedly pointed out the ruins of an old monastery, school, and library. I read and wrote during the day when it was too hot to do anything else. It was a village house, so the room at the rear had no windows; I camped out back there in the cool dark with my laptop. Village people bartered eggs and cheese and lavash. Mardi lived off what he tended in his garden. He was the happiest I had ever seen him. He was growing food through the biodynamic method, and when I tasted his arugula, it blew my mind. It was like all the store-bought arugula I had ever eaten had been such a poor imitation that I now felt like a fool for all the times I thought I had been eating actual arugula.

"Are you going to stay on this mountain forever?" I asked him. He knew it wasn't my question and that people had been gossiping. He told me he didn't want to leave. What was the point? But he didn't know about forever. Then he told me about Rudolf Steiner, whose principles biodynamics are based upon, who said that stories can make people have preconceived notions of others. "People think they already know you before you have told them anything," he said. "They are more attached to their story of you than they are to the idea of connecting with you."

After several days, I, too, didn't want to go back to Yerevan, never mind New York City. Here, on the mountain, I didn't have a story. I had fresh air and food and my writing and philosophical chats with Mardi. But I had to leave. I got on a plane, and a bedbug hitched a ride in my suitcase.

❖

I spent my first week back home feeling out of sorts. What was I doing here? Did I even like New York anymore, its fast pace, the rat race?

At some point, I told myself to accept it. I had to count my blessings. I had to find a way to like whatever experience New York was giving me.

That morning, I woke up at 5 a.m., staring a bedbug in the eye. As I said, it was a welcome distraction. I could focus on this problem. But it also seemed like divine intervention. *You're accepting New York? Then accept this.*

It gave me an opportunity to sort through my clothes, books, letters, and photos, to realize my many loves and interests, to let go of what I didn't need, and to continue to build myself back up.

❖

When I was in Armenia, I kept waiting for the moment that would end the book, that would show me how much I had changed, how much I had let go. But it never came. The dramatic arc isn't my tradition anyway. Any Armenian family knows there is no rising arc, no chain of events gradually leading to a conflict. We break out into argument easily; we confront crisis immediately and constantly. Our journey takes winding roads and detours, and what seems like home can sometimes just be a stopping place until the next war erupts and boom—you're now a member of a double diaspora, exiled twice. Resolution never comes. Reparations never made. It doesn't mean that we're not strong. One part of the body is wounded while another one heals. Villagers on a remote mountain peak helplessly stave off attacks, and a far-flung community in diaspora maintains and adapts its beautiful traditions.

When Gharib visited the mountain, we hiked down to the swift, cool river in the canyon and encountered a medieval Jewish cemetery. A plaque claimed that history had forgotten how Jews had arrived in this little village, and I couldn't help imagining that they had been seeking shelter or had been temporarily indisposed while traveling the Silk Road, finally resting at this gate through which they departed. Gharib stayed up late that night and showed me that the only guys on Viber were in Nakhichevan. He had clearly moved on, having sex left and right, while Mardi confessed to me that he hadn't had sex in months, another kind of moving on, perhaps.

The next night, friends came over, and as the Aerosmith ballad, "I Don't Want to Miss a Thing" played on the radio, Gharib found his audience. He lip-synched to the back of Mardi's head.

Gharib didn't know the lyrics, but it didn't matter. He comically mimed his mouth in time to the music. Gharib didn't seem to be professing his love for Mardi. This performance was more about mocking all the drama they had been through, all the pained love they had shared. In response, Mardi ignored Gharib's antics and stoically cut up an apple. When Gharib got to the bridge, when Steven Tyler seems to completely lose his mind, and I didn't think Gharib could go any more over the top, he did, like a maniac, thrashing his arms and bobbing his head as if his neck would break. As everyone else laughed hysterically, Mardi raised his eyes and smirked at me.

It seemed moments of connection like these made me the happiest, and I wondered if I had been destined to always be a part of an extended gay family.

Yes, that's true, but so are other realities. As much as I love my community, I recognize this notion is just another story: one I can express and celebrate, but that I don't have to get attached to.

❖

The night before the exterminators were scheduled to arrive, the water bug was still alive under the jar after two days of captivity. When my nerve built up, I slid a postcard under the jar and held the assemblage together while running to the incinerator chute in the hallway and pitching it down, hearing the jar bounce off the metal walls of the chute. Then I stepped out for the evening. As I walked home later from the subway, I realized I would miss the old coot. Under glass, it had been a quiet, intriguing pet. You couldn't help but admire it as you reviled it, eventually finding it beautiful—a survivor, a New Yorker. I opened the door to my disassembled apartment and got settled in for the night, watching TV on my sofa, when what should scuttle into the room from the kitchen but a water bug. Again, another divine intervention: *Oh, so you missed that bug? Well, here's his brother.* This one moved in an erratic way, a frantic scuffle, and when I managed to plunk a plastic jar over him, I realized why: he was missing a leg. For a moment, I was filled with horror. Was it the same bug, its leg now broken from bouncing down the chute? How in the hell did it get back up here? And why? Whatever the truth, the bug was much more excitable than the previous one, fluttering about. I did not hesitate as

I had the last time. I immediately slid a postcard under the jar and sent him down the incinerator chute.

I didn't keep him.

I know it seems as if I'm comparing my ex to a cockroach, but that's not it. The bug represents the self-loathing in my body, a test if I can let this persistent pest go. Even as I do, I know that it will always return. The question is how to live with it, to change, instead of trying to escape it.

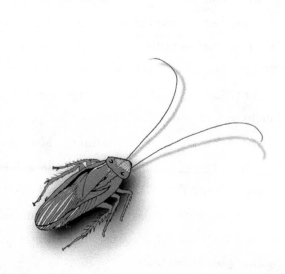

ACKNOWLEDGMENTS

I'm grateful to many people who encouraged me during the long process of drafting, revising, and publishing *The Fear of Large and Small Nations*.

Karyn Kloumann, thank you for championing this book: for your compassionate reading and nuanced understanding of Na's journey. Your editorial responses, from the overarching themes to the tiny details, helped me to find the heart of Na's strength and to bring this story home. I'm forever grateful for this collaboration.

Kimberley Lim and Ishita Bal contributed their copyediting and proofreading skills with heart and soul. Thank you for seeing the best in this text.

Catherine Kapphahn, Nita Noveno, and Cynthia Thompson: thank you my dear writing sisters and heroes, who encouraged me to write this story, seeing its value when I was uncertain. You read the earliest words and were there for me as friends.

Thank you, David Ciminello, Eric Lehman, and Laura Meyers: your kinship and feedback helped me to find the third person—my magic key.

Many thanks to the Queens Writers Lab: Picchenda Bao, Catherine Fletcher, Jared Harél, Mary Lannon, Meera Nair, and Vaughn Watson, for supporting me as a peer and a colleague, for your excellent feedback, for your sympathy during the long road to publication, and for your literary camaraderie.

Thanks to dedicated folx who read chunks or the full manuscript and offered supportive critique: Shushan Avagyan, Tim Fredrick, Nairi Hakhverdi, Nikkya Hargrove, Mary Lannon, Meera Nair, and Aida Zilelian.

Thanks to friends for writing-related advice, hospitality, kind ears, and laughter: Arpi Adamian, Melissa Bilal, Chiqui Cartagena & Jennifer Knight, Haig Chahinian & Peter Simmons, Michelle T. Clinton & G. Colette Jackson, Kim Foote, Linda Ganjian, Annette Kim, Lola Koundakjian, Gigi McCreery, Deena Patel & Walter Polkosnik, and Sweta Vikram.

Thanks to Shahé Mankerian and Pam Ward, dear friends, peers, and respected authors, for reading the manuscript, offering encouragement, and penning beautiful blurbs.

Many thanks to various institutions: The Fulbright Scholars program for making the research for this book possible. My time at Macondo was joyful and provided a means to commit to the difficult aspects of the story. Lambda Literary's Writers Retreat for Emerging LGBTQ Voices lifted me up as a queer writer. Susanna Gyulamiryan at Art and Cultural Studies Lab/Art Commune AIR program provided a space and community in Yerevan that helped me complete this manuscript. The Jeanne Córdova Prize for Queer Nonfiction recognized me at a crucial time, their monetary award helping to fund this project. The Laundromat Project and MacKenzie Scott gave an unrestricted gift that I applied to this book. The Queens Council on the Arts offered professional and financial support that kept the machine moving over many years.

Geraldine Zodo at the Jerome Zodo Gallery kindly commissioned a performance "Family Returning Blows," developed from this manuscript as a work in progress. Arno Yeretzian of Abril Bookstore and Lousine Shamamian of GALAS provided support to present a revised version of the performance. Thanks for helping to bring these words to audiences and creating conversations about domestic violence.

Students from my Writing Cross-Culturally and Writing Nonfiction on Social Change courses at the Gallatin School of Individualized Study at NYU participated in many edifying conversations about the nuances of writing creatively and politically about place and culture, which informed this work. Queens College creative writing students, through their life stories, enlightened me on the experience of navigating multiple homelands. Thanks to students in Heightening Stories, Creative Writing From Queer Resistance, Our Side, and Connected Rooms workshops who read excerpts and taught me about bravery and love. I am grateful to women workshop students in Armenia who gave me a deeper understanding of ourselves in community.

The Free Artsakh Writers shared a soothing online space across continents and borders during the Second Nagorno-Karabakh War in 2020, which helped me take final steps towards publication.

Finally, thanks to my parents, who, in coping with their forgetting, showed me what it means to be strong: to be interdependent and resilient.

Nancy Agabian's previous books include *Me as her again: True Stories of an Armenian Daughter,* a memoir honored as a Lambda Literary Award finalist for LGBT Nonfiction and shortlisted for a William Saroyan International Writing Prize, and *Princess Freak,* a collection of poetry and performance art texts. In 2021 she was awarded Lambda Literary Foundation's Jeanne Córdova Prize for Lesbian/Queer Nonfiction. *The Fear of Large and Small Nations* is her first novel.

CPSIA information can be obtained
at www.ICGtesting.com
Printed in the USA
LVHW042026200723
753059LV00005B/111

9 798985 969238